T0058789

THE
LULLABY
GIRL

OTHER TITLES BY LORETH ANNE WHITE

In the Barren Ground
In the Waning Light
A Dark Lure

Angie Pallorino Novels
The Drowned Girls

Wild Country
Manhunter
Cold Case Affair

Shadow Soldiers
The Heart of a Mercenary
A Sultan's Ransom
Rules of Engagement
Seducing the Mercenary
The Heart of a Renegade

Sahara Kings
The Sheik's Command
Sheik's Revenge
Surgeon Sheik's Rescue
Guarding the Princess
"Sheik's Captive," in *Desert Knights* with Linda Conrad

Snowy Creek Novels
The Slow Burn of Silence

Romantic Suspense
Melting the Ice
Safe Passage
The Sheik Who Loved Me
Breaking Free
Her 24-Hour Protector
The Missing Colton
The Perfect Outsider
"Saving Christmas," in the *Covert Christmas* anthology
"Letters to Ellie," a novella in *SEAL of My Dreams* anthology

LORETH ANNE WHITE

THE LULLABY GIRL

Montlake
Romance

This is a work of fiction. Names, characters, organizations, places, events, and incidents are either products of the author's imagination or are used fictitiously.

Text copyright © 2017 by Cheakamus House Publishing
All rights reserved.

No part of this book may be reproduced, or stored in a retrieval system, or transmitted in any form or by any means, electronic, mechanical, photocopying, recording, or otherwise, without express written permission of the publisher.

Published by Montlake Romance, Seattle

www.apub.com

Amazon, the Amazon logo, and Montlake Romance are trademarks of Amazon.com, Inc., or its affiliates.

ISBN-13: 9781542047975
ISBN-10: 1542047978

Cover design by Rex Bonomelli

Printed in the United States of America

For those who work so tirelessly to give the nameless back their names.

FLOTSAM

Monday, January 1

"Ty, dammit! Get your butt away from there, will ya!" Betsy Champlain, all of eight months pregnant, stood on the verge of the road and yelled into the wind for her son to come back from the water's edge. It was raining, clouds low, dusk rolling in fast with a fog from the sea. She could barely see him now, chasing their little family Maltese into the gloam along the strip of dark, pebbled beach. Panic licked through her stomach.

She spun around. Behind her, along the manmade causeway that jutted out into the water, ferry traffic was lined bumper-to-bumper for miles. Four sailing waits long and then some. Most of the earlier sailings between the mainland and the island had been canceled throughout the day because of the storms that had ridden into the polar jet stream on the coattails of Typhoon Shiori, blasting the Pacific Northwest with a roller coaster of foul weather. Plus, it was New Year's Day—a holiday in this part of the world. Which meant tomorrow was the first day back at work in the new year, and everyone was trying to get home. She was never going to make it from the Vancouver mainland back to the island tonight. Frustration ate at her. She shouldn't have come solo to visit her mom with the two kids and the dog. Ferry traffic was always insane over the holiday period.

They'd been cooped up in the car for hours, and Chloe, their little dog, had needed a bathroom break. Betsy had left the Subaru in the lineup with the window down and Emily, her three-year-old, inside, sleeping. She'd crossed over the road to where she could watch her eight-year-old take the dog down the riprap embankment to pee.

But Ty had been busting with frustrated energy after being imprisoned in the vehicle all day. He'd scuttled down the riprap, slipping and dropping Chloe's leash. Chloe had hightailed it straight to the water. Ty chased after his pet.

"Ty! Get back here! *Now!*" Conflict stabbed through Betsy. She shot a look back at the Subaru, then glanced at Ty's little ghost-shape vanishing into the mist. She spun around and waddled fast back to the car.

"Emily," she said, shaking her baby girl. "Wake up. You have to come with me."

Betsy grabbed her half-asleep child's hand and dragged her at a run back over the road. They negotiated the wet, slippery riprap down to the beach. Emily began to fall and cry. On the beach Betsy scooped Emily up onto her hip and stumbled over the rocky strip to where Ty had vanished. She was breathing hard. She also needed to pee—her bladder felt like it was going to burst.

"Ty!" she yelled. She couldn't see him. "Tyson Champlain, you get your butt over here right now, or—"

"But Ma—" He popped up from behind a rocky outcrop, holding a driftwood stick. Relief cut Betsy like a knife.

"Chloe's found something—I'm just taking a look." He disappeared again behind his rock knoll.

Heaving out a sigh of exasperation, Betsy readjusted Emily's weight on her hip and negotiated her way across a carpet of small barnacle-encrusted rocks. She came around to the seaward side of the knoll. The tide was far out, revealing a wide expanse of silt covered in slime and scalloped with brown foam. Along the lacework of foam lay lengths of seaweed as fat as her arm along with other detritus that had been tossed up in the storm. A stench of rot and brine and dead fish filled her nostrils.

Ty was crouched over something, poking it with his stick. Chloe growled, trying to wrestle the object away from him. Unusual for the dog.

She frowned, a sense of foreboding creeping into her bones.

"What is it, Ty?"

"A shoe."

Betsy set Emily down, took her hand, and came closer to see. The mist was thicker down here. Emily stopped crying and peered with interest.

"It's got something inside," Ty said, trying to shove Chloe away as he jabbed the contents of the shoe with his stick.

A memory chilled Betsy to the core—a news show she'd watched recently about severed feet in sneakers that had been washing up all over the BC coast and in Washington. Sixteen in all since 2007. No other body parts to match.

"Leave that alone!" She grabbed her son by his jacket and yanked him back. "Pick up Chloe's leash—now! Get her away from that shoe."

Ty's eyes went round at her tone. For once in his life he obeyed quickly and silently. He grabbed the dog's leash.

Together they stared at the shoe. It was pale lilac in color beneath the grime and seaweed that entangled it. Small. Stubby. A high-top sneaker with a fat, air-filled base for a sole.

Betsy turned back to look up at the rows of cars, now blurred behind a screen of rain. What should she do? Run up there and bash on windows to see if anyone could help her? Help her do what? Police. She needed to tell the police.

"Hold on to your sister, Ty," she said, fumbling in her jacket for her cell phone. "And grab on to my jacket with your other hand. Don't let go, either of you."

He didn't.

Betsy had never called 9-1-1 before. No need, thank God. But . . . did this constitute an emergency? Or would she look dumb? Her gaze shot to the little shoe lying in the silt. There was definitely something inside—like the photos she'd seen on the news.

She knew about the hoaxes, too. The running shoe that had been found with a partially skeletonized animal paw inside. Others stuffed with raw meat. But the cops would want to know, too, if this was a hoax. Right?

"Mom?"

"Quiet."

Fingers shaking, she pressed 9-1-1.

"Nine-one-one, what is your emergency?"

"I . . . uh, I . . ." Betsy's voice stuck suddenly on a ball of phlegm. She cleared her throat. "I found a shoe. I think there's a foot inside. I think it washed up in the storm."

"What is your location, ma'am? Where are you?"

"The causeway beach at the Tsawwassen Ferry Terminal. About . . . halfway up, I think."

"What is the number you are calling from?"

"Cell phone." She gave her number.

"And what is your name, ma'am?"

"Betsy. Betsy Champlain." The pressure on her bladder was suddenly intense. She needed a washroom badly. For some reason she also needed to cry. She swiped the back of her hand across her nose, sniffed.

"Are you safe? Everything else all right?"

"Yes. Yes, I'm out here with my kids and my dog. In the rain. My dog found the shoe, and there seems to be a bit of old sock and something inside. I know there are hoaxes, but—"

4

Up on the causeway engines started growling to life, headlights going on. The line of cars began to move. Someone honked at her stationary Subaru.

"Oh God, I need to go move my car—the ferry lineup is moving."

"Ms. Champlain, Betsy, could you please stay with the shoe? I've got RCMP on their way. There's a police vehicle in your vicinity now. They'll be there shortly."

"My car is in the lineup. They're honking—"

"We'll contact BC Ferries. They'll get someone out there to direct traffic around it. Betsy?"

"I'm here. I'll wait." She paused. "I . . . know about the dismembered feet," she said quietly, her attention returning to the little lilac high-top. "But this one . . . it's not an adult shoe." She reached down and gathered her children closer. "It's a child's. A size eight or nine."

"Does it show the size?" said the operator.

"No. But it's about the same as my daughter's shoes."

Betsy hung up, shivered, rain soft against her cheeks. She sat down on a rock and clutched her kids tight to her body. Too tight. So tight—because suddenly everything that was precious was right here in her arms. She stared at the kid's shoe lying in the silt. "I . . . I love you, sweethearts."

"I'm sorry, Mom." Tears glittered in Ty's big brown eyes. "I—I'm sorry I didn't listen."

She sniffed and rubbed her nose. "Not your fault, Ty. It's not your fault—it's going to be okay."

"Whose shoe is it?"

"I don't know."

"Where's the rest of her?"

Betsy glanced at the shadows of land barely discernible through the mist across the bay—Point Roberts in the United States. Behind her traffic inched along the causeway that stretched a mile into the ocean to the ferry terminal, which lay just five hundred yards short of the US water border. The ferries crossed through American waters each time they traveled from the mainland to Vancouver Island.

That little foot could have come from anywhere. Off a boat maybe? Washed from land out into the sea during the storm?

"I don't know," she said. "They'll find her."

"Who will?"

"I don't know, Ty."

CHAPTER 1

It all goes back to the beginning . . .

TUESDAY, JANUARY 2

Angie Pallorino snapped several photographs of the shadowed service entrance at the back side of the hospital. Her flash flared white against raindrops that fell soft and insidious. It was already dark in this Pacific Northwest city of Vancouver on the second day of the new year. And cold. The kind of dank cold that burrowed deep into bones and made it feel as though the chill were emanating from within.

She stepped back under the shelter of the eaves and checked her watch. 4:51 p.m. Her appointment was running late. Angie wondered if the woman would even show. Perhaps she should have arranged to meet the retired nurse someplace other than outside this service entrance in an old brick alley across from the stone cathedral. But it was here that it had all begun, and Angie needed to go right back to the beginning to find the answers about who she was, where she'd come from. It had started on a night not unlike this. Black. Wintery. Except on that night thirty-two years ago it had been Christmas Eve and it had just started to snow. Big fat flakes.

Across the alley Saint Peter's Cathedral loomed—an ominous shadow of gray rock, Gothic spires vanishing into the dense mist. Shivering slightly, she raised her camera and shot a few images of the arched windows and stained-glass panes that glimmered with hesitant light. Her father's words from a fortnight ago crept into her mind . . .

That Christmas Eve in '86, while your mother was singing with the choir at Midnight Mass, some kind of violent gang fight erupted downtown. From inside the cathedral we heard gunshots, screaming, and tires screeching. They found you in the cradle . . . long red hair. You had no shoes. It was winter, and you had no shoes—just a little pink dress. Like a party frock but old and torn and covered in blood.

Inhaling deeply, Angie returned her camera to her sling bag and gingerly massaged her left upper arm. It was tender where a bullet had ripped through flesh two weeks ago. Thankfully, the slug had missed bone and critical nerves and tendons, but just the act of raising her arm to shoot photos was making her muscles ache. She heard footsteps on the brick and jerked around.

A woman approached from the direction of Front Street where traffic was busy and lights were bright. Stocky, average height, the female wore a coat to her knees and carried a black umbrella overhead that glistened with rain. Slung across her shoulder was a large black tote. Anticipation balled in Angie's throat.

"Mrs. Marsden?" she said as the woman neared.

"Jenny—please call me Jenny. I'm so sorry I'm late." Her voice was low and husky at the edges with kindness—the sort of voice a child might imagine a nurse should have. Jenny joined Angie under the eaves out of the rain, which was beginning to come down harder now, splashing into puddles. "And I apologize for not managing to meet earlier in the day when there was more light—this place looks downright spooky in the darkness." She laughed softly as she shook out her umbrella. "Retirement is not what I thought it might be. The soup kitchen where I volunteer is running me off my feet, especially at this time of year.

When that blush comes off Christmas, there really is less giving, you know? Everyone seems to turn inward in the cold month of January when debt starts to hurt."

"I appreciate you being able to see me at all, and at such short notice."

"How could I not? When I got your call about looking into that old cradle child mystery for your friend . . ." The nurse turned to face the bolted garage doors of the service entrance behind them. She shook herself. "It was over three decades ago, and the memories still come over me like it was yesterday—Christmas Eve, the sound of that alarm going off inside the ER alerting us to an abandoned baby in the box, then the gunfire and ringing of the church bells . . ." She tilted her chin toward the doors. "They now use this entrance for hospital waste pickup. But this is where it was, the first angel's cradle. And right beside it, over there"—she pointed with her umbrella—"was the old ER entrance. Ambulances traveled into this alley until the new, larger entrance and parking bays were constructed down at Front Street." She paused. "It was the first newborn safe haven in the country. A place where mothers in distress could leave their infants safely. And as long as there was no sign of physical abuse on the baby, police were not contacted. The child went into the system for adoption." The woman turned and studied Angie in the dim light, as if searching to prove something for herself. "What is your friend's interest in this particular case?" she said.

Angie shifted her weight. She suspected this veteran nurse could see right through her reason for being here. But Angie was not ready to tell anyone that she was the cradle child abandoned here in '86. She inhaled deeply and said, "My friend was the one found inside the cradle that night. She learned only two weeks ago that she'd been adopted. For her whole life she believed she was someone else entirely. Now she'd like to know who she really is, who her biological parents might have been, how she came to be left in that baby box. Her case, as you know, was investigated by Vancouver police, but with no leads, no one coming forward with any information at all, the case finally went cold."

"And because you're a detective with the Metro Victoria police on the island, your friend asked *you* to come over to the mainland to find out more?"

"That, yes. And because I . . . have a bit of free time on my hands." Not of her own volition—Angie had been placed on administrative leave after she shot sexual predator Spencer Addams—the Baptist—to death. Her disregard of a direct order, breach of MVPD protocol, her use of excessive force, evidence of rage, and a blackout had resulted in her being stripped of her badge and gun pending an Independent Investigations Office probe. On top of that there was a separate review underway by her own Metro Victoria Police Department. Worst-case scenario was that the IIO would deem her actions had veered into criminal. The IIO investigators could hand her case over to a Crown prosecutor. She could face criminal charges.

It didn't help that she was now being sidelined in the ongoing investigation that had come out of the Spencer Addams pursuit—a case *she* had helped crack wide open.

Angie cleared her throat. "So, visiting the location and speaking to you is my ground zero, my first step." She offered the nurse a smile. "I found your name in a newspaper feature from '86 that had been digitized. Apart from a few articles, there's not much online from that *pre-everything-on-the-Internet* period," she said. "I'm sure I'll find detailed coverage in library microfilm archives, but unfortunately the VPD has purged the old files and evidence from storage, so whatever you can tell me about that night, and about the cradle itself, is going to be helpful."

Jenny nodded, her gaze still probing Angie's. "Well, the modern cradle concept was inspired by the foundling wheels of the twelfth century. When Catholic nuns in Europe sought a way to reduce infanticides, they came up with a method that allowed moms in distress to discreetly place newborns into a cylinder outside the wall of a convent.

The cylinder was then rotated, moving the baby inside. The mother would then ring a bell outside the convent and leave without ever being seen. Modern cradles, or baby boxes, work in a similar way. A mother unable or unwilling to care for a newborn—and who might otherwise dump her infant somewhere to die—can safely and anonymously abandon her baby in a hospital bassinet accessed via a secure and electronically monitored door located outside the emergency department."

"But from what I've read, the first Saint Peter's cradle was shut down?"

"Yes," Jenny said, stepping farther back under the eaves as rain pummeled down and wind began to gust. "Because of legal issues. Four months after it first opened, a healthy baby boy just hours old was dropped off. This sparked international media attention, alerting the World Health Organization. The WHO then came out claiming baby boxes contravened the rights of children to know their parental history and medical backgrounds. This, of course, is not a view that I share," Jenny said. "My take is that a child's very first claim is the right to life, upon which all other rights are contingent. I mean, what use is the right to know your birth history if you've been abandoned in a dumpster and you die?" She inhaled deeply, shaking her head. "Nevertheless, the WHO protest *did* highlight our country's lack of safe haven legislation, and the cradle was shut in '88."

"But you now have a new angel's cradle at the new Front Street ER entrance?" Angie said.

"The program relaunched only in 2010. It took a great deal of persistence, imagination, and collaboration with government and other stakeholders to get to that point," Jenny said. "And because there's still no blanket safe haven legislation, it's key that our local program works in concert with existing laws, which still hold that the abandonment of a child is a criminal offense. However, police and the attorney general's office finally agreed that they would not seek to prosecute mothers if there was no evidence of abuse on the child. Hospital staff are also under no obligation to report the abandonment or connect the baby with the parent, even if the birth mother does anonymously present to our hospital hours or days after delivery for treatment, provided her newborn was left *safely.*" Jenny paused and held Angie's eyes. "The toddler abandoned here in '86 was a whole other story. For one, she wasn't an infant." She paused, and history seemed to hang in the cold air. Wind whirled suddenly in a new direction, chasing down the alley as it whipped rain at them under their shelter.

"Would you like to see the new cradle?" Jenny said softly. "I can show you how it works from the inside. I did let the ER staff know that we'd be coming, and they're fine with it."

"Please," Angie said, suddenly reluctant to enter the old Catholic-run hospital, fearful of the memories that might confront her. But she was equally anxious to see a real cradle for herself—perhaps it *would* prod some buried memory—and that's precisely why she was here. She was *desperate* to recall more than the few dark snippets that had begun haunting her.

They made their way down the alley and rounded the corner onto Front Street. It was alive and dense with evening commuter traffic, pedestrians, buses. Tires crackled over the wet road surface. A vehicle honked. A bus exhaust puffed white condensation into the chill air. Across the street from the hospital, store windows glowed brightly, colors smeared with rain. Above those stores, apartments and offices rose up into the low cloud.

Jenny Marsden took Angie past a bank of ambulances parked outside the ER facility entrance. Under the cover of the portico, outside the ER doors, Jenny halted and once more shook out her umbrella, the ruby light from the emergency sign above the doors casting an otherworldly hue across her features.

"This is it," the nurse said as she closed her umbrella and nodded toward the wall beside the ER entrance. On the wall was a mural. It depicted a woman's head bent as if in sorrow, her hair flowing into the shape of an angel's wing—as though the angel was protecting her. Beside the mural, written in a gentle cursive font, were the words ANGEL'S CRADLE OF SAINT PETER. Beneath the words a small square door—more like a window—had been set into the wall. It was rimmed with metal and positioned just above waist level.

"This door remains unlocked at all times," Jenny said. "A mother can open it, place her newborn in the bassinet inside, and thirty seconds after the door is shut, an alarm sounds inside the ER. Staff will then respond and attend to the abandoned infant."

Angie swallowed as cold seemed to crawl deeper into her body.

"Come. I'll show you what it looks like from the inside."

The nurse led Angie through the ER reception area and down a sterile-smelling corridor lined with empty beds on wheels. They came to a set of square double doors in the wall, also at waist height. Four plastic chairs lined the wall beside the doors. Jenny stopped and faced Angie. Under the harsh fluorescent lighting, the nurse regarded Angie in silence. Angie weighed Jenny in return. The woman's hair was thick and cut into a blunt bob above her shoulders. In this light Angie could see that the nurse's skin was fine and papery. Deep lines fanned out from wide-set warm brown eyes and bracketed her mouth. The wrinkles seemed to map years of empathy and sadness. They were the lines, Angie thought, of a person who'd cared too much for far too long. Angie had once been told that empathy did not make for an easy nursing career. It was the more self-centered nurses—the ones who could easily objectify and distance themselves from their patients' pain—who fared best. It was the same with cops, in her opinion. The truly compassionate officers didn't last—or live—quite as long. It was a survival thing—the ability to cut off that part of oneself.

"What did you say your friend's name was again?" Jenny Marsden asked quietly.

"I didn't." Angie forced a smile. "She prefers to remain anonymous at this point."

The nurse considered Angie's reply, oblivious to two paramedics suddenly rushing a gurney past them. "I understand," she said finally, quietly. Her eyes shimmered with moisture. She turned away quickly and opened the doors set into the wall. "This is the interior entrance to the bassinet."

Angie came forward and peered in.

The compartment was painted a deep eggplant. It ran from waist to ceiling height. A door in the rear wall led to the outdoors. A clear plastic bassinet was positioned at the base. The bassinet was about four by three feet in size—large enough to accommodate a three- or four-year-old. Like Angie had been when she'd been abandoned. The mattress in the bassinet was covered in a soft-looking white flannel fabric. In the corner sat a yellow teddy bear dressed in a red sweater printed with the words SAINT PETER'S HOSPITAL.

The teddy's beady eyes regarded her intently. A shrill ringing began in Angie's brain as she stared into the shiny eyes. The air grew hot. Pressure increased inside her skull. She struggled to draw in a breath, to gather the onslaught of emotions swirling like an unchecked tsunami inside her chest.

Jenny leaned over the bassinet and opened the door on the far side. Cold wet air blew in. Through the opening Angie could see the lights and traffic of Front Street, a Starbucks logo in the window across the sidewalk. She felt as though she'd slid through some alternate reality, some hole in time.

"The cradle back in '86 was not much different from this one," Jenny said quietly. "It affected us all, you know, finding that bleeding and mute toddler inside. She was a beautiful child—that pale complexion, the long dark-red hair, and that tattered little pink dress with frayed lace." A pause. "We all thought someone would come forward to claim her instantly—that she had to have *some* family who was missing her. But no one did—not a soul. No mother presented at Saint Peter's with injuries later. The other hospitals in this health-care region reported nothing suspicious, either. It was a mystery. An absolute mystery."

"Tell . . . tell me more about the child," Angie said, her voice husky.

"Her mouth had been slashed open by a sharp weapon—it had sliced through both the upper and lower lips on the left side of her face. She was bleeding copiously from the wound. Blood saturated her dress, the bassinet. She was clutching the teddy we'd placed inside, like a lifeline. Blood soaked the teddy bear as well. She was in shock, gray eyes like saucers. And she made no sound at all. As though she was beyond crying and had perhaps been that way for a long time before." Jenny fell silent.

Angie looked down at her.

"Eyes the same color as yours," Jenny said almost inaudibly. Her gaze ticked to the scar that marred the left side of Angie's mouth. "Hair the same deep-red shade as yours—like Brazilian cherrywood, I always thought."

Angie's cheeks went hot. "The news feature that I read online didn't give much else beyond those same details."

"Yes—the police asked us to keep silent about the other information. They said it would aid them in their investigation. We took their request very seriously. Like I said, finding that toddler in the baby box . . . It impacted us all deeply. We *all* wanted answers, and if not talking to the media was going to help get them, we wanted to do everything we could."

Tears pricked suddenly at Angie's eyes. It scared her—this lack of emotional control. But hearing that there'd been people who'd cared all those years ago, who'd wanted the same answers she now sought, who'd done everything to help her . . . it connected her to this place. And to this nurse with whom she shared a piece of the past. It gave her a small sense of belonging, of *grounding*—something she'd begun to crave desperately since her father had dropped the bombshell of her past on her.

"Holdback evidence," Angie offered. "That's why police asked for silence. But you *can* talk now. Whatever evidence did come into the cradle with the child in '86 has since been destroyed. I visited the VPD this morning, and they confirmed this. There are no case files, no evidence, nothing. Their old collection and maintenance procedures have since changed dramatically—as is the case with many law enforcement agencies worldwide that used to routinely destroy evidence in storage after a set period of time. The lead detectives who handled the cradle case are now deceased. I'm meeting with the widow of one tomorrow, but I doubt she'll be able to tell me anything."

Jenny nodded and worried her bottom lip with her teeth.

"Can you tell me what time the cradle alarm sounded?" Angie prompted. She'd heard her father's side of the story. Now she wanted as many other viewpoints as possible.

"It was around midnight," the nurse said softly. "As Christmas Eve turned into Christmas morning—just before the cathedral bells started to peal. I was busy at the nurses' station when the alarm rang. We'd experienced false alarms before—sometimes curious folks would open the door just to see what was inside. But that night was different." Jenny stared into the bassinet, a distant look entering her eyes, as though she were seeing right back into the past. "I opened the doors, and . . . the little girl just sat there, staring at me, blood pouring from her mouth as she clutched that stuffy bear. I . . . it was a shock, like nothing I've experienced." Jenny paused, collecting herself. "She must have been taken from some place of shelter in a great hurry given that she was so underdressed for the weather. No time to even put on her shoes. And I imagine she did own shoes because the soles of her feet seemed in fairly good condition. She was very thin, though."

"What happened next?" Angie prodded.

"I yelled for help. ER staff rushed to my assistance. We got her into surgery, controlled the bleeding while checking vitals. The doctor on duty sutured her mouth. A nurse trained in forensics was called in. She . . . uh . . ."

"Did a rape kit?"

"Basically, yes. And took photos while we worked. Our primary focus, however, was patient care. Then the police arrived, asked questions. A pediatrician was brought in, and a social worker. Signs of malnourishment and possible vitamin D deficiency were present. I don't think she spent much time outdoors in sunlight. Her age was estimated to be around four—dental calcification and eruption, long bone growth, epiphyseal development, closure of growth plates and bones— it all happens at a fairly predictable pace. However, she was small for her estimated age."

Tension coiled like a serpent in Angie's belly. With a very carefully measured voice, she said, "So there were signs of neglect."

"Long term, in my opinion. Perhaps her whole life."

Angie inhaled slowly. "And . . . evidence of sexual abuse?"

"We found no overt signs of sexual trauma. No anal or vaginal tearing or perineal bruising. But that doesn't always mean . . ." Jenny cleared her throat and reached into her pocket, extracting a tissue. "There were contusions on her body. Some older, some more recent. Some on the insides of her thighs. Evidence of a fractured left radius that had gone untreated." She blew her nose. "I'm sorry. There's always the one case that gets to you. For me, this was it."

"I know," Angie said quickly. "I work in the sex crimes unit on the island. I know how it feels to be faced with an innocent child, or a young woman, helpless in the face of adult abuse, neglect." She knew it with every molecule of her being, that feeling. It was why she'd become a cop. It was what kept her in sex crimes. It was what got her out of bed every morning. But not in her wildest dreams had she ever thought that her drive—her fierce passion for justice in special victim crimes—might have been shaped and fueled by her own suppressed childhood traumas, a life of abuse that she might have endured before she was found here, in the arms of Saint Peter's cradle, on that Christmas Eve. A past she could not remember.

Jenny's lips flattened, and she nodded. "While we were working on the child, others apparently heard gunshots and screams outside the church, around the same time as the bells started. Someone said they'd heard a woman scream. Some witnesses heard tires screeching. Police interviewed everyone who'd come out of Midnight Mass and some people from the restaurants across Front Street. One of our orderlies who had been taking a smoke break out on a balcony upstairs reported seeing a dark van racing down the street, but he didn't know it had been the cause of the squealing tires. Apart from that, no one seems to have witnessed anything else. Back in the eighties, the streets in this area of the city were pretty empty at that time of night."

"What evidence, specifically, did the VPD investigators ask you to keep quiet about?"

Jenny hesitated as she cast her mind back. "There was a sweater, left in the cradle with the child." She wiped her hand across her mouth as if to obliterate something that suddenly tasted bad. "A purple woman's cardigan—buttons down the front. Size medium. Common Sears brand at the time. We figured it had been put inside the cradle to keep the girl warm." A pause. "There were some really long dark-brown hairs caught in the fabric and some short dark-blonde ones. There was also what looked and felt like small amounts of drying semen."

A sickness stirred in Angie's gut. "What made you think it was semen?"

"It fluoresced under UV light, which would have been due to the presence of molecules such as flavin and choline-conjugated proteins, indicative of seminal fluid."

"They bagged this sweater and took it into evidence?"

"Along with photos of everything, plus the girl's dress, underwear, the teddy bear, and the rape kit. They took samples from the blood smeared on the outside of the cradle door, and they found two bullets,

18

one they dug out of the wall, and there were some shell casings. None of which we could talk to the press about."

Which meant there would have been a ballistics report, lab serology results, ABO blood type analysis, microscopic hair analysis—evidence now gone forever thanks to outdated police policy. Angie swore softly. "That old evidence could be retested today using modern DNA technology not available in the mideighties."

"I'm so sorry."

Angie sucked in a deep breath. "And the child didn't utter a word, not once? The whole time she was here?"

"No. And we didn't know whether that was because of shock or a lifetime of neglect—under those circumstances delayed speech is not uncommon. When no one came forward, and she couldn't, or wouldn't, tell us her name, the cops started calling her Janie, as in little Jane Doe. She stayed at the hospital a few weeks before being released to the system. While she remained here in our care, social workers and a psychologist visited regularly. Police tried many times to question her with their assistance, but Janie Doe just stared at them. A forensic artist also came to do a sketch. She drew Janie without the wound across her mouth, and that illustration was published in all the papers, put up in posters around town, and run on the television news—all asking if anyone knew this child."

"I saw that sketch in one of the digitized articles," Angie said quietly. "So they did all that and *still* no clues?"

"It ate at me, Angie," Jenny said. "It consumed all of us who'd worked ER that night and who'd helped nurse our little Jane Doe back to health." A strange look crept into the old nurse's features. She cast a quick glance over her shoulder. "I know I shouldn't have done it. But I did." Quickly, she dug into her tote and removed an unsealed envelope. She held it out to Angie.

"It's yours. If you want it."

A feeling of trepidation unfurled through Angie. She stared at the envelope. "What is it?"

"Open it."

She took the envelope, lifted the flap, and removed an old Kodak print. In fading colors it showed a skinny little girl in a hospital bed wearing pj's too big for her. She clutched a teddy bear similar to the stuffy in the bassinet. The girl's complexion was so pale she looked almost translucent, a blue vein showing at her temple. Hair, deep red, hung lank about her bony shoulders. Unsmiling, she stared directly at the photographer with pale-gray eyes that were empty of all emotion. Her mouth was brutally swollen, bruised. Blackened by a line of stitches like some bad Halloween makeup.

"I shot that photo shortly before child protection services took her. At that point she'd been here under observation for almost four weeks, and although she still hadn't spoken a word . . . I . . . she looked at me differently that morning. I felt she was trying to communicate. So I held her hand, and I squeezed and said, 'Honey, if you're listening to me, if you can understand me, squeeze my hand.'" Emotion hitched Jenny's voice. She fell silent for a moment, blew her nose again. "And then . . . then I told her that she was going to be safe . . ." Once more, Jenny's voice wavered. "I . . . I just wanted to make *some* connection, to have her show me *some* sign that she was aware—not of what was happening to her, or had happened, but that there were people in this world who cared, really cared, and who were kind, and that the folks working in the system would find her a loving home, that one day she'd really know love." Jenny blew her nose again, her tissue going ragged. "And she did—Janie squeezed my hand."

Emotion closed Angie's throat. Quickly she turned her head away. The little bassinet blurred as tears swam into her eyes.

"Do you have children?" Jenny said.

Angie shook her head, not trusting herself to look at the nurse.

"I don't, either. I can't. But I always wanted them. I believe children validate our reason for being—they are what makes us eternal. And when I was given the news of my infertility, I felt that life for me had ended in some way." The nurse fell silent. Still, Angie was unable to meet the woman's eyes, to see in the woman's face the rawness that laced her voice.

Jenny continued, her words growing gravelly. "I'd been struggling emotionally with this news, but that day, when the angel's child squeezed my hand, I . . . I felt I'd made a fundamental contribution in this one little girl's life. I felt *validated.* Maybe I missed out not having kids, but on that day Janie Doe showed me I *did* make a difference in the lives of others, and that alone was a life worth living."

"You did," Angie whispered. "You *did* make a difference."

"Is she happy—your friend? Did her life go okay after she was adopted?"

Angie wiped her eyes with the base of her thumb and finally turned to face the nurse.

Jenny's kind brown eyes locked fast and sincerely onto Angie's gaze. "I *need* to know." She made a small fist and knocked it against her sternum. "It affected me—my heart, right here. I never stopped wondering. It's why I kept that photo. And when you phoned out of the blue just after Christmas, asking to meet with me, it was like a sign." She swallowed hard. "I thought, yes, she's okay, the angel's girl is out there somewhere, and . . . in trying to find the truth, she's finally coming home. All the way back to the beginning, as things must be. I know it sounds strange, but . . . that's what I thought. My cradle girl is coming home. Full circle."

Angie took a moment to marshal herself. "Yes," she said very quietly. "Her life went okay. She grew up in a safe and privileged home. Her adoptive parents loved—still love—her in every way they know how. She never wanted for material possessions. They sent her to the best schools and took her on wonderful vacations. And all the while, she never remembered or knew for a moment what had happened to her that Christmas Eve. Nor did she ever recall anything about her past. Until recently when she started to . . . see things. Hear things. That's when she sought the help of a therapist and when she pushed her father for the truth. He finally told her how she was found in a cradle. And now she wants to learn the whole story—the before. She wants to find her biological parents."

A kind of knowing and peace entered Jenny's face, and she nodded. It was a look Angie associated with holy people.

"Thank God," the old nurse whispered. She raised her hand to touch Angie's arm, and Angie braced—her usual response to unsolicited physical contact. The nurse noticed and lowered her hand, instead channeling it back into her coat pocket. She dug out another Kleenex and once more blew her nose. "Sometimes paths cross for a reason, Angie. I'm glad you came. So glad."

A surge of warmth filled Angie, along with a bittersweet poignancy and a sense of deep kinship. This woman was a physical link to that little girl from before—that little girl in pink who'd been haunting Angie from the murky depths of her own subconscious. The girl Angie had come to find. Herself.

"Going public—speaking about it—could help, you know," said the nurse. "People, relationships change. After all these years, someone might be ready to come forward."

"I know," Angie said softly. "But I'm not ready. Not yet. If . . . if you could please keep my visit to yourself for now, I'd really appreciate it."

Jenny Marsden gave her a long, searching look. "Sometimes we think we're keeping secrets," the old nurse said softly. "But really, those secrets are keeping us. Be careful, Angie. Don't let this secret keep you."

CHAPTER 2

Detective James Maddocks watched the six young women through the hospital ward observation window. Just teenagers by all appearances. All dark-haired save for one blonde. All emaciated. Vacant eyes. Expressionless features. All had barcodes tattooed onto the backs of their necks.

The girls had been discovered two weeks ago when police had swarmed the *Amanda Rose*, a Caymans-registered high-end luxury yacht moored in one of the city's quaint harbors.

It was Maddocks and Angie's investigation as part of a team tasked to hunt the Baptist that had led law enforcement to the *Amanda Rose*. Aboard the now-impounded vessel, they'd discovered the Bacchanalian sex club—a top-dollar international floating brothel. And in the bowels of the boat they'd found these six underage women being forcibly confined for sexual exploitation. All were foreign. Apart from this, little else was known about them—not one had uttered a word since their rescue.

Standing beside Maddocks was Detective Kjel Holgersen, along with the girls' victim services counselor and their psychiatrist.

"How long do you think before they might talk?" Maddocks asked the doctor as his gaze went from one teen to the next. The young females sat at a table with trays of hospital food in front of them. Only one poked listlessly at her meal using a fork. The others remained motionless, all clearly cognizant of the fact that they were being watched from behind the one-way observation glass. Under police custody, they were being housed in a ward that included beds and a living room area. It was here that they were being slowly nursed back to health and weaned off the opioids to which they'd been addicted. The MVPD had not disclosed their location to the press.

"No way of telling yet," said the doctor. "It could be months before they speak. Possibly years, even with therapy. They're exhibiting symptoms that include severe catatonia, or catatonic depression—they're immobile most of the time. Have trouble sleeping, difficulty concentrating and making small decisions, are fearful of sudden movements and loud sounds, show no appetite, are constantly fatigued. Just the simple act of sitting up in bed took them hours during the first few days after they were admitted."

"No communication between them?" Maddocks said.

"Primarily nonverbal interaction has been observed, and it's been limited to eye contact and the occasional hand gesture. One of our nursing staff did hear a whispered exchange between the dark-haired patient, the one pushing her food around, and the blonde," the doctor said. "But it was terminated the minute they became aware of the nurse's presence."

"Did your nurse get a gist of the language they spoke?" Maddocks said.

The doctor shook his head. "Our nurse *thinks* it could have been a Slavic language."

"Well that sure as hell is going to narrow things down," Holgersen said quietly. The lanky detective stood uncharacteristically still at Maddocks's side, his gaze fixated on the girls. "They's a complete enigma. Whoda thunk the Baptist would lead us here—to some fucking international sex trafficking mystery?"

"They have no trust," their victim services counselor added. "They've been tortured, drugged, psychologically abused, and are apparently terrified of communicating anything about themselves to the hospital staff or to myself, likely in fear of recrimination."

Maddocks returned his attention to the girl poking at her tray of institution food. High, angular cheekbones. Strong nose. Wide-set almond-shaped eyes the color of coal. Her thick dark hair was scraped back into a severe ponytail. She had to be younger than his daughter, Ginny. A sick oiliness slicked through his stomach at this thought, at the memory of almost losing Ginn to the Baptist. At everything that had happened over the past month—how he'd fallen in lust and then some kind of love with his partner, Angie. How she'd disobeyed a superior officer and breached protocol in order to save both his and Ginny's lives, how Angie might yet lose her job because of it. The fact weighed heavy on his shoulders. He also knew it was crushing Angie to be sidelined on this barcode girls investigation now. This should have been her baby, in part. Sex crimes—special victims—was her wheelhouse. And he needed a female detective with her experience on his team now.

As he regarded the dark-haired teen, a visceral image seeped through him—his dark-haired Ginny. Eighteen. Her body tightly bound in a plastic tarp, swinging by a rope strung down from a crumbling old trestle bridge in the misty darkness. Angie trying to crawl along the top of the bridge to free his daughter . . .

He rubbed his brow, forcing his focus back to the six females, effectively all Jane Does until his team could learn more.

What are your names? How were you brought into the country? Where did you originate? Where are your families, friends, homes? You must have loved ones looking for you.

Maddocks had recently been hired for the MVPD's homicide division, where his first assignment had been to spearhead the hunt for the Baptist. He'd subsequently been asked to form a new task force designed to investigate these six barcoded survivors. To assist on his investigation, Maddocks had brought in officers from the MVPD's sex crimes unit, counterexploitations, the drugs section, and the criminal intelligence unit. The case was expected to grow exponentially—these girls had likely entered the country through a sophisticated international human trafficking network. The passports found for them aboard the *Amanda Rose* had likely been forged. The documents had not been stamped or used at any Canadian point of entry, either. This made Maddocks think the passports had possibly been intended for future use as the *Amanda Rose* sailed with the girls out of Canadian waters and crossed into US and South American waters—a historic pattern of travel already established by the floating brothel.

Also still unknown were the identities of the Bacchanalian Club's owner-manager-pimp and her transgender bodyguard-assistant. The pimp was a female who looked to be in her sixties. She went by the name Madame Vee. Her assistant was known only as Zina. No identity documents had been found aboard the yacht for those two.

"How much of their catatonia might be attributed to opiate withdrawal?" Maddocks asked the doc, ignoring his phone as it began to vibrate in his pocket.

"Again, hard to say," said the psychiatrist. "Withdrawal symptoms do include anxiety, low energy, insomnia, hot-cold sweats, abdominal cramps, and vomiting, but in my assessment this is probably more a sign of prolonged trauma and abuse, both physical and mental."

"It's consistent with what we see in survivors of human trafficking," the victim services counselor said. "The control tactics employed by traffickers to retain victims in exploitative situations usually include some form of social isolation, forcible confinement, the withholding of identification documents, imposing strict rules, limitation of movement, as well as physical violence and threats of violence. Many victims believe that if they do not comply with exploitation, their employers have the ability to inflict harm on family members both locally and overseas. Some are simply terrified that their families might learn they are—or have been—engaged in sex work." She inhaled deeply. "I believe these girls were threatened with their lives and the lives of their families if they talked to authorities."

Anger, hatred coalesced like cold jelly in Maddocks's gut as he listened to the victim services counselor, who was also a highly respected therapist.

"Trust will obviously take time," he said quietly.

"For them to feel safe will take even longer."

Maddocks met the woman's eyes. "They don't realize they're free yet."

She shook her head. "They might never feel free again in their lives."

Determination, cold and hard, steeled his jaw. He looked from the counselor to the doc. "Will you call the minute there is any change?"

The doc nodded. "If any information does come forth, it will likely come from her." He nodded to the dark-haired female who'd now set down her fork. "She's the oldest, we think. And she's definitely the strongest mentally. Possibly she was procured more recently, had less brainwashing and torture, or is just more resilient. More of a survivor. You get them sometimes—the ones who just defy all odds."

As Maddocks strode toward the hospital exit with Holgersen, his phone vibrated again in his pocket. He slowed his pace and took out his phone, recalling suddenly that someone had tried to reach him earlier while he was talking to the doc.

"Maddocks," he snapped as he pressed his cell to his ear. Seeing those girls catatonic like that had snuffed his last vestiges of patience. He burned to find and nail whoever had done this to them. So far Madame Vee and Zina were squarely in his sights. They were both being held on remand in a prison up the island peninsula, but neither had spoken a single word during interrogations so far. They needed someone to crack. Needed a break.

"Dammit, James—" His ex's voice came through his phone, strident. "You spaced Ginny's appointment again."

Maddocks stopped dead in his tracks, checked his watch. Already 6:17 p.m. *Shitshit.* Ahead of him Holgersen came to a halt and crooked up his brow in question.

Maddocks waved him ahead, indicating that he needed a minute. As Holgersen slouched off with his peculiar lope, Maddocks stepped aside into a hospital waiting area that was vacant.

"Listen, Sabrina, I—"

"Don't 'listen' me—Ginn's appointment was at four thirty. I just called her to see how it went, and she told me you never arrived to pick her up, which meant she missed her therapy session altogether."

Guilt sliced sharply through him. He'd been so swallowed by the scope of managing the fallout from the *Amanda Rose* takedown and the subsequent barcode girls investigation that he'd clean spaced his agreement to drive his own daughter to her therapy appointments. As it was, Ginny's critical-incident stress therapy was a direct result of *his* role in the Baptist investigation. She'd almost died because of what *he* did for a living—hunting heinous monsters. And this time the monster— Spencer Addams—had turned around and zeroed in on Maddocks's vulnerability. His own child.

Maddocks dragged his hand through his hair.

Crap. Why didn't Ginny call and remind me when I didn't show? It hit him suddenly—maybe she *had.* Maybe it was his own kid's call that he'd ignored while engrossed in conversation with the doc, while he was trying to save the daughters of strangers.

"I'll sort it—"

"She sorted it. Ginn made another appointment on her own, but you and I agreed, James. We agreed that she could remain living alone on the island *only* if you were there for her. You promised to take her to all those therapy sessions."

Maddocks loosened his tie. "I said I'll sort it out, Sabrina. It's just—"

"It's *just* the story of our goddamn lives, and I'm sick of it. It's *just* why we couldn't make our marriage work. It's *just* why we never felt like a family. It's *just* why you're not fit—never were—to be her father. It's why Peter—"

"Enough." He ground the word out between clenched teeth, his body temperature elevating further.

It's just *the reason I moved out here and took this job—to make amends, to be close to my daughter, to build a relationship with her . . . to try to salvage what was left of my family . . . to be a good father.*

He *still* hadn't got it right—he'd let his own baby girl down again because he'd been sucked into tunnel vision over the barcode girls.

Was this what it always boiled down to in the end—focusing on nailing the bad guy, then going on to nail the next? Fighting your best fight to bring murder vics and their families justice while struggling to also build a nest egg, a home, a family, and it's worth fuck-all in the end? Was there actually a way to work a major crimes case *and* still be a devoted husband and father, still attend all those school functions, sports events, music recitals that he'd missed over the years, yet *still* give victims their full due?

He took a deep breath, exhaled slowly. "I'm going to make this work," he said coolly. "I—"

"No, you won't. You're involved in that big case, I know that. And from past experience I also know what that means, the hours you keep. I can't imagine how you're even going to care for that lame three-legged mongrel of yours, let alone manage a relationship with that . . . that cop—"

"Angie. Her name is Angie. That cop saved our daughter's life, Sabrina."

A moment of hesitation. Sabrina cleared her throat. "I . . . I know," she said, her voice softer. "And I'm grateful for it, I really am, but it was your job with homicide that landed Ginny in danger in the first place. So here's what I'm going to do. I'm getting onto the first ferry over to the island tomorrow. I'm going to help Ginn pack up her things, and I'm bringing her home to the mainland. She'll live here with me and Peter. We'll see that she follows through with her critical-incident stress therapy and that she gets all the moral support she needs. I've already arranged with a local psychologist to fit her in. This is not a good time for her to be on her own, and she can transfer her credits to UBC. The school has a much higher reputation than UVic."

His jaw grew tighter and tighter as his ex rattled on. "I'm going to hang up now," he said quietly. "I'm right in the middle of something—I'll call you back when I can talk properly."

"James—do not do thi—"

He killed the call and checked his messages. One missed call from Angie. Nothing from Ginn. He punched in Ginny's number. As the phone rang, he went to the window behind the chairs in the seating area and looked out into the parking lot. Mist shrouded the evening. Darkness came early this time of year. Rain fell soft and insidious, and water squiggled down the pane. Under a misty halo cast by a light in the parking lot, Holgersen was walking Jack-O, the three-legged mutt Maddocks had rescued after a hit-and-run last Halloween. His chest tightened at the sight of his partner with his aged, hobbling dog. The guy was an enigma. Full of odd ticks and seemingly unable to string two grammatically correct sentences together, but he was one of the most astute investigators Maddocks had encountered in his lifetime of policing. And he suspected Holgersen's idiosyncratic speech was either a tool to set people off guard or a distraction behind which he hid. But what was he hiding? That was the question. An unspecified unease whispered through Maddocks as he watched the pair. He liked Holgersen but was not entirely sure he could trust him.

"Dad?"

30

He tensed. "Hey, Ginn. I'm so, so sorry about spacing the appointment. Why didn't you call when I didn't show? Why didn't you remind me? Is everything all right?"

"It's fine, Dad. I didn't want to bother you—I know how busy you are with the investigation into those girls. And I *want* you to get whoever did this to them. I need you to do whatever it takes to put away those people who were abusing them." Her voice caught on a surge of emotion. "They're the ones responsible for hurting Gracie and Faith, and for abusing Lara, for putting them in harm's way, and for harboring a killer," she said, referring to the young local girls who'd been targeted by the Baptist. "I want you to put all of them away for a long, long time. And I'm fine. Honest. I can—I *want* to do this therapy thing on my own."

Again, the image of Ginny trussed up like a cocoon in a polyethylene tarp swung into his mind. It sent ice through his chest. His hand tightened around his phone.

"What are you doing right now?" he said quietly.

"Why?"

"I just want to know. I want to be sure that you're okay."

"I've got someone over."

"Who?"

A small beat of silence. "A friend."

"Who?"

"Someone you don't know."

"A guy?"

"Yes, a guy. Dad, it's—"

"Is your new roommate home?"

"Yes. And even if she wasn't, I'd be fine. Is this . . . this is all because of Mom, isn't it? Did she just call you?" Maddocks hesitated, and Ginny continued before he could answer. "Listen, Dad, Mom did ask me to go live with her and Peter. I said no. I don't want to go home. I don't want

31

to go backward. I want to face this. Here on the island. I like my new school. I like my new friends. I'm happy in my apartment—"

"Ginn, this is not your—"

"If you're going to say it's not my decision, it is. I'll be nineteen in four months." His mind instantly shot back to the barcode girls. Even the eldest among them was not close to nineteen. "I *need* to get over this on my own, and I told Mom so. And I won't slip on the counseling sessions, I promise. I rescheduled, and I can get myself there on public transit. I can do this, Dad."

"What time did you reschedule for?" he said.

"Next Thursday. Six o'clock, after my classes."

"Okay, this is how it's going to play, kiddo. I'll be waiting in my vehicle outside your apartment at five thirty next Thurs—"

"It's not necess—"

"It is, Ginn. For me. It's necessary for me, too, to be there. Okay? Please."

A hesitation. "Sure, Dad."

"And afterward, you and me, we go out for dinner and catch up. Promise me."

"Promise."

Maddocks signed off with his daughter, his heart tight. He checked his watch again. He also needed to call Angie. He was itching to know how her meeting with the old nurse from Saint Peter's had gone. He started to dial her number, but the hospital doors slid open and in came Holgersen, his jacket and hair glistening with rain, Jack-O tucked awkwardly under his left arm.

"Sarge!" he said, loping hurriedly over. "We're needed back at the station. Stat. Zina's counsel wants to deal—Zina's offering information on the barcodes."

CHAPTER 3

Angie watched Jenny Marsden disappearing down the dark street and into the mist. The old nurse was right—a secret could own you. A secret was powerful. But only to the degree that revelation thereof threatened one's social relations. And she did feel threatened by this one. This secret of her past painted her as victim. It made her feel vulnerable. And the old-boy cops with whom she worked in sex crimes, and homicide— where she really wanted to be—had noses for hot blood, fresh wounds. Like a wolf pack, they tended to turn on any perceived weak link among them. And kill it. A primal survival instinct perhaps, because a group was only as strong—or as fast—as its weakest link. And cops were all about depending on their pack for survival.

Angie's method of coping as the only female among the group was simple—someone bullied or baited her, she punched hard and straight on the nose before her opponent could sink his teeth into her fragile spots. It worked. Especially on misogynistic asses like Harvey Leo. Which was why she did *not* want to go public with this. Not yet. Especially not while she was under investigation for use of excessive force. She had zero intention of becoming a poster child for police brutality, either. The MVPD would hang her out to dry if that happened— she was certain of it. The force was already struggling to rebuild its reputation after internal leaks to the press during the Spencer Addams investigation.

When she saw Jenny turn the corner, Angie walked slowly back up the brick alley. Once more she stood in front of the dimly lit service entrance. She closed her eyes, feeling the cold, smelling the rain, listening to the sounds of the city, trying to take her mind back thirty-two years, trying to recall the moments right before she'd been stuffed into the baby box here.

Mist and wetness cloaked her. She could scent the dampness of the bricks and that strange metallic smell she associated with coming snow.

But no memories whispered—nothing at all.

She crossed over to the cathedral, climbed the stairs, and pulled open the heavy wood door. The space inside was cavernous, solemn. Candles flickered—little gold tongues of light licking at stained glass and shadows. Behind the altar hung a sculpture of Jesus, his head bowed under his brutal crown of thorns, hands and feet nailed to the cross. Angie tried to hear it again—the thin, sweet, angelic mezzo-soprano tones of "Ave Maria," the hymn her adoptive mother had been singing in this cathedral on that fateful Christmas Eve over three decades ago. The same song her mother had sung while rocking mindlessly in her chair at the Mount Saint Agnes Mental Health Treatment Facility on the island two weeks ago. Hearing the melody that day had started to stir to life dark memories locked deep inside the vault of Angie's soul. She called the sounds to mind . . .

Ave Maria . . .

Gratia plena, Dominus tecum . . .

But no memories rustled to life this time. Instead, the strange Polish words she'd also recently begun to remember echoed through her brain.

Uciekaj, uciekaj! . . . Wskakuj do srodka, szybko! . . . Siedz cicho!

Run, run! Get inside! Stay quiet!

The voice was a woman's. Had the woman been yelling at Angie to get inside that cradle? To shut the hell up once she was inside? Angie returned her thoughts to her dad's confession.

34

In the photos that your mother and I saw in the media, you looked exactly like our four-year-old Angie did when she was killed in the car accident in Italy in '84. The same red hair. The right age. It was haunting, the fact that she—I mean, you—were found right outside the church where your mother was singing, where in her prayer she'd felt a link to you again . . . She felt it was you, Angie. Arriving, returning, right on the cusp of Christmas Day, like a child in a manger. And your mother saw it as a sign. A very powerful sign. She believed our Angie had been sent back by angels and that we had to do everything in our power to claim you, adopt you, bring you rightfully home to us.

Angie shook herself at the memory. Her adoptive parents had inserted her into the void left by their dead child—effectively replacing the old "Angie" with the new one from the cradle. They'd even given her the same name—led her to believe she *was* the old Angie and that she'd gotten the scar across her mouth during the car accident in Italy. Talk about identity crisis.

She left the church and walked back down the alley toward Front Street, beckoned by the warmth of the brightly lit storefronts. A bereft emptiness and cold filled her as her boot heels echoed on the brick paving. It came with a sense of resignation, of heavy defeat. Maybe she'd never learn the truth. With those VPD case files and evidence gone, with the detectives deceased, her avenues of investigation were sorely limited.

Angie stopped outside the ER entrance, her attention once more drawn to the brightly lit Starbucks outlet across the road. She studied the storefront through the rain, then shifted her attention to the apartments above it, the shops adjacent. The digitized article she'd told Jenny Marsden about had been accompanied by a news photo taken shortly after the gunfight had erupted outside the cathedral. Police had cordoned off the area in front of the cathedral, and the witnesses plus a small crowd had gathered on the opposite side of the street right about where that Starbucks was. Except it wasn't a coffee shop back then.

Angie stepped farther back under the portico cover, out of the rain. She took her smartphone from her pocket—a new one she'd bought since she'd had to hand over her work phone along with her badge and gun while on suspension. She pulled up the news photo she'd clipped from the article and saved. It showed a group of about twenty people huddled in hats and coats, snow coming down, bright lights from a television news crew, yellow crime scene tape, officers in uniform. Behind them was a restaurant with a pink neon sign in the window that declared, **THE PINK PEARL CHINESE KITCHEN**.

She glanced up. The Chinese restaurant had been replaced by the Starbucks. But when? Had there been another business—or several—in that space after the Pink Pearl had vacated the premises? She could obtain that information from city planning and business license records on her next visit to the mainland, but asking wouldn't hurt. Besides, she could do with a hit of warm caffeine and sugar.

Angie pulled up her hood, stepped back into the rain, and crossed Front Street. She entered the Starbucks.

The place was quiet inside at this dinner hour. A lone male sat with his laptop at a table near the back, and two females Angie guessed were hospital employees conversed in deep chairs in a corner. Music played softly—a lyrical, jazzy tune. Pushing back the hood of her jacket, Angie ordered a cappuccino and a brownie from the young woman behind the counter. The woman sported a nose ring and a silver bar across of the top of her ear. Wrapped around the left side of her thick neck was a large spiderweb tattoo. The tat reminded Angie of a fishnet stocking struggling to contain a fat white thigh—like some *Rocky Horror* costume. Angie moved to the end of the counter, where a male barista made her coffee.

"Do you know how long this Starbucks has been here?" she asked the barista.

Glancing up, he frowned and made a moue. "Like maybe four years? Or perhaps five?" He turned to his colleague with the tat. "You know how long this place has been open, Martine?"

Martine shook her head, clearly disinterested.

"We had a water pipe burst about six months ago," the barista said, concentrating on pouring foam onto Angie's drink. "So the interior of the place has been refurbished. That's why it's pretty new looking."

"Any idea what was in this space before?"

He glanced up. "It was a Chinese restaurant. An old place that had been here for decades." He smiled. "The only reason I know is because the old Chinese dude who used to run it like forever still lives in one of the apartments upstairs."

Excitement flushed through Angie. "Do you know his name?"

"Hey, Martine, the old restaurant guy—you know his name?"

"Ken somebody," she said. "Ken Ling . . . Lee. I dunno." She wiped her hands on her apron, grabbed a silver jug, and went to the sink where she commenced rinsing it.

The barista handed Angie her cappuccino. "Like I said, he lives in the apartment building upstairs. Comes in here like clockwork every afternoon around two. Reads his paper and has a green tea latte. Always sits in that back corner if he can get the table."

"So he'll likely be here tomorrow?"

The barista snorted. "If nothing changes. I can set my watch by that guy."

Rippling with adrenaline, Angie took her coffee and brownie to a counter that ran the length of a window facing Front Street. She perched atop a barstool and sipped her drink while she studied the image on her phone again. If that old restaurateur had been working here back in '86, or if he knew someone who had, she might have her first witness. A place to start. Tomorrow morning she had an appointment with the old detective's widow on the North Shore. She could make it back into town by two in the afternoon to see if the restaurateur was here. If not, she'd begin with city records and possibly find his name and address. Or canvass the residents in the apartments upstairs in search of him.

Energized, Angie bit into her brownie and called Maddocks's number on her cell. As it rang she chewed her brownie, relishing the instant sugar and chocolate rush. Her call kicked to voicemail. Angie hit the kill button and slowly swallowed her mouthful, which was suddenly dry in her throat. He was busy on the barcode girls case. She knew that. *Her* case—or at least it should have been, in part. It was her and Maddocks's work on the Baptist case that had led to the discovery and rescue of those young women with the barcode tats. A small tang of bitterness filled her mouth. She'd saved Maddocks's life, and there he was, working one of the biggest and most intriguing investigations to hit the MVPD books in decades. And it would no doubt mushroom in scope with possible international reach. While she sat on the sidelines with her career in jeopardy.

Angie reached for her coffee and sipped as she turned her attention to the huge brick hospital across the street. Through her own reflection on the window, she studied the building. Smeared and darkened with rain and nestled up against the ominous stone cathedral, it brought to mind some Dickensian structure, a rambling place filled with galleries and passages and terrible pain and secrets. The place where she'd been abandoned. Where her new life as Angie Pallorino had begun; where her old slate had been wiped clean of her memories. As she regarded the building, the rain outside turned into fat flakes of snow. They floated down like weightless silver leaves and settled fast on the roofs of parked cars and on the cold sidewalk.

A surreal sensation sank through her—she was on the cusp of two identities. The child before. And the Angie after. With the sense of surreality came fear. It unfurled from somewhere deep down in the basement of her soul, from her buried past, fingering upward like a stranger into her present. She shook it. Because there was only one way forward now.

Ironically, it meant going backward first.

CHAPTER 4

WEDNESDAY, JANUARY 3

Angie drove over the Lions Gate suspension bridge, her wipers squeaking against the soft mist of winter rain. It was 11:30 a.m., and traffic flowed smoothly. Far below the bridge the waters of the Burrard Inlet gleamed gunmetal gray. To her left, off the beaches of Kitsilano and Spanish Banks, more than twelve tankers skulked in fog, awaiting their entry to the Port of Vancouver—delayed indefinitely thanks to a longshoremen's union strike that was now into its second week. To her right, hidden from view on days like today, lay the hazy white wedge of Mount Baker in the States. But up ahead, on the opposite shores of the Burrard, the densely forested North Shore mountains were exposed in shafts of sunlight as skeins of cloud drifted over their green flanks. Above the snowline everything was pristine white.

The widow of deceased VPD detective Arnold Voight was expecting Angie up on the slopes of one of those mountains where she now lived in an in-law suite in her daughter's home. Voight had been the lead detective on the '86 cradle case.

CBC radio played softly in the background of her Nissan Altima rental as she turned onto the off-ramp that would lead her from the bridge down onto Marine Drive. Her MVPD Crown Vic was another thing she'd had to surrender while on administrative leave. She also had to call into the department on every day that she'd normally be working—she was still being paid. Still on the clock. A suspension was not a vacation, as her superior, Sergeant Matthew Vedder, had reminded her.

Anxiety crawled into her chest at the thought of the pending IIO review ruling. Not only could it kill her career entirely, but it could also give her a criminal record. Angie didn't know how *not* to be a cop, let alone how to be a criminal.

In an effort to distract herself, she hit the hands-free phone icon on her dash and dialed Maddocks once more. He was the only one she'd told so far about her discovery that she was the angel's cradle child, and she wanted to share with him what she'd learned from the nurse. She'd tried calling Maddocks from the hotel last night, but each time she'd gone straight to voicemail.

His phone rang, and yet again her call was shunted immediately to voicemail. Angie turned onto Marine Drive as she listened to Maddocks's recorded voice. She stopped at a red light and left a message.

"Maddocks, it's Angie. I . . . give me a call, will you? I'm on my way to see the widow of Detective Arnold Voight. She lives on the North Shore. VPD has no case files." She ended the call, a hollow feeling in her gut. She missed him, dammit, and that frustrated her. She didn't want to miss anyone. She did not want to *need* anyone. Her grip tightened on the wheel. The light turned green, and she hit the gas. She'd see him later tonight anyway—they had a reservation for dinner at the King's Head to celebrate her so-called "birthday," which was today. The farce of it dug deep after having seen the cradle. Because no one knew when she'd really been born, or to whom. The Pallorinos had simply picked today, January 3, because they'd felt it was the start of a new life for her at the commencement of a fresh year. And, her father had said, because the date was set just slightly apart from the actual New Year's festivities, so she could still feel "special" on her own day.

40

As Angie took a left up Lonsdale, her thoughts turned to her adoptive parents—Miriam and Joseph Pallorino. They'd lived here on the North Shore while fostering her before the adoption had gone through. Her father had told her that a social worker and a child psychologist had visited them several times each week. A speech therapist had come, too, to help Angie learn to speak again, teaching her English, because by then they'd begun to suspect that she might have been raised in a foreign language before she'd been abandoned. Or not taught to speak much at all.

Uciekaj, uciekaj! . . . Wskakuj do srodka, szybko! . . . Siedz cicho!

She'd known instinctively that those words in her memory meant, *Run, run! Get inside!*

She believed now that she'd understood some Polish as a child, and that the voice yelling those words had possibly been her mother's, or the voice of a female caregiver.

Angie took her vehicle up a steep hill. She rounded a corner, slowed, and checked the address on a pillar at the bottom of a precipitous driveway. The widow's residence. She turned in, drove up to a rambling post-and-beam rancher painted pale gray, and parked outside the garage.

Nerves, anticipation shimmered through Angie as she looked up at the house. She was about to come face-to-face with the wife of the cop who'd hunted for her family three decades ago.

CHAPTER 5

"Please, come in. I'm Sharon Farraday. My mum's expecting you." The woman who'd opened the door to Angie was slender with dark hair scrunched up into an untidy but flattering ponytail that sent soft tendrils about her narrow features. "She's through this way."

Angie removed her boots and coat and followed Sharon Farraday through a living room with a wooden floor, vaulted ceiling, and a wall of glass that looked out toward the Burrard and the city down in the distance. The tops of city skyscrapers poked through a bank of dense cloud that had settled over land at sea level. A child playing on the floor amid a scattering of toys looked up as Angie entered the room—a cute tomboy of a girl around the age of three. She wore dungarees, a flannel shirt, and she sported strawberry-blonde braids.

"Hi," the child said, her round blue eyes inspecting Angie intently.

"Kaylee, this is Angie Pallorino," said Sharon. "She's come to visit Gran."

"Wanna see my dinosaur?" Kaylee thrust a plastic toy toward Angie. "It's a bronnosaurus."

"I see," Angie said, bending down to take an obligatory look at the toy being offered to her.

"I got it for Christmas. What did you get for Christmas?"

Angie smiled as a memory washed through her—making love with Maddocks on Christmas Day, on his yacht in the wind. Rain beating against deck. "Well, I certainly didn't get a dinosaur."

"It's vicious!" Kaylee said with a grin that scrunched her freckled nose.

"I'm sure it is." Angie straightened up, and her attention went to a series of family portraits on the bookshelves behind the child. The images depicted a happy-looking family unit consisting of mom, dad, and daughter. Another frame showed a grizzled man with thick gray hair holding a fishing rod, his arm around a slight silver-haired woman with a huge smile.

Angie nodded toward the photo. "Is that your mom and dad?" she asked Sharon.

"Yes—the great detective and his stay-at-home wife."

Angie's gaze ticked toward Sharon. Was that a tone of resentment? Sharon gave an apologetic shrug. "I don't mean it like that. But you know, growing up as the child of a cop in major crimes—well, you probably don't know. But I hardly saw him until his retirement three years ago. By then I was long grown, making a family of my own. Then eighteen months after he quit work, he died." Hesitation entered her voice, and a darkness sifted into her eyes. "Sometimes you can spend your whole life waiting for the day you leave work, the day you're going to start enjoying life, start living, start getting to know your family. But by then it's over—it's too late. You're gone."

"Wanna play?" Kaylee interrupted. "I got a tyrasaurus for you."

Angie broke her gaze with the woman and glanced at the child on the floor. She was around the same age as Angie would have been when she'd been stuffed bleeding into that cradle. Same age as the little girl in pink who'd been haunting her in her hallucinations. A chill crawled down her spine. She shook the odd emotion. "Not now, Kaylee, thank you. I need to see your gran."

Sharon pointed Angie toward a staircase. "My mom's suite is downstairs." She lowered her voice and said, "Her memory is not quite what it used to be—she gets confused sometimes. And frustrated if pushed to recall things. Please, whatever it is that you've come for, go on easy on her."

Angie's heart sank a little. "Of course." She started down the wooden stairs. Behind her Sharon called out, "I hope you like scones—I could smell her baking all morning."

At the bottom of the stairs, a door hung ajar. Angie knocked, then edged the door open a little wider. "Hello? Mrs. Voight—are you here?"

The tiny silver-haired woman from the photo popped out from around the wall. She wore an orange apron that was covered with giant purple eggplants.

"I'm Angie," she said, stepping into the open-plan living area.

"Wanda. It's good to meet you." The woman offered Angie her hand. There was a hint of England in her accent, and her hand felt cold and frail, like the bones of a little bird. "Arnold would have been so thrilled at your interest in his old case. That mystery of the cradle child really got to him." She undid her apron ties as she spoke.

"Do you know much about it?"

"Not really. Arnold didn't discuss the details of his cases with me. He liked to keep me separate from all that dark stuff that went on at his work. I made you tea—do you like tea? Please, sit down." Wanda Voight gestured toward a round table abutting a window that looked out over a small garden. On the table was a colorful cloth, atop which sat a teapot covered with a quilted cozy. Beside it was a plate of scones, jars of jam and cream, and a set of matching cups, saucers, and plates.

"I love tea, thanks." Angie seated herself at the table. "You have a nice view from downstairs, too," she said, taking in the pretty little envelope of lawn outside with its neatly trimmed edges, shrub border. A drooping yellow cedar stood sentinel over it all. Once a few pleasantries had been exchanged and tea had been poured and a hot buttered scone and jam had been set in front of Angie, she steered the conversation back to the topic of her visit, remaining careful not to angle in too directly—senior citizens did require a different level of tact when it came to interviews. They'd witnessed life in a different era. They generally needed to be made to feel relaxed, comfortable, warmed up with common interests. Angie explained again why she'd come. "As I mentioned on the phone, I'm looking into that cradle case for a close friend."

"Are you a private investigator, then?" said Wanda.

"In a manner. At least in this capacity." Angie set her cup on its saucer and leaned forward. "That case made the media. Ads and posters were sent out, yet no one came forward to claim the child, no distant relative, nothing. It must have been high-profile for a while?"

Wanda sipped her tea, thinking. "You know, it was the top of the news for a week or so, but then there was that big earthquake up in Alaska, and the angel's cradle child story sort of got swept away by it all. On top of the quake, news broke about that Boeing going down in the Pacific. There was a team of Calgary hockey players on that plane, and it was all everyone was talking about." She took another sip of her tea, then shook her head. "Arnie had nightmares about the cradle case. And when no one came for that little girl, and Arnie could do nothing more to find out where she'd come from . . . well, he had trouble letting it go. He was disturbed by his own inability to solve the mystery."

"He was the lead investigator, I understand."

"Yes. His partner at the time was Rufus Stander. They worked it together. Eventually they had to put the case aside for more pressing things."

"What happened to Rufus Stander?" Angie asked. "When I visited the VPD yesterday, they told me he was also deceased." *And I got a feeling there was more to it than that.*

A shadow crept into the elderly woman's eyes. Carefully, with two hands, she set her cup on the saucer. She wiped her mouth with her napkin. "Arnie and Rufus had a particularly difficult case several years after the angel's cradle one. An eight-year-old boy went missing from

Stanley Park. Clean vanished into thin air. Arnie and Rufus were part of the team tasked with the search. And they were the ones who found him. Just one block down from the park where he disappeared. They were searching the rental unit of a man who'd apparently been seen talking with the boy in the park shortly before the boy vanished. The man was not at home—the landlord let Arnie and Rufus into the unit. Apparently, the landlord said the tenant had not been seen since the day the boy went missing. While Arnie was talking to the landlord, Rufus opened the fridge door, to see what was in there—to judge how long the man might have been gone and whether he might be returning . . ." Her voice faded. She shook herself.

"A garbage bag came tumbling out and thudded onto the floor. The boy had been stuffed into the bag and crammed into the fridge. Rufus told Arnie later that it was the garbage bag that really got to him—the fact that someone's kid had been put into a trash bag like that. Just some rubbish to be thrown away. Why stick the child in that bag, he said, if you're going to put him in the fridge?" A long pause. Rain began to fall harder outside. The boughs of the yellow cedar sulked lower as they dripped water.

"Rufus never got over it, I think," Wanda said, her voice going raspy with emotion. "That and all the other stuff those city cops had to deal with. Years later he tidied up his affairs. Washed all his clothes. Laid all his shoes out neatly in his cupboard and in the boot room, side by side. Then he went and lay down on the railway tracks. At the bottom of North Van." Another break of heavy silence descended over Wanda. She cleared her throat. "That's when Arnie finally put in for his retirement. People don't understand the toll that job can take on a police officer or his family. They don't know how we all have to tiptoe around the ugly side of the job, the mood swings, the depression, the drinking." She looked out of the window, her gaze going distant. "Sometimes when Arnie came home after a bad shift, I couldn't talk to him for hours. I just had to let him lay on the couch and watch mindless television and have a couple of beers, and then he'd finally come around and be himself again. It wasn't easy being married to him. But I loved him." She returned her gaze to Angie. "I miss him."

Angie's chest clutched at the rawness in Wanda Voight's eyes. She hesitated, then awkwardly she forced herself to cover the woman's hand with her own. "I'm sorry," she said.

Wanda inhaled deeply. "No, I'm sorry. This was not supposed to be about me." She extracted her hand, fumbled for a handkerchief in her pocket, blew her nose, and then came to her feet. "I asked Sharon to bring Arnie's boxes up out of the basement. She put them by the sliding door for you."

"What boxes?"

"They're over here," Wanda said as she got up and made for the glass slider.

Angie lurched to her feet and followed, her pulse suddenly racing.

Wanda pointed to two cardboard file boxes that rested side by side on the floor behind a sofa. They were sealed with yellow tape. In fat black Sharpie along the side of the front box, someone had scrawled the words Box 01 Jane Doe Saint Peters #930155697-2.

Shock slammed through Angie. She bent down and moved the first box aside.

Box 02 Jane Doe Saint Peters #930155697-2

Her gaze ticked up to Wanda. "Are these the angel's cradle case files?"

"Like I said, it got to Arnie. He never did stop looking in his own way. He always wondered if that child might return one day as a grown woman to ask him questions. He knew she'd been adopted. He knew that she'd been taken in by a good, kind family. He even called the child's adoptive father a few times to check on the child and to see if she might have remembered anything about that day, or about her life before. Or whether the adoptive family had ever been contacted by anyone suspicious. Arnie also thought that maybe a relative might eventually come to him in search of the child. But no one did. He never did find her family, nor the men who'd fired the guns outside the church that night. When he learned that the evidence was going to be destroyed, he went and got these boxes. He wasn't supposed to. They used to incinerate anything in evidence that was to be destroyed, with witnesses watching. Sometimes they'd return property to families if they could find them. In this case, since there was nothing valuable in there, no weapons or anything, they let Arnie take it. He told them he was going to keep working it on his own. He brought the boxes home."

"*Did* he work on it?"

"He opened the files up several times, extracted some notes, poked around a bit. In the end he resealed the boxes. When I sold the house after he died I brought them here and they went into the basement."

Angie stared at the boxes. Deep inside her belly, her muscles began to shake.

Is it possible?

Could the forensic evidence that Jenny Marsden had told her about be inside those boxes—lab serology results, prints, ballistics info, rape kit—things she could have retested for DNA?

"I think Arnie would like you to have them," his widow said softly. "He'd like to know that someone was still looking."

Angie's heart galloped up into her throat and her skin turned hot as she continued to stare down at the two boxes on the floor. A potential portal.

To her past.

Her future.

CHAPTER 6

Angie circled the city block three times before she found street parking near the Starbucks entrance—she wanted the Nissan close by so she could keep a check on her boxes. Hurriedly she exited her car and stuffed coins into the meter. It was already past two. She jogged toward the coffee shop, her bag slung across her body. Wind blew cold, but at least the rain had stopped. Heart beating fast, she pushed open the door.

Warmth and the scent of coffee greeted her. The place was bustling, noisy with chatter, different staff working behind the counter. Excitement punched through her as she caught sight of her target—an elderly Asian man bent over a newspaper at a small round table in the back.

Angie threaded her way through the lineup and approached the table.

"Morning," she said, tempering her voice.

He glanced up. Angie judged him to be in his seventies. He was small, bent like a question mark inside his oversize houndstooth jacket. His ears stuck out like mug handles from beneath a monk's fringe of white hair that circled a smooth mahogany pate dotted with liver spots. Beneath his pronounced apple-shaped cheekbones, his jaw looked hollow, as if he might be toothless. Eyes, deep and brown, peered at her quizzically from behind small silver-rimmed glasses.

Angie offered him a smile and said, "My name is Angie Pallorino. The barista working here last night told me I might find you here today. I believe you operated the Pink Pearl Chinese Kitchen?"

He frowned. "Yes. For many years. My family owned it. I worked in the restaurant, many, many years, since my twenties."

"Could I join you for a moment? I'd like to ask you a few questions."

He frowned and adjusted his glasses, hands trembling slightly with age or illness. "I was . . . just about to leave. My show comes on television in fifteen minutes. I always watch it."

Angie's muscles tightened. "I'll be really quick."

He hesitated, then held his hand out to the vacant seat in front of him. "Please."

"Could I get you another tea?" Angie said as she pulled out the chair. "Something else perhaps?"

"No, thank you. Like I said, I'm about to go."

She seated herself, spoke quickly. "Was your restaurant here in 1986?"

"Well before that. My parents opened the Pink Pearl in '82. My sister and I sold it only five years ago. It was a piece of Vancouver history, if I say so myself. Many eras in this city that we have seen come and go."

Angie leaned forward. "Do you perhaps remember when a child was left in the angel's cradle at Saint Peter's Hospital on Christmas morning in '86? There was apparently a gunfight, yelling, screaming. Tires screeching. Maybe you were among the crowd of people who were interviewed by police or journalists?"

He frowned, his eyes going distant. "Yes. That was a big day, yes. I couldn't forget that day. Shooting. The child. The papers said it was a gang fight, yes."

"You *saw*?"

"Not me. I was back in the kitchen. We always closed late, after midnight. Things were busy all hours at the Pink Pearl with the nurses, doctors, paramedics often coming over for something to eat, or for takeout, between shifts. But my grandmother was by the cash register that Christmas Eve—she saw something. She died many years ago."

Adrenaline crackled into Angie's veins. "*What* did she see?"

A look of caution entered his eyes. He glanced at the door. Angie placed her hand on his arm. "Please, I need to know. For a friend. I'm looking into the old angel's cradle case."

"Are you a journalist?"

"No."

"Police?"

"I'm doing this in a personal capacity," she said. "Just conducting some research into the child's story. For my friend."

He held her eyes, weighing her, and Angie forced herself to temper the edge she could hear entering her own voice. "Did your grandmother give a statement to the police at the time?"

He shook his head slowly, as if still figuring out whether to trust her. "She didn't speak English. She didn't like police. She stayed away from them. Was afraid of police because of her history in China. But she told *us* what she saw that night."

"Us?" Angie urged gently.

"Me. My sister. My mother and father and my brother. She was standing over there—facing the windows. That's where the cash register used to be." He pointed to a place across from the door. "Red curtains used to run along the bottom half of the windows so that people walking past in the street couldn't easily look in at the patrons dining at the tables. It was almost midnight—the church bells had not yet started ringing. And that's when she saw the woman."

Angie's pulse spiked. "Woman?"

"In a dress. Running across the road toward the alley between the hospital and the church. She carried a child on her hip."

51

"The cradle child?"

"I think so. My mother said she took notice because this woman wore no coat, and it was cold. It had started to snow. Because of the curtain, my grandmother could only see the top half of the woman and the child on her hip. My grandmother hurried up to the window to see more, but already the woman was gone, down that brick alley. Then, just as my grandmother came up to the window, she heard yelling. She said two men then came down the street, from over there." He pointed to his left. "She said they were chasing the woman and the child. They carried handguns. Also no coats."

Angie's mouth went bone-dry. "What . . . what did she *look* like, this woman?" Her voice came out hoarse.

"All my grandmother could see was very long dark hair. The woman seemed young, she said."

"And the men?"

"Big. Muscled. They went into the alley after the woman, and then my grandmother heard gunshots, but right as the shooting started, the church bells started clanging. She heard tires screech farther away. Then a black van came past, very fast, although the van might have been unrelated, she said. It was only later—after the newspeople and the police arrived and the crowd started gathering outside the restaurant—that we learned a child had been put in the cradle."

"And *you* didn't mention this to the police—what your grandmother saw?"

"I did," he said. "The investigators asked to speak to my grandmother directly, with me as interpreter, but she changed her mind—she told me in Chinese that she hadn't seen anything at all and that she'd imagined it. I relayed her words to the police. She was eighty-two at the time, and her eyesight was not good. Cataracts. She was also prone to imagining things, and no one else had seen these men and that woman, so . . ." He shrugged. Outside the coffee shop, a bus drew up and stopped. Hydraulics hissed noisily as the bus lowered and the doors opened to let passengers out. The man's gaze shot to the bus through the window, and he checked his watch. "I must go." He folded his newspaper and pushed himself up onto his feet. "Good luck with your research." He gave a slight bow.

"Wait, wait." Angie came quickly to her feet and dug into her pocket for a business card. "I didn't get your name, and I might want to speak to you again later or call you." She handed the man her card. He studied it, then glanced up sharply.

"You *are* police."

"I work as a detective on Vancouver Island, yes, but this has *nothing* to do with my job. I promise. Like I said, it's a personal favor for a friend."

Mistrust entered his small brown eyes.

"My friend was the child left in the cradle," Angie said quietly, desperate to build trust before he departed. "She wants to know why she was left there and where she came from. I'm trying to help her. Is there somewhere I can contact you later if I need to?"

"I'm Ken Lau," he said finally as he pocketed her card. "I live in one of the apartments upstairs. We have always lived above the Pink Pearl. Now I live above the Starbucks."

"And your phone number?"

"I'm in the phone book. Lau on Front Street."

And with that he shuffled toward the door and pushed out into the winter afternoon. The door swung slowly shut behind him.

CHAPTER 7

Angie inched down the mile-long causeway toward the Tsawwassen Ferry Terminal. Her goal was to be home in good time for her birthday dinner date with Maddocks—she burned to tell him her news now—but blustery weather and high winds had delayed ferry sailings and backed up traffic. She'd also cut timing fine by having returned to the Starbucks to find Ken Lau.

As she crawled forward, the two case file boxes hunkered on the seat behind her like a heavy presence, alive and full with simmering, cobwebby secrets yearning to be addressed. But she had to wait. She wanted to open the seals in a sterile environment wearing gloves in case there was uncontaminated evidence in there that could be retested. Angie's plan was to call Dr. Sunni Padachaya, head of the MVPD crime lab, and ask her to recommend a cutting-edge private firm with forensics expertise to run any tests she might require. Money was not an issue. This evidence was priceless—and Angie had investments. She'd been shrewd with her income over the years. The discovery of these boxes was a game changer—it fueled her with renewed hope.

Angie cursed as she was forced to tap the brakes again. The lineup of cars ahead slowed to a dead halt. Impatient, she drummed her nails on the dash. Wind gusted, rocking her vehicle, driving billowing curtains of rain and mist over the road. She reached for the phone icon on her dash and pressed Maddocks's number. His phone rang several times before cutting to voicemail.

"Hey, me again. I'm in the ferry lineup heading home. Just letting you know." She'd save her news for dinner. "See you at the King's Head." She terminated the call, but that strange hollowness at not being able to connect with him stole into her excitement at having found the boxes and Ken Lau.

Angie waited for the line of cars to start moving again along the spit that jutted out into the wind-whipped ocean. The bruised sky was growing darker as clouds lowered—another front coming in. A bright light down on the misty beach caught her attention. She peered at it through the worms of rain squiggling down the driver's side window. A small group of people clustered around the light. It was unnaturally bright. That's when she noticed the CBC news van parked just off the road above the beach. Curious, she reached into her glove compartment and extracted her binoculars—cop habits die hard. She wound down her window. Rain wet her face as she trained her scopes on the group. Someone was holding a huge umbrella over a plump blonde woman who appeared to be under the interrogation of a reporter with a long black coat holding a mike. The plump woman's short hair ruffled in the wind. She had a small white dog on a leash. She wasn't just plump, Angie realized as the woman turned sideways—she was very pregnant under her blue jacket. The pregnant woman pointed to a rocky outcrop on the beach. The cameraman swung his camera in that direction. As Angie watched, a strange chill filled her, an odd sense of things closing in.

Her phone rang and she jumped. Quickly she hit the control panel on her dash, connecting the call, expecting Maddocks.

"Pallorino," she said, almost adding, *MVPD sex crimes.*

"It's Vedder," came the voice. Angie went stone still. Anxiety twisted into her stomach at the sound of her immediate superior's voice—Vedder was boss of the sex crimes unit where she'd spent the past six years. Vedder had also been appointed as the MVPD liaison between her and the Independent Investigations Office.

"Sir?" She wound up her window.

"Can you come in later this afternoon? We have a ruling from the IIO. We'd like to meet in person to discuss that as well the results of the MVPD internal review."

For a nanosecond Angie was unable to speak. She cleared her throat. "What did the IIO say?"

"We need to do this in person. You might want to bring your union rep."

Fuck. Her eyes burned. She rubbed her brow. "I . . . I'm in the ferry lineup at Tsawwassen," she said slowly. "If I make this next sailing, I could be in your office just after five. I'll call Marge Buchanan and see if that works for her."

"Confirm with me once you've contacted Buchanan."

"Vedder, who is 'we'?"

"Me and Flint."

Angie cursed inwardly. Inspector Martin Flint was head of special investigations under which the sex crimes unit fell, along with the counterexploitation unit, the high-risk offender unit, and the domestic violence criminal harassment unit. She was toast.

"You've got to give me something—let me at least prepare myself."

"I'm sorry, Angie." His use of her first name did not help. The tone in his voice told her that this was not easy on him, either. Vedder had been good to her. He'd gone to bat for her on the many occasions that Angie had butted heads with the misogynist dead wood on the force. Detective Harvey Leo for instance. She and Vedder had become close—he was one of the few guys on the force she had bonded with, someone she trusted. So, this was it. She'd suspected it might happen—that they'd fire her ass. She just hadn't anticipated it happening so soon. Her biggest worry now was the IIO handing her case over to

Crown prosecutors. She could be charged for use of excessive and lethal force. "I'm also really sorry about the timing," he added. "I know it's your birthday."

Yeah, happy fucking birthday to me. "I'll be there." She stabbed the kill button. And sat numb. Through the squiggles of rain on the window, the film crew was moving closer to the rocky outcrop. A truck behind her vehicle honked. Angie jumped. The line of cars in front of her had started to move. She flipped a bird over her shoulder and reached forward to engage her gears. It wasn't anticipation that crackled through her now as she crawled farther forward with the traffic. It was anxiety, a sense that life as she'd known it really was over.

Finally drawing up to the ticket booth, she rolled down her window. A blast of sea wind slapped her in the face, tangy with salt and restless with change.

Hers was one of the last vehicles to make it onto the *Queen of the North*. The ferry ramp made a heavy *ka-clunk* sound as she drove onto the vehicle deck. A sound of finality. As the bridge drew up behind her, a man in a bright-orange visi-vest waved his flashlight, sending her deeper down into the dark bowels of the vessel. Engines and metal rumbled. Angie parked, got out of her rental, locked it, and zipped up her down jacket. She went up to the passenger level, pushed through the heavy door to the outside deck, and braced into the gusts as she walked to the front of the boat. She stood there, hands on the railing, her face turned to the raw wind, and she didn't care about the ice-cold rain that lashed her face. Across that metal-gray water was the island. Her home. Behind her lay the mainland, her unknown past. The ferry horn blasted, and the tone of the grumbling engines shifted as the props churned white foam into the sea. The ship pulled out of the dock. Angie felt as though she was about to cross a threshold.

CHAPTER 8

Maddocks refrained from loosening his tie, although the interview room inside the Vancouver Island Regional Correctional Centre was airless. Hot. Cinder block construction. Pale institutional walls. Two-way mirror. Locked door. A male guard in a black uniform stood in front of the door, feet planted apart, shoulders square, his right hand clasped over his left wrist in a posture that indicated he was ready for anything. The name tag on his breast pocket read MORDEN. A ring of keys and a truncheon dangled from his belt. Across the table from Maddocks sat the inmate he'd come to interview—Zina, the transgender bodyguard-assistant arrested in the *Amanda Rose* takedown two weeks ago.

Seated beside Zina was defense lawyer Israel Lippmann. Observing through the two-way glass were Holgersen, a Crown counsel prosecutor, and a correctional officer.

Maddocks, Holgersen, and the Crown lawyer had driven up the Saanich Peninsula to the old Wilkinson Road jail—a max-security facility that housed both offenders who had been sentenced and those on remand. Lippmann had proposed a deal in exchange for his client being transferred to another facility and for ameliorated charges. The carrot being dangled in front of the MVPD and Crown counsel was information on the identity of the barcode girls.

It could be the breakthrough they needed to help track the suspects who'd trafficked the girls. This kind of sex trafficking usually involved some level of organized crime and international criminal cooperation. The barcode tattoos themselves indicated a level of coordinated criminal structure and ownership branding.

Maddocks regarded the aquiline features of the seven-foot-tall transgender prisoner across from him. The inmate's hair was cropped military-short and dyed silver. Maddocks had recently learned via Lippmann that the prisoner self-identified as female. It wasn't easy for Maddocks to suddenly think of this abuser, captor, and trafficker of young women as a "she." But he was working on it. *Her* skin was a strange ashen tone, her eyes almost colorless. She wore prison garb—bright-red pants, red sweatshirt with VIRECC, BC CORRECTIONS emblazoned across the back. She sat eerily still, no emotion evident in her features. Fresh purple contusions and swelling marred her left cheek. Stitches tracked across her left temple. Ligature marks ringed her neck. Ironic, Maddocks thought, given how one of her sex workers had died during a breath-play act gone wrong.

Before entering the room, Lippmann and the prosecuting counsel had hammered out the plea bargain details and interview terms acceptable to both Lippmann and the Crown.

Maddocks pressed the RECORD button, activating the camera and voice recorder. "Interview commencing with inmate known as Zina. Location, Vancouver Island Regional Correctional Centre. Time, 4:45 p.m., Wednesday, January three." He held Zina's gaze.

"For the record, can the inmate please state legal name?"

"Zaedeen Camus," she said clearly, eyes unblinking.

Maddocks's pulse quickened. They now had a name they could run. "Nationality?"

"I'm from Algiers. My mother was Algerian. My father is a French national. I hold a French passport. My permanent residence is in Paris."

Which explained her accent.

"And you call yourself Zina?" Maddocks said.

"I find the name more feminine. I prefer to identify as a female. I'm currently undergoing hormone therapy. Surgery will follow."

Which sliced to the heart of the matter—the reason they were here. During the chaos of the *Amanda Rose* takedown, it had not been made clear to arresting officers that Zina, who was born with male characteristics, self-identified as female. She'd been incarcerated with the general male population at VIRECC. Sexually assaulted and badly beaten on her first night, she was now being kept in solitary for her own protection. Lippmann had filed various complaints, among them one with the human rights commission. And he'd demanded transfer to an exclusively female pretrial facility. However, safety concerns remained over the current regulations around transgender inmates and Zina's potential transfer into a female population. Given Zina's alleged involvement in possible kidnapping, sexual assault, trafficking, torturing, drugging, brainwashing, and forcibly confining underage females aboard the *Amanda Rose*, she was not going to get an easy ride in *any* prison population. But it was why their inmate was prepared to talk now.

"Where are your identity documents, your passport?" Maddocks said. "They weren't found aboard the *Amanda Rose*."

Zaedeen Camus glanced at her lawyer. Lippmann gave a small nod.

"Madame Vee instructed me to bag my documents along with hers and to seal the bag, weight it down, and cast it overboard."

"When did she instruct you to do this?"

"As the SWAT teams swarmed the vessel."

"How did you cast them overboard?" said Maddocks. "Out of the window? Of her office?"

"Correct, out of the porthole in her office."

"Describe the bag."

"A sealable dry bag. Black. Watertight. A small orange logo on the side."

"How big?"

"Holds five liters."

"Why overboard?"

"Madame Vee felt that silence and anonymity was the safest policy if we were to undergo interrogation. She also wanted the documents protected in the event we might be able to retrieve them with a diver later."

"Anything else in the bag aside from identification documents for you and Madame Vee?"

Her eyes flickered. Lippmann moved his hand over his notepad—a sign.

"Yes."

"What else was in the bag?"

"Some other papers—only things pertaining to our personal identification."

Maddocks made note of this and of the bag's description. They needed to get police divers down below the *Amanda Rose*.

"And what is the legal name and nationality of Madame Vee?" Maddocks said, after having eased round to the big question.

Zaedeen Camus stiffened—the first overt sign of stress in the prisoner. Maddocks held her gaze. And yes, in her flat-colored eyes he could read the stirrings of fear. The female pimp still wielded power over Zina, possibly over her other employees, too. So far the mysterious madam in her sixties had given police nothing. And neither her prints nor Camus's were in the system. Nailing down her identity would be a quantum step forward.

"Go ahead," Lippmann urged quietly.

"Her name is Veronique Sabbonnier," Camus said.

"Nationality?"

"Also French."

"Where did you meet Veronique Sabbonnier?" Maddocks said.

She swallowed. "We met in Paris. She frequented a hotel where I was the manager."

"When was this?"

"Maybe five years ago."

"Was Veronique Sabbonnier working as a pimp at this time?"

Lippmann cleared his throat and said, "That question is outside the parameters of our interview agreement."

Maddocks met the lawyer's dark eyes, allowed a beat of silence, then redirected. "When did you first begin working for Sabbonnier?"

"I encountered her again two years ago at a hotel in Marseilles to which I had been transferred. She had docked with the *Amanda Rose* in a local port. She spent four months in Marseilles. I got to know her well during this period, and she invited me aboard the yacht and then offered me a job with her club."

"The Bacchanalian Club?"

"Yes. I sailed with the *Amanda Rose* at the end of what Madame Vee referred to as her Marseilles season."

"In what capacity did Sabbonnier hire you?"

Camus glanced at her lawyer. Another curt nod from Lippmann.

"Personal assistant. Bouncer for the Bacchanalian Club."

"Which was operating as a high-end sex club?"

Silence.

Maddocks opted for a side swipe. "Did Sabbonnier ask you to dispose of Faith Hocking's body after Hocking died during a sex act aboard the *Amanda Rose*?"

Lippmann leaned sharply forward. "That question is way outside the parameters of our arrangement, Detective."

Maddocks inhaled deeply, allowing for another gap of silence, for pressure to build in the overly warm room. According to the two young johns being charged with Hocking's strangulation during an erotic asphyxiation act gone awry, it had been Camus who Sabbonnier had called in to clean up and remove the body. Camus had allegedly wrapped Hocking's naked body in a thick polyethylene tarp, the same kind of tarp Ginny had later been wrapped in. Sabbonnier had then allegedly tasked yacht carpenter and deck hand Spencer Addams to take Hocking's body out in a boat that night, where he was to dump it at sea. Addams, however, had kept Hocking's body for his own necrophilic uses for a week before finally throwing her out to sea. She'd washed up in the Gorge, becoming Maddocks's first call on his new job with MVPD homicide.

Maddocks tried coming in from yet another angle. "Was Spencer Addams, the carpenter, already working aboard the *Amanda Rose* when you were hired in Marseilles?"

"He was hired shortly after. He worked on the yacht during the Mediterranean seasons and during the following seasons in Victoria, Vancouver, Portland, San Francisco, and the Caribbean."

"And from where did Sabbonnier procure sex workers for all those 'seasons'?"

"Some of the sex workers were supplied by local clubs or pimps in the cities where we docked—Sabbonnier has . . . arrangements in various cities. The women would work for the season the yacht was in port. Some would return for several seasons. Of their own volition."

"But some of the women were held full-time on the ship against their will?"

Silence.

"Okay," Maddocks said, "let's get right to the barcoded girls, shall we? There were six young women found aboard the *Amanda Rose* where it was docked at the Uplands Marina. All of them have barcodes tattooed onto the backs of their necks. All appear underage and foreign. Where do they come from?"

"Prague."

Maddocks locked his gaze onto Camus. "Just 'Prague'?"

Her Adam's apple moved. She moistened her perfectly sculpted lips. "Prague is a staging area. That's all I know."

Maddocks doubted it was all she knew, but he could come at it again later when they drilled down in further interrogations with both Camus and Sabbonnier, ideally leveraging one off the other with this new information.

"Is Prague where this so-called 'merchandise' was tattooed with barcodes?"

"From what I understand, yes."

"What do these tattoos denote? Expiry date? Ownership?"

"Ownership. The origin and age of the merchandise. And the date a girl was first put into service. The tattoos have been scanned into a computerized database for tracking. The girls go out for a fee, generally for a period of two years. They can be returned for new ones after that period, if so desired, at additional costs. Madame Vee was testing this new line of . . . merchandise, as she calls it."

Bile rose up the back of Maddocks's throat. "And who owns this barcoded merchandise?"

"A Russian organization."

"What organization?"

"I don't know. The Russians have fully taken over the sex trade in Prague from the Albanians. They're supplying the UK market now. And the North and South American markets. That's all I know."

"Right. I'm sure that's all you know. And where did the six barcoded women found aboard the *Amanda Rose* enter this country?"

"Port of Vancouver. On a container ship out of Korea. Vancouver Hells Angels members and their affiliates who work as longshoremen at the port facilitated their entry."

Maddocks's pulse spiked. He kept his face impassive and his body still. "And then, once the 'merchandise' had come into port?"

"Then the barcoded girls were taken to a holding house somewhere in BC—I don't know where. Maybe Vancouver. After that, the six came to us."

"How long were they at this holding place?"

"I don't know. Awhile—maybe a month."

"Why were they held there?"

Camus hesitated. Her lawyer nodded. "They were being . . . conditioned."

"Which means?"

Swallowing, Camus said, "Fattened up a little, maybe. Brought back to full health while buyers were sought from clubs, that kind of thing."

"So they suffered in the shipping container. How long were they at sea?"

Lippmann moved in his chair, causing the plastic to squeak. "My client has no more knowledge of the girls' transportation into the country than she has offered."

Inhaling deeply, Maddocks said, "So the Vancouver Hells Angels are cooperating with a Russian organized crime ring based out of Europe?"

"She's told all that she knows," Lippmann repeated.

"Or all that she *will*?"

"I reiterate," Lippmann said, "we have a prior legal agreement as to what shall be revealed." He paused, dark eyes lasering Maddocks's. "At this stage."

Machiavellian opportunist, thought Maddocks, steadfastly returning the lawyer's gaze. Lippmann was keeping cards to play later at the expense of six abused and terrified underage women. "What about the girls' passports?" Maddocks said, continuing to push at the boundaries of their arrangement. "We found documents for the six barcoded girls on board the *Amanda Rose*—three Israeli passports, two Estonian, and one Latvian. These girls are not Israeli, Estonian, or Latvian." In truth the MVPD had no idea what nationality the six girls were, but Maddocks was winging it. "We've also had these passports examined by forensic document experts—they're forged."

Silence.

He leaned forward. "What I'm thinking is that these young women were given passports from these countries because these particular nations—Israel, Estonia, Latvia—are among those that did not require any entry visa to Canada, until the recent changes. Now all they need is an ETA, an electronic travel authorization, which can be obtained online for a couple of dollars. Why is there no record of these passport numbers having entered this country?"

"I don't know," Camus said.

"Because they were for future use, weren't they? For when you and Sabbonnier traveled with the girls aboard the *Amanda Rose* for all those 'seasons' in the ports of different countries?"

Silence.

"Where were the forgeries made?"

"Don't know."

"How about you try and guess?"

"Maybe they're forged in Tel Aviv, by Russians there."

A hot rush of adrenaline dumped through Maddocks's blood. Slowly, quietly, he said, "So, we have Russian organized crime in Tel Aviv working in concert with Russian organized crime in Prague to traffic women internationally. And this human trafficking ring is connected to the Hells Angels on a local level?"

Silence. Lippmann was edgy now.

Maddocks said, "After the six girls had been nursed back to health in this holding place, did Vancouver Hells Angels members bring them directly to you and Veronique Sabbonnier? For a middleman cut? Or did someone else handle the financial transaction and sell and deliver the girls to you?"

Red spots seeped into the oddly colored skin along Camus's sharp cheekbones. Maddocks's blood beat faster at the tell. His own skin grew hot. A Russian international trafficking ring connected to a high-profile local biker gang? If he could get proof, this was huge. Hells Angels were notoriously tough to nail. He needed to get in touch with the Royal Canadian Mounted Police's organized crime units on the Lower Mainland. Interpol and other international human trafficking agencies would also need to be looped in. His case may well be intersecting with other investigations already under way.

Camus swayed suddenly in her chair. Apart from the hot spots, the rest of the blood in her face appeared to have drained completely, leaving her a hue of gray.

"Okay, that's enough, Sergeant Maddocks," Lippmann said, lurching to his feet and signaling the guard behind them. "We're done here. My client needs medical attention, rest. We'll sign any written statements when you're ready with them."

Maddocks remained seated while the guard unlocked the interview room door and led Lippmann and his client out.

As the door shut behind them, he blew out a long, controlled breath—this was just getting started. And now he really had the taste of the hunt in his mouth.

Maddocks exited the prison with Holgersen, copies of Zaedeen Camus's signed statement in his hand. Outside it was dark. Cold. A fine mist rained down.

Holgersen halted under the portico cover beside one of the twin stone lions guarding the entrance to the prison. He fished a squashed pack of cigarettes from his pocket. "Now there's a freaking thing," he said, battling to extract a cigarette from the packet, "if we can prove a Hells Angels and longshoremen's union connection to the Ruskie mob."

"Yeah." Maddocks nodded to Holgersen's smoke. "You going to be long with that?"

"Just a few quick drags, boss. Since I can't smoke in your vee-hickle and all." He lit his cigarette, blew a stream of smoke into the night.

Maddocks looked out at the rain, agitated with his partner's delay. "Flint is checking with organized crime divisions on the mainland as we speak. He's putting out feelers to see if anyone else has run across barcoded sex workers."

"Good thing we kept them tattoos details outta the press after the *Amanda Rose* takedown." Holgersen took a long drag and spoke around the smoke as he exhaled. "Still, my bet is on those Angels and Ruskies having already shut down whatever shipping channel they was using now that news is out about the *Amanda Rose* busts. Even with those details withheld, they'll know that we had to have found their girls, and they'll just take their next shipment of barcoded merch down some other fucking rabbit hole."

Tension balled in Maddocks's stomach. He checked his watch. 6:30 p.m. His date with Angie at the King's Head was set for 7:30 p.m. He and Holgersen still had to drive all the way back down the Saanich Peninsula to the MVPD station in Victoria, where his superior, Inspector Martin Flint, was awaiting the statement.

"So I heard the Vancouver port has this giant X-ray machine they use to screen those shipping containers coming in daily," Holgersen said, flicking his ash onto the ground. "But they scan only like three to four percent of thems that are deemed high risk. Apparently the customs guys decide which ones to scan from intel they get before them ships come in—they only target ships for inspection reported to have had unusual activity on board. How do they gets that intel, I ask you? Shit gets through those ports every day." He glanced up at the prison's castle-style turrets and crenelated battlements and nodded toward the facade of the historic prison. "Looks like a medieval castle, don'tcha think? Would never say so from the insides. Correctional officer told me they calls this place 'Wilkie' because it's on Wilkinson Road. Been in operation over one hundred years. Was the Colquitz Provincial Mental Hospital for the Criminally Insane once." He waggled his fingers near his temple. "Madhouse."

"Look, do me a favor," Maddocks said, reaching the limits of his patience. He dug into his own pocket and pulled out his keys. He held them out to Holgersen. "Go ahead to the vehicle. You can drive. I'll meet you there—just need to make a personal call. And no smoking in the car."

Holgersen glanced at the keys, then back up into Maddocks's eyes. "Pallorino?"

"What part about 'personal' didn't you hear, Holgersen?"

He gave a half shrug and stole another quick drag before stubbing out his cigarette on the heel of his shoe. He dropped the butt into a baggie that came out of his pocket. "So when's the IIO decision coming down?" he said, sealing the bag and repocketing it.

"No idea."

"Pallorino knows nothing yet?"

"Not that I know of. Now go," Maddocks said.

Holgersen observed Maddocks for another moment. Then he snagged the keys and skittered down the stairs, his big feet surprisingly agile. He flipped up the collar of his dull-gray jacket, dug his hands deep into the pockets, and slouched off into the rain. When he was out of earshot, Maddocks dialed Angie.

He swore softly as he once more got her voicemail—he'd tried calling her before the interview with Camus. He left a message.

"Angie. We're playing phone tag here—had to make an emergency trip up to the regional corrections facility." He refrained from mentioning why he'd come. Or with whom. His ongoing investigation with Holgersen—her junior partner from sex crimes—was going to be a minefield of personal conflict between him and her as they continued to move forward. "I'm on my return to Vic right now but could be running late for our 7:30. If you get there before me, have a drink on me, please. Will be there as soon as I can."

He killed the call and made for his Impala. Holgersen was behind the wheel, engine warming, heater blasting. Jack-O snoozed on his sheepskin rug on the back seat. So far brass had not complained about Maddocks bringing the dog to work. He'd deal with that if and when it happened.

As they headed down the peninsula, rain lashed harder. Maddocks's thoughts turned to Angie and the IIO ruling—and what it might do to their nascent relationship. A disquiet seeped low and cold into his stomach.

✝

CHAPTER 9

Marge Buchanan, the union rep, was awaiting Angie beside the MVPD station doors, under the roof out of the rain, right behind the carved totem pole that served as an emblematic support column.

"Thanks for coming," Angie said tersely, walking right past the woman. She yanked open the glass door. She wasn't up to meeting Buchanan's eyes right now—this woman who'd so generously and attentively sat with her through the initial IIO interrogations, who'd advised her not to exercise her right to silence in this case, who'd helped with a lawyer. Angie wasn't so sure now that *not* exercising her charter right to silence had been the correct move. Because in answering questions, she'd exposed the fact that she'd had some kind of blackout during her violent shooting of Spencer Addams—she could not recall firing her weapon so many times, nor why she had done so. All she could remember was seeing that little halo of pink behind Addams—that luminous little ghost girl in a pink dress that she'd been hallucinating. And she'd snapped. All she'd wanted to do was get the ghost kid *away* from Addams. Save her. Of course she hadn't confessed *that* part. She'd only told the IIO investigators she could not recall firing any shots after the first one. Either they'd believed this, or they might have concluded she was lying. Neither option was good.

Angie held the door open for the rep, still not making eye contact. The older woman entered the building and stopped in front of Angie, finally forcing Angie to look into her face.

"I know this is hard. Any questions before we go up?" Buchanan said.

"Probably after," said Angie. "Depending on the ruling." Her plan was to hear Vedder out, say little. And deal with the facts once she had them.

The older woman managed to keep pace with Angie's clipped stride as Angie led the way upstairs to Vedder's office, which looked out onto the sex crimes bullpen and her own desk. As they went Angie got a whiff of the woman's hairspray—her coif was fixed in a solid steel-gray helmet around her head. Buchanan had been a cop back in the day. Is that what Angie would say about herself? *I was a cop once, back in the day* . . .

Once upstairs Angie strode swiftly past the bullpen, spine erect, chin up. She'd donned a black tailored leather blazer over slim black jeans. She wore her best boots, which had a slight heel. Hair washed and sleek down her back. She knew she looked her best. She might be a loser, but she was not going to dress like one.

Dundurn and Smith were at their desks. For the past six years, Angie had been one of the sixteen detectives in sex crimes. They were divided into teams of four. She and Holgersen were one team in her unit of four. Dundurn and Smith were the other pair. Along with a training officer, a ViCLAS coordinator, an analyst, and two project assistants, they all worked under Sergeant Matt Vedder.

Smith glanced up from his paperwork as she passed. Surprise cut through his features. "Pallorino?" He started to get to his feet. Dundurn glanced up from his paperwork, his butt-ugly brown suit jacket hanging on his chair behind him. Angie felt a clutch in her throat—she never thought she'd see the day she missed those two assholes and that stinking jacket of Dundurn's. She gave them both a curt nod, adjusted the hem of her blazer, and kept on going. She knocked on Vedder's glass door. He had the blinds down. Not good.

"Enter!" came his voice.

Angie braced, then opened the door. Vedder was seated behind his desk. To his left sat Inspector Martin Flint.

"Sir, Inspector," she said. "You know Marge Buchanan?"

They nodded their greetings, and Vedder gestured toward the two vacant chairs in front of his desk. "Take a seat."

Angie met Vedder's eyes before doing so. They were expressionless. His features flat. Not good. Really not good. Slowly, she lowered herself into a chair. Buchanan seated herself in the remaining chair.

"How have you been, Pallorino?" Vedder said.

She dropped her gaze to his hand. It rested flat atop some folders. She recognized the IIO logo on the topmost one.

"Awaiting the decision." She titled her chin toward the folders. "If we could cut to the chase, sir—what's the final word from the IIO?" She felt the scrutiny of Flint intense upon her, but she refused to look his way. This was it—she could feel it. Thick in the air. The end.

"For the record," Vedder said, "the purpose of the IIO investigation was to determine whether the subject officer—which is you, Pallorino—referred to as the SO in this report, may have committed any offenses during the fatal shooting of the affected person—Spencer Addams, referred as the AP in the report—on Monday, December eighteen, in mountainous wilderness west of the old railway trestle bridge over Skookum Gorge. I've made copies of the ruling for both you and Buchanan."

He slid two files across his desk. Buchanan reached for hers. Angie just glared at the cover of her own copy, her face going hot.

"As you know, this report will be posted on the IIO website, and it will be accessible to media."

Blood started to boom in her ears. She felt dizzy. She couldn't sit still. She needed to get out of here, stat. She cleared her throat. "Bottom line, sir—can you please give me the bottom line?"

He held her gaze. "Based on his review of all the evidence collected during the course of the investigation, and based on the law as it applies, the chief civilian director of the IIO has determined there were significant issues and concerns regarding the SO's tactics, primarily relating to a direct disregard of the orders of superiors, excessive use of force, a troubling gap in memory, and what was determined to be probable evidence of rage, or at the least loss of professional control." Vedder continued to hold Angie's gaze. "The autopsy of the AP and ballistics results from the scene are consistent with the SO having shot eight rounds into Addams's face, chest, and neck. Apart from the one bullet deemed to have been fired from a distance of about twenty feet, and another from about six feet, the others were all fired into the AP at close range while he lay prone on the ground."

Angie swallowed but refused to blink. A bead of sweat pearled between her breasts and began to dribble down under her bra strap.

"However, given the exigent circumstances, the CCD believes that it cannot be said that your failures rise to a level such that consideration of criminal charges is warranted."

Relief punched her sternum so hard it stole her ability to breathe. She cast a quick glance at Buchanan, who gave a small smile and a nod.

Vedder did not look impressed. Neither did Flint. She'd gotten lucky, and she knew it.

"However," Vedder continued, "following an additional MVPD review into the incident, as required by the Police Act, the department has determined that a grievous breach of department protocol occurred, and it goes to a historical pattern of insubordinate behavior. There remains concern over your psychological frame of mind, especially after you lost your partner last summer and have not followed through with the required counseling." Vedder shifted in his chair. "It's been decided that disciplinary action will include a twelve-month period of probation where you will work as a uniformed officer in an administrative position that does not require carrying a service weapon. We're offering you the position of social media officer within the community and public affairs section at a pay grade commensurate with the position. The officer currently in that position will be away for twelve months on maternity leave starting next week—you will relieve her for that period commencing tomorrow."

Angie's throat closed in on itself. She blinked. "You . . . can't be serious?"

"This was a *very* serious breach of protocol, Detective Pallorino. In the course of our internal review, several officers expressed concern about potentially being partnered with you. Especially after the Spencer Addams shooting coming so close on the death of your previous partner."

"I was cleared in that investigation."

"One investigation too many. You will also report to an approved police psychologist for a psychological assessment and will follow through on the resulting recommended course of therapy. And you will attend department anger management courses, as well as a series of workshops designed to build better team players." He pushed the MVPD file toward her and a copy toward Buchanan. "At the end of the twelve-month probation period, another internal assessment will be conducted."

"After which I can return to sex crimes?"

"There is no guarantee. It will be contingent on behavior during your probation."

Angie's vision narrowed. Blood boomed loud in her ears.

Buchanan leaned forward. "Detective Pallorino has vacation and sick days owing that amount to a period of three months at her current pay scale—"

Vedder cut in. "If she chooses to take those three months now, the clock will only start ticking on her twelve-month probation when she returns." A pause. "The public affairs unit will have a desk ready for you to report to first thing tomorrow, Pallorino. It's a 9:00 a.m. to

5:00 p.m. position. Start time tomorrow will however be 11:00 a.m. because Officer Pepper, whom you'll be replacing, will be available from that time onward to show you the ropes. She has a school presentation before that."

Silence. The atmosphere in the closed office grew thicker.

Angie stared at Vedder.

Two weeks ago she'd been gunning for a big promotion into the elite all-male homicide division. She'd gotten so damn close.

School presentations?

A uniform?

No service weapon?

She'd *never* been that low on the totem pole. Ever. *Social fucking media? You have got to be kidding me.* It was humiliating. It wasn't even an option—*everything* that defined her was in being a detective. In working major crimes. It was why she got up in the mornings—*how* she got up in the mornings. They might as well have fired her.

Happy shitty fake birthday, Angie.

CHAPTER 10

"Hey, it's about time I finally got through. How's the birthday girl? Did you get my other messages?"

Maddocks.

Angie tightened her hand around her cell phone. It was 7:52 p.m. She'd been sitting here at this bar counter at the King's Head nursing a martini since 7:25. She lifted her glass and took a sip. "You're going to tell me you're running even later, aren't you?"

"I'm so sorry, but—"

"But something's come up? The case?"

"It's a big deal. We got a major br—"

"Yeah, a breakthrough. I get it, Maddocks." Her attention went to a narrow mullioned window that looked out into the dark parking lot. She'd chosen this stool so she could keep an eye on the Nissan with her boxes inside. Not that anyone was likely to break in and steal her cold case files, but she had a protective urge to watch over them nevertheless. She'd been champing at the bit for Maddocks to arrive—to tell him about Vedder, her probation. Her trip to Vancouver. Her major break with the cold case files. Maddocks was the only person she could truly confide in at the moment. He'd proven she could trust him. He'd had her back, and she had his.

"So how long do you think you'll be?" She tried to keep her disappointment from her voice.

"Another half hour max. Can you wait, please? You having a drink?"

Irritation, resentment, anger, hurt, all of it crashed suddenly through her in one powerful, uncontrollable wave. "Look," she said coolly, "I don't think this is going work out, Maddocks."

He hesitated at the sharp shift in her tone. "You don't think *what* is going to work?"

"Dinner. This . . . this thing between us."

"Whoa, Angie, back up—hold it right there. What's going on?" A pause. "Shit, it's the IIO ruling, isn't it? Did it come in?"

She inhaled deeply and glanced up at the heavy paneling on the ceiling of the bar, struggling suddenly to marshal her control. "Yeah," she said quietly.

A beat of silence. "And?"

"And nothing. I'll talk to you later, when you've got time. I'm going to hang up now, finish my drink, and go home."

"I'm coming to your place, after—"

"No. Don't. Please." She killed the call and sat for a moment clutching her phone. Her own image stared back at her from the mirror behind the rows of bottles across the bar. She could see deep bruises of fatigue smudged beneath her eyes, offsetting a deathly pale, gaunt complexion. She must have lost more weight than she'd realized over the past few weeks. Her hair hung sleek to her shoulders, lips painted deep red, for Maddocks's benefit. For the occasion of her birthday dinner. She'd made an effort, but all she'd accomplished was "haunted."

Who are you, face in the mirror?

An old rhyme came to her mind.

Fractured face
in the mirror,

you are my disgrace . . .

a sinner . . .

She cursed inwardly. She couldn't do this. She could not sit for one year behind a desk, doing the job of a rookie, giving talks to auditoriums full of bored teenagers or elementary school kids, when she had acknowledged skill and experience in investigating sex crimes and, more recently, in working a series of linked, high-profile homicides. She'd helped stop a serial killer. Tweeting? Facebooking? Crafting posts for the *Day in the Life of a Cop* blog? Yeah, that was seeking justice. That was using her skills.

Enduring the punishment wasn't even a guarantee of regaining her position in sex crimes.

But if she *didn't* do it—if she quit the MVPD before swallowing her twelve months of discipline—she'd never get a letter of reference. She'd never work as a detective again.

She tossed back the dregs of her martini.

"Another?"

Her gaze shot to the barkeep. He was maybe thirty, eyes liquid obsidian and densely fringed. Thick, dark, tousled hair. Olive-toned skin, smooth. Lean and muscular in the way of a triathlete. *Fuckable*, she thought suddenly. And she felt hot. She held his eyes and gently turned the stem of her martini glass in her hand.

"Who's asking?" she said.

He waited a beat, not breaking eye contact. "Antonio."

She snorted softly. "Of course. Antonio. Yeah, please, another."

"Same?"

"Yep—martini, dirty."

"Rough day?" he said, taking her empty glass from her hand, allowing the backs of his fingers to brush against her skin. The contact shot a crackle of electricity up her arm, and it felt nice. She imagined how he might look naked and cuffed to a bed with a hard-on. How she might sheath his erection with a condom. Open her thighs. Sink down on to him. Rock her pelvis, gentle at first . . . Her heart beat faster. Heat rushed to her groin. That old urge to hit the club serpentined low into her belly and sank claws deep into her throat. A good, mind-numbing, anonymous fuck—that's what she needed right now. Better than a drink. Better than coke. Better than dope.

"You could say it was rough," she said.

"Anything I can do?"

Hell yeah. "The drink."

"Be right back."

Antonio sauntered in an overtly casual fashion to the far end of the bar, where he began to fix her drink. She watched his gluteal muscles moving beneath the fabric of his tailored black pants. *Nothing like an orgasm to take one's mind off things.*

Angie forced herself to break her gaze. She knew her physical reaction for what it was. An addiction. An escape. A way of numbing other feelings. Hitting the Foxy, the adult entertainment club on the highway out of town, had been her coping mechanism for years. A place to blow off steam. All the major crimes cops had ways of doing this. The Foxy had been hers—a hunting ground where she could scope out an anonymous target, proposition him, cuff him to a bed in the adjacent motel, and screw him without exchanging names or numbers. No strings attached. And she'd leave before he could properly enjoy her in return. Power trip, yeah, but so what? She dealt with men who used women every day of her life, so this was her way of taking back control. Angie had grown increasingly addicted to this fix, the latent danger, the taste of physical and emotional strength.

Until Maddocks.

Until the Spencer Addams case.

Antonio placed her fresh drink on a coaster in front of her.

"Thanks," Angie said, avoiding his eyes this time, instead averting her attention to the ice hockey game playing on the large-screen television above the bar. She took a hard swig of her martini and focused on the warm burn of alcohol blossoming through her chest, and she breathed in deep.

The hockey game finished, and the channel segued to the 8:00 p.m. news. An image of a small, dirty, pale-lilac sneaker suddenly filled the screen. Angie stilled her glass midair. The text at the bottom of the screen said, ANOTHER DISMEMBERED FOOT WASHES UP IN SALISH SEA.

The camera cut to a young woman with a pretty, round face, blue eyes, short blonde hair blowing in wind. The woman's nose and cheeks were pinked, and her blue jacket glistened from rain. Behind her the sky hunkered bruised and low above a misty gray ocean. She stood on blackish sand that had been sculpted smooth from the outgoing tide, and she held a leash with a little white dog attached to the end. The blonde woman pointed to a knoll of rocks near the waterline where a pile of seaweed lay in a tangle. As she turned, Angie saw that the woman was pregnant.

Slowly, she lowered her drink to the counter.

I saw that today. I saw them filming while I was in the ferry lineup speaking to Vedder.

Two middle-aged men climbed onto the vacant stools beside Angie. She barely registered them.

"Man, check that out," said one male to the other. "Weird shit, those floating feet. What's that now, seventeen in the last ten years?"

"But that's just a kid's sneaker," said the other man. "A little girl's shoe. Those other floating feet were all adult size." The male leaned across the bar and called to Antonio. "Yo, could you turn that TV news up a sec?"

Antonio bumped up the sound. Angie stared, transfixed by the little high-top runner that once again filled the screen. A yellow-white mass nestled inside the shoe. Something dark and unarticulated began to unfurl at the core of her body. Anxiety rose inside her.

The camera cut back to the beach, this time to a reporter. Dark tendrils of hair blew across the woman's face as she spoke into her mike. "A decade-old mystery was reignited on Monday when the remains of another detached human foot, still in a shoe, washed up on the causeway beach at the Tsawwassen Ferry Terminal, making it the eighteenth dismembered foot to be found along beaches in British Columbia and Washington State since 2007. The shoes containing the macabre contents have been washing up like pieces of ocean detritus, and they've been found among bits of foam, candy wrappers, shells, rocks, or clumps of seaweed. Betsy Champlain was on the beach with her children New Year's Day when she made the grisly discovery."

The reporter turned to the pregnant blonde woman. "Ms. Champlain, can you tell us how you found the dismembered foot?"

"My two children and I were in the ferry lineup, heading back home to the island. It was really busy, several sailing waits. Our dog, Chloe, needed a bathroom break, so we brought her down to the beach, where she broke away from my son. We found Chloe over there by those rocks with something in her mouth."

"The shoe?"

Emotion twisted the blonde woman's face. She shied away from the scrutiny of the camera by looking down at the sand. "It seemed so small," she said softly. "So alone, just lying there on the beach. Just a child's shoe—the same size as my daughter's. That little girl is—was— probably the same age as my child."

"How old *is* your daughter, Ms. Champlain?"

"She's three."

Angie swallowed. The man seated closest to her cursed softly. "Just a kid," he said again. "How does a kid lose a foot? What in the hell happened to the rest of her?"

The camera cut back to a close-up of the reporter. "RCMP spokesperson Constable Annie Lamarre has confirmed that the brand of shoe is a ROOAirPocket, girls' size nine, left foot, and yes, it does contain what appears to be the remains of a child's foot. Lamarre said the discovery was sent to the BC Coroner's Service for further examination.

The Coroner's Service has declined comment, saying only that the case is under investigation. CBC has learned, however, that this particular ROOAirPocket high-top model was manufactured only between the years 1984 and 1986, after which it was discontinued and replaced with the ROOAir-Lift."

The image of the shoe once more filled the screen. An inexplicable nausea rose in Angie's belly. The reporter's voice spoke over the image. "In BC several of the dismembered feet found to date have been identified as having belonged to people with mental illness who likely jumped off one of the many bridges in the area. Three of the feet were linked to individuals who probably died of natural causes. Other theories have also been suggested—some think the shoes floated across the Pacific from the Asian tsunami or that they drifted from one of several small plane crashes up the Inside Passage. Others have suggested something more nefarious—a serial killer. What is unusual, whatever the theories, is that no other body parts have ever surfaced to match the feet." She paused. The camera zoomed suddenly back to her face. "And this recent ghoulish gift from the sea—the discovery of this little girl's shoe manufactured more than thirty years ago—is not quite like the others."

Angie glanced around the pub. The interior seemed to have grown darker. Colder. She felt as though she was being watched, but no one was looking at her. Yet the sense of things closing in that had besieged her in the ferry lineup was tightening its grip. Outside, the wind gusted, lashing rain against the mullioned windows.

CHAPTER 11

He sits at his metal desk writing a letter. On a shelf to his left is a small television set. It's tuned to the local CBC channel, which is airing a Canucks–Oilers hockey game. He's waiting for the news. Earlier he ate a decent-enough dinner in the cafeteria. Now is the customary hour during which he likes to conduct his correspondence, old style, with pen and paper while listening to—and occasionally glancing up at—the day's news on television. Routine. He's come to like it. Routine is life. Habits are what make a man. If he masters his habits, he masters control. It gives him power. People misunderstand power. Real power is being at peace with oneself and living in the moment—not being affected by the currents and actions of others. Once his correspondence is complete, he will do his pull-ups.

My dearest Mila,

he writes.

Did my gift arrive in time for Olivia's birthday? I asked your mother to ensure that she ordered it with plenty of time to spare and to surprise you both on the day. Let me know as soon as you can whether Olivia likes it. Perhaps you could send me a photo of Livvy with her gift?

He pauses, looks up at his small window. It's dark outside. Raining. He wonders if the air is cold.

I hope to make it in person to Livvy's birthday party next year. It might be possible. I want to believe it shall be possible. My next hearing is in five days. Tuesday. It's scheduled before lunch, which means statistically I might stand a better chance this time. Think of me then, please. Wish me luck. I am a changed man, Mila, and I will show them that. And when—

"Another dismembered foot has washed up in Salish Sea . . ."

His gaze shoots to the TV at the sound of the news anchor's voice. He stares as an image of a dirty high-top sneaker fills the screen. Pale lilac. Small. Something waxy and gray-yellow inside the running shoe. Ice filters into his chest. He drops his pen, snatches up the remote, increases the volume. He listens to the reporter on the beach recount how the girls' size-nine shoe came to be found on the causeway beach at the Tsawwassen Ferry Terminal. His mouth turns sawdust dry.

"CBC has learned, however, that this particular ROOAirPocket high-top model was manufactured only between the years 1984 and 1986 . . ." The images, the sounds, begin to blur. He blinks hard as the camera cuts back to the reporter, and he struggles to swallow as a memory torques through him.

Little feet running. Flashes of pink, purple . . . on deep-green grass. Puddles of light, rare ripples of laughter . . . a singsong nursery rhyme.

Screams. Blood everywhere. The crab pots.

The fish eating flesh . . .

Time stretches like elastic. He can no longer hear the sound of the television. All he can see in his mind—as if burned in negative upon his retinas—are the child's eyes, clear and gray, round and bright with utter delight as she opens the box and discovers the shoes—a new pair of pale-purple ROOAirPockets, nestled in the box with soft tissue paper.

No, this cannot be. Not possible. Not after all those years. Not right before my parole hearing. It's a coincidence. Has to be . . .

The newscast segues to a piece on a tent city protest in downtown Vancouver. He gets up, goes to the basin, turns on the tap. He runs the hot water until it is scalding. He washes his face, scrubbing his hands brutally over his skin, the harsh prison soap burning his eyes. He turns off the water and braces his hands on either side of the sink. Slowly he looks up into the shatterproof mirror bolted to the wall. A face looks back at him. It's not his. Not the face he knows when he thinks of himself. This man in the mirror has a complexion that is sallow and sick against his prison shirt. The eyes are lined, and the lids droop at the edges with flaccid skin. But those eyes still see things from a time long ago. And right now they see the dark shadow lurking behind the man who stands in front of the mirror. A shadow, it appears, that he cannot outrun or outlast. No matter how hard he tries.

It's nothing. Calm down. It means nothing to me. It's just a coincidence.

CHAPTER 12

Angie made several trips up from her car in the underground parkade, carrying her file boxes and the supplies she'd bought on her way home to her apartment on the top floor. Once inside with her last load, she kicked her door closed behind her and set the second case file box on the floor beside the first, wincing as the muscles in her injured arm protested. She rubbed her arm as she stared down at the boxes.

Box 01 Jane Doe Saint Peters #930155697–2

Box 02 Jane Doe Saint Peters #930155697–2

She allowed herself to feel excited as she locked her door and shucked off her rain jacket. She'd rather focus on her cold case than on making decisions about whether or not she was going to dig out her uniform and report to the MVPD's social media desk tomorrow. It also kept her thoughts from straying to Antonio behind the bar or from hitting the club. Or dwelling morosely over her failed birthday date with Maddocks and what that meant to her, and whether she wanted to fight to make a relationship work with him.

Once her coat and boots were off, she flicked on all the lights in her small apartment and got the gas fire cranked. She changed into warm leggings and pulled on a fleece sweater, thick socks, and her Ugg boots. Even so, cold seemed to linger inside her bones, as though a dank chill had crawled out of the shadows of her past at the hospital yesterday and burrowed into her very core, and it was not going to go away until she found answers.

After wiping down her dining room table with a bleach cleaner, Angie covered the surface with a shroud of heavy-duty plastic sheeting—she'd picked up the roll at the hardware store along with four-by-four-foot melamine sheets, a glue gun, and a pack of colored markers. Ideally, the case file boxes should be opened in a lab or in a similarly sterile environment in case they contained biological evidence that was still viable. Proper evidence-handling procedures should be followed. But chain of custody had long been broken. Arnold Voight, according to his widow, had opened the boxes on more than one occasion in his home. He or his surviving family members could have introduced any number of contaminants. The boxes had also been stored in a basement, which could have been damp. So whatever evidence these boxes might contain, it was unlikely to be admissible in court.

However, if she *did* discover evidence that could be retested, it might steer her toward new clues, something that *could* be used in court. And yeah, she was thinking like a cop here—not only did she want answers, but she also wanted legal retribution. A wrong had been done to that little Jane Doe—to *herself.* Men with guns had chased a young woman with long dark hair across the street in the snow—a woman who might be her mother. Jane Doe's face had been sliced, blood all over the place, semen stains on a sweater left with the kid. Shots had been fired. Witnesses had heard tires screeching, possibly from a van that had fled the scene with the woman being held captive. Or dead.

If Angie could draw any consolation from what she'd learned so far, it appeared that the dark-haired young woman had been desperately trying to save the child. The woman had *cared.*

Angie had not been abandoned—she'd been protected from the bad men.

Once the plastic sheeting had been secured around the table legs, she stepped back and examined her work. Her incident room was taking shape. She hefted the boxes from their place at door and set them upon the prepped table surface. Boxes in place, she proceeded to denude one wall in her living room of framed photographs and a painting. Working carefully yet swiftly, Angie used the heated glue gun to affix the white melamine sheets to the bare wall, creating a giant dry-erase crime scene board. It might be a bugger to remove these sheets later, but she wasn't thinking about later.

While the glue was drying, she shunted her desk and computer up against the adjoining wall. Firing up her desktop, she opened the file in which she'd saved the few online articles that she'd managed to locate on the angel's cradle child from 1986. Her goal was to make more trips to the mainland, where she would start by visiting the Vancouver library archives in search of possible microfilm copies of all the newspapers from that period.

Those articles could yield potential leads, give her the names of photographers and journalists who'd covered the story, names of the publishers and editors of the time, possible witnesses. Also an option was approaching the television stations and newspapers directly in search of archived material, but she wanted to tread very carefully before approaching any journalist types. They'd smell a story on her. She was not ready to become the news. Again.

Especially not now that she was walking on thin career ice after the Spencer Addams shooting.

Angie connected her digital camera to her desktop and downloaded the photographs she'd shot outside the hospital and cathedral. She selected a couple and hit PRINT. She then clicked open an image that she'd saved from one of the online articles—the sketch artist's rendering of Janie Doe. The caption beneath the image read, DO YOU KNOW THIS CHILD?

She hit PRINT.

While her printer hummed, Angie checked her whiteboard sheets. They felt secure—the glue was dry enough. At the top of her board, in bold black letters, she scrawled, ANGEL'S CRADLE CASE '86. Under the header she copied the case ID that the VPD had used on Voight's boxes: JANE DOE SAINT PETERS #930155697–2.

Beneath the case number she stuck the sketch artist's image of Janie Doe. Beside the sketch, Angie pasted the fading Kodak print that Jenny Marsden had given her. Next she added the images she'd shot outside the hospital.

She took a step back and absorbed the visual effect, the case now feeling tangible. Real. It channeled her focus.

Her own bruised face from thirty-two years ago looked back at her. Angie touched the scar across her lip.

Who are *you, Janie Doe? What did those eyes of yours see that was so bad that you can no longer remember?*

Angie shook herself, snapped on a pair of crime scene gloves, and picked up her camera. She returned to the table and shot several angles of the sealed boxes, ensuring that she captured the file numbers. She was going to document every step of this very personal investigation.

The term *cold case* was controversial, Angie knew. It gave the impression that unsolved cases were unworkable. But a cold case was just a concept—there was no one standard definition. It was simply a case that had been reported to law enforcement and investigated, but either due to insufficient evidence or a lack of strong suspects, no one had been arrested and charged. And because of the passage of time, a lack of fresh leads, pressures on municipalities and police departments for higher solve rates, those cases were no longer being actively pursued by investigators.

But where time was your enemy . . . She set down her camera and reached for a box cutter. *Time is now your friend.*

Conventional wisdom held that if a homicide was not solved within the first twenty-four to seventy-two hours, then the chances of solving that case begin to diminish rapidly. The reasons for this were obvious: The opportunity to retrieve uncontaminated evidence was strongest at the outset. Witnesses were still centrally located, their recollection of events fresh. They were also less likely to have had opportunity to get stories and alibis straight among themselves.

However, over the years, as Jenny Marsden had noted, relationships between people involved in a crime could change considerably. Witnesses once afraid to come forward might no longer be reluctant to talk. And with the leaps that had been made in forensic science since the late eighties, minute amounts of trace that once might have yielded nothing could now be tested for DNA. The old hard-copy *tenprint* fingerprint card system had also been revolutionized with the advent of digitalized friction-ridge imaging systems—digital scans of prints were now stored in automated print identification databases to which new files were constantly being added. '

This *could* be solved, Angie thought as she found her box cutter and began to slice carefully through the yellow tape on the first box. Her pulse raced in anticipation. It *was* possible.

She opened the lid, and disappointment stabbed—just one binder inside with some loose files, two rather skinny notebooks, and newspaper cuttings in a plastic sleeve. She told herself this did not necessarily mean the investigative files were incomplete.

It is not the size but the quality that counts.

She was lucky to have these at all.

Moving to the second, bigger box, Angie sliced the tape and opened the top. Her pulse kicked. Inside were several brown paper bags marked boldly as EVIDENCE. Almost shaking with adrenaline, Angie reached for her camera and took more photos. She set her camera down, then lifted out the bag on top. On the side the contents were marked as STUFFED BEAR, SAINT PETER'S HOSPITAL ANGEL'S CRADLE.

She hesitated, then, with gloved hands, she carefully opened the top of the bag. A teddy bear's head peeked out, fur stiff with a dried brown residue. Blood—her blood. Time slowed. Her mouth turned dry. Carefully she slid the teddy out of the evidence bag and studied it—not dissimilar to the one she'd witnessed inside the new angel's cradle bassinet that Jenny Marsden had shown her. This bear also sported a T-shirt imprinted with the words SAINT PETER'S HOSPITAL. But the letters on this little T-shirt were barely legible under the stiff brown residue. Her heart began to pound.

This is my blood I'm holding in my hands. From when I was four. This teddy was with me inside the cradle. A bolt of bright white light struck into her temple, sending mirrorlike shards of memory slicing through her brain. Pain seared across her mouth. Angie gasped. A woman screamed.

Uciekaj, uciekaj!

Run, run!

Wskakuj do srodka, szybko.

Get inside.

Siedz cicho!

Stay quiet!

Her world spiraled—as though she was driving into a blizzard at night, her car headlights bouncing off dizzying snowflake asteroids. Then came that haunting, tinny, horrorlike nursery rhyme tune.

> *A-a-a, kotki dwa . . . Ah-ah-ah,*
> *two little kittens,*
> *There were once two little kittens,*
> *two little kittens,*
> *they were both grayish-brown.*

Shock—deep, seismic—gripped her and began to shudder her body. Banging sounded inside her head. Louder. Angie couldn't breathe. *Breathe, breathe, Angie . . .*

More banging. Faster. Harder.

"Angie!"

She jerked herself back, and her gaze flared to her door. Someone was knocking—trying to get inside? Terror gripped her by the throat.

Siedz cicho!

Stay quiet!

Disoriented, she stared at the door, struggling to pull reality into focus. No one had called up to be buzzed into the building. Was it one of her neighbors?

More pummeling. "Angie? I know you're in there. I saw the Nissan in your parking space downstairs."

Maddocks?

Panic leaped through her. Her gaze darted around the apartment.

"I'm going to let myself in, okay? I'm coming in."

Keys—she'd forgotten that she'd given him a set of keys to the building and to her apartment. With trembling hands, Angie tried to stuff the bear back into the evidence bag. But the shiny bead eyes held hers. She was suddenly incapable of putting the bear's head back inside its dark prison. She took it out again.

The door opened. Angie froze, bear in gloved hands. Maddocks loomed in her doorway, all six foot four of him. Black coat. Ruffled blue-black hair. Red tie against a crisp white shirt. The day had stubbled his jaw, put shadows beneath his eyes and fatigue into the lines of his face. Under one arm he held Jack-O. In his other hand was a bottle of red wine and an envelope. His dark-blue eyes pierced hers.

"Angie—you okay?" He stepped into the room. His gaze shot first to her table, then flicked up to her whiteboard. "What's going on?" He shut the door with the heel of his shoe and set Jack-O down. The three-legged animal hobbled over to the doggie bed that Angie had positioned near the gas fireplace for when Maddocks came to visit. The pooch curled onto his bed and eyeballed her suspiciously. Maddocks approached the table. His gaze dropped to the blood-stiffened bear in her hands, and then slowly he raised his deep-blue eyes to meet hers. Compassion filled his features.

A little voice rose inside her. *You don't deserve him, a man like this. You're too jealous of him professionally. He will hurt you. You will hurt yourself by screwing this up. Better to walk first, before he does.*

"This is old evidence?" he said. "From the cradle case? You got it from the VPD?"

Angie cleared her throat and slipped the bear properly back into the evidence bag. She resealed it. "You shouldn't have come—I told you not to come."

His mouth firmed. He went over to her kitchen counter, set down the bottle of wine and envelope, and took off his coat. He hung it over the back of a chair and began opening her cupboards. He found two glasses, which he placed on the granite kitchen countertop. "Give me a chance to at least apologize for dinner and to raise a glass for your birthday." He uncorked the wine as he spoke, then poured two glasses. He brought them over and held one out to her.

She declined to accept the drink. She turned her back on him and snapped off her gloves. "I need you to leave, Maddocks."

He set the glasses back down on the counter, then placed a hand on her shoulder. It was large. Warm. Solid. Like him. She stilled.

"Tell me about the IIO investigation. What did they say?"

She didn't trust her voice suddenly. Inside her belly she started to shake again. He turned her around slowly. She looked up into his eyes.

"I'm so sorry that I wasn't there for you today, Angie." A pause. "What . . . was the ruling?" He cupped the side of her face. She ached to lean into his touch. But at the same time, she did not want his compassion or pity. That's how her colleagues would see her when they found out about her probation—as pitiful. Some, like Harvey Leo, would even derive glee from her fall to the social media desk. She had no intention of playing to their hand, would *not* become the victim, the disgraced detective back in uniform, the abused little girl left in a cradle with a sliced face and a bloody teddy bear and semen on a sweater.

He caressed the line of her jaw with his thumb. And something fierce and angry erupted inside her—a desperation to burn down her own insecurities, to kill the pain, to blind herself to the fear of what her own memories might reveal, the realities that she might have to face about what had happened to her in childhood. She grabbed his tie and yanked him closer. Drawing his head down, she reached herself up and pressed her mouth hungrily to his. His lips were cold from outside. He hesitated a nanosecond before suddenly cupping her buttocks and jerking her hips tightly up against his pelvis. His mouth bore down on hers, forcing her lips open. He slid his tongue inside, met hers. Lust blinded Angie as she felt his erection stiffening against her belly.

Desperately, furiously, she shoved him back against the wall near the door, oblivious to the pain in her arm. A picture crashed to the floor. Kissing him hard, their tongues slipping, tangling, mating, she hurriedly undid his fly and slid her hand into his pants. He was hot and hard against her palm. The big-shot homicide cop, the ex-Mountie who'd saved her ass by not reporting her mental collapse. The lover who'd broken her down and built her back up. The man who'd shown her how to submit, how to trust during sex. The man who lived on an old yacht he'd been trying to salvage like his sinking marriage and family dreams. The father whose life she'd saved along with the life of his daughter. A man she believed she could come to love—if only she'd let herself.

He moaned deep in his throat as she took his penis in her hand, working him. He attempted to move away from the wall, to back her toward her bedroom, but she resisted, instead pressing him harder up against the wall, pulling his pants down around his hips. "Now. Here," she growled against his mouth as she wiggled her own pants down over her hips, tangling them in her Ugg boots. She kicked off one boot and freed herself of one pant leg before lowering him fully to the floor.

His eyes, intense, held hers as he allowed her to pin his wrists above his head against the floor. Angie straddled his hips and slid the crotch of her skimpy panties aside. Widening her knees, parting her thighs, she sank down onto the hot, hard length of him. With a bliss-filled sigh she spread her thighs farther, making him go deep, deeper. And she began to rock her hips, creating friction deep inside the core of her body. Her breaths came fast, faster. She rocked harder. She became slick around his erection. Her body began to tingle. A hot, raw anger exploded, ripping through her gut, driving her wilder. She closed her eyes, put her head back, mouth open wide, panting, her skin going damp. And she rode him hard and fast and half-clothed, forcing her mind back, mentally reliving that very first night she'd spent with him at the Foxy Motel. She gasped suddenly, froze, then cried out as muscle contractions slammed through her in rolling waves, taking control of her body.

CHAPTER 13

Maddocks sat beside Angie on the sofa in front of her gas fire. Sipping wine, he listened as she told him first about her meeting with Vedder and Flint, her discipline, then about her trip to Vancouver and her discovery of the case files. She smelled good, fresh from their shower, and she was bundled in a soft white robe, hair damp. Rain ticked against the windows as the clock edged toward midnight. Foghorns sounded balefully out over the water.

She spoke with a toneless voice, and her complexion was wan, her eyes circled with the darkness of fatigue. She was corralling her emotion again. Only letting it escape through fierce, angry, controlling sex.

While their coupling had been exhilarating and his orgasm mind-blowing, a disquieting sensation lingered in Maddocks. It reminded him of their first sex together at the Foxy Motel when she'd cuffed him to the bed, straddled him, and ridden him to her heart's content and then gotten off him before he could come. He'd thought she was going to leave him there, naked and bound to the bed with an aching hard-on. It had made him ravenous for more. He'd wanted to get to know this woman named Angie who'd picked him up in the club expressly to screw him and leave him.

But he now knew that dominant sex was Angie's coping mechanism, her addiction. They'd gone beyond that first night. Well beyond. They'd found something tender and vulnerable based on trust. But this . . . given what she was going through right now, it was a sign of regression. He worried what it might mean for their fledgling and as yet fragile relationship.

"I can't do it, Maddocks," she said, setting her wine glass firmly down on the coffee table next to the envelope she had not yet opened. "Putting on a uniform every day, driving a desk nine to five for an entire year? Preaching to schoolkids? Social media—*me?*" She cursed softly and stared into the flames. "It's humiliating," she said quietly.

He leaned forward. "If you don't suck it up, if you quit now, there's no way you'll ever get a letter of reference. You'll never work as a cop again, Angie."

Her jaw tightened. She refused to look at him.

"Hey." He touched her hand. She tensed and pulled away, reaching instead for her glass. He inhaled deeply. "Listen," he said softly, "twelve months will go faster than you think. It'll be over before you know it. And—"

She swung round to face him. "Don't. Do not patronize me, Maddocks. Ever."

He held her gaze. "It's still policing work of value—building bonds with kids, creating awareness in young women. It's an opportunity to get in touch with our constituents, our community. You could teach self-defense. You *can* make it work, Angie, I *know* you can. You're just fighting it on principle right now."

"That's all very well for you to say, Mr. Hot-Shot Homicide Cop who's leading the task force—an investigation *I* should be working. Have they offered you Buziak's job full-time yet? You going to be the big overall MVPD homicide boss now?"

His gaze pinned hers. The undercurrents of her words swirled dark and potent between them like a lethal undertow. With it surged his own feelings of guilt. She'd done it for him—disobeyed direct orders. Still, there'd been no need to *overkill* Addams like that. Emptying her clip into Addams's face, her use of excessive force, was wrong. And the evidence of rage and a blackout—those *were* worrisome issues. As a boss he could not justifiably overlook the fact that this woman could put other officers in jeopardy in a crisis situation. She'd gotten off lightly. And she needed to visit that police shrink in order to get to the bottom of her hair-trigger rage. Her issues probably stemmed from buried childhood trauma and the more recent tragedy of losing her previous partner on a call, but that didn't make her *safe*. It didn't make the way she'd shot Spencer Addams okay.

"Let me help you, Angie," he said, voice low, firm. "We can work through this together. And if you do the probation, it will give you evenings and weekends to work through Voight's case files. If you stay on the job, you'll have access to law enforcement databases. By next Christmas this will be over. Four seasons. That's all."

She swallowed. Emotion glittered in her eyes, hard like diamonds. "You can't help me," she said softly, coolly. "You're too busy. What happened today, anyway? Why were you at the correctional center? What kept you from our date?"

"Between you and me—"

"Fuck it, Maddocks! Are you serious? You going to say that every time? Who in the hell am I going to tell anyway? Send out a tweet? Blog it from my social media desk?"

He clenched his jaw, and his pulse kicked up a notch. A little warning began to whisper inside him that maybe he *should* hold information back from her, but he told her anyway, about the interview with Zaedeen Camus and the plea bargain. The muscles in her neck grew taut as she listened. When he finished, she reached for her glass and took a heavy, hard swig, then sat for a moment staring at the fire. "So the Hells Angels and the Russians?" She cursed softly. "Who went up to Wilkie with you?"

"A prosecutor and Holgersen."

She snorted, refusing to meet his eyes. "So, Kjel Holgersen," she said so softly it was almost inaudible.

"He's a good cop."

"Yeah. Right. He can hardly string three coherent words together, but at least he doesn't go emptying clips into the faces of bad guys. At least he doesn't try stabbing his partners."

Maddocks stared at her, the memory swirling through him—her blackout after they'd questioned the Catholic priest during the Baptist investigation, her trying to stab him outside the downtown cathedral.

"Angie—"

She surged abruptly to her feet. "I need sleep. It's late. And I have a decision to make."

The unspoken hung between them. She wanted to sleep and think *alone*. He was not welcome. Not part of this big decision in her life, as much as he'd been a part of the lead-up to it. A cold feeling sank through him. Maddocks slowly got to his feet. He picked up the envelope he'd brought. "Open it."

She hesitated, then took it from him. She lifted the flap and took out a voucher.

Surprise showed on her face. "These are for a lodge, up north, in the wilderness?"

"For us. To spend some time together, far away from everything. As soon as we can."

The hard emotion in her eyes softened. She swallowed.

He reached out and cupped her cheek. "You don't have to do everything alone. Don't lock me out, Angie. Don't."

Her jaw tensed.

He nodded slowly, dropped his hand, and reached for his coat, which was draped over the back of a chair. He gave a sharp whistle. "Jack-O—it's time to go, boy."

He shrugged into his coat as Jack-O roused himself and hobbled over. Maddocks hesitated, then turned quickly, bent down, and gripped

Angie's face firmly between two hands. He gave her a hard kiss on the mouth. He felt her stiffen, resist, then yield to his kiss. It sent a punch of relief to his gut—she still responded, still wanted him. Their connection remained, at least on some level. He broke the kiss, held her gaze. "Sometimes you do need to stop fighting."

He scooped Jack-O up under his arm and made for the door. It was past midnight as he and Jack-O rode down in the elevator. He knew there was no way Angie Pallorino was going to sleep. She would not be able to resist the siren call of those boxes on her table. This was going to be a rough ride. On all counts.

He also remembered all the things he loved about her—her independence, strength. Her beauty inside and out. The fire that burned inside her to help the vulnerable. How she could be so gentle if she wasn't so afraid. Their sex. All reasons he still wanted this to work.

CHAPTER 14

THURSDAY, JANUARY 4

The door snicked shut behind Maddocks and Jack-O. Angie dragged both her hands over her damp hair. What in the hell was she doing? Trying to sabotage this delicate thing between her and Maddocks before it even had a chance to grow? Before *he* could leave *her*? She was not being fair to him—this was her problem. The fact he was still working on *their* case while she'd saved his life and ended up on probation—it was her fault, not his. She needed to own that. She'd dug her own grave because she *could* have saved him and Ginny without using excessive force in killing Spencer Addams.

Nevertheless, Maddocks's compassionate, calm, commanding presence just seemed to rub salt into her own feelings of inadequacy and failure.

You don't have to do everything alone.

Well, yeah, you do have to do some things alone. You come into this life alone, and you go out alone. At the end of the day, it's just you.

Angie reached for her glass, swigged back the last of the dregs. She then scraped her hair back, tied it up with a hairband, snapped on a fresh pair of crime scene gloves, and returned her attention to the box holding the evidence packets.

Setting the bag with the teddy bear to one side, she lifted out the next bag. It was marked as containing a purple women's cardigan. Angie paused as she caught sight of a binder tucked down along the inside of the box. She placed the bagged sweater onto the table and reached for the binder, opened it. The front page itemized everything that was supposed to be inside this box.

She scanned the list.

One teddy bear. One girl's dress. One pair of girls' underwear. A purple women's sweater. Dried and vacuum-packed blood samples, ABO blood-type analysis, preserved biological stains taken from the sweater, mounted slides of hair evidence—some short ash-blonde hairs and some long dark hairs. Photographs of bloodied patent fingerprints and handprints from the scene. Images of dusted latents. Photos of Jane Doe's contusions and mouth wound. Rape kit. Ballistics report. Angie's blood grew hotter and hotter as she read. This was a breakthrough.

If there was hair in here, while a trace examiner might have said in the eighties that there was either a match or no match, given new technology, hair samples as small as two millimeters could now be tested for mitochondrial DNA and eventually compared with known individuals. Hair as old as four decades had been successfully tested.

And preserved samples of blood, semen—if the evidence had been adequately processed and stored, she might get DNA profiles. She should not open another thing. Given that there was indeed preserved biological evidence in this box, she needed to get it straight into the hands of a good forensics lab without further contaminating it. First thing tomorrow she'd call Dr. Sunni Padachaya. The MVPD crime lab head was renowned for her early starts to the day and her late finishes. She'd once informed Angie that she had no life apart from her lab work.

Angie got Sunni. Because she didn't have much of a life apart from her work, either. Which was why it sliced so deep to be put on probation, to risk losing her career.

Suddenly exhausted, her vision blurring, Angie glanced at the clock in her kitchen. Almost 2:00 a.m. She replaced the binder, followed by the bagged sweater and teddy bear. She snapped off and trashed her gloves. If she was lucky, she might be able steal a couple hours of sleep. She shunted the dead bolt home on her door and clicked off the lights in her living room. She went into her bedroom and took her uniform out from the back of her closet. She hung it on the outside of the closet door and sat down on the edge of her bed. She stared at it—the black pants, black shirt, the badge on the sleeve, the name tag on the left breast that said, PALLORINO.

The last time she'd worn it was on a sweltering July day just over six months ago. For her old partner Hash Hashowsky's funeral. Her chest tightened at the memory of the lone riderless horse with Hash's boots hanging symbolically from the stirrups. A sea of uniformed officers, some in black, some in red Mountie serge, had followed the horse to the plaintive tune of Scottish bagpipes and the cry of gulls. The downtown part of the city had come to a stop. Emotion flooded her eyes, and she swiped it away angrily. He'd been her mentor. Her friend. She'd loved Hash like a father. At least *he'd* never let her down like her adoptive father had with his lies. And heaven alone knew who her real biological father was. The thought struck her—what would Hash advise her to do in the face of probation?

He'd tell her she'd worked her ass off to become a damn fine detective, and throwing it away now over a twelve-month period of discipline would be a fool's game. Angie inhaled deeply and squared her shoulders. She clenched her hands over her knees. And Maddocks was right—if she did swallow her discipline and stay with the MVPD, she'd have access to law enforcement databases that would otherwise be closed to her.

She could take it one day at a time. And she didn't have to start until 11:00 a.m. tomorrow. That gave her time enough to potentially get her evidence to a private lab before reporting for duty. At least the techs could commence working on her samples. Just the idea of pending results—new clues—would keep her going through the first day. And then when she returned home tomorrow, she could dig into Detective Voight's case notes and other material.

Angie brushed her teeth, crawled into bed, and clicked off her bedside lamp. As she drifted into the darkness of sleep, a faint and distant sound reached her. A female voice. Singing. Soft, like a lullaby . . .

Ah-ah-ah, ah-ah-ah,
były sobie kotki dwa.
A-a-a, kotki dwa,
szarobure, szarobure obydwa.

Ah-ah-ah, ah-ah-ah,
There were once two little kittens.
Ah-ah-ah, two little kittens,
They were both grayish-brown.

Ach, śpij, kochanie,
jesli gwiazdke z nieba chcesz-dostaniesz.
Wszystkie dzieci, nawet źle,
pogrążone są we śnie,
a ty jedna tylko nie.

Oh, sleep, my darling,
If you'd like a star from the sky, I'll give you one.
All children, even the bad ones,
Are already asleep,
Only you are not.

She could see a dark room. A shut door. A small band of purplish light seeping through a barred window up high near the ceiling. She was lying on a bed. A hand held hers. Skin cool. Soft. It was a nice feeling. Another hand brushed hair back from her brow . . .

Ach, śpij, bo wlaśnie
księżyc ziewa i za chwilę zaśnie.
A gdy rano przyjdzie świt
księżycowi będzie wstyd,
ze on zasnął, a nie ty.

Oh, sleep, because
The moon is yawning, and he will soon fall asleep.
And when the morning comes,
He will be really ashamed,
That he fell asleep and you did not.

CHAPTER 15

Kira Tranquada loved her job.

She was the youngest identification analyst with the small identification and disaster response unit—the IDRU—at the BC Coroner's Service, and she'd come into work the instant she'd heard about the latest floating foot discovery. That was four days ago. The lab had gotten to work immediately on the evidence brought in by the RCMP to see whether a viable DNA sample could be extracted.

It wasn't the first dismembered foot she'd worked with. Determining the origin and identity of these notorious floating feet was complicated. Ocean currents could carry the dismembered body parts as far as sixteen hundred kilometers—or around one thousand miles—and the currents in the Strait of Georgia where the majority of the feet had been found were highly unpredictable. Human feet also had a tendency to produce adipocere, a soaplike substance formed from body fat, which could conceal the scientific clues that helped determine postmortem interval. Under optimal conditions, a human body might remain intact in water for as long as three decades, meaning that the feet could have been floating around for years. But that length of time in water could also degrade DNA.

The driving force in aquatic taphonomic patterns—the rate at which a body decomposes in water—is oxygen. In highly oxygenated water, a corpse can be reduced to a skeleton within half an hour to a few days, consumed by scavengers ranging from sharks to smaller fish and squat lobsters, Alaskan prawns, Dungeness crabs, and small amphipods commonly called sea lice, plus other organisms. In those instances, feet encased in protective shoes would disarticulate from the skeleton, and if there was air in the soles, they'd float to the surface pretty fast. But for a body lying in an anoxic underwater area, for example in a deep gulley full of silt and sediment, anthropophagy—the consumption of a corpse by organisms and predators—would be virtually nonexistent. This, plus an alkaline pH and anaerobic bacteria, would be ideal for the formation of adipocere from body fat—more frequent in a child. And while adipocere, which is sometimes referred to as grave wax, could make determining postmortem interval very difficult, it did preserve other forensic evidence. Bottom line, Kira and her team had managed to get viable nuclear DNA from this little foot without using terribly lengthy or complicated procedures. She now had a profile, and it was being run through their geographic information system.

"It's not going to go any faster if you hang over my shoulder like that, Tranquada," Ricky Gorman muttered as he tapped at his keyboard. "Why don't you go get me a coffee or something and chill?"

Kira punched Ricky in the shoulder in mock rebuke. He was the IDRU's GIS whiz. Most armchair crime aficionados tended to associate GIS with the geographic profiling of the hunting habits of serial killers, but Ricky's expertise lay in the compilation of a multifaceted database of unidentified human remains and missing persons reports from around the province. And BC had the highest number of unidentified bodies in the country. This was partly due to the wild, mountainous terrain, the raging rivers, the miles of shoreline riddled with coves and islands, hostile weather, and sheer size—uninhabited for the most part—with borders that stretched from the Washington to Alaska and the territories. It was why the IDRU had been formed under the Coroner's Service umbrella in 2006, and they consistently had about two hundred files under open investigation, with more added as others were solved.

Ricky was among the first to have created a GIS program that specifically used Google maps for human remains investigations, and his systems had helped find an identity match for many of the floating feet, which had made headlines around the world.

"Sugar and cream?" Kira said.

"Hmm."

Kira went over to the coffeepot. She poured two mugs of fresh brew. It was the second pot she'd put on since coming into the office at 6:00 a.m. It was now almost 9:00 a.m.

"What did the anthropologist say?" Ricky said as she brought the two mugs over to his desk.

"Left foot bones of a three- or four-year-old child. No sign that it was removed by mechanical means—no tool marks like a knife or a saw." She set Ricky's mug down beside him. "Grave wax makes it tough to tell how long the foot has been out there, but the CBC news appears to have been on the mark with the manufacture period for that brand of shoe." She sipped from her mug, watching Ricky's bank of monitors. "That ROOAirPocket-Zero high-top model was produced only between 1984 and 1986 before it was discontinued."

"Doesn't mean the kid went into the water then," Ricky said, reaching for his mug.

"No." Kira took another sip and nodded toward the monitors. "I met a cop the other night who still thinks this GIS stuff is a crock. He figures there's not much more you can do with GIS that he can't do with a big ol' map and pushpins. He said smart cops have been doing the pushpin thing for years—they figure out patterns in their brains."

"Luddite." Ricky set his mug back down beside him without taking his eyes off his work. "Old-school law enforcement said the same thing about Vancouver cop Kim Rossmo. He went on to become the first officer in Canada to obtain a doctorate in criminology, and his dissertation resulted in the geographic profiling methodology and software now being used by the FBI."

"Yeah, I told him. I also explained that if a plane crashes and there're no bodies found, but we know that there were passengers and a pilot on that plane, our system keeps track of that, too. If a foot washes up fifteen years down the road, or a piece of finger bone is found in fishnet a decade later, we're going to be able to tell right away if it came from that crash. Just like that body that was pulled from the Fraser River in Coquitlam a quarter century ago," she said, taking another sip. "It was identified as a Prince George man whose corpse floated downstream nearly eight hundred kilometers. No one had even thought to look for a match against missing males *that* far north—investigators were shocked."

Ricky froze. "Shit," he muttered. He leaned forward sharply, hitting his keys. "We got it. We got a cold fucking hit!"

Chills raced down her spine as she peered over his shoulder. "Holy—" She grabbed the phone on the desk, hit the number for the head of the IDRU. "Dr. Colbourne, you're going to want to see this. We got a direct cold hit on the kid's foot." She spoke fast, her gaze riveted on the information being displayed on Ricky's monitor. "And the person is not missing." She paused as new information populated Ricky's screen. "Not deceased, either. She's very much alive."

CHAPTER 16

Maddocks received the call at 8:18 a.m. Thursday—one of the barcode girls had agreed to speak to him. She appeared to understand some English and had indicated to their victim services counselor that she was Russian. Maddocks had immediately contacted a female interpreter and arranged for her to meet him at the hospital where the girls were being held. He and Holgersen had driven over, stat.

Maddocks and Holgersen now strode alongside the victim services counselor and the interpreter toward the room in the wing where the girls were being treated.

"She's the oldest one?" Maddocks asked, thinking of the girl who'd been poking at her plate of food while the others sat listless.

"She appears to be," the counselor said, leading the way. "And she's definitely the strongest mentally." She came up to a closed door, stopped, and turned to face the detectives and interpreter. "She's waiting inside with a female orderly. I'll sit in on the interview. The orderly will not. If at any time I feel that our survivor is coming under stress, I will call the interview to a halt. Is that understood?"

"Loud and clear," said Maddocks.

She hesitated. "Possibly two males interrogating her might be too much."

Maddocks turned to Holgersen. "Why don't you go hang in the cafeteria until I need you?"

"Anything you says, boss." He turned and loped away, fiddling in his jacket for his nicotine gum as he went. Maddocks inhaled, mentally preparing himself, striving for a calm, nonthreatening demeanor from the outset. Ideally, he'd have liked to have had Angie conducting this interview. But there were no other females on the task force right now who were qualified to handle this delicate situation, and the last thing Maddocks wanted was to wait and have their victim to clam up again.

The counselor reached for the door handle but paused once more. "She's still twitchy—still being weaned off the narcotics they were giving her."

"Understood," said Maddocks.

They entered. The girl sat with a nurse at a small round table under a long window that cast them in a wintery light. It was the one who'd been poking at her food. Her dark hair was once again scraped back. No makeup. Today she wore a simple gray hoodie over a white T-shirt, yoga pants, and slippers that someone must have brought for her. Maddocks felt a clutch in his chest—in this light she looked much younger than his Ginny. Barely sixteen. That she was the oldest of the six sliced even deeper.

The nurse placed her hand over the girl's and then got up and left the room. The interpreter took the nurse's seat and introduced herself to the girl in Russian, explaining why they were here.

Maddocks placed his file and notebook on the table. "I'm Detective James Maddocks," he said. "Do you mind if I remove my jacket and take a seat?"

The interpreter relayed his words in Russian.

The girl nodded. Her hooded black eyes flicked nervously around the room, and she fidgeted with her nails in her lap. They were chewed to the quick. Visible around the thin column of her neck were fading bruises. A taste of bile rose up the back of his throat as he recalled his interview with Zaedeen Camus.

What do these tattoos denote? Expiry date? Ownership?

Ownership. The origin and age of the merchandise. And the date a girl was first put into service. The tattoos have been scanned into a computerized database for tracking. The girls go out for a fee, generally for a period of two years. They can be returned for new ones after that period, if so desired.

He draped his jacket carefully over the back of the chair and seated himself. "You're a long way from home," he said.

Again, the translator conveyed his words.

The girl nodded.

Maddocks said, "I want you to know that you can stop talking whenever you want to, okay? Just let me know. You can raise your hand like this." He raised his hand, palm facing the girl.

She listened to the interpreter, then nodded.

"Are you okay that we record this interview?"

Fear darkened her eyes as the interpreter explained the question.

Maddocks leaned forward, kept his voice calm, quiet. "I want you to know that we will do everything we can to protect you, and the more information you can give us, the better we will know who to protect you and the others from. Recording this interview will go a long way toward helping put them away. Are you okay with that?"

She said something in Russian to the interpreter, who in turn said, "She wants to know if she will have to face the men in court if she speaks about them on tape."

"We can make sure that doesn't have to happen. We can protect your identities," he said. "Okay?"

The girl nodded. Only then did Maddocks place the recording equipment on the table. He pressed the button, and the red light came on. She stared at it.

"Can you tell me what your name is?"

She listened to the interpreter, then glanced at the victim services counselor, who nodded.

"Sophia Tarasov."

"How old are you?"

"Seventeen this month."

"And where is home, Sophia?"

"Novgorod in Russia."

"Do you have family in Novgorod?"

She glanced down and shook her head.

"How about somewhere else? Is there someone we can inform that you're all right?"

She shook her head harder.

Maddocks nodded. Not only was she afraid, but she was also embarrassed perhaps. He'd come back at that angle later, because someone had to be missing and worried about this teen. "Can you tell me how you came to be on the yacht called the *Amanda Rose*?"

She inhaled deeply and began to speak while staring at a crack in the table. The interpreter relayed Sophia Tarasov's story in Russian-accented English.

"I answered an Internet advertisement for modeling. I phoned the number. They told me to come to an address in Novgorod. A man took pictures of me and gave me food, something to drink. He seemed nice. And then I woke up inside some kind of van. I was hurt. They had raped me. I was bleeding. They gave me water, and there must have been drugs in it because I passed out again and remember nothing. I don't know how many days I was in the van. Taken to Prague. I only knew it was Prague from something one of the men said. In an apartment in Prague, I was beaten and raped many times over by different men. And I was drugged. I was kept chained to a mattress on the floor, no clothes."

Maddocks swallowed. "There were other girls in this apartment?"

"In my room, yes. Three more on mattresses. And in the other rooms. I heard them. Crying. Sometimes they screamed. I don't know how many days it was, maybe a month, and then they took twenty of us in a truck. It was a long journey."

"The same men who brought you to Prague?"

"Different men. They spoke a Russian dialect."

"Would you be able to describe any of these men?"

"I don't know." She was silent for a while, then said, "One man had a blue crab, here, a tattoo, on his arm." She patted her forearm. "They took us to city with port. They put us on boat."

"Do you know which city?"

"It was Russian. Maybe Vladivostok—I heard this name when the men talked quietly when they thought I was knocked out from the drugs." This answer came from Sophia directly, in broken English. The interpreter glanced at Maddocks in surprise.

"Jump in if and when you need to," he said quietly to the interpreter, then turned back to Sophia.

"You speak English?"

She nodded. "Bit. I learn at school."

"What kind of a boat?"

"Fishing boat. Crab. Rusty, old. Bad smells."

"What makes you think it was a crab fishing vessel?"

"I know from my grandfather. He was crab fisherman. King crab. Sea of Okhotsk. Long time ago. He told us stories and had pictures, how American boats from Alaska have square crab cages and throw them over the side one at a time. In Russia we use ones shaped like this." She made a cone shape with her hands. "Russian fishermen slide cages off back of boat."

Adrenaline quickened in Maddocks. This was very specific information they could check.

"And from there—maybe Vladivostok—twenty of you sailed on this crab fishing vessel?"

She nodded. "We were in bottom of the ship. No light. It was many days. Bad storms. We got sick. One night they shook all of us awake, told us put on all warm clothes. They tied our hands, like this." She brought her wrists together. "They brought us up to deck. There was another ship close. Could see it through fog."

"Also a fishing vessel?"

"No. Like cargo ship. Containers on the deck. Piled high."

"Did you see any names on the hull? Anything to identify the vessel?"

"Only when we were brought on board new ship. They took us over side in fishing boat and across to cargo ship in the smaller boat. I saw flag from South Korea on cargo boat."

Maddocks's heart beat yet faster. "Are you certain?"

"Yes."

"What else did you see?"

"Very little. Getting dark. It was foggy. No moon. Lights on the boat nearly all off. It was very cold. Windy."

"What language did the crew aboard the South Korean vessel speak?"

"Some Russian. And an Asian language."

She reached for a glass of water in front of her and took a long swallow, hand trembling.

"They transferred all of the twenty women from one ship to the other?"

"Yes, and some other cargo. It took long time. I don't know what other cargo was. Maybe crab."

"And once you were aboard the Korean cargo vessel?"

She shook her head, her eyes going distant. Her face tightened. "They kept us in container, all twenty of us. We had two buckets for toilet. A man with scarf over face come once per day with new buckets and some food and water. We got very sick and thirsty. I lost all track of time and the days. One girl, she died. She took long time to die. They left her body inside container with us."

Maddocks rubbed his jaw. The interpreter shifted uncomfortably in her chair. Maddocks sensed that Tarasov's victim services counselor was going to cut him off any second now—she was also getting edgy. But he didn't want to rush Sophia Tarasov. If he paced things carefully, she might speak to him again on several more occasions. He might get more in the long haul through patience. Nevertheless, urgency nipped at him—because the longer things took, the more time it gave the organized crime rings to bury evidence.

"Where did the South Korean ship take you?"

She shook her head, looking down at her fidgeting fingers. "Maybe port in South Korea. Then another ship, which stop maybe China. Cargo change. Then Vancouver."

"When you docked at the Port of Vancouver, how did they take you off the ship?"

"Some men opened container, make us hurry out. We were already on land with other containers all around. Dark. It was night. The men in big rush, watching everything. They take us to another dock, put us in another boat. Small one."

"How small?"

She sniffed and wiped her nose. Her shakes were intensifying. A sheen of perspiration was beginning to gleam on her brow. "I . . . I don't know. I . . . was not well. Throwing up. Passing out. I remember little. Just blur. There were nineteen of us got off ship. Only ten put on smaller boat."

"Where did the other nine go?"

"I don't know. Maybe truck."

Maddocks cleared his throat. "How long were you on the smaller boat?"

She shook her head. "Don't know."

"What do you remember next?"

"Waking up in place with four rooms. There was small kitchen and bathroom, but door to outside was locked. Windows had bars up high. We have nice food now. Fish. Vegetables. Fruit. Water. A woman would bring."

"Can you describe this woman? What nationality?"

"She old. Maybe eighty. She was all dressed in black. When I ask her question, she say in Russian that they will cut my tongue out if I talk. Like they told us in Prague they would do if we ever speak to anyone about men who brought us there. In Prague there was woman with no tongue."

A tightness clamped Maddocks's throat. It came with a thin spear of red-hot anger.

"What could you see through the windows of this house?"

"Big trees. Lots of trees. Like forest. Through the trees, water."

"Anything else? Sounds? Traffic, airplanes?"

"Very quiet. No traffic noise. Sometimes small plane up high. And engines sometimes, like from boats. One time helicopter."

"Did you see anyone else in this place, apart from the old woman?"

Now her whole body began to shake.

"Only one man. He come when it is dark a few times. He very big. He wear hood, and he make lights dim. He say he come to test all the merchandise. Very rough. Not young, but very strong. Powerful. He barely say two words."

"Accent? Language?"

"English. American accent, like you."

"He got naked apart from the hood?"

She shifted uncomfortably in her chair, nodded.

"Was he circumcised?"

She glanced at the interpreter, who translated in Russian.

Sophia shook her head. "He wear protection."

"Was there anything else distinctive about his body?"

"Here—" She touched the side of her neck and slipped into Russian.

"Tattoo," said the translator. "Like a crab. Same as the one she saw on the fishing vessel from Vladivostok. Same as a man in Prague. But she says he kept the room dim whenever he visited. His hood looked like an executioner's hood, black with a slit for his eyes. She glimpsed the crab only when his hood slipped a little during a sex act."

117

Adrenaline spiked through Maddocks. Calmly, he said, "Sophia, would you be able to describe this crab tattoo to a sketch artist?"

She nodded. Maddocks reached into his pocket for his phone. He called Holgersen.

"Can you bring in a sketch artist, stat?" he said as soon as Holgersen picked up. "Get Cass Hansen if you can. I've used her before—she's good. And she lives two minutes away from the hospital."

He killed the call and turned back to Sophia.

"What happened next?"

"Madame Vee, she come on a plane."

"How long were you in this place before she arrived?"

"I don't know. Maybe three or four weeks. Madame Vee come with Zina."

So Camus had lied about not going to the holding location. They could use this.

"They make us stand naked and turn us around. They talk in French. They pick six of us. We were put on small plane, seaplane. We landed in harbor and were taken by small boat to *Amanda Rose*."

"When the seaplane took off from this holding place, what did you see from the air?"

She shook her head, and her eyes filled with tears. "Nothing. They used blindfolds."

"Did you see the pilot?"

She shook her head.

"How long did this flight take, Sophia?"

"Maybe hour?" She lifted her shoulders. "Or two—I scared. I don't know."

"Did you ever leave the *Amanda Rose* after you first boarded the yacht?"

"No. They lock us inside cabins. Keep us apart from the other girls. Only when police come and raid the boat and took us did we leave *Amanda Rose*." She wiped her eyes, but tears kept streaming down her cheeks.

The victim services woman leaned forward. "Detective Maddocks, I think we might have had enough for today."

He nodded. "Just one more question, Sophia. The other girls who are here with you at the hospital now, where are their homes, what are their names?"

"No name." She shook her head wildly. "No give name, I promised, no names."

"Okay, okay. Can you tell me where they came from?"

Her brow furrowed into tight wrinkles. She looked terrified.

"Please," he said softly. "It will help."

She stared at him for what seemed like a full minute, then slowly said, "Two from Syria. They were taken from refugee camp in Greece. They were promised passage to Germany, jobs. One from Austria—she Turkish. Other two from Russia, like me. Other parts Russia."

Maddocks's jaw tightened. A knock sounded on the door. The counselor got up to open it. It was Hansen, a sketch artist the MVPD used regularly.

"Thank you, Sophia. Thank you very much. You've been a tremendous help." Maddocks came to his feet and went to Hansen at the door.

"I came as soon as I could," Cass Hansen said quietly, looking flushed from her rush over. "Detective Holgersen said it was urgent."

Maddocks lowered his voice to almost a whisper. "We need an image of the tattoos Sophia saw on several men. Seems like the same tattoo on all of them. And if she can describe anything more about the men, especially the big guy who wore a hood when he assaulted them sexually."

Hansen nodded. "I'll try," she said softly.

Maddocks closed the door behind Hansen, his pulse pounding. This was it—the breakthrough they needed. Sophia Tarasov would provide more down the road; he was certain of it. She might get the other girls to talk, too.

✝

CHAPTER 17

From the warmth of his car, through the rain-streaked windows, a man watches the entrance of the medical building that hunkers dark and wet under the low cloud and rain. Leafless deciduous branches outside the hospital walls wag gnarly fingers in the wind.

As the two detectives exit the building, he sits up sharply in the driver's seat. For a few days now he's been tracking the lead detective, who was in the news in connection with the takedown of the Bacchanalian Club aboard the *Amanda Rose*. The papers and TV stations claimed several young women from the boat had been taken into MVPD custody. He knows from his boss they're barcode merchandise. But he didn't know where they'd been taken. Until now.

He thinks he's found the girls. They're in that hospital.

The tall skinny detective in the ugly bomber jacket and combat boots stops to light a cigarette. The boss cop—the taller one with pitch-black hair and pale skin, the one he's been tracking—is dressed in a classy wool coat. Behind them come two women. The man knows that the dark-haired woman is a Russian interpreter because the detectives waited for her to arrive before going inside earlier, and once they were inside, he'd jimmied open the car she arrived in. In her glove compartment he found business cards with her address and photo. He fingers one of these cards now as his gaze settles on the second woman, committing her to memory. Blonde. Short. Athletic build. He doesn't know who she is. She arrived later. The group converses outside the hospital entrance for a few minutes while the skinny cop grabs a few fast drags on his cigarette, exhaling in a cloud of smoke and condensation. They start down the stairs. The skinny guy drops his smoke, grinds it out with his boot, then picks it up again and puts it in a bag. Drawing up his collar, skinny cop follows his boss-partner to an Impala parked in the lot. The two women go separate ways.

He lights a cigarette of his own—the skinny detective's smoking has given him the urge. The Impala pulls out of the lot and turns down the street. He continues to wait in his nondescript sedan, his plates carefully obscured with splattered mud. His skill, his art, is patience. Discretion. Even in the face of a ticking clock and pressing urgency. He gets big money for completed jobs. This is a big job.

For this job he's been told to send a message. He never questions why. He never feels stress or emotion. He only takes pride in a contract neatly executed.

When the interpreter drives out of the lot in her little blue Yaris, he extinguishes his cigarette carefully in his ashtray and starts his own ignition. He puts his car into gear and drives slowly behind the interpreter's vehicle, his tires crackling on the wet streets as he holds a safe distance.

CHAPTER 18

A pixielike woman with purple hair and a white lab coat poked her head out of the lab door and peered at Angie. "Our receptionist is not in yet."

Angie felt hot and bothered in her uniform as she stood holding her evidence box in the reception area of Anders Forensics, the firm that Dr. Sunni Padachaya had recommended. Her arm ached. Traffic up the peninsula had been a beast. And urgency nipped at her—she still needed to make it back to Victoria before her 11:00 a.m. start, or she'd have a black mark against her on day one of her probation. This nine-to-five noose was going to suck even more than she'd imagined.

"I'm here for Dr. Jacob Anders," she said. "He's expecting me—I called earlier."

"Oh, *you're* Angie Pallorino?" the pixie said, eyeing her beat uniform.

"Yeah."

"I wasn't expecting a police officer."

"Right."

"Jacob is through this way." She led Angie down a sterile concrete corridor lined with vast windows that overlooked a bay ruffled with whitecaps. The building smelled new. It also reeked of money. Sunni had said Dr. Jacob Anders would be pricey when Angie had reached her by phone early this morning. Sunni had personally vouched that Anders was one of the best in the business—a newly relocated British expat with a breadth of LE-related experience abroad and in North America. He'd also contracted in the past to the FBI and the RCMP as well as other police organizations.

The purple-haired lab pixie opened a door. "His office is through this way. Go ahead."

Angie carried her box into an office suite walled with smoked glass. Here, too, expansive windows looked out over the gunmetal-gray bay. A glass-and-chrome desk was positioned in front of the windows. No chair behind it, only one in front of it. Shelves of books lined one wall. Another wall hosted a bank of monitors and a large smart screen. Several of the monitors showed what appeared to be live black-and-white surveillance footage from inside his labs and the exterior perimeter of the building. One screen displayed what seemed to be an underwater feed filming a whitish object trapped beneath a curved cage. There was no one in the room.

"Hello? Dr. Anders?"

"Detective Pallorino, welcome," came a deep and resonant voice. Holding her box in front of her, Angie swiveled around to the source of the sound. From behind a partition appeared a man in a wheelchair. Surprise rippled through Angie as she was forced to lower her gaze to the man's face. He wheeled forward and proffered his hand. "Please, call me Jacob." His accent was British, the kind Angie associated with upper class and sophistication.

Angie balanced her box on her left hip and shook the man's hand. His grasp was firm, calculated. It brought to mind the resoluteness of a surgeon coupled with a pianist's sensitivity. Everything about him whispered *paradox*, from his overt physical disability, to the power he seemed to exude, to the intelligence and kindness in his gray eyes. Angie judged Jacob Anders to be in his late forties, possibly early fifties given the silver that flecked the dark hair at his temples and the lines that bracketed his strong mouth. Movie-star handsome but just slightly off-center in a way she could not immediately articulate. His assuredness made her square her shoulders.

"Thank you for meeting with me at such short notice," she said.

He appraised her, taking in her uniform, clearly shaping a question in his mind for which she did not feel like providing an answer.

"Take a seat," he said. "You can place your box on the desk over there. How can I help you?"

"You come highly recommended by Sunni Padachaya, with whom I work at the MVPD lab," Angie said as she set her box on the glass surface. Anders wheeled himself around to the other side of his desk while she lowered herself into the chair in front of it.

"Sunni's a good friend of mine," he said. "We met at a forensics conference in Brussels many years back and have kept up a connection ever since."

"I consider her a friend, too." Which wasn't saying much, as Angie didn't do girlfriends, or at least not very well—the relationships never lasted when she tried. She cut right to the chase because she was squeezed for time. "I'm looking into a cold case from 1986 for a friend." She explained to Jacob Anders what she knew of the cradle case to date and how she'd come into possession of the evidence and files.

"I did open one of the evidence bags, the one with the teddy bear, which I probably shouldn't have, but I used gloves, and it was done in a fairly sterile environment. What I now seek is interpretation of the old lab reports and to see if there's any viable biological evidence worth testing for DNA using current technology and whether the photographic images of the bloodied handprints and fingerprints can be digitized. Given that the VPD was going to destroy the evidence before the detective took it home, and given that he reopened the boxes at home and his family has been storing the boxes in a basement, even if there is viable evidence in there, it could be compromised."

He sat back, relaxed as he assessed her and the merits of her case.

"Would you be interested in taking it on?" she said, glancing at her watch, pressure ratcheting up.

"You're aware of our fee structure?"

"It won't be a problem."

He moistened his lips, watching her features. Angie felt her cheeks begin to redden—the man could tell she was hiding something. She adjusted the collar of her uniform and bit the bullet. "In full disclosure, there is something else I should add." She paused, her gaze locked on his. "It's confidential."

"We treat all our work as confidential," he said. "Confidentiality, discretion—it's a necessary and absolute cornerstone of our business."

She wavered. "I . . . I am the child who was found in the cradle, but I have no recollection of the event, nor of my life preceding the event."

He didn't blink. Not a thing changed in his face. It gave her an odd rush of relief at having gotten it off her chest, as if handing this information over to him lifted some of the dark weight she'd been shouldering in secret. This had to be how her suspects felt on the other end of her interrogation table when they finally confessed to what they'd been trying to hide from police.

"And you're certain?"

Angie blinked. "You mean, am I certain that *I* am the cradle kid?"

"Yes."

"I . . . from what I understand, from what I've been told, yes." Her brain reeled in a totally new direction. This was something she had not thought of.

"And you say that the cradle child's DNA is likely in this box?"

She nodded. "Her blood is on the teddy bear and the dress. There could be hairs, too. She had—has—the same color hair as me. I mean, if it was me, it's my hair. And I have the scar on my mouth—same as in the photos."

"To be a hundred percent certain, we should take a fresh biological sample from you before you leave. We'll compare it against the DNA contained in the evidence. Is this acceptable to you? I can have my tech provide you with our contract, which includes a full disclosure statement and the relevant privacy clauses."

Anxiety twisted through her belly. "Yeah. Sure, yes. I do want to be certain." A shadow moved in the corner of her eye. Angie's attention shot to the monitor on the wall that showed the underwater footage. She stared as an elastic, amorphous thing stirred up a cloud of silt and grainy detritus, expanding to smother the cage, making it disappear from view. Tentacles came into view as it then contracted to squeeze itself through one of the small square gaps in the cage wiring. Octopus. Once inside the cage it expanded again, and a cloud of white maggotlike organisms erupted and squiggled wildly away. The octopus smothered the white object inside like a blanket.

She leaned sharply forward. "What *is* that?"

He turned to the screen. "Ah." He smiled as he wheeled closer to the monitor. "Giant Pacific octopus. Come to feed on the porcine flesh being secured to the seabed by the cage. This is part of our underwater taphonomy study being conducted in conjunction with Dr. Karen Schelling at Simon Fraser University." He turned to face Angie. "She's an entomologist who—"

"I know who Dr. Schelling is. She often gives talks to law enforcement. I've been to one of her lectures on what insects do to corpses."

"Well, she's trying to learn more about the rates of decomposition in various marine environments. This is her equivalent of an underwater body farm. Except we can't put human donors out there in the open water, so we use pigs fresh from the butcher to approximate decomp rates on human bodies. Underwater taphonomy is a field a lot less studied than taphonomy on land, and there are so many more variables."

"So this is a live feed? From out there?" Angie tilted her chin toward the bay beyond his window where a series of docks led out into the water. At the end of one of the longer docks was a small building being lashed by wind and rain.

"Correct. Karen, however, is based at SFU on the mainland, but she can operate her underwater cameras remotely from anywhere in the world. I have a feed here, but anyone can log on to the project via the Internet and watch live."

A chill crept into Angie's bones as she regarded the octopus now feeding on the dead pig trapped underwater in the cage. She thought of that little shoe on the news and imagined a child lying on that seabed instead, being consumed by sea lice and crabs and octopuses and fish. The chill in her bones turned to ice, and a strange pressure filled her lungs. Clearing her throat, she said, "I . . . I should probably get back to work. I apologize for the rush, but I'm on a fixed schedule at the moment."

His gaze ticked briefly to her uniform. "Understood." He reached across his desk to press an intercom button on his phone. "Maryanne, could you bring Officer Pallorino one of our contracts to sign and take her through to the lab for a buccal swab and blood sample."

"On my way," came a woman's voice.

Jacob Anders released the button and said to Angie, "When did you learn that you were the cradle child?"

"A few weeks ago."

Something acute and unreadable entered his eyes, as if he were seeing her anew, recalibrating his initial assessments of her. It made her uneasy. He was probably going to run his own background check on her as soon as the door shut behind her.

"How soon might we have results?" she said.

"I can expedite things if it's urgent, but it will depend on how well that evidence was packaged and stored. While DNA is incredibly resilient and can last thousands of years if buried a few feet below ground, or even a few hundred thousand years if frozen in ice, any exposure to heat, sunlight, water, or oxygen will have degraded it. And the more degraded the DNA, the more complicated and lengthy the lab work.

Sometimes the decay makes it unworkable. I'll give you a call and an idea of timelines once we've made a full assessment of the evidence."

"Fair enough."

A knock sounded the door. It opened, and in came the purple-haired pixie, a file clutched in her hand. Angie got to her feet.

"Thank you again, Dr. Anders, for—"

"That's Jacob to you," he said with a smile as he wheeled out from behind his desk. He offered his hand.

Angie shook it, sensing once more that peculiar combination of power and finesse in his grip.

"My pleasure." His smile deepened. It exposed his incisors. It put light into his pale-gray eyes. And those eyes reminded her of a wolf. Cunning and watchful.

CHAPTER 19

Driving back to the station, Maddocks replayed for Holgersen the interview with Sophia Tarasov. Holgersen fiddled to free a nicotine gum chiclet from its packaging as he listened. Once he'd liberated his tablet of gum, he popped it into his mouth and said, "So, Vladivostok, eh? Jeezus, you sure I can't smoke in here, boss?"

"When are you going to stop asking?"

He grinned around the green wad of gum between his teeth. "When it stops annoying you."

"What do you know about Vladivostok?"

"It's about eighty klicks north of the North Korean border—a hub for secondhand Jap cars. And Ruskie king crab, most of it poached and sold via South Korea and China to the US market."

Maddocks shot Holgersen a hot, fast look.

"*What?* Jeezus, you's like Pallorino. Thinks I knows nothing. I knows stuff, okay? I got interests."

Maddocks eyed him a second longer before returning his attention to the wet road and traffic. "Go on."

"I's also seen a picture of ink like Tarasov described—a light-blue crab. It's a thing for a group of the Ruskie crab Mafia.

"Crab Mafia? That's a *thing?*"

"Sure it's a thing. Everyone knows."

"I didn't know that was a thing."

Holgersen shrugged. "Anyone who's in the seafood industry or who invests in it knows. I's from fishing folk—my folk all know. My great-gramps fought with the Ruskies in the Resistance during World War II, when the Krauts occupied the far north of Norway. See?" He made as if his hands were scales weighing a balance between the two. "Fishing, criminals. Ruskies. Like I says, I got interests—parta my background."

Maddocks threw Holgersen another look. "Your great-grandfather was Norwegian?"

"Yep."

"Guess that explains the name Kjel Holgersen."

"Yep." Holgersen turned to look out of the rain-streaked window and drummed his fingers on his bony knee. "My gramps and pops was both direct from Norway. They came over to Canada after my gramma died—they had relatives in what used to be a Norwegian fishing community way up the north coast, above Bella Bella, just shy of the Alaskan border. Wanted to start over and all that. I remember my gramps from when I was little. He told us stories about the Ruskies up near Lapland—guess I's been interested since then. Fishing. Ruskies."

"Who was us?"

"What?"

"You said he 'told us' stories."

"Oh . . . no, just me I guess," he said quickly. "And my pops. The moms wasn't real interested."

Maddocks detected the almost imperceptible shift in Holgersen's tone and body language—he'd let slip something and was covering up. It piqued Maddocks's curiosity—if you understood the motive, you understood the man. "So that's where you're from, then, north of Bella Bella?" he prodded.

His partner opened the window to a sudden blast of cold air, spat his gum out into the street, and wound up the window. A diversion tactic.

"Yeah, so, Vladivostok," he continued as if the personal exchange had never occurred. "Going to Vladivostok to ask about poached crab is like going to Colombia to ask about cocaine. You gets your head chopped off, or your house is firebombed, or you gets gunned down in the street. You got all these abandoned and illegal pirate boats in the harbor there. Some is used for the gray fishing fleet—full of forged documentation and shit but condoned by Soviet authorities as legit, or the Ruskie officials turn a blind eye for some good vodka and a few hookers. But the black fleet—now thems the real pirates. Crew could be from anywheres—Indonesia, China, Russia, Sudan. The black ships are registered in places like Cambodia, Somalia. But both the black and the gray crab harvests go the same route, basically. Live crab hauled from the Sea of Japan is transferred from a fishing vessel to a legit cargo vessel and taken to South Korea."

He groped again in his pocket for his gum. The guy never stopped fidgeting. Like it was physically impossible for him to be still. Holgersen cursed as his green gum wad popped from its packaging to the floor. He bent around his seat belt, groping on the floor of the passenger side.

"Hah! Bastards, these packages." He wiped the wad with his thumb and stuck it in his mouth.

"Are you saying what I think you're saying?" Maddocks said. "That the barcode girls could have traveled the same route as poached crab? They were smuggled with seafood imports?"

"Sounds like, from what Tarasov told you. A while back there was a bust in Seattle—a US seafood distributor was found with a warehouse filled with king crab marked as having come from China. But it was illegal Russian crab, routed via South Korea and then through China, where it was repackaged and got a from-China stamp. The US seafood distributor claimed he didn't know the crab's origin, and the prosecutor had nothing on him. Whole thing was dropped. Happens all the time." He scratched his head and chuckled. "Crab laundering. Through China."

Maddocks said nothing. His brain was racing. It actually did fit with the route Tarasov had described. He pulled up at a red light.

"Like money laundering," Holgersen reiterated. "You get it?"

"Yes, for Chrissakes, I get it. We need to run the crab tat that Hansen sketched for us through the gang insignia databases."

"Yeah. My bet is if we start looking at what crab or seafood imports came into the Port of Vancouver from China or South Korea over the past coupla years, we might nail our ship. But tracing back—now that's gonna be a big international kinda job, and those Ruskies are full of fake documents from nonexistent government entities. They don't even have a definition for organized Russian crime, it's so tangled into government."

"Your father still in the fishing business?" Maddocks said, circling back to whatever Holgersen might have been hiding with his slip earlier.

Holgersen measured Maddocks with his gaze. "No," he said slowly. "You knows how it goes with them old resource-based communities— fishing industry in my hometown was decimated by international fishing practices and open-water salmon farms. My pops lost his job. Whole fucking place died. Virtually everyone took off—like a ghost town up there now."

"Where's your dad now—the rest of your family?"

Holgersen gave a dismissive shrug and changed the subject. "Rounds and about. And you know what else? Tarasov just handed us Sabbonnier and Camus on a plate. If Tarasov testifies that Camus and Sabbonnier was witnessed in this holding place, and that's where they procured the six girls from that big hooded dude, then that pimp bitch and her bodyguard are going so dooooown, man." He made a sliding motion with his hand.

Maddocks turned into the station lot. "She's not testifying. But we do have her statement. We can use that."

"What do you mean?"

"I told her she wouldn't have to testify." He parked, checked his watch. Almost 10:30 a.m.

Was Angie going to swallow her probation and come into work at eleven?

The thought made him edgy. But right now he needed to brief Flint on the breakthrough with Sophia Tarasov. Holgersen's theory about the crab was also worth running up the flagpole. If there was anything to it, and given Camus's allegations about a Russian link to the Hells Angels, this case wasn't going to last long in the MVPD's hands. Whatever agency asserted jurisdiction, Maddocks was determined to keep his finger in. For the girls, all younger than his own daughter.

For Sophia Tarasov, who was so damn brave.

And yeah, for Ginny. Maybe this was slightly misplaced, but Maddocks needed justice, retribution, for his kid. In his mind it would balance the scales—he owed his daughter after the Baptist case had nearly cost her life. This is where the Baptist case had led him. He was going to see it all the way through.

Which reminded him—he had to take Ginn to her appointment this afternoon, and he'd promised her a dinner date after. He exited the vehicle with Holgersen, beeped the lock. Drawing his collar up against the blowing rain, he strode toward the station building, his partner's long legs easily matching his gait.

"If them other barcode girls start talking, too," Holgersen said, "we might still be able to convince Tarasov to testify down the road."

"Yeah. Why don't you start running the sketch of that crab ink through the databases, see if we can positively ID it as Russian crab Mafia insignia." Maddocks reached for the door handle. "And check out the gang intelligence databases—see what else you can dig up on the Vladivostok connection. I'll catch up with you as soon as I've looped Flint in."

As Maddocks entered the station, Holgersen hung back, stepping under the eaves for a proper smoke. Maddocks was once more assailed by the notion that the odd detective was studying and judging him, using his speech and nicotine habit as a smokescreen. And a buffer to whatever he was hiding.

✝

CHAPTER 20

Angie bought a coffee down the road from the station, and after pulling into the MVPD parking lot, she sat in her car for a moment, gathering up her spine to run the gauntlet, because she could see Holgersen and Harvey Leo from homicide taking a smoke break outside the entrance along with some junior detective whose name she could not recall. She checked her watch—10:56 a.m. She couldn't delay any longer.

Day one, Pallorino.

Only three hundred and sixty-four more to go.

Stick it out, and you can avail yourself of exclusive law enforcement databases.

Flipping down the visor mirror, she smoothed her hair back, tightened the bun at the nape of her neck, and reached for her coffee. She got out of the Nissan and shut the door, forgetting her uniform hat. Irritated, she opened the back door, snagged the hat off the back seat, and swung her door closed. Hat in one hand, coffee in the other, she strode purposefully toward the MVPD entrance, wind cool against her face, determination fierce in her stomach.

"Palloreeeno, hey, how goes?" Holgersen said, coming forward from under the eaves with a big smile that showed the gap between his front teeth. "Welcome back. I tried to call yous—left a coupla messages—"

"Sorry. Been busy." She returned his smile with a grimace of her own. All she could think about was how he'd taken her role on the barcode girls investigation, how he'd briefly been her junior partner in sex crimes and was now working hand in hand with Maddocks, who was being positioned for a management role in homicide. It rankled. She shot a quick nod toward Detective Leo and to the young plainclothes with him.

"Nice duds there, Pallorino," Leo said, taking a long drag on his cigarette and blowing out a stream of smoke. "You look just the same as you did on your first day as a rookie." He took another slow drag, his eyes holding hers. "Well, almost the same. Too bad we can't turn back time and erase the wrinkles to match the beat cop outfit, eh? Wonder if mine would still fit me. So where they got you working now? Traffic control? Parking tickets?"

"Missed you, too, Leo," Angie ground out through gritted teeth. "And I doubt you'd fit into yours—you've put a few kilos around that girth since you wore it to Hash's funeral. Guess it's the whiskey, eh?" She turned her back on him and reached for the handle of the glass door.

"Social media." He chuckled darkly. "Now *there's* a thing. Lonehorse, hot-headed Pallorino who doesn't play nice with others is now the sweet smiling face of the MVPD, bridging gaps with the public, helping da boys in blue be *social?*"

She stalled dead in her tracks, then spun abruptly and took two fast strides toward the old detective. The steel toe of her boot caught against a piece of paving. She stumbled, flailing toward Leo as she tried to regain her balance. Her latte burst the lid off the takeout cup and gushed hot, creamy, brown liquid onto Leo's crotch and down the front of his thighs. He lurched back in shock, his butt hitting the wall. "What the *fuck!*"

"Oh my goodness," Angie said sweetly. "I am *so* sorry, Detective." She stabbed her hand into her pocket and grabbed the napkin she'd put there when she'd purchased her coffee. She started to dab the napkin at Leo's wet crotch. "Holgersen, you got another Kleenex for me there?"

Holgersen bent double with laughter, slapping his bony knee like a cartoon.

"Get your fucking hands off my groin." Leo slapped her arm away, unable to back out of her reach because Angie had cornered him up against the wet concrete wall.

Slowly, Angie came erect. Her mouth tightened. Standing toe to toe with Leo, her eyes level with his, she said quietly, "I can be so clumsy, especially with my sore arm. Gunshot and all. I do hope you have a spare pair of pants in your locker, Detective."

Wariness crept into his weathered face. He did not move a muscle, and there was little doubt in Angie's mind that he was suddenly recalling the last time he'd overstepped the line with her at the Flying Pig Bar and Grill and she'd grabbed his balls and squeezed. Hard. "You watch that mouth of yours around me, Leo," she whispered.

Stepping away from him, she tipped her empty coffee cup into the garbage, yanked open the door, and entered the building. Her heart was racing.

As the glass door swung slowly shut behind her, she heard Holgersen call, "Hey, Palloreeeno, remember, no feeding the trolls. Social media one-oh-one—play nice."

Her blood spiked as she found her way down the hall to the ground-level office with a sign on the door that read, COMMUNITY & PUBLIC AFFAIRS UNIT.

Taking a deep breath, she pushed open the door, entered.

The room was small. Four desks were cramped inside and topped with computers. Windows looked out onto the parking lot. Two females, late twenties, were seated in civilian clothes behind two of the metal desks. Angie guessed one to be the art director, the other the graphic designer-videographer. A very pregnant cop wearing an MVPD-issue maternity smock over her black uniform pants stood at a row of bookshelves. The shelves were stacked with glossy brochures, flyers, books, rows of DVDs—so-called MVPD collateral, Angie presumed. The pregnant officer glanced up and smiled. She waddled forward, her left hand supporting the small of her back as she extended her right hand. "Welcome. Marla Pepper—social media relations officer."

Only three hundred and sixty-four more days.

"Pallorino," Angie said, shaking the officer's hand. Then as an afterthought, she added, "Congratulations. How far along are you?"

"Any day now." Another smug smile. "Can't wait to get out of here and put my feet up. Next week can't come fast enough—you should be up to speed by then. Let me start by giving you the basic rundown, and then you can just start shadowing me, ask questions as we go. Good enough?"

"Yeah."

"It's nothing too complicated, really. This is Diana Bechko, the unit's art director." Pepper motioned to the woman at the first desk. "And her graphic designer, Kosma Harrison." Both women offered their greetings, smiled, but Angie could see that they were eyeing the newcomer in their midst with curiosity, maybe even a level of wariness. No doubt they'd been fully apprised by the MVPD grapevine of her quick temper, her proclivity toward rage, violence. Her punishment. Angie returned the necessary pleasantries but without a smile. She was not here to be their friend. She was here to get through her sentence. Sooner they cottoned on to that and left her alone, the better.

"And this will be your station," pregnant Officer Pepper said as she showed Angie her own desk, at which she'd pulled up a spare chair. "You can use the laptop for now, then transition to my desktop once I'm on mat leave."

Angie set her hat on the corner of the desk and said nothing. An awkwardness entered Pepper, which was good because it took the edge off her annoying pregnant perkiness.

"So . . . basically these are the tools of my trade—the computers, I mean," Pepper said. "You'll be responsible for managing the MVPD

Twitter, Facebook, and Instagram accounts and for updating the events page on the MVPD website. You'll also craft posts for the *Day in the Life* blog." Pepper offered another smile, but more hesitant now, her gaze weighing Angie a little differently. "Social media is such a huge component of an organization these days. Something I take very seriously."

Angie nodded in silence. Pepper cleared her throat, then tried a different tack. "I was in operational policing myself for six years. Most of those driving a K9 SUV, tracking bad guys with my police dog. But many of the basic elements of policing still play here. I jumped at the social media opportunity as soon as we decided to try and fall pregnant, of course."

Angie's eyes snapped to Pepper's. The woman was from another planet as far as Angie was concerned.

Pepper's cheeks flushed. "I couldn't in good conscience be out there endangering an innocent civilian, a baby's life. A bullet-suppression vest goes only so far, you know?" A pause. Her blush deepened. "Kids are important. They're our future."

The memory of Jenny Marsden's words slapped Angie cold in her face. She inhaled, her mind shooting to Tiffy Bennett, the toddler she and Hash had been unable to save last year, to that old Kodak photograph of herself as a child with the cut and swollen face in Saint Peter's Hospital. To all the other kids—special victims she'd met through sex crimes. Guilt at her judgment of Pepper twinged through her. She smoothed her hand over her hair. "Right."

Pepper weighed Angie, reading her shift in tone. "It'll be okay," she said. "You'll get used to it." She held her hand toward the chair. "Take a seat."

As Angie seated herself, Pepper pulled up the various MVPD social media accounts. "In addition to overseeing these, you will work closely with the MVPD's two spokespersons. Technology and news cycles no longer require a daily press conference, but our unit does field hundreds of calls every week from local, national, and international media for

information and interviews. You'll channel those requests accordingly . . ."
A movement outside caught Angie's eye.

Maddocks and Holgersen leaving the building, striding toward his Impala.

She felt hot, swallowed, tried to focus as Pregnant Pepper droned on. But all she could think of suddenly was her coupling with Maddocks last night. Self-recrimination snaked through her. She was trying to hurt him. She needed to find a way to make things right again. As she watched the Impala drive off, she resolved to find Maddocks after she punched out today. Maybe they could go grab a bite to eat.

"Our unit also produces the print publication *Beyond the Call of Duty*—collateral that plays a major role in crime prevention. What I've found on Twitter is that there are two basic camps—those who *love* the police and those who despise us. I'm talking about those who detest law enforcement on principle and who let us know it via our social media threads." Pepper glanced at Angie. "Nothing I can say is going to change the minds of those trolls."

Social media one-oh-one—play nice.

Angie glanced at her watch as Pepper prattled on. Only seven more hours before she could clock out, maybe meet up with Maddocks, go home, and start working on Voight's case files.

CHAPTER 21

At 4:35 p.m. Angie found herself sitting momentarily in an empty office. She reached quickly for her phone and dialed Maddocks. Her spirits lifted when he picked up right away.

"Hey," she said. "I was wondering—"

"Ange, can I call you right back? I'm—"

"I'll be quick—want to meet for dinner later? Rain check for last night?"

"I . . . I can't. Got a date with Ginn. I promised her—"

"It's fine. I've got stuff I need to do." She killed the call and sat at her desk holding her phone, a strange cocktail of emotions circling through her. *Fuck it.* She slotted her phone back into her duty belt she was now wearing sans firearm.

Stupid mistake, calling him. I knew he was busy.

She returned to struggling with her blog post. She was determined to finish it before she punched out in a few minutes.

"Detective Pallorino?"

Angie glanced up.

One of the civilian MVPD receptionists stood in doorway. Big breasts. Big, bouncy eighties hair—bleached blonde. BB is what Angie mentally called her.

"There's an RCMP officer here to see you, ma'am," the woman said. "He's with someone from the Burnaby coroner's office."

Angie frowned, then came sharply to her feet. "They say what they want?"

"No. They're out front."

Angie followed the big blonde to the reception area. Through the bullet-resistant glass above the counter she saw a male in his thirties seated in a chair beside a slight, mousy-looking female. The male wore plain clothes, but Angie could see the police badge on his belt where his jacket folded back. A file folder rested in his lap. A thread of trepidation curled through Angie. She unlocked the side door and entered the reception area. The man stood immediately.

"I'm Angie Pallorino," she said. "How can I help you?"

"Constable Shawn Pietrikowski, RCMP missing persons," the male said. "And this is Kira Tranquada, BC Coroner's Service."

The young woman stepped forward and extended her hand. Her rain jacket bore the Coroner's Service logo on the left breast. "I'm with the IDRU—the identification and disaster response unit," she said.

"What's this about?" Angie said as her brain raced through past cases she'd worked, trying to figure out if these two were here because of something she'd been investigating.

"Is there somewhere private we can talk?" Pietrikowski said.

Angie hesitated. "Come this way." She led them through the reception door and down a long corridor toward interview room B. They entered, and she shut the door behind them. It was one of the smaller rooms. A two-way mirror hid a tiny observation area. A table was pushed up against the wall, three chairs around it. Mounted up the far corner near the ceiling was a discreet camera and audio feed.

"Take a seat," she said, pulling up a chair for herself.

Tranquada set her bag down on the floor beside a chair and removed her jacket. As she draped it over the back of the chair, she glanced pointedly at Angie's boots. The sense of trepidation deepened in Angie.

The pair seated themselves. Pietrikowski positioned his folder squarely on the table in front of him. He flicked a glance at the two-way mirror and cleared his throat. "To confirm, for the record, you are Angela Pallorino, adopted daughter of Joseph and Miriam Pallorino?"

His words hit Angie like a mallet. Blood rushed from her head.

"What *is* this about?" she snapped. "Is it my mother? Has something happened to my father?"

"So that's an affirmative—you are Angela Pallorino?"

"*Yes*, I'm Angela Pallorino," she snapped. "Daughter of Joseph and Miriam Pallorino. And yes, I was adopted. How do you know this? What relevance is this?"

Po-faced, the RCMP officer carefully opened his file. On top of the documents contained inside was a photograph. He unclipped the photo and slid it toward her.

Time stood still. Angie stared at the photo—the same dirty little high-top runner from the news. The one that had washed up at Tsawwassen. Something grayish-white inside. Nausea began to rise in her belly along with a fierce urge to flee.

Uciekaj, uciekaj! Run . . . run . . .

"Do you recognize this shoe?"

Pulse racing, she slowly raised her gaze to meet the Mountie's. She turned to look at the woman from the coroner's office.

I'm with the identification and disaster response unit . . .

"This looks like the shoe I saw on the news," Angie said carefully.

"It was found—"

"I know where it was found," Angie said, voice clipped, anxiety rising. "I said, I've seen the news."

Tranquada swallowed and shuffled uncomfortably in her chair at Angie's sharp retort.

"You haven't seen that shoe anywhere else?" Pietrikowski said. "Maybe you remember it from some years back?"

"What in the hell *is* this?"

Tranquada leaned forward and touched the photograph gently. "We managed to obtain a viable DNA sample from this foot. We got a cold hit to a known individual in our system."

A buzz started in Angie's head.

"The DNA is a match to yours, Ms. Pallorino," said the officer. "An identical match."

CHAPTER 22

Angie stared at the photo of the shoe—a little life raft. A preservation container. Its contents safe from underwater scavengers. It could have floated for miles and miles and miles from anywhere. She felt like Alice going down the rabbit hole, falling, falling, spinning, spiraling downward, and nothing was making sense. Silent, the dour-faced Mountie assessed her. Tranquada watched her, too.

Angie leaned forward, opened her mouth, shut it, then opened it again and said, "I don't understand." She looked up from the photo and met Tranquada's dun-colored eyes. "*Identical* DNA? What does that even mean? Are you saying I could have had a monozygotic *twin*?"

"If you've still got two feet, yes, it's possible," said Tranquada.

"Of course I have two feet," Angie snapped.

"The other alternative is that there's an error. Or an adventitious match, which is a match obtained when the DNA profiles from two individuals match just by chance." Tranquada's dun eyes were gleaming. This novelty, this cold hit, was exciting to her. Angie got that, on a professional level. But to her, this was a whole other animal right now.

"Also," Tranquada continued, "antiquated RFLP analysis was used on the original sample, which was standard from 1986 to around 2000, so we'd like to take a new sample to confirm the match. We can take a buccal swab now, if that's okay with you?"

Twice in one day—you have got to be kidding me.

"Why is my DNA even *in* your IDRU system?" Angie said, voice clipped, blood pressure rising. "It's not like I'm in the National DNA Data Bank for convicted offenders, either."

"Your profile was provided to the IDRU by the Vancouver Police Department," Officer Pietrikowski said.

"I . . . didn't know that the VPD has my DNA profile on file."

"They don't," the Mountie replied. "Detective Arnold Voight submitted your DNA to the IDRU before he retired from the VPD."

"He submitted an MPQ," Tranquada explained. "That's a missing persons query. It included your DNA from the angel's cradle case." She reached down into her bag and pulled out a biological evidence collection kit as she spoke. "The IDRU was created expressly to identify human remains found in this province and to do it in a coordinated fashion." She placed the kit on the table. Angie tensed.

"Prior to the IDRU, things were handled piecemeal with individual police departments doing their own thing. However, in order for the IDRU to be able to investigate, we needed information on missing persons, which of course falls under police mandate and not the Coroner's Service mandate. So the IDRU came up with a system—our office sends out MPQs, or missing persons query forms, to various police agencies. Officers will then dig up old files—cold cases, missing persons reports on anything from newborns to seniors—and they'll fill in the forms providing us details like name, height, weight, possible tattoos, information from dental records, DNA profiles, and any other pertinent information. It all goes into our GIS database. It's rare for us to get a cold hit like this, but when we do, it's a total rush."

Angie couldn't breathe. Her skin prickled with heat under her uniform. "Fine," she said slowly. "I'll provide a sample."

Tranquada didn't hesitate. She opened her kit, snapped gloves onto her hands, extracted the buccal swab from its sterile packaging, and came to her feet. Angie opened her mouth, her eyes on Pietrikowski as Tranquada gently rubbed and rotated a sterile swab against the inside of her cheek. Five to ten seconds. Standard timing to ensure the entire swab tip made proper contact with skin—Angie knew the drill. Except this time she was on the other side of the interview table. Sitting in her rookie uniform.

"I half wondered if we might find you wearing a prosthesis," Tranquada said as she extracted the buccal swab from Angie's mouth, careful not to touch it to her lips, teeth, or any other surface in the process. She inserted the swab into a dry collection envelope and sealed it. "I figured maybe you'd lost your leg as a child in some freak event—like a boating accident or a plane that went down into the water, and the foot finally floated free of the wreckage."

Angie wiped her hand over her lips. They'd gone dry. "Any idea how long that foot has been in the water?" she said.

"Hard to say given the formation of adipocere. It's—"

"I know what adipocere it is."

Tranquada nodded. "Well, it helped preserve the DNA, but it makes it hard for our anthropologist to gauge time in water from the bones. That girls' shoe model, however, was manufactured only between 1984 and 1986. It's possible it's been in water all this time."

"Age of the child?"

"Around four. No tool marks or any signs of mechanical removal."

Angie rubbed her brow. 1986. Age four. Same as her when she'd been abandoned in the cradle.

"And you're *certain* you have no memory of a shoe like it?" Pietrikowski said.

"Yes," she said quietly, struggling to reframe everything she'd just learned through this new window. "How did you connect the cradle Jane Doe's DNA with me?"

146

"Detective Voight provided the details of your adoption and the identity of your adoptive parents on the MPQ," Tranquada said.

So I've been sitting there in a database all this time, just waiting for a hit.

"Can you recall anything at all of your childhood prior to the cradle event?" Pietrikowski said.

Her gaze flared to the cop. "No. Nothing. I told you."

Apart from hallucinations. A ghost girl in luminous pink. A Polish song. Strange words. It struck her suddenly like a bolt of light from the dark—Alex, her psychologist friend and old mentor from her college days, had suggested the girl in her hallucinations might be a projection of Angie herself, a subconscious attempt to recall repressed memories, her child self from the past reaching out to her adult self in the present, but . . . could it be the memory of a sibling? A little ghost girl doppelgänger in pink reaching out for help, needing to be laid to rest properly? Needing a heinous wrong avenged?

My sister. A twin.

Angie's heart skipped a beat at the concept. The Asian guy, Ken Lau from the Pink Pearl Chinese Kitchen—his grandmother had seen a woman with only one child on her hip. But there'd been a curtain obscuring the bottom half of the woman. What if the young woman in the snow had been holding the hand of another little girl as they'd fled across the road?

Ah-ah-ah . . . two little kittens . . . there were once two little kittens.

Uciekaj, uciekaj! . . . Run, run!

Wskakuj do srodka, szybko . . . get inside.

Screams.

Angie struggled against a sudden urge to throw up.

"Have you attempted to search for your biological parents, Ms. Pallorino? Ever been contacted by a biological family member?"

"I only learned that I was the cradle child a few weeks ago," Angie said. "I've never been contacted, and I've only just started my own search for my biological parents."

"I understand from Detective Voight's widow that you've taken possession of the angel's cradle case files along with the evidence that Voight removed from the locker prior to scheduled destruction," said Pietrikowski.

Something inside Angie went stone still. Her gaze snapped back to his. "That's correct. I took my case files."

"The RCMP requests that your transfer those files and evidence to us. We're reopening the cradle case in conjunction with the discovery of the child's foot because of the DNA match."

Adrenaline, conflict whipped through Angie. Yes, she wanted her investigation reopened. She wanted the full resources of the RCMP thrown at the floating foot case. And her own. But she also didn't want her personal inquiry to be cut off at the knees. She could *not* handle being completely disempowered. Not now. She regarded Officer Pietrikowski, taking in his cold, classic cop demeanor. His overt lack of emotion and empathy.

"I'd like to be involved in that investigation," she said.

His gaze touched quickly on her uniform, then returned to her eyes.

"I'm a detective," she said. "I'm with MVPD sex crimes. I'm just wearing this uniform temporarily." And she hated herself instantly for having stooped to explain her predicament to this cop.

"It's an RCMP investigation at this point, ma'am. As the victim, we will keep you apprised of—"

"I am not a victim." She leaned forward, gaze drilling into his. "Let's get that one thing straight, Officer Pietrikowski. I'm a survivor. That's special victims one-oh-one." She paused, waited for him to blink. "You don't call them victims to their face. You don't give them the burden of that label. Then again, you've probably never worked sex crimes or with special victims, have you?"

He repositioned himself in his chair. Tranquada remained motionless. The Mountie held Angie's gaze, then reached into his pocket, taking out a card. "As I said, the RCMP will keep you apprised of any developments. And the IDRU will let you know the results of the buccal swab in about four to five days. Feel free to call me if you have questions or if you remember anything from the cradle event or your childhood prior to that." He pushed his card across the table toward Angie. "When I have further questions, I will be in contact. Now, if you could hand those case files and evidence over, Ms. Tranquada and I could potentially head back to the Lower Mainland before the last ferry leaves."

"The file boxes are not on these premises," Angie said, coming to her feet. "And I need to return to my workstation. I could possibly have them here for pickup in the next few days." Urgency crackled through her. How long could she stall this Mountie? Long enough for Anders Forensics to complete the tests?

"I can come by your residence this evening." Pietrikowski closed his file and stood up.

"They're not at my residence, either. They're off-site, in safe storage. I'll need to retrieve them, and my hours are currently budgeted." She snagged his card off the table, held it up to his face. "I'll call when they're ready to be collected."

A wariness sharpened his eyes. His shoulders stiffened. "Those are police files in a now active investigation. Obstruction is a—"

"Those files were as good as destroyed, Officer. They were no longer VPD property. They were given to me and are now my property. I'll get them to you as soon as possible."

"I'll return to collect them tomorrow," Pietrikowski said coolly. "Do I need to come with a warrant?"

Tension twisted through her. He was probably going to put in for a warrant anyway at this rate—it had to be the reason he wasn't forcing her hand right now. She needed to get home—copy and digitize everything tonight, save it all to her computer before morning. If the Anders Forensics techs could document the evidence and take whatever samples they needed for testing, and if they could make copies of all the lab reports, she could perhaps hand the boxes over tomorrow without having to forgo her own independent investigation. "Fine. They'll be here. Now, if you'll excuse me?" She reached for the door, opened it, and waited for the pair to exit, her heart slamming against her ribs.

Tranquada gathered up her bag and DNA kit, and the two departed the room. Angie followed them down the hall. Once she was certain they'd left the building, she returned quickly to her now-empty office. The others had clocked out for the day, much to her relief. Hurriedly she dialed Anders Forensics. She paced up and down in the tiny space between the desks while the phone rang.

CHAPTER 23

"There, that's it," Holgersen said, rolling his chair aside to show Maddocks an enlarged image of a pale-blue crab tattoo on his computer monitor. "A known symbol for a subsect of the Russian crab industry historically involved in organized criminal activity. They'll do anything and align with anyone for profit. Rough dudes, those—like chop-your-body-parts-to-send-a-message rough. This group originated out of Vladivostok but evolved through them so-called bitch wars in Stalin's gulags, according to that law enforcement intel." He nodded toward the computer screen.

"Bitch wars?" Maddocks said, taking a seat beside Holgersen and pulling his chair in closer to examine the details of the tattoo.

"Yeah. Says there that powerful criminals worked their way up in them Soviet labor camps to becomes 'thieves-in-law.' But when ol' Hitler invaded the Soviet Union, Stalin gots desperate for more warm bodies to fight the war, so he offered gulag inmates freedom if they joined his army." Holgersen popped a tablet of gum into his mouth, chewed, and spoke around it. "Them thieves-in-law showed their status through a system of tattoos and symbols still used by the Ruskie mobsters today."

Maddocks scrolled to an image of another tattoo. Same size. Same detail. This particular one had been photographed on an inmate from

Montreal, incarcerated for firebombing a hair salon owned by the wife of the rival Irish Mafia in Quebec.

"Identical to the tats Sophia Tarasov described to Cass Hansen," Maddocks said.

"That Stalin was a thug," Holgersen said, nodding toward the monitor. "Gang database says when the war was over, just like that, he ships all them prison vollies back to gulags. Wham bam, thank you, ma'am. So those who'd refused to fight for Stalin and remained in prison, they go calling the returnees traitors—bitches—and them bitches get sent to the bottom of the prison hierarchy. Those bitches then go forming their own power bases by collaborating with prison officials. That gets them nice cozy positions on the inside, and it turns the old-school thieves-code guys even more bitter. It erupts into a series of bitch wars from '45 to '53 with heaps of inmates killed every day. Prison guards egg the violence on—a real easy way to get rid of inmates and free up prison cells." He spat his gum into the wastepaper basket.

Maddocks flicked a glance up at him.

"Overdosing on the nicotine," he said, waggling his fingers at his mouth and pulling a face.

"Go on," Maddocks said.

"When Stalin finally kicks the bucket, around eight million gulag inmates are suddenly set free. Them who survived the bitch wars becomes a new breed of criminal no longer bound to the old thieves' code of conduct—an every-man-for-himself bunch who cooperate with government when necessary. Black markets thrive. Then, as the Soviet Union starts to collapse in the seventies and eighties, the United States goes an' expands immigration policies. These guys begin to leave Russia in droves for places like Israel, the United States—many popping up in an area of south Brooklyn. Brighton Beach—Little Odessa. From there Russian organized crime began to spread in the United States."

"Good job," Maddocks said, checking his watch and coming to his feet. He reached for his coat. "Flint contacted the RCMP gang unit on the

Lower Mainland, told them about our barcodes. They immediately connected him with a lead investigator on a special integrated task force—"

"What task force?"

"Investigator wouldn't say. Apparently he was guarded. They're
sending two members over to the island to meet with us in person
tomorrow afternoon to see what we have."

Holgersen angled his head. "What did Flint give them?"

"Only that we had six barcoded females in our custody who might
have been trafficked through the Port of Vancouver from Prague with the
assistance of Hells Angels. This task force is interested in cooperating."

"Cooperating? You mean as in actually sharing the details of *their*
ongoing investigations with *us*? Or just taking whats we have?"

Maddocks shrugged into his coat. "We'll see tomorrow."

"Whoa right there. I knows how it goes—they's the Mounties, the
feds. No doubts they're already working with Interpol on this one, and
maybe the Feebs also, given as the *Amanda Rose* and its brothel plied up
and down the US coast. And we's just the little ol' metro force. My bets
is they yank this carpet right out from under our asses now and takes
our case lock, stock, and barrel."

"Let's call it a night, shall we? Deal with it tomorrow." Maddocks
clicked his fingers, calling Jack-O out from his basket under his desk.
He scooped the animal up.

Holgersen reached for his own jacket. "Wanna catch a beer and a
burger at the Pig?"

"Got a date with my kid. See you in the morning."

As Maddocks strode from the room, Holgersen stood motionless,
watching him. Maddocks pushed through the door, wondering again
what drove the guy and just how far he could trust him. Something
about the detective always felt off-center and left him uneasy.

CHAPTER 24

Kjel Holgersen pushed through the doors of the Flying Pig Bar and Grill, a joint down the road from the MVPD station named tongue-in-cheek for the police fraternity that frequented it. He scanned the place, his eyes adjusting to the muted light. It was packed. Colm McGregor, the burly Scots owner, was manning the bar himself, as per his custom. Leo, with his thatch of white hair, was hunkered over a glass at the beaten-copper bar counter, his head bent in close conversation with some guy seated on the stool beside him. As Kjel approached, the man behind the old detective came into view. Surprise washed through Kjel—he hadn't realized Leo was friendly with forensic shrink Dr. Reinhold Grablowski.

As Kjel neared the pair, he saw that Leo was showing Grablowski an A-4-size piece of paper with something printed on it. Leo folded the printout in half, then in half again. He slipped it into the breast pocket of his jacket. Grablowski patted Leo on the shoulder, came to his feet, and turned to leave.

"Heya, Doc," Kjel said. "Don't go leaving on my account."

Eyes as black as night met Kjel's through silver John Lennon–style frames. "Detective," Grablowski said in his slight German accent. He gave a quick feral smile that did not reach those beady eyes. "I'm running late. Enjoy your evening." He brushed past Kjel.

Climbing onto the vacated barstool, Kjel said, "Didn't know yous and Profiler Grablowski was tight."

Leo knocked back the dregs of a whiskey and motioned to McGregor to bring him a refill. The detective's eyes were bleary. He must have gotten an early start today.

"I had something of interest for him."

"Like what?"

The veteran cop eyeballed him, deliberating whether to tell, which made Kjel even more curious. He switched approach, figuring he'd come at it again later, when the drink had loosened Leo up even more.

"So you's cleaned up your pants, I see?"

"Fucking bitch, that Pallorino," Leo muttered. "Had a spare in my locker."

McGregor set a fresh glass of whiskey with ice in front of Leo. Kjel asked McGregor for a Heineken and a vegetarian burger with onion rings.

Leo grabbed his glass, took a deep gulp, and sat silent. "How's the barcode investigation going?" he said finally.

McGregor placed the Heineken in front of Kjel. He reached for it, took a deep swallow straight from the bottle. "Ah—nothing like that first sip, eh?"

Leo studied him.

"Investigation's going good," Kjel said.

"Just 'good'?"

"Yeah." Kjel took another pull on his drink.

Leo swore. "At least you're still on it. If your boss-buddy hadn't put me on that homeless guy homicide, I'd still be working it. Figure Maddocks wanted me out 'cause he's screwing Pallorino and she has it in for me."

Kjel cocked a brow. "Even them homeless needs justice—someone's gotta do it."

"Fucking Pallorino," Leo said again, and then he glanced over his shoulder, lowered his voice. "You want to hear something good?"

"About Pallorino?"

"Yeah, about Pallorino."

"If it's gonna get me in trouble," he said, tipping the beer bottle to his mouth, "then maybe I don't wants to know. I prefers my coffee inside my mug, not down my crotch." He chuckled, then took a swig.

"Or maybe you're brownnosing, eh? Trying to stay in new-guy Maddocks's good graces."

"Oh, fuck off. Tell me. What is it?" Kjel knew Leo would come around to it soon enough.

"So I was in that little observation room next to interview room B, and suddenly in walks Pallorino with an RCMP officer and this woman from the coroner's office in Burnaby, and they start to talk."

"She walked into the interview room?"

"Yeah. And audio was on."

Kjel held the detective's gaze. "Audio was . . . just like . . . on?"

"Yeah. Yeah, someone had left it on."

He studied Leo, a wariness creeping into him. "What was you just happening to be doing in the observation room?"

Leo slid his hand into his jacket pocket, pulled out a slim silver hip flask.

"You's shitting me. Jeezus fuck, Leo—you wanna get your hairy ass fired before you max out on your retirement plan or what? Why you telling me this? I don't wanna know you tipple on the fucking job."

"I'm telling you so that you don't figure I followed her in there on purpose to fucking spy on her, that's why."

Kjel weighed the old detective. There was more. Had to be. Leo was feeding him this information as some kind of test.

"So," Kjel said quietly, "what you hear?"

"Pallorino's DNA is a dead match to that little kid's foot found at Tsawwassen."

Kjel stilled his beer midair. "What?"

"Yeah, God's truth. The Mountie and the coroner's woman came over to inform her they got a hit, and they wanted another sample for proof. They've opened an investigation into the foot, and she's a part of it."

"You's shitting me."

"And why would I do that?"

"Pallorino's got, like, two feet—real feet. I mean, not like I actually *seen* her bare feet with my own eyes. But—"

"A twin maybe," Leo said. "Pallorino's adopted. She was left in that baby box at Saint Peter's Hospital in Vancouver back in '86 when she was four. The Mountie was questioning her about it. I looked it up after." He pulled the piece of paper from his breast pocket again—the one he'd been showing Grablowski. Unfolding it, he laid it in on the bar counter. "Printed it from the Internet."

Kjel pulled it closer and read the article, a dark sensation leaking into him. He looked up at Leo. "How long was you just sitting in that observation room that you's managed to hear all this?"

"Long enough."

"You showed this to Grablowski?"

He shrugged.

"What in the hell for?"

"Pallorino fucked up his book deal by going and killing the Baptist. The doc had to pay back his mega advance because his deal was contingent on face-to-face interviews with Spencer Addams—to talk direct with the Baptist about all his rapes while traveling the world aboard a floating brothel and about his upbringing, his mother, father, all the freaky religious stuff. So I figured as compensation Grablowski might like first shot at breaking the Mystery Twins story—one twin sliced across the face with a knife and stuffed into an angel's cradle during a gunfight on Christmas Eve, the other twin's foot found floating in the sea over thirty years later." He took a hard swig of his drink, wiped his mouth with the back of his hand. "And then the cradle child ends up a sex crimes cop? The same cop who goes and overkills a serial killer. No memory of her past until now, bam, this foot floats up? Tell me there's not a major true crime book in that. Who better to write it than Grablowski, who helped profile the killer she shot and who worked with the cop twin on the case?"

"You angling for a cut on this new book deal?"

"I don't need the money. But hey, if it comes my way, I ain't gonna turn my back on it." He sucked back the last of his whiskey, plunked the glass down a little too heavy-handedly. "No matter how you slice it, Pallorino is the cradle kid. And once that story breaks, it's gonna run away from her anyway. Might as well give Grablowski a shot first."

CHAPTER 25

Angie worked fast, like someone in the manic phase of bipolar disorder, racing to outpace the vortex of emotions threatening to overwhelm her in the aftershocks of the DNA bomb dropped on her by Pietrikowski and Tranquada.

Jacob Anders had told her on the phone that his staff had started documenting everything in her box from the moment she'd brought it in. They'd made good headway by the time she'd called him this afternoon. He'd committed to having his techs work overtime and through the night if necessary in order to meet her request for them to log, copy, digitize, and garner whatever samples they could to be tested later. For an additional price.

This was priceless to her, she'd told him. She was desperate to have it all saved before she had to hand the evidence to the RCMP.

It's not just for me now. I had a sibling. This changes everything.

And Angie did not doubt for an instant now that Tranquada's new DNA test would come back positive. Because it fit—all the strange disjointed memories in her mind slotted into this scenario. And it just fed her urgency, the fire in her belly to find answers. Why had *she* been the one to survive and not her sister? And yes, she doubted her sister was alive somewhere wearing a prosthetic, although anything was possible.

But it was more likely the little girl in the lilac high-tops had come to terrible harm at the hands of one of those men with guns outside the hospital. One of those men, Angie believed, had slashed her mouth and taken both the young dark-haired woman and the other child.

Up on her whiteboard, next to the photograph that Jenny Marsden had given her, Angie stuck a photo of the dismembered foot. She'd clipped and printed it from an online *Vancouver Sun* news article.

Stepping back, she studied the growing collage of images. Her nerves popped and sparked at the seismic shift in her paradigm.

Two little kittens, two *little kittens* . . . The woman singing in the dark room—a memory that Alex had coaxed out with hypnosis—the sense of another presence in the room, a little girl calling with her hand reached out to Angie. *Comeum playum dum grove* . . .

Her eyes filled with sharp emotion. She swiped it angrily away.

Focus.

She checked her watch. The clock was ticking—she had to scan every single page in Voight's files before morning. Then she needed to drive out to Anders Forensics and pick up her evidence before Pietrikowski arrived at the station to take possession of her boxes. Before he slapped her with a warrant and started rumbling about obstruction charges, because that was *not* going to sit with well with Vedder and the rest of the brass, who'd love any opportunity to cast her adrift, especially now. And she wanted back in sex crimes when all was said and done.

Angie set up her printer-scanner beside her computer and began to work through the files in the box, scanning and digitally filing each page as she went. Her scanner was slow and the process tedious. She told herself she could not afford to waste time in reading any of the details right now. She could go through it all on her computer later.

Inside Voight's binders were the reports from the initial responding officers. Results of a neighborhood canvass. Witness statements taken from parishioners exiting the cathedral, other statements taken from people across the street, from the nurses and docs in ER. On the surface everything seemed to tell the same story: A woman screaming. Gunfire. Men yelling. The cathedral bells clanging, followed by the screech of tires on a street somewhere behind the hospital.

In her quick survey of the statements she was scanning, Angie noted nothing mentioned about anyone else actually seeing a dark-haired woman without a coat being pursued by two big men across Front Street. She hoped that Ken Lau's grandmother had not just made this up, as she'd later claimed.

It was almost 1:00 a.m. when two newspaper articles slid out of a plastic sleeve and wafted to the floor.

Angie bent down to retrieve them. Clippings from the *Vancouver Sun.* She read the first. It was short—basically a caption under a photo of a charred wreck of a van. It was dated 1998—twenty years ago. The piece reported that an explosion had alerted CP rail workers to a vehicle fire near a train yard in the Burnaby area. Firefighters had extinguished the blaze by morning, and in the glove compartment of the burned-out black Chevrolet cargo van RCMP had found a Colt 1911 semiauto-matic pistol, .45 caliber. At the time of going to press, the police had offered no further details, saying only that the vehicle blaze was under investigation.

Angie frowned. Why was this article in here?

What had Voight been thinking?

That this particular van could have been the one heard screech-ing outside the hospital almost seven years earlier? The one Ken Lau's mother and the orderly smoking out on the hospital balcony had possi-bly seen? Did Voight suspect the Colt .45 was the handgun fired outside the cathedral?

Angie read the second newspaper clipping—a short article about a drug bust in Vancouver's east side that occurred November 20, 1993, twenty-five years ago. A VPD officer had been shot in the head, and an innocent bystander had taken a bullet in the lower back during the bust. Both had been transported to hospital. Two men had been arrested on scene. Another two had fled in a van. The report stated that more details would follow as they emerged.

But there was nothing else in the plastic sleeve. Angie chewed the inside of her cheek. Perhaps Voight had been working on some theory that had not panned out, and he'd dropped it. Hence no follow-up articles. Possible these clippings were totally unrelated to the cradle case and had been inadvertently included in the binder—these things happened. She'd drill deeper into this angle later, but right now she needed to keep scanning.

It was past 3:00 a.m. by the time she'd copied and digitized everything.

Her vision blurry with exhaustion, Angie clicked off the lights in her apartment and crawled into bed with her track pants and sweatshirt still on. As fatigued as she was, she could not fall asleep. Outside wind gusted. Rain hammered in waves against her windows. Her brain circled around and around everything she knew about her case to date, and she tried her damnedest to remember something from her past. Anything. She even tried to conjure up the ghost of the little girl in pink again. But nothing came to her. She punched her pillow into shape, determination steeling her. Whatever it took, she was going to get answers. Not for herself, but for that little girl who could be her sister.

As she dozed she thought she heard the little girl's words finally whispering through her mind again . . .

Come. Come playum dum grove . . . come . . .

Or was it the wind?

CHAPTER 26

Friday, January 5

"Doctor," the nurse says with a nod as the man strides past the reception area. He wears a medical coat, a name badge clipped to his pocket, a stethoscope around his neck.

He knows from the Russian interpreter where the girls are being held in the institution, what ward, what room. He knows protocol of entry. He reaches the room and tilts his head politely toward the uniformed officer sitting outside, guarding the occupants. A momentary look of question enters the officer's face. It's placated by his quick smile and his assured reach for the door handle. Confidence. It's the art of the trickster. It's 12:49 a.m. as he enters the room. The officer is perhaps tired and sluggish because of the hour.

A small night-light casts a faint glow near the back of the ward. The girls are afraid of the dark, it seems. But the glow is not bright enough for him to see what he needs, so he takes a small Maglite from his pocket. He goes bed to bed. One by one he checks the charts hanging at the ends of the beds. One girl stirs as he moves past. He casts her an avuncular smile, waits. She turns over and goes back to sleep. He suspects they've had medication to aid slumber.

He finds the chart he's looking for. His target is asleep on her back, features slack and calm under a blanket of oblivion. Pretty thing. She must have brought in top dollar. He knows from the interpreter that she's the one who spoke to the lead detective named James Maddocks. It's via her that the man will now send a message from his boss. He removes his lab coat, lays it neatly on a chair near the bed. He snaps on latex gloves. Going up to the side of her bed, near her pillow, he bends down and places a gloved hand upon her shoulder. Gently, he tries to rouse her. "Sophia," he whispers in her ear.

She moans slightly, stirs. He tries again. *"Sophia."*

Her eyes snap open wide. She sees him. Terror twists into her face. He slaps his gloved hand hard over her mouth. "Shh," he whispers, holding his Maglite to his lips like an index finger. Then in Russian he says, "Be very quiet. Do not move, or I will kill all the other girls as they sleep. Do you understand?"

Her eyes flare sharply toward the younger ones, whites showing huge around her irises. She's protective over them, he realizes. This is helpful. "Do you understand me, Sophia?" he says again in Russian, close to her ear.

She nods. Terror has muted her flight-or-fight response. It's numbed her. She fears for her life and is compliant because of it. She's been well conditioned. He places his thin Maglite between his teeth and holds it there so he can see what he is doing while using both hands. He takes from his breast pocket a prefilled syringe. He uncaps the needle, taps it. With a swift move he smothers her face with his hand, twisting her head brutally sideways. She writhes and squirms and struggles to breathe under his palm, and it makes the vein down the side of her neck bulge. Deftly he sticks the needle into the vein and pushes the plunger on the syringe. He waits a few seconds, and she starts to relax and go limp. He releases his hand. A soft sigh escapes her.

"Feels good, no?" he says softly in Russian, stroking her cheek. Her eyelids droop. He returns the syringe to his pocket and then unsheathes the hunting knife that hangs on his belt. He sharpened it well before coming. She's fading, starting to pass out. It won't be long now.

Clamping his palm down over her brow to hold her steady, he forces the back of her head firmly into the pillow. Maglite still in his mouth, he shines light upon her lips. He sticks his gloved fingers between her lips and pries her jaw open wide. He holds it open as she begins to gag. Her eyes flare to life again, just for a moment, and fear flickers in them, but she's no longer able to resist.

"You know what happens to girls who talk," he whispers.

He brings the hunting blade up to her mouth.

CHAPTER 27

Angie remained standing in front of Jacob Anders's desk. She didn't have time to sit. It was 8:11 a.m. She was in a rush—going to be late for work.

"It's all back in here," Anders said, patting the side of the box on his desk. "We've taken all the blood and hair samples we could, and it's possible that we'll have some DNA results for you in a few days. The semen stains might not prove viable, though. We'll try, but it will take longer. There appear to have been two different sources."

"Of semen?"

"Yes."

"On the sweater? *Two* contributors?"

"Correct."

A sick, bitter taste rose up the back of her throat. It steeled her determination. Whatever had happened that Christmas Eve over thirty years ago, she was going to find out. She was going to get those two men.

Dead or alive.

Anders watched her face intently as he said, "There was also a lab report on evidence from a rape kit conducted on Jane Doe."

She inhaled deeply. "What did it say?"

"No evidence of sexual activity, although there was evidence of earlier vaginal tearing."

Angie's gaze shot to the window. Her heart raced, and she clenched her fists at her sides. She glared at the stormy ocean. It didn't prove anything. She could have been injured some other way. Didn't mean it hadn't happened, either. But clearly, whatever had occurred in her early childhood had been bad enough to wipe her memory clean in a merciful act of self-preservation, creating a blank slate upon which her adoptive parents had written a totally new life and identity.

"Thanks," she said softly.

"All the paperwork from the box has been logged, copied, and digitized. The evidence has also been logged and photographically documented. What samples remain have been returned to the packaging."

"And the prints?" Angie asked, referring to the images of the bloody finger and hand patents that had been captured on the outside of the cradle door.

"Also digitized."

A spark of adrenaline knotted into her anxiety—those digitized prints could now be run through automatic identification databases.

"This is your copy of everything we have on file now." Anders slid a memory stick across his desk toward Angie.

"I can't thank you enough, Jacob," she said as she snagged the storage device off his desk and slipped it into her breast pocket. She reached with both hands to grasp her box.

"Why is the RCMP reopening this?"

She stilled, met his wolfish eyes. She'd told him about being the cradle child, but she wasn't sure she wanted to tell anyone about the floating foot match yet. It might still prove to be an error. She broke his gaze and glanced at the underwater feed of the pig carcass covered in a cloud of sea lice. The carcass seemed bigger, rounder today. More bloated. A Dungeness crab shuffled spiderlike on long skinny legs across the seabed toward the pig. As she watched, the octopus returned, swooping into view from the top-right corner of the screen. It swamped its body over the crab. Silt exploded in a cloud as they struggled and lice scattered. She stood momentarily numb as she watched the octopus smother the crustacean to death and begin to consume it. Angie swallowed as she recalled Jacob Anders's words.

Confidentiality, discretion—it's a necessary and absolute cornerstone of our business.

She moistened her lips and said, "Did you hear the news about the dismembered child's foot found five days ago?"

"I did."

"The DNA of that foot is apparently a dead match to mine. The VPD detective on my cradle case submitted my DNA profile to the identification and disaster response unit at the coroner's office before he retired. They got a cold hit between the two."

A beat of silence. When Anders spoke again, she heard the subtle shift in his tone. "That is interesting. I presume they're doing another DNA test to confirm the hit?"

"Correct."

"Is this going to cause problems?" He nodded to the box. "With the RCMP."

"Not for you. The evidence was mine. I provided it to a private lab for testing. Now that I've been asked, I'm handing over what has not been used." She gathered the box into her arms, wincing slightly. "Thank you again—I need to get to work."

"I'll be in touch," he said.

But as Angie reached his door, she turned and said, "Monozygotic twin DNA—it's not absolutely identical, is it?"

"Identical twins come from the same fertilized egg, so they do share the same DNA. Which makes monozygotic twins indistinguishable using the standard panel of thirteen STR loci. However, as each twin embryo grows and develops in utero, and the cells continue to multiply, the replication of each twin's DNA isn't perfect. Minor errors or variations begin to occur so that by birth each twin's DNA is subtly different from its sibling's. And as life goes on, each twin is subjected to different environmental stresses, which in turn alter each one's DNA replication. These variations can now be picked up by a newer DNA technique known as single nucleotide polymorphism, which gives the examiner a complete DNA sequence of the strand being analyzed."

"So given changes due to environmental stresses, even my own adult DNA could potentially have minute differences from my childhood DNA?"

"Technically—" The phone on his desk started to ring. "I need to take this," he said, reaching for the receiver. "I'll call as soon as we start getting results."

"Thanks again."

Angie left his office and hurried for the building exit. She pushed through the door holding her box. Wind and rain slammed into her as she stepped into the cold air. Sheltering her box with her body, she made for her Nissan rental. Once inside the car, she started the engine and put her foot on the gas without giving it a chance to warm up. Her pulse was galloping. Even without traffic she was going to be late for work now.

Vedder and company were not going to approve of her actions on the job so far. And now she *really* needed to keep her job in order to run the pending test results. The first thing she was going to do the instant she found a break today was get those digitized patent finger and palm prints taken from the cradle crime scene into the automated fingerprint identification system.

CHAPTER 28

"What?" Maddocks blinked in disbelief as the person on the other end of his phone repeated the news. Maddocks killed the call and fired a hard look at Holgersen. "She's dead," he said, feeling numb. "Sophia Tarasov is dead. Hospital staff found her unresponsive in a pool of blood in her bed at 7:30 a.m. Coroner and pathologist are en route to the hospital now."

Holgersen shot erect in his chair, eyes wide. *"What?"*

Maddocks surged to his feet, raw shock pounding through him. He grabbed his coat, shrugged into it. "Get an ident team out to the hospital. Stat. Then meet me out in the lot."

"What . . . what about the others?" Holgersen said, coming to his feet.

"Terrified. Not saying a thing, but they're alive." Maddocks fished his old dog out from under the desk. "Get hold of the interpreter, too. Get her to meet us there. We know at least one of the other girls speaks Russian." He barked the order as he made for the incident room exit. Jack-O under his arm, Maddocks strode fast toward the elevator, his mind reeling, sweat breaking out over his skin. He jabbed the elevator button. While he waited for the elevator, he placed a call to one of the first responding officers still on scene at the hospital.

"Constable Dutton," came a male voice.

"Sergeant Maddocks here," he said as he entered the opening elevator doors. He pressed the button for the ground floor. "I'm the lead on this. That uniform guarding the girls' room last night—I want that officer's name, the hours of his shift. If he's still there, keep him there. If not, bring him in. If another uniform replaced him—or her—on a shift last night, I want that officer in, too."

"Affirmative, sir."

Maddocks exited the elevator and made hurriedly for Flint's office, his shock morphing quickly into white-hot anger. He rapped on the door, opened it.

Flint glanced up sharply from his desk, his eyes flicking to the animal hooked under Maddocks's arm.

"Sophia Tarasov," Maddocks said. "She was found dead in a pool of blood in her hospital bed this morning. No one saw a goddamn thing. I'm on my way there now with Holgersen."

Flint blinked and came abruptly to his feet with his typical bearing that screamed *military background*. He hid his surprise well. "Keep me updated from the scene. And work fast. This isn't going to last long in our hands—we need to gather whatever we can if we want to follow through on our own successful prosecution of our local cases."

Maddocks held his boss's steely eyes. "The investigator from the mainland you spoke to yesterday," Maddocks said, "from the integrated task force—"

"Yeah. They know something they're not sharing, at least not over the phone." His boss's faced tightened as he spoke.

"Could that knowledge have prevented this?"

Flint met Maddocks's glare. The man's mouth flattened, and his eyes turned cold and hard. "I hope to hell not. But my gut is screaming maybe."

Shit.

"I'll let you know what I find on scene," Maddocks said, turning to go.

Outside, Maddocks found Holgersen smoking and pacing like a caged cheetah next to the Impala. Holgersen flicked his butt aside as soon as Maddocks neared and beeped open the lock. They drove with the siren going and wipers doing double time as rain deluged the city and flooded parts of the streets. They arrived at the hospital within fifteen minutes.

Pulling in outside the entrance, Maddocks parked tightly behind the coroner's van.

"Looks like Doc O'Hagan and company are already here," Holgersen said with a tilt of his chin toward the van. They exited the car, leaving Jack-O inside, windows down slightly. A uniform at the hospital doors checked their badges and entered their names on a crime scene log. Maddocks and Holgersen strode fast down the corridor toward the ward.

Outside the door a male doctor conversed quietly with the victim services counselor, who was white-faced and hollow-eyed with shock. A uniformed cop stood off to the side.

"*How* could this happen?" the counselor said as soon as Maddocks approached. "There was a guard, for heaven's sake—an *armed* MVPD officer posted outside their door. Why? *Who* would do this?"

"Where are the other girls?" Maddocks said to the counselor as he reached into his pocket for a pair of nitrile gloves.

"The first responding officers took them to another room. I've got a psychologist in with them now."

"The interpreter arrive?"

"No," said the counselor.

Maddocks spoke to Holgersen as he snapped on the gloves. "Call Dundurn or Smith—get one of them in there with the girls." Holgersen stepped aside to call the sex crimes detectives. "And chase up that interpreter."

Maddocks turned to the man in the white lab coat. "Who are you?"

"Dr. Tim McDermid. These patients have been under my care—"

"When did you last see your patients?"

"I checked in before I left for the night yesterday—around 9:00 p.m."

"How were they?"

"Fine. Alive. Sophia was better than she'd been since she was first admitted. I . . . I thought she might be one of the lucky ones who would be able to pull through what she'd endured to regain some semblance of a normal life. She was so young, just a teen." Emotion glittered in the man's eyes.

Maddocks firmed his jaw. "Was there a nurse on duty last night?" he said.

"On call for this ward—the patients had progressed to a point they were sleeping through the night."

"I want a list of everyone on duty last night. Can you go get that for me?"

"I . . . yes, yes of course."

"When you've got it—" Maddocks raised his gloved hand high and summoned a uniform over from down the corridor. She hurried over.

"Sir?"

He glanced at her name tag. "Tonner, accompany Dr. McDermid here—get the names of everyone who was working in this hospital yesterday. Start calling them into the cafeteria. Seal off that area. And find someone to cordon off this wing."

"Sir."

Holgersen came forward, snapping on his own gloves. "Dundurn is on his way. No word from the interpreter yet—not answering her phone."

The officer stationed outside the door logged Maddocks and Holgersen into the room and handed them each a set of booties.

Once their shoes were encased in the booties, Maddocks turned toward the door, inhaled, and entered. Holgersen, uncharacteristically silent, followed behind him.

A forensic tech was taking photos inside. Another was dusting for prints. Pathologist Barb O'Hagan was beside the bed upon which Sophia Tarasov's body lay. A sheet covered Tarasov's body from the waist down. She wore a simple white nightgown. Her arm hung over the side of the bed, palm up. Her face was turned toward the door. Blood covered her open mouth and ran onto her white pillow. Her eyes were wide and sightless. The white hospital sheets were drenched almost black with her blood. It had dripped to the sterile tile floor. A tech had placed yellow crime scene markers where the drips had fallen.

The doc looked up. "Morning, Sarge. How are we this fine day?"

"Doc," Maddocks said, standing still, absorbing the scene.

The room was warm. A white drape billowed slightly over a heating vent. Rain fell outside. The other beds were empty with untidy sheets. One bed looked as though it had been wet.

"Jesus fuck," whispered Holgersen. "How in the hell could this happen? With five other girls in the room and a uni outside, and no one hears or does a thing?" He went over to the wet bed, sniffed. He glanced at Maddocks. "They were terrified. One of them peed their bed. Maybe they saw who did it?"

"Even if they did witness the act, they were too afraid to call staff until someone came to do the rounds in this room at 7:30 a.m."

Holgersen swore softly again. "If they's wasn't talking before, they sure as hell ain't gonna be talking now."

Maddocks went over to the body. O'Hagan was peering at her thermometer over the top of her glasses.

"Alphonse sends his regards," she said, recording the temp in her notepad. "He left me here while he had to attend another call."

Charlie Alphonse was the region's coroner. Barb O'Hagan worked as one of his forensic pathologists—a crusty older woman with a passion for speaking for the dead. Maddocks had gotten to know O'Hagan well during the Addams investigation. She and Angie were pretty tight, and they both shared a dislike for Harvey Leo.

"What you got, Doc?"

"Didn't want to pull back the sheeting until you got a look at her in situ, but I took a reading from under her arm. Rigor is not complete. Given her temperature and the warmth in this room, I'm going to say postmortem interval is anything between six to nine hours."

He checked his watch. It was 8:11 a.m. "Which would put time of death somewhere between 11:00 p.m. yesterday and 2:00 a.m. this morning."

"Sounds about right," she said, returning her thermometer to the bag on the table at her side. She picked up a small flashlight. "There's something you need to see."

She shone her light on the decedent's mouth and used a wooden spatula to clear aside some of the blood pooled inside the cavity.

"Take a look inside," she said.

Maddocks leaned forward and peered into the mouth. Shock jerked through his body. His gaze flared to the doc.

"She's got no tongue," he said. Just a bloody stub of muscle, sliced clean through.

"It's been excised."

"Where's the rest of it?" Holgersen said from behind him.

"Don't know yet," said O'Hagan.

Maddocks stared at Sophia Tarasov's face, the open maw pooled with blood. *Shit.*

"You think that's what killed her?" Holgersen said. "Exsanguination from an excised tongue?"

"She could conceivably have choked—drowned—in her own blood with her head tilted back like that. I'll know more once I get her up on the table," O'Hagan said.

The unspoken hung thick and dark in the room as Tarasov's words snaked through Maddocks's brain.

When I ask her question, she say in Russian that they will cut my tongue out if I talk. Like they told us in Prague they would do if we ever speak to anyone about men who brought us there. In Prague there was woman with no tongue.

"A warning," whispered Maddocks. "Sophia Tarasov crossed the line, disobeyed the rules. And someone hunted her down to send a message."

"How in the fuck did they find her, get in here? How would they even know she talked?"

Maddocks shook his head. "I don't know. A leak. Or maybe they didn't know that she talked, but they were aware that we had them and wanted to be sure no one *did* speak."

"And they just picked Tarasov? Coincidence like?"

"Maybe she's given them trouble before—the others are younger, more frightened. And killing them all—maybe there just wasn't enough time."

"But those surviving girls witnessed it," Holgersen said, glancing back at the bed that had been wet. "And now they believes they can be tracked down anywhere."

CHAPTER 29

"He entered the ward shortly before 1:00 a.m. I . . . thought he was a doctor," said the wan-faced officer who'd been stationed outside the door when the suspect had entered. "The docs did rounds at night when the vics were first brought in. It wasn't that unusual to see a doctor or nurse enter at that hour."

Maddocks was seated opposite the officer in a small room that the hospital had made available to the MVPD for their investigation. Meanwhile, Holgersen was going through closed-camera security footage with hospital security. Other employees who'd been on duty last night were being interviewed in the cafeteria. The decedent's body had been taken to the morgue. The postmortem would commence this afternoon. Maddocks had every intention of being present when O'Hagan got Tarasov up onto that table.

"Description of the male?" Maddocks said coolly.

"He was average. Average height—about five ten. Caucasian. Maybe in his thirties. Or forties. Average complexion."

Christ.

"Hair? Don't tell me—average, too?"

The young cop wiped a sheen of perspiration from his brow. He smelled bad in these close quarters. Of fear and possibly a few too many drinks the night before. A hangover could have lulled him into complacency, Maddocks thought.

"Dark-brown hair," the officer said. "Cut short—a conservative cut. Thick hair." He wiped his face again. "I didn't know the girls were at risk like that. We should have had better security protocol. We should have been checking the IDs of all doctors who went in and out from the get-go. That wasn't my brief."

Maddocks tightened his jaw. He hadn't known the extent of the risk that the young barcode survivors faced, either. All the suspects found aboard the *Amanda Rose* had been taken into custody—there was no threat from them. The barcode tattoo detail had never made it into the press. Nor had the location where the girls were being treated been disclosed. But given Tarasov's and Camus's statements, and Holgersen's trafficking route theory, this could be the work of the Russian mob. Whoever had sold the so-called merchandise would have known that these specific girls had gone to Madame Vee and were aboard the *Amanda Rose*. And when the traffickers had learned in the news about the MVPD takedown of the yacht and the Bacchanalian Club, the mob would have put two and two together. Possibly they came to reclaim their merchandise. Or at least stop the girls from testifying. And perhaps to send a warning to others. But which others? More girls like this? Here in BC? The rest of Canada? The United States?

He kicked himself for not having initiated a tighter security protocol from day one, nevertheless. He'd bet his last dollar that this integrated task force investigator who was so keen for members of his team to meet with Maddocks had known the risks. Yet the lead investigator's secrecy, his refusal to give Flint a heads-up right away as to what they might be dealing with—it could have cost Sophia Tarasov her life. Anger curled thin and hot through Maddocks's blood.

"Build?"

"Average build. Not thin, not fat, not overly athletic. Confident walk."

"What about eye color?"

"I . . . I don't recall."

Maddocks heaved out a breath. "We'll get you in with a sketch artist. And you heard nothing while the suspect was in there? No scuffles, screams?"

"Nothing. He was inside for about twenty minutes. When he came out, he looked as normal as he did when he went in, wearing his lab coat, no blood on him, nothing."

A knock sounded on the door. It swung open wide. A red-faced uniformed officer entered and held up a bag with a white garment inside. "Sarge, sorry for the interruption. Found this in the dumpster outside—lab coat," he said. "Blood on the inside and a stethoscope and security badge for a Dr. Martha Taluswood in the pocket. Dr. Taluswood reported a vehicle break-in to security yesterday evening. It happened sometime between 6:00 and 10:00 p.m. She said her coat, stethoscope, and badge were on the passenger seat of her car, along with a security card. They were gone when she returned to her vehicle."

"Where was she parked?"

"Staff lot E—a silver Toyota RAV4, plate NT3–87B."

Maddocks cursed and lurched to his feet. "Log that evidence. Get it to the lab, stat." He turned to the officer he'd been interrogating. "You, wait here. I'm going to get someone to help you with an identikit."

Maddocks left the room and strode down the hall, making for the security room. He jabbed the elevator button and called Holgersen at the same time. The elevator doors slid open. He stepped in. Holgersen answered.

"Yo, boss."

"I'm on my way up. We're looking for footage that covers the dumpsters outside and the staff parking lot E from around 6:00 to 10:00 p.m. Our suspect broke into a doc's vehicle during that time frame and took her coat and security clearance to gain access to the hospital. Looks like the coat was left in a dumpster outside the hospital. Given the blood found on the *inside* of the coat, the suspect could have removed the lab coat to assault Tarasov, then re-covered himself with the coat after he was done, hiding any blood that he'd gotten on his clothes so he didn't attract undue attention while exiting the building." Maddocks watched the elevator buttons light up in succession as he spoke. "This guy is organized. Calm. This is no neophyte."

"Hit man," said Holgersen. "For the mob."

The elevator doors opened. Maddocks stepped out. "Yeah, possible." He stopped, turned around in the corridor. "Where is the security office located? I'm on the fourth floor."

"West wing. Far end."

"Did you get hold of the interpreter?"

"Negative, boss. Called her office direct. They said she phoned in late yesterday afternoon to say that she was taking an impromptu long weekend trip across the island to go winter storm watching. She's due back Monday."

"Find someone else, then." Maddocks killed the call and strode westward down the sterile-smelling corridor, his brain churning. None of the surviving five girls were speaking, as expected—wouldn't even look a female officer in the eye. They were terrified and in medical distress from the trauma.

His phone rang as he neared the security office, which he could see up ahead—glass walls, banks of monitors showing closed-circuit surveillance footage. Maddocks connected the call, put his phone to his ear as he walked.

"Maddocks," he said.

"It's Flint. We've got a problem. You need to stand down."

Maddocks stopped dead in his tracks. "What?"

"The integrated task force, which includes the RCMP, has asserted jurisdiction over the Tarasov murder and the surviving barcodes."

"They have the authority?"

"They do. The order just came down. They're sending RCMP members from the island division to temporarily secure and take over the scene. They'll be bringing in their own crime scene techs and will take possession of the decedent's body to conduct their own postmortem. You need to stop everything you're doing, Sergeant. Pull everyone back. Stat."

Fuck.

"I want you and Holgersen back at the station this afternoon for that meeting we still have scheduled with two members of the task force. They'll be wanting a full debrief."

Heart pumping, Maddocks killed Flint's call and entered the security room, where Holgersen was sitting with two uniformed members of the hospital security team. They were watching grainy grayscale footage on the banks of monitors. Holgersen glanced up as Maddocks entered. He pointed to one screen. "Take a look."

Maddocks leaned forward, watching over Holgersen's shoulder. A male in a white lab coat. Walking toward the hospital entrance from the parking lot. The time stamp showed 12:45 a.m. Adrenaline thumped into his veins, burning the image of the man into his brain—his stride, the way he held his head, the angle of his neck, the roll of his shoulders, the swing of his arms. As the uniformed officer had said—average. Not remarkably thin nor overly built. Neither tall nor short. He kept his face turned away from cameras as he entered the hospital. Sure, direct. Like he belonged. Like he knew where the cameras were located.

"Stop. Stop right there. Back it up," said Maddocks.

The security guy did as he asked.

"There." Maddocks pointed. "Watch carefully—see how he walks."

Holgersen stuck his nose up close to the monitor. He gave a soft whistle. "He's gots a slight limp . . . like his left leg is maybe a tiny bit shorter than the right?"

Maddocks rubbed his jaw as he watched. "Something," he said. "Something is just off-center with his gait."

"Figure that's a wig he's wearing?" Holgersen said, hunched over and peering at the image like a cat watches a mouse.

"Could be," Maddocks said quietly. "So far no wigs have been found in the dumpster, but if he's a professional, he took that with him. We'd stand a good chance of getting DNA off that. Still could get some off the coat."

"There!" A security guard pointed to another camera. "1:25 a.m. He's exiting out the back of the building. He's carrying the lab coat."

They watched in silence as their suspect opened the dumpster and tossed the coat inside. He kept his face turned from cameras.

"Why?" said Maddocks. "Why not just take it with him? We could still get something off it . . ." His voice trailed as it really hit him. This was not their case. Not anymore.

"Because he's not hiding," said Holgersen. "He knows there's cameras on him. Maybe he thinks any DNA trace on the coat will be compromised because it's gonna be mixed with the owner of the coat's DNA and the blood from Tarasov? Or he doesn't care. He's sending a message not only to the girls but also maybe to us, and he's staying just this side of safe, 'cause look how he keeps his head turned away from the camera at all times. He sure as hell knows exactly where them cameras are."

Maddocks said nothing, just watched, absorbing everything he could as the man walked away from the camera toward the back parking lot where the light grew dim. There was definitely a very slight lilt to his stride. It's one thing people in disguise had a tough time hiding—the way they walk. The man disappeared into shadow.

"He come up on any other cameras?" Holgersen said.

"We need to stop right there," Maddocks said quietly. He turned to the security guys. "We're going to need all that footage. There'll be an RCMP team in shortly to take possession."

"What?" Holgersen came to his feet. "What you mean, boss?"

Maddocks jerked his head toward the door, indicating that Holgersen should step out. Once outside in the corridor, he lowered his voice and said, "That integrated task force is taking over. It's no longer ours. We've been ordered to stand down, stat."

"You're kidding me, right? I . . . shit . . . this . . . they *needs* us—we needs to work together on this. We've done all the groundwork all the ways back to the *Amanda Rose* takedown, the Zaedeen Camus plea bargain, Sophia Tarasov's statement. Like what about all that shit now? We just sits down and they interrogate us, takes all our files? No, no fucking way." He pointed his finger at Maddocks. "What I tell you? Huh? They's assholes. Dickheads. Fucking feds."

"Go outside, Holgersen, have a smoke. Take a nice deep breath of tobacco and cool off. I'll meet you at the vehicle."

"What you going to do?"

"Wrap up here."

CHAPTER 30

"It's all in there," Angie told Officer Pietrikowski as he stood in the MVPD reception area holding her boxes one atop the other. "I had to retrieve them from a private lab. I'd started having my own tests run on the old evidence."

He opened his mouth, but her hand shot up, palm facing him.

"Before you go telling me I've compromised anything, those boxes came out of home storage where they'd been opened and reopened. The lab I used is experienced in forensics. If there is anything compromised, it did not come from the lab or me. And you have my DNA profile should you need to rule me out. Or in."

Pietrikowski was not impressed. "We'll be in touch," he said, mouth grim as he left the reception area and shouldered open the exit door. As soon as he'd vacated the building, Angie hurried back to her desk and picked up her phone. It was lunch hour, and the public affairs office was empty. She hit the extension for Stacey Warrington, the ViCLAS—Violent Crime Linkage Analysis System—tech in sex crimes. She'd always been Angie's go-to person for anything database oriented.

"Stacey, I'm sending some files to your computer—prints. Can you do me a favor and have them run them for me?"

"Hey, Angie, I thought they had you on the cushy social media desk job for a while," Stacey said.

"They do. This is for an old case I'm still working—the prints are from over thirty years back. I had a lab digitize images of friction ridge detail taken of bloodied patents left at a scene. When you have time," she said. "As a favor. I'll owe you."

"Yeah, yeah, right. Send them now. I've got a hole in my schedule. I can get on it right away."

Angie opened up her personal laptop, which she'd brought with her to work. She plugged the memory stick into a USB port and uploaded the files from Anders. She attached the first set of images and hit SEND. "Sending as we speak."

Officer Pepper entered the office, taking off her coat. "How's that blog post coming?" she said as she hung it up.

"Great." Angie attached the next set of files, sent those, too.

"Need a hand? Any questions?"

"I'm good, thanks," Angie said without looking up.

"It needs to go live before the end of the day—needs to be out there for the weekend."

"Yeah, I got it." *Like anyone cares if an MVPD blog post goes live on Monday instead of Friday.* Nevertheless, Angie shut down her files as soon as the images had gone through. She switched computers and reopened the document containing her blog-in-progress. She tried to focus on finishing off her blog post, but anticipation hummed in her blood.

It was 3:23 p.m. when the phone her desk buzzed. Internal call. She lunged for the receiver.

"Angie, it's Stacey. We got a hit. He's in the system."

"Serious?"

"You sound surprised."

"No. No." Chills raced over her skin. "It's a *he*? The patents belong to a male?"

"The one set, yes."

Angie shot a glance at Officer Pepper, who was casting a watchful eye her way. "Who is he?" Angie said quietly.

"Name's Milo Belkin."

"So he's got a record—he's *alive*?"

"And kicking. On the inside. He's doing time at Hansen Correctional Centre for a series of charges ranging from criminal negligence causing death, to possession of an illegal firearm, to possession of narcotics with intent to traffic. He's got another six months remaining on his sentence. Seems like he's going right to his WED date."

"Can you forward me the details—and whatever else you can dig up on his arrest, charges, anything and everything?"

"Gotcha. Looks like he was charged prior, too—for sexual assault and battery. But he was acquitted when the complainant suddenly refused to testify and dropped all charges."

Excitement exploded through Angie. One of the men who'd chased the woman into the alley. *Alive*. And not going anywhere for at least another six months. This was it. This was her breakthrough. She ran her hand over her hair, almost unable to sit still. "Okay, thank you—and anything else you can dig up on those prior charges, too."

"No problem."

She hung up and made a fist pump.

"The blog post going well, is it?" Pepper said.

"Oh yeah," Angie said with a smile. Almost shaking with excitement, she located the number of Hansen Correctional Center and called to confirm that an inmate named Milo Belkin was indeed incarcerated there. She set up a visit with Belkin for noon tomorrow. The Hansen institution was on the Lower Mainland. It was the weekend tomorrow. She could be on a ferry tonight, stay in a Vancouver hotel, drive out to Hansen first thing in the morning.

This—*this* was why she needed to keep this social media desk job. She had weekends off, and she could still play the police card when she interrogated her suspect. And if this Belkin was serving his criminal sentence right up to the warrant expiry, or WED date, he clearly hadn't been meeting requirements for early parole—he was making someone unhappy.

And now she was going to repay Milo Belkin the favor.

CHAPTER 31

Maddocks carried his laptop under his arm as he and Holgersen strode with Inspector Martin Flint toward the conference room at the end of the top floor corridor. Maddocks cast Holgersen a quick glance. The guy loped with his shoulders hunched into his scruffy jacket, chin jutted forward, his hands digging deep into the pockets of his gray jeans. His combat-style boots were scuffed and spotted with muck from the streets. He looked like a scrappy junkyard dog jonesing for a fight.

Flint, by contrast, was all spit and polish in a white uniform shirt with lapel insignia, tie secured with a gold tie pin, pressed black pants—his military history evident in his deportment and fastidious attention to detail. Ordinarily Flint functioned as the MVPD's head of special investigations, which fell under the major crimes umbrella, but he was currently standing in as the major crimes boss until someone was officially hired to replace disgraced Inspector Frank Fitzsimmons, who'd been leaking sensitive MVPD information to the media during the Baptist investigation in an effort to unseat the chief. Flint was also temporarily overseeing the homicide unit, which also fell under the major crimes umbrella. This was a hole left by Jake Buziak, whose online gambling habit using MVPD equipment had been revealed during an internal investigation into the MVPD leak. Maddocks had taken over the Baptist task force from Buziak shortly after he was hired, and it was being made clear to Maddocks that he remained number one in line for Buziak's job as head of homicide once the barcode girls investigation was wrapped.

As they approached the room, through the glass walls Maddocks saw a male and a female seated at the long conference table. Behind them a bank of windows looked out over the city. Clouds boiled puce along the horizon. Rain spat against the panes.

Flint pulled open the glass door. They entered, and Flint made brief introductions while Maddocks went to the head of the conference table. He connected his laptop to a large smart screen at the end of the room.

The male cop at the table introduced himself as Sergeant Thomas Bowditch, an RCMP officer with a long history of investigating organized crime and human trafficking in the Lower Mainland. The female, Constable Vicky Eden, had most recently worked with the RCMP's international operations in Europe before being detailed to the task force. Both veterans bore guarded features and expressionless eyes. They'd been sent by task force lead investigator Sergeant Parr Takumi, who was stationed in Surrey on the mainland and had been appointed to head up the team. Takumi's prior post had been in Quebec, where he'd earned accolades for investigations into the Irish West End Gang, the Montreal Mafia, Hells Angels, and Colombian cartels.

Holgersen slumped into a chair across the table from the pair and folded his arms over his chest. He glowered at them. Maddocks remained standing at the head of the boardroom table. Outside the windows the late-afternoon sky was darkening and fog was blowing in.

Bowditch got right to it without preamble. "Everything you've got on your barcode case to date, we need it. And we'd like you to give us an overview now."

Flint nodded to Maddocks, who pulled up his computer file and hit a key, bringing the smart screen to life. The group listened in taut silence as he gave them a bare-bones briefing on their investigation.

Rain ticked against the windows as wind gusted wickedly around the outside corners and crevices of the concrete building. The distant sound of a foghorn reached them. Another storm front was closing in.

Maddocks pointed at the row of mug shots displayed across the screen. "These are the six barcoded females who were forcibly confined aboard the *Amanda Rose*." All were thin. Haunted looking. All dark-haired, save for the one blonde. Below their faces were images of their respective barcode tattoos.

"Sophia Tarasov." Maddocks pointed to the first image. "Killed last night around 1:00 a.m. COD as yet unknown. Postmortem pending. Her tongue was excised. Originally from Novgorod. The only one who has given us a statement so far. According to Tarasov, the girls were threatened with having their tongues cut out if they spoke."

Eden and Bowditch exchanged a fast glance, tension evident in their bodies.

Maddocks hit another laptop key, and a large map filled the screen. "From Tarasov's statement, this is a possible route taken by the six barcoded victims into the country." With his finger, Maddocks drew a line across the smart screen between Prague and Vladivostok, which lay just above the North Korean border. "From Vladivostok, twenty young women were transported in a crab fishing vessel. Somewhere in international waters they were transferred to a cargo ship flying the South Korean flag." He moved his finger across the map, drawing a line down to South Korea. "Tarasov said one of the women died at sea, leaving nineteen. They docked in what she thought could have been a city in South Korea, possibly Pusan. She believed they were then taken to China and then across the Pacific"—he drew a long line over the ocean—"to the Port of Vancouver here on the North American coast." He paused.

"One helluva trip," muttered Holgersen.

Maddocks said, "Detective Holgersen has noted that this journey coincides with traditional Russian king crab import routes—both legal and illegal harvests from the Russian far east. It's an industry that has traditionally been dominated by organized crime—the so-called crab Mafia—which has deep roots in Russian government organizations." He hit another key, and the image of the pale-blue crab tattoo filled the screen.

"Tarasov described this tattoo to a forensic artist. It matches the tattoo used as an insignia by a subsect of the crab Mafia. Tarasov witnessed identical ink on one of her male captors in Prague, on one of the crab fisherman out of Vladivostok, and on her captor-pimp in what we think is a remote BC coastal location where nine of the girls trafficked from Vladivostok were held for maybe a month. From this holding location, it appears six of the nine girls were sold—or hired out—to Veronique Sabbonnier, owner-manager of the Bacchanalian Club brothel, which she ran aboard the *Amanda Rose*. Sabbonnier brought the six barcoded women here, to Victoria."

The female officer—Eden—jotted a note on the pad in front of her. Bowditch typed a text on his phone and sent it. Maddocks waited for the cop to finish texting. Bowditch looked up, his features studiously benign, but Maddocks could read sharpened interest—excitement even—in the eyes of both officers.

Eden cleared her throat and leaned forward. "Did Tarasov say how they got from the Port of Vancouver to this remote coastal location?"

Maddocks inhaled deeply. He glanced at Holgersen, then Flint, and then he skirted the question. "We got a statement—as part of a plea bargain—from Sabbonnier's assistant, Zaedeen Camus. Camus, who self-identifies as female, said the Russian traffickers were collaborating with Hells Angels members entrenched as longshoremen at the Port of Vancouver. The Hells Angels members facilitated the girls' removal from the cargo container, and they apparently initiated transport of the girls from the dock to this remote coastal location."

Both Eden and Bowditch stiffened. They exchanged a hot, quick glance. "We'll need to interview Camus ourselves," she said. "And as agreed, we'll need *all* written statements, recorded interviews, logged evidence, everything. We'll take possession of the remaining barcoded women, and—"

"Camus is being transferred to a Lower Mainland pretrial facility," Flint said. "The information she has given to date is part of a plea bargain that includes the transfer." He paused. "The legal arrangement with her counsel is in connection with local crimes that we're prosecuting locally."

"We can handle it all from here," Bowditch said, starting to push his chair back.

"Your task force—what is the scope?" Maddocks said, leaning forward and pressing his knuckles onto the table. His eyes lanced Bowditch's and then Eden's. "What is the purview of this?"

"I'm afraid I'm not at liberty to share this information without the necessary security clearance," Bowditch said. "It's a highly sensitive interagency operation involving international and national agencies as well as specialized local units. It's drawn under one umbrella several investigations that have been years in the making, and it includes deep-cover detail that cannot be compromised, for the safety of our UC officers."

Maddocks bristled, tension building hot and low in his belly as the image of Sophia Tarasov's body washed back into his mind. Tarasov's image morphed suddenly into his memory of Ginny trussed up in that polyethylene tarp, bloodied and swinging by a rope hung from the trestle bridge. He recalled the mutilated bodies of Faith Hocking and Gracie Drummond on O'Hagan's autopsy table. Both young women, Victoria locals, had worked as prostitutes through the Bacchanalian Club, where they'd come to the deadly attention of the Baptist—a man who was harbored by Veronique Sabbonnier and Zaedeen Camus. Those two had made the Baptist's crimes possible.

Sometimes, Maddocks thought as he met the gazes of the two veteran officers, it wasn't just bad guys who hurt young girls, it was

bureaucracy. Pride. Territorialism. Because if he let this out of MVPD
hands now, there was no doubt in his mind that Gracie Drummond's
and Faith Hocking's families would not see justice done at a local level.
The local johns involved with the Bacchanalian Club and the strangulation death of Faith Hocking would not be prosecuted. These two
cops had bigger fish to fry. The MVPD case to which Maddocks and
his colleagues had given so many hours of their lives, to which Angie
might have sacrificed her career, which had almost cost the life of his
daughter, would end up mere collateral damage, swept under the rug
in some plea deal.

Voice low, he said, "We can help you in more detail if we can
understand the parameters of your investigation."

"Yeah," Holgersen said, moving his gum from one side of his mouth
to the other. "Like, maybe we has theories that don't quite add up, but if
we knew more, *ka-ching*, the bits an' pieces that might not be in them
case files you're getting—they suddenly slots into place."

Bowditch's mouth twitched. His eyes narrowed. "If the implication
is that you're withholding evidence, theories, I must—"

"The withholding of evidence," Maddocks said, slowly, coolly, his
gaze lasering Bowditch, "is probably what cost Sophia Tarasov's life."

Silence slammed thick into the room. Bowditch cleared his throat.
"That's—"

"There are other barcode girls out there, am I correct? Tattooed sex
workers your team knows about?" Maddocks said with another quick
glance at Flint. "Here on North American soil. And they've come to
harm at the hands of the Russian mob, right? Did any of them have their
tongues excised? Perhaps when they tried to help law enforcement?"

Silence.

"You both knew exactly what kind of danger Sophia Tarasov
and the other five barcode survivors were in," Maddocks said crisply.
"Instead of informing the MVPD when we were first put into contact
with you, which would have dramatically altered our security protocol

for those young women, you arranged this meeting"—he wagged his hand between them—"to come and see what we had while you put in motion the requisite legal steps to assume jurisdiction of our case." He paused. Thunder rumbled in the low fog outside. Rain lashed afresh against the darkening windows, in which they were beginning to see their own reflections. "And before you could even get here, Tarasov was murdered. In what appears to be a mob hit." Another beat of silence. "You killed her—*you* killed that young woman—and I can make a case for it."

Eden cleared her throat. She tapped the back of her pen rapidly on the table. Bowditch glowered at Maddocks, hot spots rising in the skin along his cheekbones.

"Possibly your task force has an appetite for collateral damage in order to catch bigger international fish," Flint said quietly. "But we don't."

"We had a duty to Tarasov," Maddocks added. "And we remain committed to seeing justice done for the local Victoria women who were hurt or murdered in connection with the Bacchanalian Club. We need *local* offenders successfully prosecuted for *local* crimes perpetrated in connection with that club. And to meet these objectives, we need to keep working on this investigation from a local angle."

Silence pressed heavy and simmering over the room.

"What do you want?" Bowditch said finally, his face dark, eyes narrow.

"Full cooperation. Same as you want."

Flint leaned forward. "We'd like inclusion on your task force."

Bowditch's mouth opened. He glanced at Eden.

"It's out of the question," Eden said.

Maddocks reached down and shut his laptop. The image on the screen died. "Thank you for your time, Officers," he said. "We have nothing further to discuss." He started to leave the room. Holgersen pushed his chair back.

"We have *legitimate* jurisdiction over this case," Eden snapped, coming to her feet, her eyes shooting sparks. "You will suffer the—"

Maddocks spun to face her. "Take it up with whatever body you wish," he said calmly. "I'll be happy to outline to whomever how the MVPD was undermined in the protection of Sophia Tarasov." He pulled open the glass door. Flint remained seated. He was letting Maddocks set himself up to take the brunt of any retaliatory measures that might now boomerang their way, as had been agreed prior to the meeting. Maddocks was more than happy to suck it up. He'd hit a wall. With his kid, his marriage, his job. Angie. His leaking old boat. Caring for Jack-O. The posttraumatic effects of nearly losing Ginny in the Baptist takedown. And he was allowing it all to zero in on Sophia Tarasov. She was the last little straw. The image of her pale, thin body—that gaunt, brave face with its tongue cut out because she'd spoken to *him* . . . It was going to haunt him for the rest of his life. He was furious with these two cops at the table. And if he couldn't hold on to a family, a wife—if he couldn't be a good enough father or make a romantic relationship work with a woman he was coming to love—he sure as hell *could* fight for the Sophia Tarasovs out there.

CHAPTER 32

Angie left the station building at 5:00 p.m. on the nose, urgency rustling beneath her skin like a trapped live thing. She'd have to make up for her late start this morning on another day. The blog post would have to wait until Monday, too, because she'd spent the latter part of the afternoon reading the information Stacey Warrington had provided her on Milo Belkin's arrest along with his trial transcript. She was wired on what she'd found.

Belkin had been arrested in Vancouver's east side in 1993—twenty-five years ago—when Vancouver police acting on a tip had stopped a white commercial cube truck in which Belkin was traveling with three other males. A gun battle had ensued. A VPD cop took a .45 slug in the skull and died en route to the hospital. A ricocheting .22 bullet had struck an innocent bystander in his lower back, rendering him a paraplegic. Belkin—who'd been shooting a 9-millimeter handgun at the scene—was arrested with a man named Semyon Zagorsky—who'd been firing a .22 pistol. The two other male accomplices had fled toward an unidentified black Chevrolet van that had drawn up behind the side street where the shootout was occurring. The two men escaped the scene in that Chevrolet van.

Inside the white cube truck in which Belkin had been traveling was a flower delivery. Stashed among the flowers, cops found 50.5 kilograms of cocaine, 14.1 kilos of heroin, and 6 kilos of hashish. The drugs were estimated to have had a street value of almost $9 million.

Angie now knew why Voight had saved those two newspaper articles. According to those old clippings, five years after the drug bust and shoot-out, a Colt .45 had been found in the glove compartment of a burned-out black Chevrolet van in a railyard.

Voight had suspected the burned-out Chevy van and Colt .45 were linked to the Milo Belkin shoot-out and drug bust with its getaway van and the .45 slug that killed the VPD officer. Voight must have also suspected Belkin and his accomplices were somehow linked to the 1986 cradle case with its getaway van.

Had that Colt .45 found inside the gutted van been the weapon fired outside Saint Peter's Hospital that Christmas Eve? Had the two men escaped with Angie's mother and twin in that black Chevy van? Had one of the men been Milo Belkin?

But if Voight *had* suspected this, he'd not been able to link Milo Belkin directly to the cradle case as Angie had just done, because the fingerprint comparison technology had not yet been in place.

Darkness was complete as Angie headed for her car, lights reflecting in puddles. Rain blew sideways in the wind, and thunder rumbled up in the clouds. Bits of tree debris pelted her as she neared her vehicle in the lot. Abruptly, a shadow cut in front of her.

She caught her breath and stepped back, her hand instinctively moving toward the sidearm in her holster—but her weapon was no longer there.

"Detective Pallorino," came a deep German-accented voice. "How are you?"

She squinted into the dark. "Grablowski? Is that you?"

"Can we talk?" the profiler said, stepping into view, the light from the parking lot lamp standard catching his face. He wore a long double-breasted raincoat with deep pockets, wide belt. His customary herringbone cap protected his head from rain. His round glasses glinted in the dark.

"What about?" she said, suddenly uneasy. "Were you waiting for me out here?"

"I know that you knock off at five now—demotion and all," he said. "Could I tempt you with a drink at the Pig down the road? We can talk there."

"Look, I'm in a rush." She proceeded toward her Nissan. "I need to be on the last ferry to Vancouver tonight. It'll have to wait."

"I don't think you'll want it to wait."

There was an edge to his voice. Caution whispered through Angie, along with curiosity. She stopped, turned to face him. Whatever the forensic shrink had to say to her, she didn't trust him—there was something sinister about this man who delved into the minds of monsters for a living and who was eager to profit off them in search of his own academic acclaim.

Thunder clapped, then grumbled away into the distance. "Want to wait for what?" she said quietly.

"I know that you are the angel's cradle Jane Doe."

Something dropped like a cold stone through her stomach. Ringing began in her ears. "I . . . don't know what you're talking about." She turned back toward her Nissan, key fob in hand, a kind of panic rising inside her. *How* could he know? Someone had to have told him. But *who*? Why?

She beeped her lock. He came up behind her. "I also know that your DNA matches that tiny little child's foot that floated all alone up onto that beach in Tsawwassen.

She froze.

Her heart began to jackhammer.

Jacob Anders? Maddocks? Jenny Marsden? She hadn't told anyone else that she was the cradle child. And she'd told no one about her DNA match to the foot—only Jacob Anders. She spun to face Grablowski. "Where did you hear this?"

"My source is reliable."

"*Who?* Tell me!"

He stepped backward, raising both hands, palms out in self-defense. "No need to get aggressive, Detective. We all know of your proclivity toward violence. I simply have a proposition in the face of this breaking news. Give me the exclusive on your story—allow me to interview you as the RCMP investigation continues to unfold. It will make for gripping true crime drama. It has all the feels—might even secure us a movie deal."

Us?

Fury lashed up inside her. She stepped toe to toe and eye to eye with the forensic shrink. "A proposition? So *you* can make money off *my* life? When you won't even tell me where you got this information? Fuck you, Grablowski." She whirled back to her car and yanked open the driver's door. He clamped his left hand on top of the door.

"We split the profits. Fifty-fifty."

"Get your hand off my car before I break all your fucking fingers," she growled through gritted teeth. Her eyes were burning. "And if you go public with this, I'll sue your shrink ass off."

"I'm not the only one with this information, Detective. But I'll hold off on going to the media if you agree to work with me on the book. And then once the story breaks, the publicity will be advantageous to sales, of course. Think about it." He panned his right hand out into the darkness as if to denote a billboard up in lights. "The mystery angel's cradle baby is separated from her twin at age four. Unaware of her past, she grows up to become an aggressive sex crimes cop, unrelenting, fierce in her drive to save all the broken women and children out there without realizing what propelled her to into policing in the first place, and possibly into the sex unit specifically. Her temper is lightning quick. She's uncompromising. She is the as-yet-unnamed MVPD officer who hunted down and violently shot to death a heinous lust-based serial killer. Whom I, the author, profiled. And then she finds out that she has—or had—a twin. What happened to that twin, Detective Pallorino? What happened to *you* prior to Christmas Eve 1986? *This* is the journey we shall take our readers on."

Inside her belly she began to shake. "Is that a threat? You're going to name me in the press as the Baptist's shooter—because not even the IIO publicly named me? You're going to break the personal story of *my* past?"

He said nothing. She couldn't read his eyes behind the shine of his spectacles in the darkness. But his silence held her paralyzed. She was doomed. Whether she cooperated with him or not—this was *all* going to get out there, one way or another.

"Sleep on it for a day or two, why don't you?" He paused. "And consider this—I can do this story justice. I have a specific interest in twins. It's been an area of academic expertise for me. Look up the old papers I wrote on cryptophasia."

"What?"

"Twin talk. It's an *idioglossia*—an idiosyncratic, private language invented and spoken by only one person, or between very few people, usually children. When it's spoken solely between twins, it's referred to as *cryptophasia*. It can grow out of delayed childhood development or reduced verbal stimulation and interaction with adult language models. Perhaps you even had a special language with your twin, Detective."

A memory sliced through her.

Come playum dum grove . . . Come down dem . . .

Angie could see her suddenly, the little girl from her earlier hallucinations, awash in a luminous glow of pale pink, no discernible face, long red hair, her small white hand reaching out, beckoning . . . A singsongy voice filled Angie's ears . . .

Two little kittens . . . two little kittens . . .

The childish, tinky-tonk tune crashed and died in a horrible cacophony, like piano keys all being smashed at once.

She shook herself, cleared her throat. Very quietly, she said, "I'm going to ask you one last time—who told you?"

"You've got my number." He adjusted the bill of his sodden hat. "Take care, Detective Pallorino."

She glared after him as his shadow merged into the dark, rainy mist. She was shaking. Cold. Wet. She got into her car and rubbed her hands hard over her damp face. She'd kill whoever had spilled her personal news to that creep. And now that it was out, there was no way that she was going to be able to cram that genie back into the bottle.

Even more troubling was who in her very close circle of trusted confidants would have done this to her?

She reached for her ignition, started her vehicle. And it struck her—she had to go tell her dad. About her DNA and the child's foot. If this was all going to blow up in the news, her father needed to prep himself. Reporters would hound him. The secret that he and her adoptive mother had been harboring all these years would be exposed to his friends, his colleagues at the university. He'd also have to find a way to protect her mom, who—in her schizophrenic-dementia state—could find it all terribly disturbing. Especially if reporters tried to get to her.

Angie rammed her car into gear and spun out of the parking lot, tires squealing as she hit the road. *Shitshitshit.* She smacked the wheel in hot frustration. What would this mean for her social media position now? Her probation? If it got out that *she* was the MVPD cop who'd been under IIO investigation. That it was her who'd emptied her clip into Spencer Addams's face in some blackout rage. It wasn't exactly the smiling face of an Officer Friendly on the social media desk.

Perhaps you even had a special language with your twin, Detective?

She punched a button on her console, connecting her phone via Bluetooth. She drew to a stop at a red traffic light, hit Alex Strauss's number.

The instant her old psychologist friend and mentor answered, she said, "Alex, it's me, Angie. I need you to put me under again—take me back in time with hypnosis. Tonight if you can, because I need to be in Vancouver early tomorrow morning." She realized if she went past her father's house now and spoke to him before going to meet Alex, she wouldn't make it home in time to gather up her things and drive up the peninsula to catch the last ferry. She'd have to rise at 5:00 a.m. Saturday instead and catch the first ferry out. It would still give her time—just—to reach Hansen Correctional Centre by noon tomorrow.

"Are you certain, Angie?" Alex said.

"Dead certain."

"It could be risky—you went into distress last time. I had to bring you out early, remember? And you did not come back easily."

She smoothed her hand over her wet hair, recalling the terror of being in that dark place in her mind where Alex had taken her. Edginess nipped at her nerves. She had to do it. Everything she'd experienced, everything she'd felt and seen and remembered, now took on a different context with the bombshell that Tranquada, the IDRU woman, had dropped on her.

Come playum dum grove . . . Come down dem . . .

It *could* be her sister, calling from beyond a watery grave. For help—to come find her. In a special language only the two of them had used to communicate. Angie's eyes filled with sharp emotion.

"I *need* to go back again, Alex. Deeper. And it's not just for me—"

Now she was doing this for someone else—a little girl who was finally taking shape. It changed everything.

"It's for my twin."

CHAPTER 33

"Come on in," Alex Strauss said, stepping back and holding the door open wide for Angie.

"Thank you for seeing me at such short notice," she said, shucking off her uniform jacket as she entered. He took her wet jacket and hung it on a hook near the door while she sat on the mudroom bench and removed her boots.

"I confess you had me at twin," he said. "Uniform looks good on you, Angie." He nodded toward her gear.

"Yeah, right." She came to her feet. "I'd have changed but had to go see my dad right away, tell him this story could break. He's going to have to face friends and colleagues and prepare my mom somehow for when the story of my life goes public. Media will hound them both, and I don't suspect reporters will go easy on either of them for having hidden my past from me."

"How'd he handle the news of a possible sibling—the little foot?" Alex said, leading the way into his living room.

She followed him. Nerves nipped as she caught sight the big old wingback in which she'd sat for her previous hypnosis session with him. "It hit him hard." She blew out a stream of breath and carefully seated herself in the chair. Alex had a wood fire burning, and his living room was warm. He dimmed the lights.

"It was bad enough with them pretending I was their dead kid, trying to insert me into their deceased toddler's life. The fact I could have a dead biological double just drives it all in deeper and weirder. He wants answers, too, about that little foot."

"Have you considered that media coverage might be advantageous? Someone might recall something, come forward."

"It would also expose me as the cop who killed Spencer Addams should Grablowski make good on his threat. Nothing good can come of that. And it could also have an adverse effect in that it might tip off persons involved in the old crimes, send them further into hiding. I just want to move as quickly as possible with my own investigation to see how far I can get *before* all the shit hits the media fan and before the RCMP ties my hands and cuts off my access to potential sources."

Alex motioned to the teapot on his table and the two cups beside it. "Tea?"

"No thanks."

"Anything else before we get started?"

She shook her head, tension winding tighter. "I want to get right to it. I still need to pack for a trip to the mainland tomorrow." And she wanted to go by Maddocks's yacht. She needed to see him before she left the island for the weekend, tell him about the RCMP and IDRU visit and the floating foot DNA.

Alex seated himself opposite her. "Phone off?"

"Yes."

"Comfy?"

She took a deep breath, rested her arms on the armrests, and wiggled her socked feet, relaxing her toes. The fire crackled, and rain drummed softly against the tin awning outside. She nodded.

Alex spoke softly, his voice deep, calm. "Close your eyes. You're going to feel increasingly relaxed. All the tension of the day is draining out of your chest and funneling down into your arms."

Angie shut her eyes and sighed deeply.

"You can feel the tension flowing down your arms. All the way down to your wrists. It's in your hands now. In your palms. It's leaving your body through the ends of your fingers. It's washing from your pelvis down your legs, to your feet. It's seeping out from beneath the soles of your feet into the carpet."

Angie focused on the physical sensations in her body, following his cues. Her muscles, her mind, began to relax.

"You're taking a deep, deep breath and releasing it all from your lungs. And again. Comfort is soft, like a warm blanket enveloping your shoulders . . ."

He continued speaking in a soft monotone. Angie concentrated on his words, the reactions in her body. She felt the tightness of the day begin to blur at the edges. Her mind opened up.

"Your brain is like a spring flower, blossoming, opening, turning its face to the warmth of sunlight. You're drifting into the arms of that comfort, Angie. Deeper. Deeper. Into the past."

Time stretched. She had no sense of how long he kept talking. She felt herself sinking down, down, down to a warm place. Her eyelids fluttered.

"Okay, now, tell me what happened the last time you went back in memory, Angie."

She moistened her lips. "I . . . was lying on a bed. In a dark room. There was someone with me in the darkness, holding my hand. A female. Her skin was cool. Soft. She was singing sweetly, gently, like a lullaby . . . those words about two little kittens. In Polish. Then she suddenly stopped singing. Someone had come in. I was scared. The room went blacker." Tension curled around her throat as an image slammed back into her brain. "There . . . there was a man in the room on top of her. Big, big man."

"On top of who, Angie?"

"I . . . don't know. The lady singing. He was grunting like a dog on her, and she was crying softly. Very scared. Wasn't nice. Horrible."

"Okay, okay, but then I gave you a magic key to get out of the room, remember?"

She noticed the key suddenly in her palm. A big brass one she'd seen in a fairy-tale book. She nodded. "Yes. I remember."

"You unlocked the door to the room, and you went outside."

She nodded.

"Let's go back there, to that door. I will repeat what we did last time, and remember, when I count backward from four, you will start returning to my living room again. You will have your key at all times. It's a magic key, Angie. You will always be safe. If at any time you feel stuck, just say the word 'home,' understand? Or use that key."

"Yes."

"All right, your breathing is becoming even slower, more and more relaxed. Breathe in and then out. Slower and slower. Deeper. Air is sinking low into your lungs, deeper. You're going down, down toward a comfortable place. Back to that door. Now open the door again with your magic key."

Angie was there, in the dark room. Fear started to claw at her. It smelled hot. Her breathing quickened.

"No. Slow. Relax. Look at the key in your hand."

She did.

"Use it."

She stuck it in the big lock that appeared in the door in front of her, and she stepped out into bright white light, just like last time.

"Go through the door, Angie. Go outside."

She blinked into the blinding brightness. And once again, instead of stepping out, she turned to look back into the darkness of the room, and she held out her hand. "Come um," she whispered. "Come playum, dum grove."

"What are you saying, Angie?"

"She must come and play. She must come with me to the berry bushes in the grove and to see fish place. Bring basket." Suddenly there was a woven basket in her hand. *"Jesteśmy jagódki, czarne jagódki,"* she sang.

"What does that mean, Angie?"

She began to sing the words in English now. "We are small berries, little black berries. We are small berries, black berries."

"Who are you singing to? Who are the berries?"

"She must come, to play. We go to dum grove, down indum. Trees. Bring baskets. Berries. Go see fish pens. Not allowed." All around her, huge drooping conifers loomed way up high into the sky. So high. Like skyscrapers. Green moss and orange and yellow lichens grew on rocks. And bright-yellow dandelions were scattered everywhere on lush emerald grass that grew long and tickled her bare shins. She bent down to pick some of the smiling yellow flowers, and the smell was heather and honey. She put them in her basket. A child's laughter sounded behind her, and she whirled around, feeling the warm air on her thighs as the hem of her dress lifted like a spinning tent. Through the bushes and trees she could see docks out on the water. Several docks. A little house on one. Like she'd seen outside Anders's lab building. Boats. Her heart began to race. "Not allowed to go to the big house with the green roof. Or go fish pens. Red man is there."

"Red man?"

She shook her head wildly. "No, no, no . . . Must come play . . ."

"Who must come play, Angie? The lady who was singing?"

Angie's chest tightened. Her head felt as though it was going to implode. Pressure on the inside of her skull. Noise in her ears. "She . . . she's there," Angie whispered hoarsely. "I can see her." She began to shake.

"Who?"

"Me. It's me."

"Your sister maybe, who looks like you?"

Angie's eyes burned. Fear was suddenly a noose. The little girl with long red hair and a pink frilled dress held out her hand. "Come um dum dem grove," she said. Their language. Their own special language. And this time Angie could see the child's face. Her gray eyes were her own eyes, and they pleaded. "Come playum . . . help . . . help me . . . help . . ." The girl began to fall backward. Her berry basket dropped. Dead dandelions all about her feet. Angie shot her hand out to catch the girl. But the girl started to fade, shattering like glass into the air. Angie screamed, spun around, then ran. And the skyscraper trees whirled like a roundabout above her head, a blur of yellow and green and black all beginning to lean inward, blocking out the blue sky, making it all black.

Uciekaj, uciekaj! . . . Wskakuj do srodka, szybko! . . . Run, run! Get inside!

Angie shook her head wildly from side to side. Cold now. Very cold. "I . . . I've got to go after her! She fell down. In the snow. Need to save her! *The man is taking her!*" Suddenly Angie was racing through the forest after . . . after . . . she couldn't see. Wind tore at her hair. Terror boiled in her veins. Her legs were pumping, grasses and brambles scraping her skin open. Her feet were cold as ice. She thrashed through berry bushes, going deep into the forest which became gray buildings and she was on a cold street with snow, and there were Christmas lights . . . *and she could see the girl's shoes . . . little purple high-tops . . . running and slipping in the snow . . . and the sound of Ave Mari-aaaa . . . bells . . .*

"Her shoes," she whispered, voice hoarse. "They're her shoes." She shook her head from side to side, mouth open, panting. She looked down at her own feet in the snow. Same shoes. Matching shoes. A face flared into her mind, sharply and in focus. A man's face. Big face.

"I . . . I see someone—a man. Big man. He's holding a box out to me. He's smiling. He's happy."

"The red man?"

"Other man."

"Take the box, Angie."

She shook her head. "Roksana."

"Angie?"

"No, Roksana."

"Who's Roksana?"

Tears spilled into her eyes. She shook her head wildly. Inside her skull everything hurt. Blood coming out of her mouth and ears and eyes.

"Do you want to come home, Angie?"

"Roksana," she said again. "Want box."

"Are you Roksana, Angie?"

She nodded, crying.

"Take the box from the man, Roksana. Open it."

She did, ripping off the purple ribbon that bound it up in a big bow. There was tissue paper inside. Pink. She pulled it apart. "Shoes. New shoes!" She clapped her hands together at the sight of the little lilac high-tops, and suddenly they were on her feet in the snow again. But they weren't. Left them inside. It was icy cold. Bare feet. No time. A woman's screams cut the air.

Wskakuj do srodka, szybko! . . . Siedz cicho! . . . Get inside! Stay quiet!

Bells. So loud. Loud! She put her hands tightly over her ears. She was panting, hyperventilating. Banging.

"Tell me, Roksana," Alex said. "What are you doing?"

"Inside. Get inside. Bells." Tears streamed down her cheeks. She couldn't breathe. "The knife is coming. Big shiny knife . . ." She screamed. Pain sliced over her face. Blood! Everywhere. Banging from the guns. *"Mila!"* she screamed. "Gone. Mila!" She began to sob. "Home, home, home!" She searched wildly for the key. Key gone. Gone . . .

Vaguely she heard a word. Four. Three. Then louder. *Three!*
Two.
One.
"You're coming up, Angie. You're safe. Warm. You're back. *Safe*. In a comfortable chair, back in Alex Strauss's house, my house. Safe. All safe."
Her eyes flared open. Her gaze shot to her palms. No blood. She felt her mouth, her scar, her ears. No stickiness. No hot blood. No coppery smell. Her entire body was shaking, and her face was wet with tears.

CHAPTER 34

After her session with Alex, Angie drove straight to the marina to find Maddocks, but he was not at his yacht. So she'd gone home, showered and changed out of her cop uniform, and grabbed something to eat at Mario's—her favorite little Italian restaurant in old Victoria. She found Maddocks home when she returned to the marina closer to midnight.

They now sat on the sofa in his cabin, dog at their side, sipping a fine whiskey as waves slapped and chuckled at the wooden hull of his old schooner and halyards chinked against masts outside. Maddocks absently ruffled Jack-O's ears as he listened in heavy silence to Angie's account of the day's events—everything from Jacob Anders and his lab, to the floating foot DNA bomb Pietrikowski and Tranquada had dropped on her, to Milo Belkin and the hit on his prints, to Grablowski and his threats, and how his mention of twin-speak had driven her to a shocking hypnosis session with Alex. How she'd heard the names *Mila* and *Roksana* and seen a man's face clearly in her mind. A man who'd gifted her shoes in a prettily wrapped box, just like the little shoe that had washed up in Tsawwassen containing her DNA profile.

She drew her socked feet up under her butt and curled into the warmth of Maddocks's body as she spoke. His solid comfort, the feeling of having an ally, reminded her of all the reasons she did love having him in her life and why she *did* want to fight to keep him there. Yet she still felt as though something was slipping away—like fine hourglass sand through clenched fingers. And his mood was different tonight—she hadn't seen him like this before. Something was simmering hot and fierce just beneath his very controlled and cool exterior.

"You okay?" she said, looking up at him.

He nodded. "How about you? How're you handling this? How do you feel?"

She gave a snort. "Like the truth is locked inside me, and I can't quite get it out. I . . . I self-identified as *Roksana* in my memory," she said. "Alex and I looked up the name afterward—it *is* Polish in origin. And I screamed the word *Mila*. It's also a Polish girl's name. I saw more of my surroundings this time. I—we—Mila and I, I think—were in a clearing in a forest. Surrounded by exceptionally tall trees. Wide trunks. Way wider than my outreached arms. Cedars, I figure, in retrospect—droopy branches with reddish bark that looked stripped into shreds. A big ancient cedar grove. Moss, lichen, dandelions. A clearing where berry bushes grew—blackberries. There was water, ocean beyond the forest. A big building with a green roof where a red man lived. Docks. Several, making square shapes in the water. One with a building on it. I thought of them as fish pens."

"Red man?"

She looked up at him. "I have no idea what that means."

"And the docks?"

"A fish farm maybe? They reminded me of the docks outside Jacob Anders's lab buildings."

"The trees could have seemed extra tall because you were small in the memory," he said, taking a sip of his drink. "Sometimes when you return to places of childhood, something like an old family house that once appeared so large can seem tiny, shrunken."

She swirled her whiskey glass, watching the play of yellow against gold in the liquid. "I know. The man who gave me the shoe box was also huge. And I saw his features clear as day—they're burned into my brain now. I'll never forget them. A roundish face. But not a flabby round—strong. A wide, aggressive brow. A nose that looked as though it had been broken a few times. Eyes set deep under that ledge of brow. Dark-blond hair cut military short. Very bright blue eyes, all twinkly bright."

"So he wasn't the red man?"

"I didn't get the sense that he was. The red man . . . I felt the red man was bad. The man with the shoe box was nice."

"Twinkly? As though you liked him?"

"I don't know."

"To describe eyes as twinkly—that's not a perception born out of fear or of someone dark and nasty."

"I guess not. But then after I took the shoes from him, my memory flipped right into a black and negative nightmare. The terror I felt was real. I had a sense it could have been him after us in the snow."

Maddocks inhaled a deep, slow breath of air. "This is heavy stuff, Ange. But maybe you're also extrapolating—having seen photos of the ROOAirPocket high-top, having received news of the possible DNA match, and after having seen Anders's docks, you might be inserting this into your other memories. That DNA match still has to be proved—it *could* still be an error."

She shook her head. "I *saw* her, Maddocks. My twin. It *had* to be her. A mirror image of myself. Me but not me. I now feel in my bones, with every molecule of my being, that the DNA test will come back positive. And seen through this new paradigm, I believe that my memories are all starting to make some logical sense now. I feel less crazy. And if one of the DNA profiles on those semen stains or the hairs also comes back as a match to Milo Belkin, we've got him right there. DNA and prints. We can use this to crack him wide open—make him talk, make him tell me what happened that night, who that other man might be." She paused. "Who my parents were."

"So it wasn't Belkin himself you saw in your memory?"

"No. I've seen Belkin's mug shot. It wasn't him. I've got a meeting with Belkin at noon tomorrow at the Hansen Correctional Centre."

Maddocks's gaze flared to hers. "Is that wise?"

"How can I *not?*"

He held her gaze, long and steady. In his eyes she read worry, and she hated seeing it there.

"The RCMP is not going to be pleased with you hitting their persons of interest first," he said quietly. "Because it's just a matter of time before Pietrikowski gets the same hit on the bloody patents that you did. They're going to want to be the ones interrogating Belkin in connection with their floating foot case."

"Their case is *my* life. And any civilian has the right to go visit an inmate."

He held her gaze. "Thin ice."

"I've got to do this, Maddocks. You know I do. The RCMP investigators are not going to loop me in the way that I need to be—"

"Or want to be"

"*Need.* Okay? I *need* this. This is my sister. My other half. *My* DNA."

"Maybe," he cautioned. "It must still be confirmed." He got up, went to the counter in his small galley, and snagged the bottle of whiskey. He held it up. "Another?"

She shook her head. He poured himself a second tot. He was quiet as he recorked the bottle. Oddly so. He turned and looked out of the portlight above the sink as he took a sip. It was black as pitch out, rain tapping against the pane as the yacht rocked gently in the wind.

"Maddocks?"

With his back still to her, he said, "You could leave it all in the RCMP's hands, you know, Angie. Offer them what you have so far. Your memories, what you got from the hypnosis sessions—do an identikit of the blue-eyed man you saw or use a forensic artist. If the cradle case is solvable, they can and will solve it without your active involvement."

He turned to look at her. "You don't have to do this yourself—maybe you shouldn't."

She did not like the feeling that the look in his eyes—or his words—put into her stomach. Just the thought of dropping this case now filled her with dread, claustrophobia. She could not tolerate sitting at that social media desk, twiddling her thumbs, if she did not have this case to occupy her. She needed to *do* something, anything, before Grablowski went to the media and the story broke all around her. She would *not* be a sitting, reactive victim. She had to *act*.

"It's going to hurt your probation," he said quietly. "Messing in the RCMP's case. How long do you think it'll be before they contact Vedder about it? You already cut it fine holding back that evidence. You're lucky Pietrikowski did *not* slap you with a warrant. You need to stay clean if you want a future as a cop, Angie."

Irritation sparked in her. "I'm just going to the mainland for the weekend. I'm going to visit a man who might have known me from before the cradle incident, that's all. I'm going to ask him if I had a sister, a mother, what happened to them. As a civilian, never mind a cop. That's my right, Maddocks."

He looked doubtful. "Like I said, thin ice. Because you're not just a civilian. You're a cop on probation. Tell me you didn't use the fact that you are law enforcement in order to get that interview with Milo Belkin tomorrow."

She thunked her glass onto the table and lurched to her feet, unwilling, unable to face the aggravating logic in his words. "I need to leave. Got to try to grab a few hours' sleep. It's late. Ferry leaves early." She reached for her coat, which hung on a hook by the stairs that led up to the deck.

"Stay, Angie," he said quietly. "Finish your drink. Stay the night, please."

She hesitated, her hand on her jacket.

He set his glass down and came up behind her. Turning her around, he looked down into her face. Her chest crunched at the sight of the hot, dark emotion simmering in his gorgeous deep-blue eyes, those dense, dark lashes.

"I can't let you leave like this, angry." He slid his hand under her fall of hair, cupped the back of her neck. His grip was warm. Assertive. Demanding. Again she wondered about his unusual mood, that strange energy that seemed to be simmering in him tonight. He traced the line of her jaw with his thumb. Heat rushed into her belly. Want—fierce and sharp and sudden and desperate—erupted inside her. For something beyond sex. A raw yearning for deep connection. It was a feeling she couldn't articulate, and it was powerful and overriding and terrifying, so she resisted it, pulling up her cop coping mechanisms instead. Distance. Intellectualization. Walls that were high and cold and safe, that protected her feelings from the rest of the world.

"I can't," she said coolly, ducking out from his touch and taking her coat from the hook. She shrugged into it, wincing as the motion tore at the injured tissue in her arm. "It's almost 1:00 a.m. I need to be up at five to catch the ferry, or I won't make it to Hansen by noon."

She started up the stairs. "See you Monday," she called over her shoulder, not looking back. She pushed out of the hatch. Salt wind slapped her face with rain. As she climbed off the yacht and onto the dock, Angie felt as though she'd just crossed a threshold, taken a step away from all that was light and warm and good to embark on a journey she could only take alone. If she turned around and looked back into Maddocks's eyes, she'd be swayed by his logic, and she'd not have the strength to do it.

And she *had* to do it.

CHAPTER 35

SATURDAY, JANUARY 6

Maddocks grabbed his coat and rushed up onto the deck after Angie. She was already striding along the rain-swept dock, wind whipping her hair and the hem of her coat.

"Angie!" he called as he clambered over the side of his boat and went after her.

She stopped, turned. Her face appeared ghost-white under the mist-haloed dock lights.

"Phone me," he said, nearing her. "Promise that you'll call and let me know how it went with Belkin."

She hesitated. Wind lashed a strand of wet hair across her face. And she looked so alone, and he loved her—everything about this irascible, lone-wolf-rogue woman. He respected her, and he loved her. And he felt as though she was slipping away. And he was worried about her. Maddocks at heart knew that he was a rescuer—he wanted to rescue Angie as much as she didn't want him to save her. Because she wanted to rescue herself. Yet she was having trouble doing it.

"Okay, sure." She turned, hesitated, and then swung back to face him. It sent a punch of relief through his stomach.

"I never did ask how it went with Ginny—your dinner."

"Fine. It went good. She's getting on with her life, doesn't want her dad's help and all that." He smiled ruefully. Wind gusted and rain came down harder. He blinked against it. "So basically it's business as usual," he said. "Although her mother would rather she moved back home and is making damned sure I know it."

Something shifted in Angie's face—a hesitancy at the mention of his ex-wife. "You didn't tell me how the barcode case is going, either," she said.

He hadn't wanted to. He was still reeling over Sophia Tarasov's murder, at having the RCMP and task force swooping in, emasculating their team. Telling Angie would have been too much on top of what she'd just endured over the last few days. Guilt pinged through Maddocks at another sudden, darker realization: Tarasov's tongue being excised, a possible Russian organized crime hit, the secretive task force—it was all highly sensitive and confidential stuff, and maybe, just maybe, a part of him deep down inside didn't fully trust Angie with it all right now. She still needed to see that shrink, sort a lot of things out.

"It's moving forward," he said. "How 'bout I catch you up when you return Monday."

Her eyes narrowed. She pushed wet hair back from her face, weighing him in the dim light and mist. "You sure everything is okay?"

"Yeah."

She frowned slightly, wavering again, as if torn by some inner conflict. "Thanks for listening," she said. "I'll come by Monday night, see if you're home, let you know how it went." She stepped closer, reached up, placed her palm against the side of his wet face. "And then you can catch me up on your case and . . . everything else."

He swallowed as her words churned a cocktail of conflicted emotions and desire through his gut. "Look after yourself, Angie."

She smiled. "Yeah. Yeah, you too." She turned and strode with renewed purpose for the gangway that led up to the marina security gate.

"You *better* be back Monday!" he called impulsively after her.

She raised her hand without turning back, and then she was gone up the gangway, through the gate, and along the walkway, where she was swallowed by a swirl of mist and darkness. A foghorn sounded out in the harbor, deep and sonorous and lonely.

He stood there, silent in the rain, watching the mist where she'd disappeared. A chill of foreboding sank through him. But before he could probe it, the cell in his pocket rang. Maddocks spun and made for his yacht. He answered the call as he got down inside his cabin, Jack-O still sleeping, oblivious to all on the sofa.

"Maddocks."

"It's Flint. Sorry to wake you—"

"I'm up."

"Good. Just got word. You're in. You've got full security clearance. You're being temporarily assigned as the sole MVPD member on the integrated task force. They want you for a full briefing in Surrey Saturday at noon. Chopper will be waiting for you at the heliport at six."

CHAPTER 36

The helicopter banked and lowered through skeins of cloud that wrapped around mountains like sleeping dragons. Suddenly, beneath the clouds, to Maddocks's right, lay the city of Vancouver, gleaming silver in the wintery light and shimmering with rain. On the opposite side of the Burrard was the Lonsdale area development marching up the flanks of the North Shore mountains. But above the snowline there was just dense, endless forest blanketed by white and stretching clean up to Alaska.

The pilot's voice came through his headphones. They were about to land.

As the bird descended, a squat sea bus pulled away from its North Shore mooring and began to ply a foamy wake across water toward the city.

The chopper angled past a white giant of a Norwegian cruise ship docked near the city's landmark convention center and aimed for the small heliport near a railyard. The pilot brought his craft down with a neat and sudden bump dead center of a white X that marked the waterfront heliport landing.

As Maddocks disembarked and ducked beneath the rotors, carrying his bag, he reached into his pocket for his phone. He called Flint as he made his way up the long wooden gangway that led to the small terminal building. Up ahead in the heliport parking lot, he could see a Mountie in uniform waiting next to a squad car—Maddocks's transport to Surrey.

As soon as Flint picked up, Maddocks said, "Did they agree?"

"It took some convincing, but yes, they've conceded—no one on the task force interviews either Sabbonnier or Camus without you being present."

A bite of victory punched through him. Whether Sabbonnier or Camus would say another word to anyone was highly doubtful, but Maddocks was heading into his first briefing bearing a grudge against Sergeant Parr Takumi, the task force lead investigator, who'd failed to alert Flint and the MVPD of the potentially lethal danger facing the barcode girls. This was now personal.

He killed the call, jogged up the steps to the lot, and approached the squad car. He introduced himself to the young Mountie, who took his bag and said that he was Constable Sammi Agarwal.

As Agarwal drove through the city and onto the highway that would take them to Surrey, Maddocks watched the urban scenery unfold, and his chest grew tighter and tighter. Surrey was his old home. It was where he and Sabrina had married and where they'd started their dreams of building a family. Where Ginny had been born. Where it had all gone wrong.

His mood turned sullen as he recalled Sabrina's words from her recent phone call about Ginny's missed appointment. They'd cut like a knife, ramming home all his failures, reminding him of his scuttled dreams of spending an early retirement with his wife, his naive visions of buying a yacht, sailing with her up into Desolation Sound, camping on remote islands, fishing, while Ginny went to college. Instead, Sabrina had begun her affair with Peter, an accountant with regular hours, a good paycheck, a family inheritance, weekends off, and a passion for opera. How could he beat a fucking passion for opera? And then had come the shocker—Sabrina had filed for a divorce. How'd he not seen *that* coming?

Now he was back here on the mainland while Ginny was on the island, alone. While Angie was in Victoria working a desk job. While his old yacht was probably springing another leak in the windswept marina. Conflict churned through him. And as the rain and clouds pressed in, so did that odd sense of foreboding that had assailed him while he'd watched Angie disappearing into the fog. He was losing her, too.

He checked his watch. She'd be driving out to Hansen right now. He hadn't even asked what Vancouver hotel she'd be staying at upon her return tonight. Tension twisted through him.

CHAPTER 37

The guard brought the inmate into the room where Angie waited at a table. Milo Belkin was not tall—maybe five foot six—but he was broad across the chest and thighs. The fifty-six-year-old had clearly been working out in his cell or in the exercise yard. He was dressed in a prison sweatshirt, loose pants, white runners. His gray hair had been trimmed in a short buzz around his skull.

"Milo Belkin," she said as he stepped into the room.

He froze as he caught sight of her. His face went white. He shot a glance at the guard, as if suddenly desperate for escape.

Angie's pulse quickened at his reaction.

The guard's features remained impassive as he took position in front of the door. The inmate turned slowly back to face Angie.

"I'm Angie Pallorino," she said, closely watching his face, his eyes. "I'm an officer with the Metro Victoria Police Department." Maddocks's voice played through her head as she said the words.

Tell me you didn't use the fact that you are law enforcement in order to get that interview with Milo Belkin tomorrow.

Belkin slowly seated himself in the chair across the table from Angie, his gaze riveted on hers. His body language screamed reluctance.

But he said not a word. The color of his eyes was dark brown—so dark they looked almost black. Intense eyes, set too close on either side of his big beaked nose.

Excitement trilled through her.

"You know why I'm here, don't you, Milo?" she said quietly. "You recognized me the instant you walked in," she said.

The man swallowed. A vein bulged at his neck, which was corded with muscle and tension. He had a tattoo on the left side of that thick neck, she realized—the ink just poking into her line of vision.

"How *do* you know me, Milo?"

Silence.

She placed a copy of the Kodak print that Jenny Marsden had given her onto the table. She pushed it toward him. "Can you tell me now?"

He refused to glance down at the photo.

She leaned forward and jabbed the print with her index finger. "That there is the angel's cradle child. Janie Doe. Abandoned at Saint Peter's Hospital, Christmas Eve 1986." Angie waited.

Slowly, cautiously, Belkin glanced down toward the image. He inhaled sharply. His eyes ticked back to Angie's face.

She touched the scar that bisected the left side of her lips. "Did you put this here, Milo? Do you perhaps remember me as Roksana?"

He shot another glance over his shoulder at the guard, who remained impervious, sullen, staring straight ahead, one hand clasped over the other in front of him.

"You chased a young dark-haired woman across Front Street that night in '86, Milo. In the snow. You and at least one other man. The woman had two children with her, didn't she? One of the children was barefoot. No coats."

His Adam's apple moved in his throat as he swallowed hard. She pushed a Styrofoam cup of water toward him.

"Dry mouth?" she said. "Can be a sign of stress. Does my presence stress you, Milo?"

He said nothing, did not reach for the water. Instead his attention returned slowly to the photo. He stared at it. Angie's heart beat even faster—he had not denied that there were *two* children present. Or that he might know her as Roksana.

She leaned forward and lowered her voice. "What did you do to that woman and the other child, Milo, the little girl who did *not* make it into the angel's cradle?"

Silence pressed thick and heavy into the room. She could smell him—sweat tinged with the unique stink of fear. She waited. But still he remained mute.

"The other little girl, her name was Mila, wasn't it?"

Tiny pinpricks of moisture beaded his upper lip as he continued to stare at the photo.

"Why do I scare you so much, Milo Belkin?"

He refused to make eye contact again. He was going to wait her out, possibly hoping she'd leave sooner than later. This felon was six months out from his WED date. And once he was released after he had served out the very last day and hour of his sentence, not even the parole board would have jurisdiction over him. He could disappear into the ether a free man. There was no way in hell he was going to say anything that would incriminate him in a crime that would garner him a whole other set of new charges. And fresh prison time.

Angie leaned farther forward, forcing him to look directly into her eyes again. "See, Milo, here's what I'm thinking—when you walked into this room, you just about wet yourself. Because I look just like someone you used to know, isn't that right?"

A muscle began to twitch in the corner of his left eye. Adrenaline pumped into Angie's blood. She kept her voice low, calm. "I resemble that woman you chased across the street, except for coloring maybe. The hair—hers was dark brown. Mine is red. Like the twins."

Her words seemed to make the last of the color drain completely from his face. The pace of the twitch at the corner of his eye doubled. He broke eye contact, stared hard at the table.

"And then when you saw this scar across my mouth, you knew, didn't you, exactly who I was. When you walked into this room, you looked like you'd seen a ghost, and you had. Because I've come back to haunt you, Milo Belkin. With this—"

She placed onto the table a printed copy of the crime scene photograph showing the blood-smeared outside door of the cradle. Beside it she placed another photograph—this one a close-up of a palm smear and clear bloody fingerprints on the door.

"This, Milo." She slid both prints right under his nose. "Whether you want to tell me what happened or not, *this* is proof that you were there that night in '86. You chased that woman and her children. You struggled with the woman outside that cradle as she fought to put both her girls inside where they would be safe. You fired shots—a Colt .45 maybe. You escaped in a black Chevrolet van."

His eyes darted back to her face.

Excitement cracked through her. "You cut my mouth, because my blood was on your hands when you touched those cradle doors as you battled to get me out of the bassinet. But then the church bells started ringing, and people began exiting the church across the alley. Maybe you heard sirens coming, too. And you grabbed the woman and the other child and ran. To the Chevy van waiting at the top of the alley on the back side of the hospital, and you fled the scene."

He lifted his hand and slowly wiped the perspiration from above his lip.

"All the old evidence from that crime scene is now being retested using new science," she said quietly. "That's how we got a hit on your prints left in that blood on the cradle door. That's how I found you, because your prints are in the system as a convicted felon. In a few days we'll also have DNA results from semen on a purple sweater that was found inside the cradle with the child. When that semen stain comes up as a match to your DNA profile, which will also be filed in the national DNA database for convicted offenders, you're going to be charged all over again, Milo Belkin. And this time"—she pushed her last photo toward him, the little lilac high-top that had washed up on the beach— "it'll be for murder." She paused. "Life."

His gaze darted to the photograph. His eyes widened. His lips parted. His breathing quickened.

"That's the remains of my sister's foot still in that shoe. You know exactly what happened to her. And to our young mother."

His eyes watered as he continued to stare at the image of the dirty little high-top. And he did *not* deny that the dark-haired woman was the mother of the two children. This set a fire under Angie.

She leaned forward and dropped her voice to a whisper. "I'm going to haunt you, Milo Belkin. I'm going to do whatever it takes to find out what happened that night. I'm going to get you. I'm going to nail your ass to the wall for what you did to my mother and sister."

"Guard," he said very quietly, his gaze still riveted on the photograph of the dismembered foot in its little shoe.

"And not only do I have more evidence coming in," she said, "but I'm also starting to remember. Things from that night. From before. On top of this, the RCMP has opened its own investigation into that little floating foot, and they've already connected it to me and the cradle case, so it's going to be better for you all around if you talk to me now."

"Guard," he growled loudly, surging to his feet. "Get me out. Now." As he turned away from her, Angie saw the tattoo on the side of his neck. A pale-blue crab.

The guard glanced at her. She nodded. The prisoner was led out.

As Angie watched Belkin go, her heart thumped in her rib cage. She could barely breathe. She had just looked into the black eyes of a man who'd seen her past. She'd smelled fresh blood on him, hot and raw in her nostrils. And like a pit bull with the taste of a red, meaty bone in her mouth, there was no way in hell that she was going to let this drop now.

CHAPTER 38

The energy in the briefing room was palpable as Maddocks entered carrying his laptop and files. He seated himself with the other officers around a long horseshoe-shaped table, and he nodded to Bowditch and Eden, who sat across from him. They were the only officers he recognized. Their response was tepid. At the head of the room, two large smart screens flanked a traditional whiteboard. Across the top of the whiteboard, in black marker, the words OPERATION AEGIS had been scrawled.

The briefing was to begin at 12:00 p.m., and that's precisely when a black-haired male officer in RCMP uniform—pale-gray shirt with lapel insignia, dark pressed pants, dark-blue tie, weapons belt—entered the room and went to the head of the table.

The uniform reminded Maddocks of something his facilitator had said back at Depot Division in Saskatchewan, where he'd undergone his police academy training. Day five was the first day that the cadets had been permitted to don their Mountie uniforms. Their facilitator had asked them to look down at their shirts and ask themselves why they were gray when most other police agencies around the world wore white or blue or black. He'd gone on to say that the cadets should see in their shirts a symbol of what law enforcement was about. Because policing doesn't always have black or white answers, he'd said. Sometimes the answers are gray, and in their future careers the days would come when they needed to look down at their shirts and remember that.

"Good afternoon, everyone," said the officer up front. "For those who don't know, I'm Sergeant Parr Takumi, in charge of Operation Aegis."

The man who'd withheld intel that could have kept Sophia Tarasov alive. Maddocks was dead keen to hear the extent of that intelligence now.

Takumi made introductions around the table. Present were RCMP members from gang crimes, human trafficking, vice, a representative from border security, and another from Interpol.

"And joining us today is Detective Sergeant Maddocks from the MVPD, where he's been leading an investigation into the Bacchanalian sex club aboard the *Amanda Rose*," Takumi said, meeting Maddocks's gaze. "Six barcoded underage sex workers were discovered forcibly confined aboard the *Amanda Rose*. They were taken into MVPD custody and held at an undisclosed location. One was found dead yesterday with her tongue excised. Operation Aegis has since asserted jurisdiction."

Not one around the table murmured or showed surprise, Maddocks noted. This team was clearly familiar with barcoded women, and with cut tongues. And his case. He flexed his hand under the table. It helped him remain outwardly cool, calm.

"Detective Maddocks's team is also continuing its investigation—and bringing possible further charges—in the homicides of two Victoria females in relation to the Bacchanalian Club. Some of the key suspects who were on the *Amanda Rose* have yet to cooperate fully with the MVPD, including two French nationals, Veronique Sabbonnier and Zaedeen Camus. Both helped harbor a serial rapist and lust killer on board the yacht, who came to be known as the Baptist. The murders of the two young Victoria women are unrelated to Operation Aegis. However, Sabbonnier and Camus remain persons of interest to Operation Aegis."

Takumi held his hand out toward another officer at the table. "We also welcome today Detective Corporal Nelson Rollins, who has been heading up Project Gateway, a year-long undercover investigation into Hells Angels collaboration with the longshoremen's union at the Port of Vancouver in facilitating the entry of Columbian narcotics and precursor chemicals. It was the work of Maddocks and the MVPD that resulted in Project Gateway being brought on board—the MVPD interview with Camus brought to light a link between the Hells Angels at the port and the Russian criminal network that Aegis has been investigating for the past eight months. Up until now we were not aware of this link," Takumi said.

"For those new to the table, Aegis was formed after the bodies of five unidentified young sex workers employed by Russian-affiliated clubs were found with their tongues cut out. One body was discovered by a barge operator in the Fraser River near the Vancouver airport early last winter. She was naked. COD was strangulation. She had a high level of alcohol in her system along with heroin. The body of a second woman turned up in a vacant Burnaby lot four months later. COD was heroin overdose. Both had their tongues cut out. Both had barcodes tattooed onto the backs of their necks. The tongue and barcode details were held back from the media. The same MO surfaced in Montreal last summer, where another barcoded female body was discovered with no tongue. Another turned up in Brooklyn, New York, and one in the desert outside Las Vegas last spring. The FBI also withheld details of the barcode tattoos and the missing tongues. No ID on the bodies. No DNA or prints or any other identifying factors in the system, until we got in touch with Interpol and linked two of the Jane Does with missing person cases out of Europe. The operating theory now is that these girls are coming from a Russian operation in Prague, which took over the sex trade in that city from Albanian organized crime. Contact with law enforcement in Prague, and again with Interpol in Europe, has confirmed that underage barcoded women are being sold or rented into sex slavery in the UK market and across Europe, and since last year, they've been showing up across Canada and now in the United States. But to date it is unknown how these women are trafficked from Prague—which serves as the supply hub—and it is unknown where these women have been entering North America." Takumi turned to Maddocks.

"Detective Maddocks here provided us with a theory that the barcoded females might be coming into the Port of Vancouver with seafood imports, both legal and illegal, from Vladivostok via South Korea and China. Project Gateway has since expanded its investigation specifically into the seafood trade and the vessels arriving from South Korea and China. It's early days yet, but it could provide the breakthrough we've all been looking for."

Takumi opened a file on the table in front of him. "Before we go to Detective Maddocks's briefing, a few quick updates." He scanned the top page in the file. "The five surviving barcoded victims from the *Amanda Rose* have all been moved to an undisclosed location on the mainland. None are speaking. Sabbonnier and Camus have been transferred to pretrial holding facilities, also here in the Lower Mainland." He scanned farther down the report. "Security footage from the hospital in Victoria has been examined by our techs. Footage was enhanced, but no biometric identification on the suspect was possible—he never allowed his face be captured on camera. Techs believe he was wearing a wig. Our suspect left no other forensic trace at the hospital scene that could identify him." Takumi looked up. "This suspect was experienced. A professional. Consistent with a Russian mob hit designed to send a message." He returned his attention to his report. "An autopsy was performed on Sophia Tarasov early this morning. COD is consistent with heroin overdose. Her tongue was excised antemortem—she was alive, likely lucid during the act."

Someone at the table cursed softly.

Takumi glanced up. "Detective Maddocks, will you brief the team on the MVPD angle?"

Maddocks leaned forward and cut right to it. "Until the death of Sophia Tarasov, the MVPD had no knowledge of the existence of, or the murders of, other barcoded women and thus no knowledge of the gravity of the threat against the six survivors in our custody, nor were we apprised of an international interagency investigation into the murders of barcoded females, until now."

Takumi glanced sharply up from what he was reading in the file. Maddocks continued. Takumi frowned.

"With this new intel, however, and with MVPD inclusion in Operation Aegis, we can now approach our investigation from fresh perspectives." He opened his laptop and linked it via Bluetooth to the smart screen. He clicked his keyboard to bring up the map of the Pacific and the Russian far east that he'd shown Bowditch and Eden earlier. He explained how Tarasov's description of crab tattoos on her assailants, plus Camus's statement that Hells Angels at the Vancouver port were involved, had led the MVPD to consider the possibility of a trafficking route aligned with illegal Russian king crab imports to North America.

He pulled up a second map on his computer, the one he'd withheld from Bowditch and Eden. A GIS rendering of the coastline from Washington, through BC, and up to Alaska.

Eden tapped the back of her pen on the table as she scowled at the map.

"Tarasov described being transported by a small boat from the container at the Port of Vancouver here"—Maddocks highlighted the port on the screen—"to a remote location somewhere along the coast, where the girls were held for what Tarasov believed was a few weeks. Tarasov couldn't recall how long the boat trip took to reach their destination— the women were all very ill and weak at that point—but it's to this remote coastal location that Veronique Sabbonnier flew in by floatplane to select her six girls from the nine who'd been transported by boat to the holding location. The other ten who came from Vladivostok were taken elsewhere, possibly by truck. Sabbonnier then flew the six females blindfolded to the *Amanda Rose* in Victoria. That flight by floatplane took maybe an hour or two. Tarasov was shaky on the timeline. Which puts this entire coastal area into play." He clicked a key on his computer. An area of his map washed with yellow. It included Vancouver Island, the Gulf Islands, the San Juan Islands, the entire British Columbia mainland coast, plus the Alaska panhandle and parts of northern Washington State.

Eden said curtly, "That entire area is riddled with inlets, coves, islands, endless uninhabited wilderness." She was clearly irked that Maddocks had not given this information to them yesterday. Had he done so, he'd likely *not* be sitting at this table today, part of Operation Aegis.

"Did Tarasov offer *anything* else that could narrow it down?" she said.

"Not before she was murdered," Maddocks said with hard look at Eden, whose mouth twitched in response. "Apart from a description of their accommodations and an old Russian-speaking woman in black who attended to them. Plus a vague description of a large Caucasian male, maybe in his late forties or fifties, perhaps early sixties, who'd worn a hood over his head and dimmed the lights when he came to 'test the merchandise.' Tarasov described the same crab tattoo on his neck." Maddocks clicked his keys and brought up an identikit image of a man.

"This came in after we'd already transferred the case files to Aegis," he said.

Takumi's attention shot to the male face on the screen. The cop's features turned dark. He glanced at Maddocks.

"This is the description of the male suspect in Tarasov's death. It was provided by our MVPD officer who was stationed outside the hospital ward when the man entered wearing a medical coat."

The group around the table regarded the image in silence. It showed the square face of a male in what could be his late fifties without any overtly distinguishing features. Eyes evenly spaced. Straight nose. Balanced lips, neither fleshy nor thin. Average chin. Caucasian. "Unfortunately, our witness could not provide eye color and is uncertain as to how accurate this identikit is. But it shows what our suspect is not."

Takumi cleared his throat. "This is all valuable intel. Up until this point, it was thought that the girls found here in BC might have entered North America via the East Coast and been trafficked through Montreal over land or by air. Until now, the Port of Vancouver and the Hells Angels in particular had not been identified as players or collaborators with the Russians. Tarasov's and Camus's statements have put this all directly into play. Along with that coastline." He pointed to the yellow area on Maddocks's map. "Somewhere in that area there is a holding facility, a key North American hub, where these girls from Prague are being processed and sold into service. We need to find that location." Takumi turned to Rollins.

"Detective Rollins, can you brief us on the latest intel to come via Project Gateway?"

Maddocks disconnected his computer from the smart screen, allowing for Rollins to make his own laptop connection.

Rollins leaned forward so that all around the table could see him properly.

"We were informed of the potential sex trafficking route being linked to Russian-Chinese-Korean seafood import connections by Sergeant Bowditch late yesterday afternoon. Our officers have since worked around the clock collating port data within the possible time frame that Tarasov and the other barcoded women might have docked with cargo vessels. We have identified two companies of prime interest, Atlantis Seafood Imports and Orca Products. Both received shipments in that time frame of king crab product labeled as having been produced or made in either China or South Korea." Rollins hit a key, and the profiles of the two seafood import companies displayed on the screen.

"Both companies are owned by a complex tangle of subsidiary holdings. We have techs presently untangling the ownership structure and attempting to attach specific names to bank accounts. Additionally, we've put round-the-clock surveillance on the warehousing facilities of both outfits, and on the managers of those facilities. We've also had contact from our deep cover officer who infiltrated the longshoremen's union nine months ago. He reports there is word among longshoremen affiliated with the Hells Angels that a 'Special A' shipment is due. The guys are apparently on edge. Potentially the shipment is one of trafficked women. And potentially the women are being held in cargo aboard one of the ships still awaiting port entry due to the strike." He cleared his throat. "We're working with the requisite authorities to gain access to the international vessels currently anchored in the Burrard, but any move will need to be made in concert with other UC operations so that we do not tip off the suspects."

Takumi interjected. "This cannot be stressed enough. No move can be made. *Zero* information can escape this room. Not only will it compromise the safety of our UC guys, but we also want to follow this 'Special A' shipment through to its maximum conclusion—the location of that coastal hub where the Sophia Tarasov and the other barcoded females were processed and resold." He turned to Rollins.

"Thank you, Detective. In the meantime, Aegis has its own UC officer out of Quebec, where he infiltrated a Russian organized crime ring two years ago. The same ring manages the club where one of our deceased barcode victims worked. The UC was subsequently seconded to Operation Aegis. He traveled west and has now gained access to a Russian club here in East Vancouver that is loosely affiliated to the Montreal club. The supper club and adult entertainment venue is called

Club Orange B. It's located in East Vancouver, and it's been a gathering place of suspected criminals with Russian backgrounds since the 1970s. Intel from our UC is consistent with intel from the docks—something big is coming. Soon. But nobody seems to know exactly when. Which is consistent with the port strike theory. Those at the club believed to be connected are reportedly tense, impatient. The longshoremen's union has been offered a contract by the port, and it's possible an agreement will be ratified by the union members soon and the strike will be over. As soon as this occurs, those ships will start coming in. We need to be ready. To facilitate intelligence gathering, early this morning, at 3:50 a.m., our UC managed to cause a small fire inside a supply room at Club Orange B, which set off fire alarms. Our surveillance team moved in under cover of responding firefighters who cleared the premises and cut electrical supply while our team installed surveillance devices in key areas of the club identified by the UC. It was a quick operation with minimal damage to the supply room. We now have live surveillance footage from inside the club."

"And the Russians don't suspect anything after the fire?" Maddocks said.

All eyes at the table glanced his way.

"We have no indication at this point that they do," Takumi said. "The installation appears to have gone smoothly. The live surveillance footage from inside the club is being monitored 24-7 by a surveillance team in the building across the street. They're watching for indication that a 'shipment' is imminent. It's possible that this club is connected to the holding facility that Tarasov described."

With that, Takumi shut down the briefing. As everyone cleared out, he called Maddocks over and handed him a fat dossier.

"Now that you have requisite security clearance, this is to catch you up. Background." His narrow black eyes bored into Maddocks, his energy visceral. "Thank you for joining us."

Maddocks took the dossier. "The inclusion is appreciated."

But Takumi held on to his end of the dossier a second longer. "Nothing leaves Aegis, understand? You use this information to steer your local investigation, but you do not give out or leak this information."

Maddocks held the man's eyes and said nothing. He didn't have to—the lines in the sand between the two men were clear. Neither fully trusted the other. Takumi released his grip on the file.

"I'll be up to speed by morning," Maddocks said, and then left the room.

Takumi watched him go.

CHAPTER 39

Maddocks cracked open the lid of his pad Thai noodle carton. He inserted wooden chopsticks and delivered a helping to his mouth. Chewing, he popped open a can of cold pop. He hadn't eaten since grabbing a coffee and doughnut on his way to the heliport. He swallowed his mouthful, took a deep swig of his drink, and opened the dossier Takumi had given him in order to familiarize himself with the scope and details of the massive Aegis investigation. To do this, Maddocks had commandeered a small L-shaped workstation in the corner of the incident room at the Surrey RCMP station where he was partially screened from the rest of the bustling room by a partition. In front of him was a phone, to his right a computer, to which he'd been given a security code unique to his badge number. The computer was linked to a confidential database of files and other relevant documentation associated with the operation.

Grabbing another chopstickful of noodles, he ate as he began to read. A noodle escaped his sticks and fell to the floor, and for a second he felt a knee-jerk instinct to tell Jack-O to get it. He already missed the irascible three-legged beast. And he worried a little because Holgersen had offered to babysit the dog, at least until Maddocks knew how long he might be stationed in Surrey and could thus make longer-term arrangements. Maddocks wasn't certain that Holgersen had ever cared for an animal. But he'd vowed to take Jack-O with him to the station every day, where the dog could sleep in his basket under the desk in the incident room—as long as no one complained. He was an old hound. He didn't need much exercise and was more than happy to make up for time spent as a stray on cold streets by sleeping in a warm bed. As long as Holgersen budgeted for regular bathroom breaks, took him home at night, and fed and watered him, Jack-O should be okay. Besides, Maddocks told himself, those two suited each other. He figured like Jack-O, Holgersen had a dark and dismal past that no one could know about, and both were twitchy and slightly off-center because of it.

Maddocks ran through the content list of the dossier, then turned to the intelligence section that listed suspected Russian organized crime members and associates along with their allied businesses and holdings.

Strings of names filled the pages and connected in a series of family-tree-style diagrams that detailed a suspected web linking across the country from Vancouver, to Toronto, to Montreal, and down into the States.

He focused on the Vancouver section and began to peruse the supporting material compiled by RCMP and FBI analysts based on intel from various investigations and UC operations in both countries.

As Takumi had noted, Russian organized crime in Vancouver tended to circle around Club Orange B—possibly ironically named after a discontinued food dye that was used to color hot dog sausage casings bright red until the FDA declared it unsafe due to the presence of carcinogenic contaminants. Maddocks snorted—the lethal Reds. Ruskies, as Holgersen would have it. The mob was known by various other colloquialisms, including the Red Octopus. Maddocks scooped up his last mouthful of Thai noodles.

The intel noted that Club Orange B offered exotic dancers and Russian cuisine, and it ran an escort agency from upstairs rooms—a front for prostitution.

Maddocks skimmed the information. Like the seafood import companies mentioned in the briefing, Club Orange B was held by a complex assortment of numbered companies and holdings. Numerous criminal investigations and criminal charges against the club had never resulted in anything of significance sticking, although individual members had been convicted of various felonies. The club's legal business appeared to be handled primarily by one firm—Abramov, Maizel, and Dietch.

Maddocks turned to the information on the law firm and whistled to himself. They had branch offices in Vancouver, Montreal, Ottawa, and Toronto and had defended several high-profile criminal cases across the country—those tried had been suspected of Russian mob links. He reached for his pop and took a drink as he turned the page, running through the list of cases. The list went back decades, with the firm adding or subtracting partners to the title as the years passed, but always two names remained consistent—Abramov and Maizel, passing the banner on to sons. And the farther back in time, the smaller the cases, but even in those cases many of their clients were highlighted in the dossier as being—or having been—suspected mob affiliates. The firm was founded in the late seventies by Abramov, a Russian expat who'd emigrated from Israel. He appeared to have started small, handling cases for fellow Russian expats. The early cases ranged from robbery, to sexual assault and battery, to illegal weapons and narcotics possession. Over the years, Abramov had taken on meatier criminal battles until he'd built his company into a massive outfit that defended and managed alleged mob business.

Maddocks ran through the list of Abramov's early cases, and . . . stilled.

He reread the name of a client charged for sexual assault and battery in 1991. *Milo Belkin.* Flagged as a mob affiliate. Maddocks's pulse quickened—*the felon Angie was going to see in prison.* The same man whose prints had been on the outside of the angel's cradle door in 1986. Maddocks checked his watch. *Shit.* Angie would have already interviewed Belkin by now—she'd be on her return trip to Vancouver. He quickly scanned farther down the document.

Belkin's 1991 sexual assault charges had mysteriously been dropped just days before he was due to appear in court when the complainant— Nadia Moss, an exotic dancer at Club Orange B—had recanted everything, saying she'd mistakenly identified the defendant. Moss had later ended up as a bar manager at the club.

Abramov was also the lawyer who'd later defended Belkin in the 1993 drug bust and shooting charges. Additionally, Abramov served as defense counsel in a second trial for one of Belkin's accomplices arrested and charged in the drug bust—Semyon Zagorsky.

Belkin had refused to identify two other suspects who'd fled the scene in a black Chevrolet cargo van, one of whom was believed to have killed a VPD officer in the shoot-out. Belkin was up for release in six months, having served time almost to his WED date, no doubt because he'd refused to cooperate with law enforcement on the identity of a cop killer. This told Maddocks something—if the drug haul confiscated in the bust *had* belonged to the Russian mob, Belkin had remained loyal throughout his sentence. This meant he was likely going to be repaid for his loyalty and looked after by the mob once he got out.

Semyon Zagorsky, his accomplice, had been slapped with a longer sentence than Belkin. The prosecution had successfully argued that the ricocheting .22 slug that had hit an innocent bystander in the spine came from Zagorsky's gun—he'd been the only one firing a .22 pistol. Zagorsky, too, had refused to name his associates who'd fled the scene. While his WED date was some years out, he was up for a parole hearing in two days.

Maddocks swung his chair around to face the computer and logged in with his access code. He wanted more detailed information on Belkin and Zagorsky. He typed MILO BELKIN. A mug shot of the convicted felon came up instantly, with details of his arrests and charges. A paleblue crab tattoo decorated the left side of his neck. Maddocks's mouth went dry with adrenaline. He punched in SEMYON ZAGORSKY. Same tattoo, but smaller and on his wrist. His name had been flagged as being part of an active new investigation. Maddocks hit the link.

A chill washed through him.

The civilian bystander who'd been rendered a paraplegic by the .22 bullet from Zagorsky's gun was Stirling Harrison. He had perished just three nights ago in a gas line explosion that resulted in a house fire in Squamish, a town along the highway heading north out of Vancouver into the mountains. His wife, Elaine, also died in the fire. Both Elaine and Stirling Harrison—parents of toddlers at the time of Stirling's injury— had delivered powerful victim impact statements at Zagorsky's sentencing. And they'd appeared at each and every one of Zagorsky's parole board hearings since, delivering similar impact statements.

Until now.

Now they would not be giving victim impact statements at Zagorsky's parole hearing in two days because they were dead.

Which meant that this time Zagorsky might actually prove eligible, since he appeared to be a model prisoner in every respect and had been moved into the general population section a few years back.

Maddocks reached for his can of pop and tilted it to his mouth before realizing it was empty. He set it down absently, scrolled farther. The house fire "accident" was classic mob MO. According to the intel on the screen, similar gas explosions had destroyed rival mob businesses in Montreal for years. The Stirling blaze was currently being investigated for proof of mob connections. This fact was marked as classified.

The mob had killed a paraplegic and his wife in order to help Zagorsky gain parole? Payment for his silence?

Maddocks sat back, rubbed his jaw.

What in the hell had Angie gotten into? These guys were lethal. Her questioning Belkin would only threaten him. Or already had. An inmate hitting his WED date was not going to welcome fresh allegations. And if she let on that she'd begun remembering things from the past . . . the Stirling house fire demonstrated the lengths the Russians might go to shut her up.

Maddocks came abruptly to his feet. He stared out of a narrow window overlooking a street, his brain racing. This was top security intel. The only reason he had access was because of his clearance for Aegis. Belkin and Zagorsky had been incarcerated for years—they were likely in no way directly connected to the barcode trafficking case, but they *were* connected to the mob. And leaking information from the Aegis intel files would be a serious breach of protocol. It could cost Maddocks his career. He could face criminal charges if it was discovered that he'd done it.

He couldn't tell her.

He also couldn't *not* warn her. He had to find a way to get Angie to stand down, but he knew Angie—she wouldn't heed some unsubstantiated warning. She'd want facts, proof.

Conflict torqued through him. He glanced at his watch, tension heating his body.

Her life could be at risk—these guys meant business.

CHAPTER 40

It was late afternoon Saturday at the Vancouver city library. Angie had returned from the Hansen Correctional Centre and was combing through the microfilm copies of newspaper archives from 1993. Her brain was hopping. There was not a doubt in her mind that Milo Belkin had known who she was the instant he'd laid eyes on her. Which *had* to mean that he'd known Angie's mother—that she bore a striking genetic resemblance to her biological parent. She could not even begin to articulate how this had rocked her. It was like she *belonged*. To someone. Was truly genetically connected to some family tree out there. She'd had a sister, who now needed justice. It altered every perception Angie had ever held about her own self-identity.

Her goal now was to find any and every old newspaper article associated with Milo Belkin's drug bust in 1993, his criminal associates, the deceased VPD officer, the injured bystander, and the ensuing court case. She would then search for more on the burned-out van with the Colt .45 found in 1998.

When Angie returned to her hotel tonight, she'd work through the evidence on the memory stick that Jacob Anders had given her, but this had to be done first, in part because of the library hours, and also because she had to be back in Victoria before Monday morning to endure another week of her discipline. She glanced at her watch, antsy for Anders to call with DNA results—anything extra that she could use to pressure Belkin in addition to the fingerprint evidence. But it was way too early. Those results could be several days out yet. She was now in a race against time with Pietrikowski, because he'd be getting the same DNA results from his lab soon, too. And when he found that she'd already hit up Belkin, he *would* take action. And that action could involve Vedder, because Angie had used her police ID to interrogate an inmate while confined to an office job on probation. She'd be in big shit, but having looked into Belkin's black eyes and seen his shock . . . it was worth it.

Her cell rang on the table beside her, and she lunged for it, hoping it might be Anders, but an unidentified number displayed. Angie frowned and connected the call.

"Pallorino."

"It's me."

"Maddocks?" A punch of warmth went through Angie. She'd called him earlier to let him know how it had gone with Belkin but had once again been kicked to voicemail. "What's with the different number?"

"Burner. Personal call." His voice was clipped, terse.

A whisper of warning slid through Angie. "I tried to call—"

"Was in a meeting. Been tasked to an interagency force based out of Surrey."

"Surrey? What? Which force? *Why?*"

"It's something that grew out of the Victoria investigation. Look, I can't talk about it, Ange—not on the phone. I—"

"It grew out of the barcode girls? The *Amanda Rose* investigation?"

He cleared his throat. She could hear what sounded like a television set murmuring in the background.

"Where are you, Maddocks? What's going on?"

"I'm in a hotel. In Surrey. I don't know how long I'll be stationed out here. Tell me how it went with Belkin." His tone brooked no argument, and there was an edge in his voice she hadn't heard before.

Surrey. Where Sabrina lives. His old neighborhood—he is stationed out there while I'm heading back to the island to drive a desk. That initial punch of warmth turned cool. "Where's Jack-O?"

"With Holgersen. For a while, at least until I know how long I might be out here. Angie—"

"You trust *Holgersen* with your dog? Why not me?"

"'Cause you're not there, Angie. And Holgersen probably likes Jack-O more than you do."

Irritable now, she said, "What about Ginny? I thought you didn't want to leave her alone?" She cursed to herself even as the words came out of her mouth. This was not like her, but she couldn't seem to stop herself. It struck her hard and sudden: *I've already allowed myself to fall too deep for this guy. I'm feeling bitter, jealous, possessive. That's not cool, and it makes no sense.*

"Ginn's fine," he said. "She wants me to do this—pursue this to the end."

"So it *does* have to do with the barcode case, then? With human trafficking, sex slavery. On an international level, because the barcodes are all foreign, and that's why you've been roped into an interagency force out of Surrey. Have you got an ID on them now?"

"Listen, I don't have much time. Tell me about Belkin," he said again, terse, cutting her off.

Her jaw tightened. She inhaled deeply. "Hang on a sec." She took her laptop and bag and moved to a quiet alcove in the library from where she could watch her notebook, which she left at the microfilm station to reserve her place. Seating herself in a deep chair designed for comfy reading, she described her meeting with Belkin, keeping her voice low as she watched the rain coming down behind the library's floor-to-ceiling windows.

"He recognized me, Maddocks. Without question. He knew instantly who I was. Which convinces me that he knew my mother and that I look just like her. He *knows* what happened that night. His fingerprints prove he was there. It's all inside his brain, and he won't spill. I just need to find a way to crack him open, make him tell me who I am and what happened to my family. Right now he's shit-scared. He knows that what I have could put him right back into prison, maybe for murder this time. For life."

Maddocks was silent for a beat, and then he said very quietly, "The ink on the left side of Belkin's neck was a blue crab."

Angie frowned. "I didn't tell you about a tattoo."

He swore softly. A cold, inky feeling of disquiet feathered into her chest. "What is this?"

Another moment of hesitation. The chill of disquiet snaked deeper. "Maddocks, *talk* to me."

"You need to stop, Angie. Now. You need to stand down from your personal investigation. You have to trust me on this—you're in danger if you continue. *Especially* if you're threatening Belkin's freedom. And I'm not just talking your job. I'm talking about your life."

Whoa. Angie blinked, reeling at the blow he'd just delivered out of left field. His secrecy didn't help. It underscored the sinister tone of his warning. And it got her back up—the fact he was not being open with her. She'd made a damn fine detective because she would not—*could not*—drop a puzzle until it was solved. The more complex the problem, the more it fired her to find the solution. Angie leaned aggressively forward in the chair.

"You can't do this to me, tell me to take something on blind faith like this—give me a warning that my life is in danger and not say why."

Silence.

She surged to her feet, clamped her arm tightly across her chest, and stood in front of the window streaked with rain. "Maddocks, what are you telling me? Is . . . is this because you came across some privileged intel associated with this task force? Something on Belkin?"

"I'm serious, Angie, I'm not at liberty to talk. But I'm asking you, please—*leave* this alone. At least for now. Do the right thing. Get the first ferry home and be at that social media desk on Monday morning. Keep your head down, and . . . keep vigilant. Lock your doors."

Tightening her grip on the phone, she closed her eyes and inhaled deeply through her nose. Her brain scrambled to piece facts together. "Okay," she said slowly. "So you came across some privileged information, and it involves Milo Belkin. You know about Belkin's tattoo, and it's key somehow. It's a symbol of affiliation to something, maybe a gang? And Belkin and this tattoo somehow ties to human trafficking at an international level, because that's the root of your barcode investigation. And now, because it's gone international in scope, and because the nature of global sex trafficking generally involves organized crime at a high level, there was probably already an interagency investigation open. And you've been co-opted into this investigation, which requires top-level security clearance. Right?"

Silence.

It fueled her frustration. It also told her she was on the right track.

"The patent prints confirm that Belkin touched that bloodied cradle door in '86, Maddocks. He was there. He *knew* my mother. He knows what happened to my mouth. Seven years after I was found, he's busted in a drug shoot-out with narcotics worth $9 million hidden in a cube truck. There's a level of organized crime that goes into that kind of haul, too. Yet Belkin never snitches—never reveals the identity of his associates, one of whom shot and killed a VPD cop. Are you telling me that Belkin—or his group—was also involved in organized sex trafficking back then, in 1986? That my mother might have been trafficked . . ." It hit her. She placed a palm across her brow. "Jesus, Maddocks, I remember *Polish* words, a woman screaming at me in Polish to stay inside that cradle and stay quiet. We were foreign." She swore as possibilities clicked into place. "When the forensic artist's sketch of me ran in all the papers, no one came forward. Not one soul in this city, or even the country, came to claim me as family. We might not have even been in the country legally—*that* would explain the dead silence, wouldn't it? That would explain why I couldn't speak any English to the nurses . . . why my life could have been so bad that my kid memory wiped itself clean in an act of pure survival."

Maddocks cursed on his end. Angie heard movement and what sounded like a door closing. The sound of the television grew suddenly muted. When he spoke again, his voice was lower, quieter. "Angie, I'm not going to tell you anything that's not already out there. And the only reason I'm saying anything at all is because I *need* you to stand down, and I know that you won't do it without some solid argument." He wavered, then said, "When you return to Victoria, to the station, you'll hear that one of the barcode girls was murdered in hospital while under MVPD guard—"

"*What?* Which one?"

"The eldest. She was the only one who talked to me. She gave a statement and was killed that same night, in her hospital bed. Her tongue was cut out while she was still alive."

Angie swallowed, feeling ill.

"Then this interagency task force under the auspices of the RCMP swooped in and asserted jurisdiction—took her body right off O'Hagan's table, kicked out our forensics guys, took possession of all evidence."

Her heart quickened. "How's Belkin connected?"

He cleared his throat. "Listen, I can't—"

"Maddocks, don't do this to me. Is there anything else in the public realm that you can clue me in to—anything I could conceivably have come across myself?"

"Angie—"

"Jeezus, come on, please! Give me something. Because there is no way in hell I'm going to just stand down now without a more compelling reason, Maddocks."

Another curse. A beat of silence. Then he said quietly, "This will be in the media—public knowledge—a couple in Squamish burned to death in a house fire three nights ago. The fire is thought to have been caused by a propane line explosion." He paused. "The deceased male was a paraplegic named Stirling Harrison. He was the innocent bystander who was injured in the 1993 Belkin drug shoot-out." Another pause. "Follow Belkin's legal counsel."

Her mind hustled to join these disparate pieces into a cohesive picture, but she couldn't. Not yet. But she could look this stuff up.

"Look, I know you, Angie. I know that you want to resist, to march to your own drum here, but I'm sticking my neck out. I'm telling you this because . . ." He swore again, viciously this time. "Because I think I'm coming to love you, okay? And I *care*, dammit. I want you around and in my life—I want to find you safely in Victoria when I get back. I want you around after your probation. I want to . . . to share"—his voice caught, turned hoarse—"spring, summer with you, Angie, get those kayaks out. Get out onto the water—work on the old boat, have barbecues on the deck, have you and Ginny there with me. I want to spend fall and next winter with you, dammit. I want a normal relationship when things settle down. I want us to see if this can work. And you need to stay alive."

Shock slammed through her. Emotion pricked into her eyes.

His dream. The one he's been trying to salvage. His old wooden boat, family . . . his vision of sailing up the coast. He wants me in it.

"Be there for me, okay? I'm here for you."

Angie couldn't speak—her voice was choked in a ball in her throat.

"I trust you," he said quietly. "I trust you'll do the right thing."

I could screw up his career if I act on something privileged that he told me.

She pressed her hand over her mouth. She didn't know how to handle this. His words, so rough with emotion, had come out of the blue, and they were dizzying and they stole all her breath and she couldn't think. They stripped her to the core. A maelstrom of feelings burned in her chest—fondness, fear, sadness, ferocity. "I . . . I've got to go, Maddocks," she said quickly and hung up.

Angie stood there, rain streaming down the windows as the sky grew blacker and lower and an evening mist crept in. A precipice—she felt as though she were balanced at the very edge of a cliff and below her was a black maw and she was being asked to lean in, and to let herself fall into that unknown.

Trust me.

He wasn't just talking about the case. He'd asked her to take a leap, and she didn't know if she could. Or even *who* she wanted to be. Whether she could be anyone at all if she did not have knowledge of who she really was. Her very sense of self-identity had been ripped out from under her when she'd learned that she'd been abandoned in that cradle, and then again when she'd been told that she'd had a twin. How could she love him, wholly, if she herself was broken?

She *had* to find her other half—her twin—first. She *had* to seek and define that dark shadow that haunted her whenever she looked in the mirror—the owner of that little lost foot.

An old rhyme came to mind, as it had before, usually after she'd hit the sex club on the hunt for an anonymous lay.

> *Fractured face*
> *in the mirror,*
> *you are my disgrace,*
> *a sinner.*

No. Not a sinner in the mirror. *My sister. My missing half. My DNA. Out there somewhere.*

Rain lashed suddenly against the library windows, and wind whistled through the building pillars outside. In the sound of the wind she heard the small voice whispering again.

Come . . . come playum dum grove. Help. Help me, Roksana.

Maddocks glared at his reflection in the hotel bathroom mirror, his hands braced on the vanity, his burner cell lying in front of him next to the basin, the television murmuring in the next room. He'd left the station to come and call Angie in privacy. He'd said stuff he hadn't intended to. The words, feelings, had just come out of his mouth, almost of their own volition, and now they could not be put back or unheard. And while he hadn't meant to say them, he meant them—he could not handle losing her, being responsible for not warning her. Like Takumi had not warned him of the dangers facing Sophia Tarasov and the other barcode girls.

But was it enough?

Would he regret not being harsher, more forcible? Giving her more information? Or less? Would he pay for not reporting to Operation Aegis what he knew from Angie—that Milo Belkin was connected to the 1986 cradle case and the disappearance of a little Polish girl, a twin whose foot had been found in Tsawwassen last week? And that Angie Pallorino and her sister and their mother might have been victims of Russian human trafficking involving Belkin and his accomplices?

Would it come back to bite him that he'd not reported to Aegis that Angie had visited with that inmate?

He dragged both his hands over his head, reminding himself that Belkin had been incarcerated for decades. It was unlikely that he was actively linked to anything directly relating to the Aegis investigation. It was simply his connection to organized criminals that put her in jeopardy—the fact the mob looked after their own and might have killed Stirling Harrison and his wife to do so.

And if Pietrikowski got his act together, the DNA from Voight's old case files would soon lead him to Belkin anyway.

Maddocks just had to trust that Angie would listen to him—that she'd see the links in the clues he'd given, see the danger, and shut up and sit tight.

CHAPTER 41

A female voice sounded through the library intercom. "The Vancouver Library will be closing in twenty minutes. If everyone could please finish off . . ."

But Angie barely heard. A dog with a bone now, she tuned out the woman's voice and quickly punched into a search engine a series of keywords: HOMICIDE, SEX WORKERS, TONGUES CUT.

She hit ENTER.

A series of links to news stories populated her laptop screen, among them references to a mythological method of murder called the Colombian necktie. She ignored those links and clicked on a CBC news story out of Montreal. Last summer the naked and badly bruised body of an unidentified female had been discovered in a vacant lot with her tongue excised. She was a dancer employed by a Russian nightclub with known mob connections. There was speculation that the woman's murder had been a mob hit, the excised tongue sending some kind of warning. Angie searched deeper for more news on this homicide, but she found nothing more in the media. Granted, her search was cursory, but on the surface it appeared that no arrests had been made, and there was no coverage of the body ever having been identified.

She drummed her fingers on the desk. If this task force that Maddocks had been detailed to was top-level clearance, and if this missing-tongue murder fell under that task force purview, it was likely that further details—like a barcode tattoo, perhaps—would have been withheld from the media.

"The library will shutting in ten minutes. If everyone could please proceed with their books to checkout . . ."

Urgency crackled through her. She could pursue this from her hotel later, but she was unable to stop.

Follow Belkin's legal counsel.

Hurriedly she typed, DEFENSE COUNSEL MILO BELKIN.

Angie clicked open the first news link in the search results—a news story covering Belkin's drug bust trial. His defense counsel was Viktor Abramov of the firm Abramov, Maizel, and Dietch.

She typed into the search field, ABRAMOV MAIZEL DIETCH.

Surprise whipped through her as the results populated her screen. The same counsel had defended Belkin's drug bust co-accused, Semyon Zagorsky. The firm, it appeared, was infamous for its defense of alleged Russian mobsters in high-profile trials in Montreal and in other parts of the country, including Vancouver.

Lawyers for the Russian mob? Is that what Maddocks was telling me? That Belkin and Zagorsky were known members of Russian organized crime, and their thug connections on the outside might have burned Zagorsky's paraplegic victim to death?

Hurriedly, Angie typed, VIKTOR ABRAMOV. She narrowed the search field to the eighties and nineties. She clicked open a 1991 digitized news article from the *East Side Weekly* on an exotic dancer's "mistake."

Club Orange B Dancer Retracts Rape Allegations

EAST VANCOUVER: Days before East Vancouver resident Milo Belkin was due in court on sexual

assault and battery charges, exotic dancer Nadia
Moss told reporters that she had mistakenly identified her attacker, who raped and badly beat her
with a baseball bat—breaking her nose, cheek-
bone, arm, and leg, and leaving her for dead in an
alley near the club at which she worked. Moss had
been due to take the stand at Belkin's trial when
she retracted her statement to police. East Van
activists had taken up Moss's cause and provided
her with pro-bono counsel.

Vancouver police, however, are not looking for new
suspects, said VPD media liaison Leanne Benton.

Moss, who is slowly recovering from her injuries,
now works as a bar manager at Club Orange B.
She told reporters she is thankful to her employers, who stood by her and who offered her a position that would help her recover fully from her
injuries.

Belkin's counsel, Viktor Abramov, said that his client has always maintained his innocence and is
grateful that Moss had the courage to come forward and admit her error.

Angie frowned. A club promotion for Nadia Moss as payoff for
withdrawing her assault and rape charges? She typed, SQUAMISH GAS
EXPLOSION FIRE, DEATH.

Top of the list was a recent *Vancouver Province* article. She clicked
it open and read.

Couple Die in House Fire

SQUAMISH: Firefighters responded to a blaze in
the Valleycliffe subdivision in the early hours of
Wednesday morning. A 9-1-1 call was received at
3:10 a.m. after residents in Eagle Street heard an
explosion, then looked out of their windows to see
the property of Stirling and Elaine Harrison fully en-
gulfed in flames. The badly burned bodies of the
Harrison couple were discovered in the aftermath
of the blaze. Arson investigators were called in, but
so far Squamish fire chief Eddie Beam is saying
that it looks like a tragic accident.

A witness who tried to enter the burning house said
he'd seen Elaine Harrison out on her lawn earlier,
but she'd reentered the burning building in a bid to
save her paraplegic husband.

Angie typed STIRLING HARRISON into the search field. Her heart
kicked at what came up—articles referencing the November 20 drug
bust twenty-five years ago and the arrests of Milo Belkin and his associate Semyon Zagorsky.

Stirling Harrison had indeed been the innocent bystander who'd
caught a ricocheting .22 slug in the back, which had put him in a
wheelchair for the rest of his life.

"The library doors are closing . . ."

Angie scanned quickly through the articles, heat prickling over her
skin as she read. Shortly after receiving the news that her husband would
never walk again and that he would lose his high-paying job as a BC
Hydro technician who worked at high elevations repairing and main-
taining the province's hydro towers, Elaine Harrison tearfully vowed

to a journalist that she and her husband, a young father, would give the most powerful of victim impact statements at Semyon Zagorsky's sentencing. Zagorsky was the one, she'd told the reporter, who'd been shooting the .22 pistol in the East Vancouver gun battle.

Elaine Harrison had additionally promised that she would push her husband's wheelchair into every single parole board hearing that Zagorsky ever qualified for—and she and her husband would both make it known to the parole board how Zagorsky had destroyed their livelihood and their family as they'd known it.

Angie searched deeper, then froze.

Semyon Zagorsky was currently incarcerated at Kelvin Maximum Security Institution in the BC interior. He was up for a parole board hearing in two days. And this time, his victims—Stirling and Elaine Harrison—would not be present to object. Because they were dead.

Angie punched in the name SEMYON ZAGORSKY.

A news photo from the time of his arrest took shape on her monitor.

Her heart beat in her throat. She stared at the image. Could not breathe. A high-pitched ringing began in her ears, and her vision narrowed, a halo of blackness closing in as she swirled down, down, down . . . into that dark place of her childhood where Alex had taken her with hypnosis. Suddenly she was there again, among the giant cedars, running on sunlight, upon dandelions, salt wind through her long hair, her dress billowing like a tent in the breeze. Glimpses of blue ocean between the trunks. Little shoes ahead of her—she was chasing them. Legs, white under a pink dress with frills, pumped ahead of her, darting through the emerald grass.

"*Mila!*" she called. "*Stop, Mila, wait. . .*" A tinkle of childish laughter. "*Berries, berries, blackberries . . . baskets . . . two little kittens . . .*"

"*Happy birthday, little ones!*" The male voice stopped the scene dead. Everything went gray. Then out of the grayness the box came at her. Shoe box. Bound by a big pale-purple ribbon. Huge hands held it, hair on the backs of those hands. A crab drawing on the inside of one wrist.

Pretty crab. Pale-blue crab, like a spider. And suddenly she was looking at the underwater footage on Jacob Anders's live feed, and down
from the corner swooped the octopus. Slammed over the Dungeness
crab. Killed it and devoured it a mushrooming cloud of silt with sea
lice scattering.

Fear closed a noose around Angie's throat. Slowly, very slowly, she
glanced up from the blue crab on white skin, all the way up. Into the
eyes of the man who was offering her the box with the purple ribbon.
Twinkly eyes. Blue like the crab. Bright blue. Friendly. Kind. She looked
deep into the piercing, sparkling blue eyes . . . and right into the face
that was staring out of her computer.

A hand slammed down on her shoulder. A voice boomed in her
ears, inside her head. *"For my Mila, and a matching pair for Roksana."*
He had a smile so big and broad. It put warmth in her heart. But . . .
all of a sudden she was running from him. Terror in her stomach. The
forest and sunshine and ocean spiraling into a kaleidoscopic vortex,
sucking her away . . . and she was in the snow . . . Running . . . She
saw those shoes running in the snow . . . *Home, home, home, got to get
HOME . . . "Alex, get me HOME!"*

Uciekaj, uciekaj! . . . Wskakuj do srodka, szybko! . . . Siedz cicho! A
flash of silver, pain . . . Angie screamed . . .

"Ma'am. Ma'am." The hand shook her shoulder harder. "Are you
all right?"

She blinked. Her gaze shot up. It was the librarian. A young guy.
Dark hair. Worry in his face. "Do you want me to call for help?"

"I . . . I, God, no." She jerked to her feet. Her skin was wet. She
could smell her own sweat, fear on herself. She slapped closed her laptop
and started blindly gathering up her things. "I'm fine."

"You screamed."

"I . . . I'm so sorry." She quickly slipped her laptop into her tote
along with her notebooks and files. She shrugged the bag handle over
her shoulder. "I'm really sorry. I must have fallen asleep and had a bad

nightmare." She scooped up her coat and hurried down the stairs, making for the library exit. She pushed out the doors, her face red-hot.

Once outside, she stopped and let the cool evening rain kiss her face and the winter wind pull at her hair. Inhaling a shaky breath, she wiped her sleeve across her mouth.

It was him. The man she'd seen under hypnosis. A man with a crab tattoo exactly the same as Milo Belkin's, but on his wrist. It was Semyon Zagorsky who had given her—and maybe her sister—those shoes. As a gift. With a purple bow. Zagorsky, Belkin's associate, knew who she was, too. He'd cared enough to give her presents. She'd liked his eyes. Had he been at the cradle with Belkin that night? The second male, perhaps? Or if he wasn't, he had to know what had gone down, given his continued acquaintance with Belkin over the subsequent years—at least until the 1993 drug haul.

Could *he* be her father?

No way in hell was she *not* going to drive out to Kelvin first thing tomorrow. That man, mob links or not, was part of her past and could be her dad. She *needed* to look into his face. Into those blue eyes. And even if he told her nothing, maybe the sight of him would make her remember everything.

CHAPTER 42

"I know it's late and a Saturday, but I'm also aware you've been waiting—"
The voice that came over Angie's phone was that of IDRU tech Kira
Tranquada.

Angie's hand tensed around her cell.

"It's a match," Tranquada said. "The child's foot DNA is identical to
yours, apart from the minor epigenetic variations consistent with those
of a monozygotic twin."

"No mistake?" Angie said.

"It's not an adventitious match, no. We conducted detailed analysis
that went beyond the accepted standard thirteen loci. We repeated the
results with a second sample. There's no mistake."

Angie killed the call and stared out of her hotel room window. It
was dark out. Through her reflection on the pane she could see lights
from the yachts in Coal Harbour below. A sheen of rain glistened on the
wings of wet floatplanes moored at the dock. Beyond, to the east, the
lights of cargo vessels and tankers twinkled and played peekaboo with
mist—the crews inside no doubt edgy for the port strike to be resolved
so that they could enter and discharge their imports.

She'd known that when Tranquada called this would be the news. But
still, the cold, hard scientific evidence dropped like a weight through Angie's

chest. A twin—who'd somehow ended up in the Salish Sea, possibly deep under water, just lying there on some seabed for years, decomposing, being consumed by sea life, her left foot finally disarticulating, the air in the small ROOAirPocket floating it up to the surface where the tides and wind and currents had bobbed it along on a journey . . . for how long? From where?

Had she suffered?

Had their mother suffered?

Who was Semyon Zagorsky to them all?

She swallowed and checked her watch. She'd already phoned the warden at Kelvin Maximum Security Institution and arranged to visit Zagorsky tomorrow. It was a six-hour drive into the interior where the prison was located. She'd need to start early. She was unsure what time she'd manage to return. She could drive back through the night if she had to, make the ferry at the crack of dawn on Monday, be in her uniform and at the MVPD station by nine.

This wasn't about disregarding Maddocks's warning, she told herself. This was about looking into the blue eyes of a man who could perhaps be her father, who might help her remember. Nothing in this world could stop Angie from doing this now—her need to know was too powerful. It was a fire consuming her.

She opened the minibar and took out a small bottle of cold white wine. She poured a glass and carried her drink back to the window. She raised it to her mirror image reflected in the dark pane. *Here's to you, Mila, my other half. I'm going to find you. I'm going to lay you to rest in a place where we both belong. I'll find that place.*

She sipped her wine as she watched Vancouver grow darker. And as it did, her reflection looking back at her grew more apparent. A stranger. A sister.

She had a sister.

Come . . . Comeum dum . . .

No matter the cost, no matter what she learned, the truth would be preferable to what she had now—silence. And ghosts.

Angie took another sip and jumped when her phone buzzed in her pocket.

She fished it out, cleared her throat. "Pallorino."

"It's Sergeant Vedder."

She stilled. Her boss. Calling on a Saturday evening? The tone of his voice did not bode well. Nor did the fact he'd announced his rank. Slowly she set her wine glass down on the table in front of the window.

"What is it, Sarge?" she said quietly.

"Sometimes I think you *want* to self-destruct, Detective," came his voice. He was angry, clearly angry. "You were on probation. Do you understand what that means? It means a period of detention from which you can be released *subject to good behavior under supervision.* I went to bat for you, d'you know that? I argued for your continued employment while others at the MVPD wanted you gone. All you had to do was report to that desk for a period of twelve months. You haven't even lasted one day. I stuck my neck out for *this?*"

"Sir?"

"I just got a call from the RCMP's E-Division. You were asked to hand over evidence and stand down from messing in an active investigation. But you went and compromised the evidence before returning it, and you interrogated a key suspect today, an inmate who now refuses to cooperate in any capacity with the RCMP. And you did it using your MVPD badge while on disciplinary measures."

She shut her eyes, took a deep breath, counted to three, and released air slowly from her lungs in an effort to stop herself from countering her superior. Or from trying to explain her personal situation to him. She was beyond this. She couldn't play this game any longer.

"The RCMP will be taking its own action against you, but you leave me no choice. You were in clear breach of your probation. I expect your badge on my desk first thing Monday morning. Your position with the MVPD has been terminated."

Her chest clamped tight. She swallowed. "Yes, sir."

Angie killed the call and swore violently, hurling her phone at the hotel bed. She then snagged her glass off the table and downed the remaining wine in one long swallow. Her eyes watered as she wiped her mouth, and she caught sight of her mirror image in the pane again. *Face in the mirror . . . Face of a sinner.* She swore again and grabbed her sling bag. She rummaged inside it for her makeup.

She found her lipstick and eyeliner at the bottom under her notebooks. She took the makeup into the bathroom, where she washed her face and brushed out her hair. Carefully she applied the eyeliner, good and thick and dark. She slicked on deep-red lip color. Moistening her lips together, she opened the top buttons of her shirt. What she saw in the mirror would have to do—it was the Angie she knew. The sinner. She stuffed her wallet in the rear pocket of her black jeans, pulled on her heeled boots, grabbed her leather coat, and stepped outside the hotel room door.

CHAPTER 43

Angie strode through the historic brick alleys and streets of Gastown, night lights and store windows smeared by falling rain. Vedder's words dogged her, playing like a loop in her head.

All you had to do was report to that desk for a period of twelve months. You haven't even lasted one day . . . I expect your badge on my desk . . . Your position with the MVPD has been terminated . . .

Sometimes I think you want to self-destruct, Detective.

Was this *it*? Was this the end of everything she'd worked so devilishly hard for? Had her hunt for her past blinded her this badly? Was this what she got for struggling to define a sense of herself outside of policing? She had no idea who she was anymore—hadn't even managed to hold on to being a cop.

She walked blindly past the homeless begging on corners and crouched in doorways, hands out for a few pennies. She marched by pairs of lovers of all sexes who laughed as they gravitated toward clubs on this Saturday night in the city. She went past the hissing steam clock, past the touristy gaslight-era lanterns haloed with mist, into the edgier, decidedly untouristy part of town—Hastings Street. Downtown Eastside. The city's oldest neighborhood, known for its open-air drug trade and riddled with sex workers, poverty, mental illness, homelessness, infectious diseases, crime. An area notorious for decades worth of missing women and for being the hunting ground of pig-farmer-serial-killer Robert Pickton.

Fog grew thicker. Litter appeared in shadowed doorways. The nightclub and restaurant clatter and bustle coming from Gastown quieted. She became conscious of her boot heels echoing on paving. Wind darted down alleys and tugged at the hem of her black coat as if trying to pull her back, warn her against going forward. And now Maddocks's words chased her into skid row, into this seedy and lost corner of destitution and sin.

You need to stop, Angie . . . You have to trust me on this—you're in danger . . . I'm not just talking your job. I'm talking about your life.

She strode faster. His words hounded her still deeper into Downtown Eastside.

Keep your head down, and . . . keep vigilant. Lock your doors . . . I'm telling you this because . . . Because I think I'm coming to love you . . . I care, dammit. I want you around and in my life.

Anxiety, claustrophobia tightened her chest, crowded her brain. And a mad kind of desperation rose inside her—a cry for relief. From this shit inside her head and her heart—these feelings she had for Maddocks that terrified her .

She saw it up ahead. A pink neon sign. RETRO ADULT LOUNGE CLUB. The letter *L* flickered. The last letter *E* had died. Red triple XXXs blinked wildly across the top of the club entrance. And next to the triple-X banner was a rooms-by-the-hour sign. VACANCY.

A bouncer stood, feet planted apart, at the door—bald head, black leather jacket with shearling at the collar. No lineup. Quiet street. A ripple of heat coursed through her.

Angie made for the door. The bouncer admitted her with a nod.

Inside, a small lobby was bathed in red light. A reception area was tucked into an alcove on her right. It was hot inside. Music throbbed below the linoleum-covered floor and pulsed up from a stairwell that led underground. On the reception counter a sign read, COAT CHECK. Another beside it declared, ROOMS FOR RENT. A musty smell of mold and old alcohol and stale cigarettes filled her nostrils. She noticed another set of stairs leading up behind the reception area, presumably to the rooms upstairs.

Angie hit the bell on the counter.

A woman chewing gum stepped out of a small room at the back.

"Yes, love?" the woman said in the husky and scratchy voice of a heavy smoker. Her skin was dulled and heavily lined. Half-moon bags sagged beneath her blue eyes, and aquamarine shadow plastered her lids. She wore a green sequined jumpsuit circa 1970, and her overtreated, red-dyed hair sprouted in a frizzy halo around her worn features.

Angie blinked at the woman, her world feeling suddenly tilted.

"Want a room?" the woman prompted as she scratched at the side of her arm with chipped carmine-coated nails. The bass of the music from the club reverberated below Angie's boots, heavy with promise.

"No. Thanks. Just want to check my coat." She shrugged out of her coat and handed it over the counter to the "concierge." Rings glittered on the woman's fingers as she grasped for Angie's long leather garment. She offered Angie a numbered ticket in return. Angie pocketed the ticket, wondering if she'd ever see her coat again. She turned to go, then hesitated.

"How much are the rooms?"

The woman angled her head, assessing Angie. She grinned slowly. A gold incisor glinted under her upper lip. "For you, nineteen dollars for two hours. Want one?"

"Ah . . . I'll take a look downstairs first. Thanks." She headed for the throbbing stairwell. Heat emanated up the well with the sound.

As Angie descended into the pulsing, smoky miasma of the basement club, something made her stop. She glanced back over her shoulder. The concierge smiled at her again, then slowly the woman's grin faded as she held Angie's gaze. Shrugging off the odd sensation that she'd just been afforded a glimpse of a future version of herself through some hideously distorted funhouse mirror, Angie turned and resumed her way down the stairs. But the sense of disquiet followed her below ground.

Angie stopped at the bottom. The area was dimly lit with a hazy red glow. Music was from the eighties. A bar counter fronted by plush stools ran the entire length of the back wall. In the floor space in front of the bar, smaller tables and booths faced a stage that was lit from the bottom, colors undulating and shifting across the surface. Upon the stage two topless women wearing only G-strings and Perspex platform heels gyrated and swung from chrome poles as the light pulsed beneath them. About two dozen patrons, more males than females, nursed drinks as they alternately conversed and ogled the dancers.

Angie felt as though she'd stepped back in time into some seedy Las Vegas strip club.

She made for the bar at the rear, slid up onto a vacant stool, and ordered a vodka tonic. The bar guy smiled, but she ignored him. Turning on her stool, she sipped her drink, watching the dancers for a few moments, wondering how they'd gotten here—who they were. She shifted her attention to evaluating the obviously single and hunting males in the establishment.

"Drink?" said a deep voice near her ear. She jumped and spun her head—she hadn't even seen or heard him approach. She was off her game. The owner of the voice smiled. Light-hazel eyes. Good haircut. Gym body. Small gold cross nestling in chest hair between the V of a pristine white golf shirt. Maybe early forties, she guessed. Her attention flicked briefly to his hand resting on the bar, a little too close to her. A slightly paler indent marked his ring finger. It was also devoid of hair. Long-term wear from a band. Her gaze ticked up to his face.

"Sure. Vodka tonic."

He waved to the barman and indicated another for Angie and a refill for himself. She swigged back her drink and picked up the second, a nice buzz beginning to lift the edge off her brain and ease her body.

"I'm Andy," he said.

"I'm sure you are." She gave him a seductive smile.

He hesitated. Uncertain. Then laughed. It was a nice laugh, a nice look. It warmed her. "I suppose you're waiting for the *Do you come here often* line?" he said.

"I was hoping for something a little more original from a married father from the suburbs."

His smiled faded. A dark look flickered through his eyes. And she wondered, is this what it came down to—the until-death-do-us-part-in-sickness-and-in-health shit? She'd encountered enough "Andys" and "Antonios" in her life to know the farce of that promise and the futility in thoughts of happy-ever-after. No doubt "Andy" here had himself stood in front a priest or marriage commissioner and made the same vow. Maybe he'd actually believed it at the time. Now here he was. Did it matter—a bit of sex on the side? Anonymous. Edgy. Thrilling. A risk. A break from the humdrum.

Would it relax him? Make him a better dad and lover at home? Keep him nice because he had a *secret*? Or would it just excite him—fuel him only until he started jonesing for another fix? Perhaps he didn't get any at home, poor boy. Wifey might be too busy feeding kids, dropping them off at day care, struggling to put in a full-day's work, and falling into bed each night exhausted. Or wifey was happily fucking her own lover in the tennis clubhouse or doing some underage stud from her classroom where she taught at some secondary school. Or maybe she'd hooked up with a first love she'd rekindled via a surprise *I-found-you!* Facebook connection that reminded her what it had felt to be seventeen and in lust and have the world at one's feet.

The thoughts flattened her nice booze buzz, so she took another deep sip of her drink and turned to watch the strippers. And the men watching them.

I want a normal relationship when things settle down. I want us to see if this can work . . . I'm coming to love you . . . I care, dammit. I want you around and in my life.

James Maddocks's face shimmered into her mind. Those deep-blue eyes. The warmth of his touch. The power in his movements. What he could do to her in bed.

Wasn't it just the same timeless farce playing out?

He'd already tried to play the game. To be a good dad. A husband. And failed. Maybe like Andy here he'd also hit the clubs for a bit of fun after Sabrina took up with that accountant of hers, hell knew. What was it to be human, to love? To be touched, to commit, to copulate. It could both nurture and hurt. It could create life, and it could kill.

She glanced at Andy. He was watching her intently. She imagined him naked. Upstairs on a bed. Two hours. Cuffed. Get her fix. He goes home to wifey. She goes . . . back to her hotel. No job.

She sucked back her drink, plunked the glass on the counter, and waved at the barman, eyes watering slightly. When the barkeep looked her way, she jabbed her finger at the empty glass. He nodded, reached for the bottle.

"Hitting it hard tonight?" Andy said, still watching her keenly. He touched her arm, trailing his finger along it. His pupils darkened as he held her gaze. "What *does* bring a woman like you here tonight, then?" he said.

"Sex."

He blinked.

"You?"

"I ah . . . yeah. Let off some steam."

Conflict warred inside her. Should she do it? Pick someone up again? Blow her brains out and numb her body and emotions with hot intercourse? Or should she draw her line right here, right now, get up and walk away, go home to the island, drop her walls and allow herself to love Maddocks . . . and brace for the pain that might cause her?

Should she take that dizzying tumble into that abyss, just to see if she could survive?

"So, Andy," she said, reaching for her third glass of vodka tonic, speaking more slowly now as the edges around her tongue blurred. "Does it work for you?" She sipped, watching him.

"What do you mean?"

The music changed. Fresh girls on stage.

"You come here. Get laid with . . . with some anonymous bitch, go home—helps you be, like, what? A good dad, husband? Until the next fix?"

His brow crooked up. "You're kinda weird."

"So they say." She sucked back another sip. *Do it. Get blind drunk. Screw this guy senseless. Do it to hurt Maddocks, to kill this thing between us that's messing with my head and heart and mind . . . just like I've damaged every other relationship I've attempted. Angie Pallorino—the black thumb to relationships.*

She raised her glass, chinked it with Andy's.

I want to share spring, summer with you, Angie, get those kayaks out. Get out onto the water—work on the old boat, have barbecues on the deck, have you and Ginny there with me. I want to spend fall and next winter with you, dammit. I want a normal relationship when things settle down. I want us to see if this can work.

She stilled the glass halfway to her mouth. And it struck, in drunk, blinding clarity as she caught her image in the mirror behind the bar—shocked a little at what she saw—she wanted to try.

She wanted to be better than that drunk ex-cop looking back at her from a seedy bar mirror. Better than the sum of her past, her childhood. She wanted to go back in time. To that grove of trees in her memory. To find the answers, and her twin. And to dust off and try to start again. From whatever that start point might be.

Yes, James Maddocks. I want to try. I want to try to be normal. Her eyes burned.

I'm going to finish this search and then go home and try.

If she died in her effort to revisit her past, well that was her lot. She needed to stare death in the face in order to be reborn, as drunkenly philosophical as that might seem. If there was a threat to her life out there—bring it on. She wasn't going to mess in anyone else's sandbox of an investigation—she was just going to look into the eyes of Semyon Zagorsky. And ask.

She stood abruptly, then steadied herself with her hand on the counter.

Andy came to his feet beside her.

She shook her head, not looking at him. "Go home," she said with a clumsy wave of her hand. On second thought, she glanced up at him with bleary eyes. "It's not worth it, Andy, so not worth it. Trust me."

She pushed herself off from the counter and tried to hold a straight line as she navigated her way around the strippers' stage, aiming for the stairs that would lead back above ground.

CHAPTER 44

SUNDAY, JANUARY 7

It was Sunday morning, and Kjel Holgersen had the day off. Pressure was easing with the bulk of the *Amanda Rose* barcode case having moved with Maddocks to Surrey. If Kjel had a life or a half-decent apartment or some hobby or something, he might have stayed at home. But he didn't. Staying home alone without being blind-tired and crashing into bed or without something to fully occupy his brain was dangerous—he'd been down that road before. That's when the shadows crept out of the closets of his mind. That's when those demons started to dance and beckon with enticingly dark promise. So he was here, at 11:00 a.m., hungry for the Flying Pig Bar and Grill's Sunday brunch mashup—a low-priced, high-carb, full-fat fry-up replete with sausages, maple syrup, bacon, and eggs with a stack of lumberjack-size flapjacks on the side. And all-you-can-drink coffee.

He pushed through the old wooden pub doors and drank in the aroma of sizzling bacon and freshly brewed caffeine and the familiar buzz of the police bar.

"Homes from home, Jack-O, ol' boy," he said as he made his way to the bar to place his order. Jack-O didn't stir in the infant carry pouch into which Kjel had stuck him. The pouch hung warm against Kjel's hollow stomach, halfway zipped into his bomber jacket. Dog knew a good thing when he saw one—probably figured if he moved, he might get chucked out. The sensation of the old pooch's little beating heart—his warm three-legged body cuddled close and trusting—sent an odd punch through Kjel. It stirred things he really couldn't handle having stirred because it could just tilt him back over the edge, and this time he'd no freaking clue whether he'd scrape back up that interminable hill again.

"Yo, Colm," he called to McGregor. The big redheaded bearded Scotsman came up to Kjel's end of the bar, his apron du jour stretched around his strapping torso, different one each day. His shtick. Today's said, BRUNCH = EXCUSE FOR DAY DRINKING.

"What'll it be, Detective?"

"The number one mashup times two. One packaged to go."

McGregor wiped his hands on a white towel, rang the order into his system. "Got a wee hole in your stomach today then?" He glanced up, did a slight double take. "What's that you got in there?" He tilted his bearded chin at the baby carrier.

"That's who gets mashup number two."

"A kid?"

Kjel angled himself sideways so McGregor could peer into the carrier. "Look like a kid to you?"

McGregor frowned, then guffawed. "That be Maddocks's hound," he declared in his great booming Scottish accent.

"Boss has gots me babysitting."

The pub owner raised a bushy thatch of red brow. "It trusts you then? To sit like that in a wee bairn pouch."

"Everybody's gots to trust somebody."

Kjel turned to survey the scene and find a table while McGregor bellowed his order through the hatch to the kitchen. He spotted the odd couple again—Leo and Grablowski. Ensconced in a secluded booth near the back of the pub, huddled over coffee mugs and partially eaten plates of food in front of them. A sinister sensation unfurled in Kjel. It tasted of distrust, suspicion. Curiosity. His mind went to the article that Leo had shown him on Pallorino being that angel's cradle kid.

He ambled over to the booth.

As he approached, Grablowski made a call on his cell phone. Leo was watching, leaning forward with interest.

"Yo," Kjel said. "Whassup, dudes? Can we's join you?"

Grablowski's head shot up. His brow lowered, and he glanced sharply at Leo as if to say, *Get this fucker away.* Leo opened his mouth, but before he could protest, Kjel was sliding himself and Jack-O onto the padded seat in the booth beside the crusty old detective.

"What in the hell is that?" Leo said, his gaze shooting to the baby pouch.

Kjel threw him a grin. "You know how cold it is out? Flippin' winter. Old three-legged little man here don't like to be cold. Ain't so speedy hobbling on a dog lead, either. So I gots him a carry bag."

"A *baby* pouch? Are you kidding me?"

"*Ergonomic* baby pouch. Boughts it at Mountain Equipment. Pricey Gore-Tex shit. Good for the momses back and all. Ands for baby posture."

"It's a dog, Holgersen. You're not even using the damn leg and arm holes."

Kjel tilted his chin toward Grablowski, who'd turned in his seat in an effort to shut Holgersen off from the conversation he was trying to conduct on his cell.

"He's on the phone. Do you mind?" Leo said.

"He can go talk somewheres else—" Kjel stopped midsentence to listen.

"I'm just giving you one last chance," Grablowski was saying, his back turned to Kjel and Leo, "to get in on the deal . . . Yeah. Yeah, I know it's your life story, Detective, but it's going to be out there. If not through me, then through someone else. This way you have control—"

"Fuck off, Grablowski."

He heard her voice, loud and clear, yelling at the shrink. "Pallorino?" he said softly to Leo.

Leo shrugged. But the bastard had a little gleam in his eyes.

"I heard the scuttlebutt when I checked in at the station this morning," Kjel said. "Heard she's out on her ass."

Leo snorted. "'Bout fucking time. It's given Grablowski the push he needed. Now he doesn't have to worry about the MVPD not hiring him because he won't be exposing a cop. She's a disgraced ex-cop."

"*You* have something to do with her being axed?"

"I wish."

"So what was it?"

"No clue."

Kjel regarded Leo steadily. "You do too have a clue."

"Serious. I don't."

Grablowski said into his phone, voice clipped, "Fine. You have until midnight tonight to come on board. The official book offer came in Friday. I met with my agent yesterday. We sign Monday, with or without you. Also got an offer pending from DayLine TV. They do that cold case series. They're interested in a podcast plus regular televised updates, interviews as the investigation unfolds. My publicist will hit media outlets with my book deal news Monday."

Kjel heard Pallorino's retort through the phone. "Break my story and I break your back, asshole."

Kjel smiled. She had spunk, that girl.

Grablowski killed the call. He turned in his seat. His face looked hot. He removed his round glasses, polished them with a napkin, and replaced them on the bridge of his beaked nose.

The waitress arrived with Kjel's coffee.

"Oh, look at that," the server cooed as she reached for the baby carrier to pet Jack-O's head, which was peeking out now. The Jack Russell cross pulled back his lips and growled. The waitress yanked back her hand.

Kjel shrugged, but admittedly he felt a little smug at the dog's defensive stance. "Old. Whats can I say?"

"Well, he clearly likes *you*."

"Yeah." He gave her a warm grin. She returned his smile. It lit her eyes prettily and put pink in her cheeks. "Be right back with your order."

"Gig kinda suits me, eh," he said to Leo as he watched the waitress go.

"Yeah. Right. Turns you into a veritable babe magnet."

Kjel reached for the sugar and poured an unhealthy stream into his steaming mug. He snagged up a spoon, stirred.

"Too bad you're celibate. What's with that, anyway?"

Kjel ignored Leo and said to Grablowski, "So, you gets pleasure out of a book deal on Pallorino's story, then, on top of the money?" He took a sip from his mug.

"That's right."

Kjel stilled, mug midway between mouth and table. "You're still burned overs the fact she cost you the Spencer Addams book deal. Is that what this is?"

Grablowski slipped his phone into his breast pocket. "Pleasure aside, this is an even better deal than the first. She'd be well advised to climb on board."

"It's her fecckin' story."

"And it's going to run out of her control. This way she has a measure of input, direction over the content."

"An' she gets to work with you. Whoo—bonus."

Grablowski locked his gaze with Kjel's. "And you, Detective? What do *you* want?"

"Some good company for brunch." He threw Grablowski a wild grin.

His food arrived—one meal packaged to go, another on a large plate with a side of flapjacks. Kjel reached for the syrup and smothered the lot with a hefty pour of maple-y nectar. "Fresh tapped from them trees in Quebec, I'ms sure," he said, raising the bottle before he set it down on the table. He lifted his knife and fork and caught sight of the black Sharpie scrawl across the lid of the takeout carton. MASTER JACK. "Hey, well, look at that, Jack-O boy." He pointed his knife at the print and said, "*Master Jack*. I likes that."

Dog didn't even poke his head out of the carrier. Kjel tucked in.

"That a mashup for the dog?" Leo said.

"Yup."

"Dogs need dog food," Leo muttered.

"Yeah, you'd know, right, Leo?" He jerked his chin to Grablowski as he chewed. "Where is she—Pallorino?"

He shrugged. "In a car. Driving somewhere."

"What happened with her job and Vedder?"

Grablowski picked up his mug. "Don't know yet."

"It'll all make for a freaking good story when this breaks first thing Monday morning, right?" Holgersen said around his mouthful.

"Right."

Kjel studied the shrink's face as he swallowed, then delivered another forkful of syrup-drenched sausage and egg to his mouth. He chewed, thinking that Pallorino was in for a rough ride. MVPD wasn't going to come to her defense when this story hit the fan.

He reached for his mug, washed his food down with a hot swig. The company at this booth was leaving a really bad taste in his mouth. As he cut into a flapjack, his cell rang. He set down his fork, wiped his mouth with his napkin, and answered his call.

"Holgersen."

He stilled at the news on the other end of his call. He shot a glance at Leo, who was watching him.

"Yeah. On my way," Holgersen said. He killed the call.

"What was that?"

"Russian interpreter, the one who helped take the statement from the dead barcode chick—theys just pulled her little blue Yaris outta Duck Lake off the highway to Sooke."

CHAPTER 45

Angie swore as she killed Grablowski's call. Fisting her hands on her wheel, she increased pressure on the gas as the empty ribbon of highway began to climb and curve through smooth, rounded hills of dun-brown wintery grasslands. She was making her way to Kelvin Maximum Security Institution. She glanced at the clock on the dash—making good time at that. Her anger with Grablowski just fueled her forward faster.

Cooperate? Asshole.

This was *her* story, one thousand percent. She owned it; *she* was going to finish it.

Nevertheless, Grablowski's ultimatum had set the clock of urgency ticking, because once the news hit about her being the mystery cradle child and a sibling to the floating foot, plus the disgraced and terminated cop who'd overkilled Spencer Addams and narrowly missed prosecution herself, her hands would be tied. She had to look into Zagorsky's eyes before Pietrikowski or anyone else joined those dots.

Angie floored the gas as she overtook a semi lumbering up the pass. As the elevation increased, snow turned the landscape white. On either side now, as far as her eye could see, brutally clear-cut forest was band-aided with the purity of snow. She crested a ridge, and wind suddenly slammed into her vehicle. Up ahead a road sign stated the elevation—she'd hit the peak of the pass. Rounding the bend, she caught sight of the valley unfurling below. Fine dry snow blew off the landscape and swirled in drifts across the road. Angie reached for her water bottle and took a long swallow, eyes on the road. She felt gross, hungover, yet remarkably clear-eyed about where she was headed now. She'd made a decision.

As she began a slow descent through the endless hills with no sign of life apart from a scattering of oncoming cars and the odd rancher's truck, her phone rang again. She hit the button on her dash connecting the call via hands-free.

"Pallorino," she snapped.

"It's Jacob Anders. We have news."

Her pulse kicked. "Yes?"

"We managed to obtain two nuclear DNA profiles from the two different semen samples—the old lab samples had been well enough packaged and preserved. We also obtained a profile from the blood evidence on the teddy bear and the dress. The blood DNA is a unique match to the sample you provided here at the lab. You were in that cradle, Angie."

She swallowed as she steered into a hairpin curve. Her tires slicked slightly on black ice. She corrected, slowed. "Is it possible the blood could also be my twin's?"

"Yes. Possible. More complex testing could determine that, if necessary."

"And the hair evidence?"

"Insufficient DNA for routine STR typing, but we did obtain mitochondrial DNA profiles for both the long dark-brown hair and the short ash-blonde hair. The '86 lab reports indicate that the hairs were examined by microscope at the time, but since the nineties, mtDNA analysis has been made possible on hair samples that were historically unsatisfactory for STR profiling. However," he cautioned, "mitochondrial DNA is not a unique identifier in the way that nuclear DNA is—it's maternally inherited. All a woman's offspring, her siblings, her mother, and other maternal relatives will have the same mtDNA profile. It can, however, rule *out* a maternal connection if there is no mitochondrial match."

Angie hesitated. "Does . . . my profile show a mtDNA match to the dark hair?"

"It does."

Her stomach tightened. So did her hands on the wheel. "So the long dark hair could have been my mother's?"

"It's not ruled out."

Emotion burned in her eyes and nose, her feelings so close to the surface. She was not used to this. Clearing her throat, corralling her self-control, she said, "What about the ballistics report?"

"The two bullets retrieved at the scene were a .45 caliber. Rifling shows both were fired from the same gun. We ran the results through our own growing database, but no hits."

"Can you forward the DNA profiles and ballistics report to the personal email address I provided you?"

"Hitting SEND as we speak, files attached."

"Thank you, Jacob." She wavered slightly before asking the next question. "That underwater study you've got on the monitor in your office—do you have any info on how far a disarticulated and buoyed foot could float in the Salish Sea?"

"That foot could have come from anywhere, Angie," he said softly. Kindly, she realized. "Those currents in the Strait of Georgia are highly variable and fed from rivers all over the place, from Alaska down to Washington, with a maze of islands and inlets in between. It could theoretically even have drifted across the Pacific from the Far East." He paused. "Okay, looks like the email has gone through—should all be in your inbox."

"Thanks again." She killed the call, saw a pullout ahead, and slowed. Drawing off the highway, Angie came to a stop. She checked her email via her phone as the raw wind buffeted her Nissan. As soon as she saw that Anders's emails had come through, she forwarded them to Stacey Warrington's addy at the MVPD station. She then called Warrington's work number and left a message.

"Stace, it's Sunday—I know you're not there—but I've forwarded some DNA profiles and ballistics imaging to your email. Any chance . . ." It struck her right then and there, like that ice-wind hitting her Nissan . . .

I've been terminated. I'm not a cop anymore. I'm not working an MVPD case. My badge and clearance is invalid. Stacey can't do this for me.

"That you could run them through the system for me? If there is . . . any problem, please, let me know. I . . . I'll owe you, Stace."

She hung up, blew out a chestful of air. New game. New rules. This was going to be her new life. How she would fill it afterward, she didn't know. All she could do now was go forward one step at a time. She reached down and re-engaged the gears. Checking her rearview mirror, she pulled back onto the highway. This section of road felt lonely all of a sudden on this chill winter Sunday morning. Nothing but snowy pastures, forest. Not even a cow in sight. As she descended the pass, the snow faded into brown grassland. Cowboy and cattle country. Nerves and adrenaline rustled under her skin as she caught sight of the frontier-style town nestled along a twisting spine of river. Beyond that town lay Kelvin Max Security, gray and sprawling like a scar across the earth.

Angie took the off-ramp.

CHAPTER 46

Angie signed the visitor register form. She handed it back to the correctional service staffer, who then checked her police ID and handed her an official visitor card, which she pinned to her shirt. She'd left her phone in her car. Weapons were not an issue because she was not carrying. Once she'd passed through a metal detector and ION scanner for drugs, a female officer escorted her to the inmate visiting area.

"How long has Semyon Zagorsky been in the general population wing now?" Angie asked her correctional service escort as they passed through a second set of electronic security gates. They shut behind her with a clang. Keys jangled on her escort's hip as they walked down the corridor, fluorescent lights flickering slightly above them.

"Four years," the officer said. "He's a model prisoner. Teaches woodwork and sewing. They make their own uniforms, plus jeans and lingerie for companies that contract with the prison for labor." She opened another electronic door into the general population visiting area. It was arranged like a cafeteria, with round tables painted a primary blue and bolted to the floor. Round seats were affixed to the tables—some tables with two seats, others with four. A handful of inmates occupied various tables with their visitors. Security personnel watched from behind the mirrored glass of an observation room.

"That's him over there." The officer pointed to lone male sitting with his back to the door. He wore a sweatshirt and loose-fitting pants. Broad back. Thick neck. Bald.

Adrenaline crackled through Angie. "Thank you," she said.

The officer departed, the electronic security door closing behind her.

As Angie approached the lone male, she moved her loose hair so that it hung forward over her shoulder, obscuring her visitor ID card. She stopped behind him.

"Semyon Zagorsky?" she said.

He turned, looked up. Bright-blue eyes met hers. A bolt of recognition slammed through her as shock twitched through Zagorsky like an electrical current.

It's him. Definitely him. The man who gave me the shoes in the box with the big purple bow. A voice sounded in her head as she looked into his eyes. Deep, sonorous, rising up from her buried past as if the iron door locking her childhood secrets in a subterranean basement had just creaked open. *For my Mila, and a matching pair for Roksana.*

And she knew. Angie knew that Semyon Zagorsky was also seeing a ghost from his long-ago past. Just as Milo Belkin had.

His eyes remained lasered on hers as she moved slowly around the table and took the seat facing him. Angie sat in silence, absorbing his face as bits of memories like tiny colored beads snapped and twitched along long-dormant neural pathways, forming bigger pictures, scents, sounds. The grove in the forest. The berry brambles full with ripe, juicy blackberries. The taste of them—a sweet-sour explosion in her mouth. The sound of a little girl's laughter sending birds scattering in trees. A deer, watching them silently as they picked the berries and small yellow flowers. Glimpses of sparkling ocean through trees. The dark room with bars on a high window. A faceless woman with long dark wavy hair who smelled of grass and apples. *Mother.* The sound of her crying. Angie swallowed while her heart stuttered, then raced.

Outwardly she struggled for cool, for composure, as she absorbed Zagorsky's features.

His was a pugilistic face with the broken nose of a boxer and a fighter's brow that protected eyes set in deep sockets. And those blue eyes from her past were still as bright and keen as in her memory, despite the passing of more than thirty years. Angie lowered her gaze to his hands. Another jolt of memory sparked through her—his hands holding the box out to her. The shape of his fingers was burned into her mind.

"Can you turn your left hand over?" she said with a voice that came out husky and didn't seem her own.

He turned his hand. The blue crab was there, on the inside of his wrist. She raised her gaze back to his face.

"Roksana?" he whispered.

Tears seared into her eyes, the well of emotion so sharp and sudden it scared her. The feelings that roiled together inside her were a conflicted tangle of love, fear, confusion. The bitter taste of betrayal.

He reached his hand slightly forward across the blue table surface as if to touch her, to see if she were real in flesh, but his eyes ticked toward the mirrored glass of the observation room, and he drew it back.

"Do I look like her?" she said. Needing to know. Desperate. "Do I look like my . . . mother?" She could hardly say the word. Afraid it was all a dream, that she'd come this far, was getting this close, and now it would shatter like a delicate glass ball into mere shards of memory that could never be made whole again.

Moisture pooled in Zagorsky's eyes. He nodded. "Yes," he whispered. "Like Anastazja."

Angie began to shake. "Her name?"

He nodded.

She swiped an errant tear from her eye. "What was her last name?"

He shook his head, staring at her as if still unbelieving. "I don't know," he whispered. "She never said. I never asked."

"What happened to her? What happened to Mila?"

His body twitched. His eyes darted again to the mirrored glass of the observation room. He was afraid. Tension twisted through her.

"Please, I *need* to know."

He touched his fingertips to the left side of his lips, as though to mirror her scar.

"Did you put that there, Semyon? Did *you* give me that scar?"

He closed his eyes a moment, as if the memory caused him pain, remorse. He shook his head.

"Did Milo Belkin do it?"

His eyes flared open wide. Now she saw terror.

Shit. Mistake. Backtrack. Fast. Before he clams up. Before it hits him that he has a parole hearing in two days and anything he tells me could be used to charge him afresh.

"Is she alive—my mother?" Angie said quickly, steering the conversation back again, trying to keep her voice neutral but failing.

Subtly, slowly, he shook his head.

"And Mila?"

The moisture pooled in his eyes leaked down his cheeks. He did not bother to wipe it away.

"What happened to my sister, Semyon? Who hurt her? Was it you? Did *you* kill that little girl and throw her body into some river or ocean like a piece of garbage? Is that why her foot floated up in Tsawwassen the other day?"

"No." He thumped his fist on the table, holding it there, his face turning thunderous, his jaw clenching tight, neck muscles like cording ropes. "No, I did not hurt her. I'd never have hurt her." He ground the words out between his teeth.

"*Who* did it, then?" Angie leaned forward, heart palpitating.

He glowered at her, a thunderstorm of emotions rippling in the tension of his muscles under his skin. He was fighting himself not to talk. It was visible, visceral—he wanted to share as much as he did not.

Angie leaned farther over the table. "You know what happened to her, Semyon." Her gaze pinned his, the edges of reality and time blurring around her. "You cared for us once, Semy. You were fond of me and Mila." Surprise cut through Angie at her automatic use of his abbreviated name. Another bolt of recall hit her out of left field—a woman's voice saying his name. *Semy.* The same voice that had sung the lullaby, the same voice that had screamed for her to get into the cradle and be quiet.

"She liked you, too, Semy. Didn't she? My mother. Anastazja."

His lips thinned, started to quiver.

"You regret what happened, don't you? You regret it deeply."

He lowered his head and turned his palms face up on the shiny blue table. He stared at his hands as if they did not belong to him, as if he was confused by what those hands might have done. A giant in a cage, a bear of a man. An odd spurt of sympathy went through Angie.

"Semy." She touched his fingers. His gaze jerked up.

"Tell me who did it, who hurt them."

Again, she could see that war inside him—a growing fear of criminal repercussion fighting with a desire to share the past with her. It was raw and tangible and powerful. A desperation rose in Angie—she was losing him. He'd said all he was going to say.

"Semy," she said again, earnest, leaning in yet closer. "Are you the father of Roksana and Mila?"

His mouth twisted in some kind of agony.

"A DNA test *will* tell, Semy. Your profile is already in the system. It'll be a simple—"

"I'm not your father, Roksana," he whispered. "But I was more a father to you two than he was."

Bam.

"*Who* was?"

He inhaled deeply and glanced at the windows behind which the officers watched. He turned to look at the door. He was seeking escape. From her, from her questions, from the past. From guilt, maybe. From himself.

"Did you love her? Did you love Anastazja?"

He made a move to get up.

She gripped his arm. "Please, don't go. Not yet. You gave me and Mila those shoes—little high-tops. Lilac. You wrapped them in boxes with purple bows. We *liked* you, Semy, I remember. Yet you chased us with guns and knives across that street in Vancouver. You took my mother and sister—"

"I was a guardian," he said very quietly, his eyes still tracking around the room, watching everything. Worried. "Your protector. It was *not* supposed to go that way. *She* made it happen. It was her fault that she and Mila were killed. After that . . . there was nothing I could do to save her or Mila." He paused, then said almost in a whisper, "You were the lucky one, Roksi—the one who got away from him. Ana could save only one of you that night. And it was close. Too close. She almost lost you both. It was a stupid move." He pushed himself to his feet, looked down at her. "Now go home, please, and stop looking. Because if he knows that you came here, and that you are searching for him, he *will* kill you." He turned to leave.

"No, wait!" She leaped up and grabbed his arm. A guard stepped out of the observation room. Angie quickly withdrew her hand. The guard held back. "*Who* will kill me?"

He looked down into her face—he was very tall, a colossus of a man. Russian in genetics and culture perhaps, but not in accent. Her brain raced. She had to run background checks on Semy, look for any information she could find on this man—his past residences, acquaintances, friends, family. She needed to find them all, talk to them.

"You have to stop," he repeated. "Promise me you will stop looking."

"I will not. I can't. I *will* find him, Semy—whoever he is—with or without you. Because I'm starting to remember things that are guiding me forward," she said. "I remember *you*. I recall you giving us those shoes. I remember the look in your eyes when you handed me the box—it was kind, gentle. It made me happy inside. And now one of those little lilac shoes you gave us has floated up with the remains of Mila's foot inside. The RCMP have opened an investigation, and they've already tied it to the cradle case in '86 and to me. They know my DNA matches Mila's, that she had a twin. Which means the cradle case has been reopened, and the old evidence from that case is being retested using new science. The fingerprints from the case have already led me to Milo Belkin, and the RCMP are close behind. So don't think your people on the outside can shut me up by firebombing my house and burning me to death like they did with your victim, Stirling Harrison—"

He blanched. Angie bit back the rest of her words as it struck her.

He doesn't know. Shit! I should have kept my mouth shut. The mob connection to the Harrison fire is privileged. It came from Maddocks.

Angie immediately tried to switch direction. "And if you didn't kill my mother and sister, you better say who did, or *you* will go down for it. Murder times two. Two consecutive life sentences. You might as well write off that imminent probation hearing, because you're going to die in here, Semy."

He leaned down, bringing his mouth close to her ear. "Be careful, Roksi. Be very careful," he whispered. Then he turned and made for the door. "Guard! Get me out of here!"

"Who is he?" Angie yelled after him. "Who wants to kill me?" The guard who'd stepped out of the observation room earlier went forward

to assist the inmate demanding to leave the visiting area. *"Who was my father, goddammit!"*

He exited.

The door shut behind him.

A female officer appeared from the observation room and came to her assistance. Angie was shaking.

The man who killed my mother and Mila is alive. He is out there. And he doesn't want me looking.

CHAPTER 47

Semyon Zagorsky dials a number from the inmates' phone at the bottom of the stairs in the medium-security range. As he waits for his call to pick up, that cold, coiled thing that he felt awakening from hibernation when he saw the little ROOAirPocket on TV rises inside his belly like a cobra ready to strike.

It isn't *a coincidence.*

It's real.

The past has come back to claim me, and now I face a terrible choice.

He's a man being led to the gallows as his call is connected.

"Mila?" he says quietly into the receiver at the sound of his daughter's voice. His head bends in toward the phone booth so others won't hear him. "Can you put Livvy on to talk to me?"

He just wants to hear his four-year-old granddaughter's voice. Hearing her sweet, innocent voice will enable him to make the decision he knows he must but can't. Just can't.

"Gampy!"

Emotion sparks through Semy's chest. He closes his eyes, fisting the receiver. His brow touches against the metal box that shields the phone. He takes a moment to marshal control of his body.

"Livvy—" His voice cracks nevertheless. In his mind he can see them—the twins—as if it were yesterday. Two little kittens, Ana called them, running, running down to the clearing in the forest, their laughter a rare slice of sunshine that tinkled like the pure sound of freedom and goodness itself. The little shoes . . . little lilac shoes running through the snow. The other one with bare feet. Ana had no time to put on Roksana's shoes. She'd fled with Roksi on her hip, her free hand gripping onto Mila, whom she'd dragged behind her. Her sweater was marked with cum from the two men she'd let use her so that she could lull them into complacency, escape to that cradle another sex worker had told her was down the alley between the hospital and the cathedral.

He sent Livvy—his own granddaughter—shoes for her fourth birthday. He can't say why. He can't say why he named his own daughter Mila, either. Possibly it was a desperate attempt to keep little Mila's memory alive, to honor the child who'd been murdered in front of his very eyes. Possibly it was because of the guilt that haunted him like his own shadow. If he hadn't cared so much for Ana, she wouldn't have been able to dupe them all with her attempt to escape that night—her desperate bid to save her children from her own fate, from working as sex slaves for the rest of their lives.

Roksana was right. He'd loved the twins. Like a father. It was him who made sure they got out sometimes to play in the sunlight and sea air. It was him who sneaked Ana out of the room when the twins' father was away.

"Did . . . did you get your present, Livvy?" he managed to say.

"Uh-huh."

"Do you like them?"

"Make me run *fast*, Gampy!"

Not fast enough. Little Mila's lilac high-tops did not move her fast enough that Christmas Eve. They did not save her while her sister screamed in pain and terror as her face was cut in the struggle to tear her away from the cradle.

"Are you going to come out and visit us soon, Gampy? Mommy says you might come one day soon now."

He swallows hard.

"Yes, Livvy, maybe. Soon." But it will never happen now.

His mind goes to his pending parole board hearing and what Roksana told him about Stirling Harrison's death. He's been set up—his chance of parole is doomed. They'll tie Harrison's death to the mob. The parole board will say that Zagorsky remains a threat, that he's still connected to criminals on the outside. Semy has always been suspicious of where the tip came from that led to his and Milo's arrests in that drug bust. Now, after Roksana's news that the paraplegic and his wife have been burned to death, he's certain. Oly.

Oly tipped off the cops and put him in here.

Oly ordered the death of Stirling Harrison. Which means Oly intends for him to remain here.

Oly is also the one providing protection on the outside for Semy's wife and his daughter, Mila, and his little Livvy. Oly bought them big houses side by side on the mountainside overlooking the city. He provides them with bodyguards, security cameras, servants—they want for nothing.

We always take care of family, he'd said. *Right, Semy?* The implication being, *Do not talk, and all will be fine with your wife and your progeny on the outside.* Oly is probably also screwing his wife. Bile rises up the back of Semy's throat as something else strikes him—maybe the bastard is fucking his daughter, too. That would be his style. That would be his revenge for Ana and the twins—for Semy letting one escape. Inhaling deeply, he says, "Everything is happy at home? And safe?"

"Yes, Gampy!" At the sound of that spirited little voice, his mind is made up. He must do what he is about to do so that Livvy can continue to grow up safe. Or she *will* be killed. Like Mila. Like Ana. Like Roksi will if she does not stop hunting. For his red "brother" is ruthless.

Semy hangs up. He makes his second call. To his lawyer, Viktor Abramov. Prison officials are not supposed to listen in to an inmate's calls to his lawyer. As Abramov's phone rings, Semy knows he is signing Roksana's death warrant. The irony is not lost on him. After all these years, she's *not* the one who escaped. She's come full circle. The little floating shoe has found her after all these years. Mila's ghost is drawing her twin home . . . and now their father will get her in the end.

It all goes back to the beginning.

CHAPTER 48

Oly listens to the voice coming from Kelvin Maximum Security Institution. It's being relayed via a complex rerouting system through his law firm's Vancouver office. He stands at his office window, computing the incoming information while he watches his guests disembark from three of his boats that have docked in time for cocktails—a twenty-five-foot Welcraft, a thirty-foot Grady White, and a twenty-five-foot Trophy. His guests are all men, and they're garbed in the all-weather suits supplied by his high-end luxury fishing lodge.

Judging by the apparent weight of the coolers his guides are offloading, his staff managed to put his guests onto a good run of winter springs, halibut, or maybe Coho. Across the steel-gray water, on another island also owned by him, wreathes of mist finger through conifers that grow dense on slopes. A bald eagle circles lazily up high. He hopes his guides also managed to locate the orca pod sighted offshore yesterday. His guides carry the catch toward the stainless-steel cleaning stations at the end of the dock. Tonight's meal of lobster and Alaskan king crab is being prepared by his chefs. The women are ready to give massages—and more, should guests desire—in the spa. His is one of the oldest and most established luxury fly-in fishing lodges along the Pacific Coast. A guaranteed five-star West Coast experience. The sea has always been the source of his bounty.

"What name did she give?" he says quietly.

"Roksana."

"She knows her old name?"

"She's starting to remember things. She recalls me—remembers that I gave her those high-tops with air pockets in the soles. She says there is old evidence from the cradle case crime scene currently being retested using new DNA technology. The RCMP have already matched her DNA to the dismembered foot. And fingerprints from the cradle already led her to Milo."

A sinister prescience fills his gut, of things coming full circle. Of inevitability. He reaches down and fingers the bone letter opener on his desk. "So . . . she's been to see Milo?"

"I . . . don't know for certain."

"This is why loose ends can never be left, Semy."

"This is why I am calling you."

"What is her name?" he says again. "She must have an adoptive name."

"She only said Roksana."

Some of his guests are coming up the gangway now, making their way toward the main lodge building. The tallest guest, the one with black hair, the man from Dubai, is the guest he most needs to talk business with. The irony of that man's presence here on this day that Semy is calling is not lost on him—it was the man's cousin from Saudi Arabia who'd wanted Ana and the twins all those years ago.

He repeats, "What name did she sign into Kelvin with? What did her ID badge say?"

"I didn't see her badge."

"Where does she live? What is her profession?"

"I . . . it was a shock to see her. I didn't ask. She didn't say."

He swears to himself but says very calmly, quietly, "That's all right. Relax. We'll sort it all out. I appreciate the call." He pauses. "What does she look like?"

"Like Ana. Just like Ana. I thought it was Ana come back. But her hair—"

"I know." Her hair is the color of his own hair but darker. Same pale skin as his own. Pale-gray eyes like his. It was these features in duplicate that had intrigued his client from Saudi Arabia. The prince had paid top dollar for the twins. He'd had to return the payment when he was unable to deliver them. Thanks to Semy.

"How tall?" he says quietly.

"About five nine. Slender. She has the scar across the left side of her mouth."

"What did you tell her?"

"Nothing—nothing that she isn't already remembering."

"Thank you, Semy." He pauses, thinking that all those years ago, when he read in the papers about the angel's cradle child and learned that she had no memory or language, he'd thought he was safe. He'd let it go. He shouldn't have. "Goodbye, Semy."

He hangs up. His gaze goes to his bookshelves, to a framed photo. Ana. At sixteen. Her tummy rounded with his progeny. His possession. Ana was the one he'd kept for himself for a while and who surprisingly bore him daughters in duplicate, which had intrigued the narcissist in him. For a time. Until a better offer came along. And then Ana had crossed him. She would not have been able to do it without Semy.

His guests are entering the lodge now. No time to waste. He goes to his desk, unlocks a bottom drawer, and from it he removes a fresh burner phone. He will discard the phone once the contract he's about to initiate is concluded. A separate phone for each contract. Always.

He makes his call and leaves a message for his man. "I have another commission," he says. "Times three. Top level."

Once his call is complete, he pours and downs a shot of vodka. He checks himself in the mirror, then goes to welcome his guests back from a successful day out on his charters.

Downstairs everything is in impeccable order. Champagne, oysters, and vodka are all on ice. Music is discreet in the background. A woman in her early nineties comes shuffling around the corner, carefully carrying a silver platter of finely sliced smoked salmon. She is dressed all in black, and she shakily sets the platter upon the table beside the oysters.

"Mama!" he says, opening his arms in a wide magnanimous gesture before clapping his big hands together. "It is marvelous, as usual."

As he speaks, the dark-haired man from Dubai enters the room. He turns to face the man. "Ahmed! Come, come on in and meet my mother, Elena, the ever-gracious hostess."

The old woman bows and then backs hurriedly away before Ahmed can address her.

"And your beautiful wife?" Ahmed says. "She is not here this time?"

"Irina is at our residence in the city. For her the remote luxury lodge life is fine enough, but only for a time—there is shopping to be done in the boutiques." He laughs.

Ahmed laughs, too. The other males enter, smiling, chattering about their catch.

"Come, come, everyone. Let us go in and have a drink where the fire is warm."

As he leads his guests through, he feels his burner cell vibrate in his pocket.

Message received.

CHAPTER 49

MONDAY, JANUARY 8

Kjel Holgersen slipped on the grassy incline that sloped down to Duck Lake. It was from the muddy waters of the lake that the little blue Yaris registered to the Russian interpreter had been pulled yesterday morning. Divers had been dragging the silt-filled lake since in search of her body. Kjel had gotten word they'd found it. In his effort not to land on Jack-O, who was nestled in the pouch under his jacket, he fell hard on his skinny ass in thick black mud.

"Fuck!" He struggled to push himself up, but his hands kept sinking almost a foot deep into slimy gunk. Rain pelted down. It made a slapping sound on the muck around him. Traffic sent a cloud of spray down from the highway above. Kjel managed to come upright and slip-slide the rest of his way down the slick long grass to where Leo stood with coroner Charlie Alphonse.

Leo had managed to arrive ahead of him and was smoking, flicking his ash onto the wet ground, which irritated Kjel, because it made him want one and because it was a fucking stupid thing to do at a crime scene. Maybe bringing a dog wasn't so cool, either, but what was he to do on short notice? He nodded to Leo, then the coroner. "Alphonse," he said.

"Detective. Nice weather we're having, eh?" Alphonse looked up into the rain. "I've called O'Hagan. She's on her way."

"Evidence of foul play?" Kjel said, trying to wipe his muddy hands off on his soaked jeans as he looked out over the brown rain-pocked surface of Duck Lake.

"Dive captain called for homicide," Leo said. "Not sure why yet—they located her at the far end over there." He pointed his cigarette, which was going soggy in the rain. "Where the lake drains into a stream. That area is choked with reeds and bulrushes. Silt and shit at the bottom is like a meter deep. She was buried in it, which is why it took a while to locate her after her Yaris was found. Body must've floated out of the shattered window of the Yaris or something. Current at the lake bottom apparently flows that way."

"There comes O'Hagan now." Alphonse nodded up toward the highway.

Kjel turned in time to see the squat pathologist sliding down the bank on her ass, trying to hold her bag aloft. He laughed as she slid in.

"Oy there, Doc, nice entry. Glads to see I'ms not the only one with style."

O'Hagan muttered a curse as Kjel offered her a muddy hand to help her to her feet.

She adjusted the bill of her cap marked CORONER after she came upright. "Where is she?"

"Bringing her up at the far end," Alphonse said.

They watched in silence in the pelting rain as three divers broke the surface and began swimming the body of the Russian translator toward the bank. Yellow crime scene tape fluttered along the top near the road where the barrier was damaged and where tire treads gouged muddy earth and uprooted grass, showing where the Yaris had left the road.

"What's that?" O'Hagan said.

"What?" said Kjel.

"Under your jacket."

"Master Jack-O." He grinned.

"Maddocks's dog?"

"Yep."

"Where's Maddocks?" she said.

"Gots a big case in the big smoke."

"Mainland?"

"Yup. Surrey. His old stomping grounds."

The pathologist eyed him. "To do with the barcodes?"

Kjel nodded, his attention going back to their floater. "There she comes now."

The divers brought their DB in floating facedown. She wore a tan-colored sweater and a tweedy skirt. Stockings. No coat. No shoes. Her hair drifted around her, brown like the water. Alphonse turned and waved up to the body removal guys to come down from the bank with their metal litter basket and body bag. Flashes popped as the crime scene photographer snapped images of the decedent being guided in.

The divers slipped and sloshed as they struggled to walk the body through the silt and reeds along the shore. A duck squawked and scattered from rushes, little wings flapping like crazy as it tried to lift its fat body off the water. Morning commuter traffic hissed along the wet highway up above. Life going on as normal. People heading to offices, kids to school.

They brought her up onto the slick grass, turned her over. Her mouth gaped. A black weed hung out of it. Her skin was garish white, covered in slime. Her eyes stared milky and sightless up into the drumming rain.

"Shit," Kjel said. "That's her all right—the Russian interpreter who helped us with Sophia Tarasov." He squatted down next to the body alongside O'Hagan, taking care not to squash Master Jack under his jacket. The pathologist wiped her hands on a cloth from her bag and struggled to snap on her gloves in the rain. Gently, she moved wet hair off the woman's face and neck. Kjel tensed.

"Fuck," he whispered. "Her throat's been slit. Clean across."

"Almost to the spinal column," O'Hagan added. She moved the hem of the woman's shirt aside, made a nick under the rib, and inserted her thermometer. She read the liver temperature. "Postmortem interval could be seventy-two hours or more. Hard to say without knowing the temps at the bottom of that lake. I'll know more when I get her into my morgue."

"So she coulda died Friday," Leo said as he stood a safe distance behind Kjel. The old homicide cop never got too close to a DB if he could help it. "When her car bust through that barrier and came down that bank?"

"Yeah," Kjel said, leaning closer to the body. "But I don't see a corpse with a slit throat and no shoes driving that Yaris through any fucking barrier." He pointed to a small, circular, reddish-black wound, purulent-looking, on the inside of the woman's wrist. "What's do you reckon that is, Doc? Burn, maybe?"

O'Hagan drew back the sleeve, revealing more marks of similar shape along the tender white flesh of the decedent's inner arm. "Consistent with cigarette burns." Her hand stilled. Kjel saw it at the same time.

"Shit," he whispered.

The interpreter was missing a pinkie finger and a ring finger on her right hand.

"Cut clean off above the knuckles." He glanced up at Leo. "Looks like she was tortured. And resisted. And he had to burn her *and* take more than one finger." He fell silent, thinking.

The barcode girl. Sophia Tarasov—that's who the interpreter's killer wanted. That's how he'd known where to find the girls in the hospital and how he'd known which one had talked to Maddocks. And this innocent civilian had fought with her life to keep the information from him. To keep Tarasov safe. But she'd lost. They'd all lost.

He wiped water from his face with his sleeve. "Better get her into your morgue, stat, Doc, because my bets is this body is gonna be snatched off your table like Tarasov was."

He came to his feet. They watched in silence, rain drumming and plopping on water and mud as the body was bagged and carefully placed into the litter basket, and the body guys slipped and staggered up the steep grassy bank with their cargo.

Jack-O wiggled inside his pouch. Kjel opened up his zipper and peered in. "Okay, ol' boy, I'll take yous for a pee as soon as we gets outta here."

As they started up the bank, O'Hagan held Kjel back and said quietly, "What's the deal with Angie?"

"I dunno," he said. "All's I heard is she got axed." He glanced up at Leo, who was grabbing fistfuls of slimy grass as he tried to haul his fat hairy ass up the bank.

CHAPTER 50

Maddocks set his triple-shot coffee on his desk in the Surrey incident room and shrugged out of his jacket. He draped it over the back of the chair. He had not been able to sleep. Angie was not taking his calls, which was bad news. He was about to phone the MVPD social media desk to check on her when his cell rang.

He grabbed it. Caller ID showed Holgersen, not Angie.

"Yeah?" he said, connecting his call as he took a seat and reached for his coffee.

"Divers found her body—the Russian interpreter."

Maddocks stilled his coffee midway to his mouth.

"What?"

"Yep—she's dead. She never did make it across the island to go watching storms or nothing. They pulled her little Yaris outta Duck Lake off the highway on the way to Sooke yesterday. Divers found her body this morning. Like mud soup, that water."

"She went off the road?"

"Murdered, by all appearances—throat cut clean across, almost down to the spinal column." A pause. "She was tortured, boss—cigarette burns and two fingers cut off."

Maddocks swallowed and slowly set his coffee cup down. "Tarasov's killer," he said quietly. "That's how he got to her. That's how he found her. Through the interpreter."

"That would be my working hypothesis. He followed the interpreter, forced her to phone her office with some ruse about going away for the weekend, then tortured her for info on the barcodes."

"How did he find the interpreter in the first place?"

"Figure he's been watching us, boss. Them Russians gotta know we gots their barcode merch. I reckon they's been tailing our investigation to find where we stashed the girls. O'Hagan's waiting on word from you. She wants confirmation that this one is hers, or if once you pass on this news to your task force they're gonna be nabbing the DB off her table like they did Tarasov."

Ice seeped into his veins. He rubbed his brow and glanced up at where Takumi was talking to another officer across the room. "Dot every *i* and cross every bloody *t*, Holgersen, because you're right. The moment I pass this on to Takumi, it's outta your hands. They're going to want everything you got."

"Yous getting anywheres over there in Surrey, then?"

"Moving forward. Any witnesses yet? Anything that places our Tarasov suspect near, or with, the interpreter?"

"Nothing so far. Your task force has all the CCTV footage from the hospital, so we can't go looking there to see if the interpreter was followed after she left the Tarasov interview with us."

"I'll get that hospital footage pulled up on this end." Maddocks's gaze shot to the incident room door as it was flung suddenly open. Rollins from Project Gateway burst into the room, two officers hot on his heels. Takumi waved them over. They all bent heads in urgent conversation. Takumi reached fast for a phone, placed a call. Something was going down.

"I gotta go. Tell me quick, is Jack-O okay?"

"Ol' Master Jack ain't wanna go back to you, boss. Living the high life here." He hesitated. "Pallorino good?"

A jab of fear. "Why?"

"Because of what happened—"

"*What* happened?"

"She gots the guillotine. Vedder terminated her."

Maddocks's brain reeled. Fear sliced deeper. "You mean she's not *there*? Not at the social media desk?"

"I thoughts you knew, boss."

Christ. "Did Vedder—*anyone*—say anything about why she was terminated?"

"Mums the words here."

"Call me stat if you hear anything." Maddocks killed the call, took a gulp of tepid coffee, and surged to his feet. He went straight to Takumi and drew the man aside. He informed him about the Russian interpreter.

"I want to look at the surveillance footage," Maddocks said. "From when the interpreter left the hospital with me, Detective Holgersen, and the sketch artist."

"I'll get someone else on that. Right now I need you on surveillance at Club Orange B. Two developments—longshoremen just voted to ratify their agreement with the port. Strike was over as of ten minutes ago, and things are moving fast. The first cargo vessels that were anchored offshore are preparing to enter port as we speak. Word from Rollins is that his UC made contact, informing him that the longshoremen affiliated with the Hells Angels are edgy. Something's about to go down, but no one seems to be able to nail exactly when—maybe in the next twenty-four to seventy-two hours. His UC suspects a shipment of smuggled women is about to enter port aboard one of those offshore vessels. Word from my UC at Club Orange B has also just come in—same thing, something's hotting up there. We think it's tied to the port action. Suits have been coming and going at the club. Two cargo vans have been brought in and are parked in the lot beside the club. Two females have been bringing in cases of clothes. And a hairdresser and makeup person were seen going upstairs. The upstairs rooms have been declared off-limits to the rest of club staff. UC thinks some kind of auction is going to happen. Maybe buyers being lined up for the women coming in."

"You mean they're cleaning up the women and selling them right out of the container, after weeks at sea?" Maddocks said, his mind shooting back to Tarasov and how her group had been fed back to health at a remote holding facility before being sold to Sabbonnier and the Bacchanalian Club.

"This strike might have thrown them off schedule. They're cutting right to the delivery maybe."

Maddocks swore.

"We've got emergency response teams getting into position around the port," Takumi said. "We've got interagency ERT guys ready to respond near Club Orange. I want you in a command position at our surveillance location across the street from Club Orange B. You're to take charge in that room. We don't give the ERT a green light a moment too soon—if this is an auction of females, we wait until all the girls are inside that club, we wait until all the buyers are in place, and only then do you give the order. Understand?"

"Understood."

"Full briefing with the rest of the team in—" He checked his watch. "In fifteen." He raised his hand. "Bowditch? Over here—anything more on those inmates?"

Bowditch came over fast. "So far nothing, sir. Appears inmate Milo Belkin was stabbed in an altercation in the showers. Bled out fast. None of the inmates are saying anything. Correctional officers don't appear to have seen anything. CCTV on the showers mysteriously went down when it happened."

Maddocks's heart stopped, then jackhammered. "What's this about?"

"Two inmates tied to our Russian group died simultaneously last night, two different institutions." Takumi turned back to Bowditch. "What about the other one, Semyon Zagorsky? Anything more on him?"

"Pathologist is saying it looks like suicide," Bowditch replied. "Found hanged in his cell early this morning. Used strips of his pants to fashion a rope. What appears inconsistent with suicide, however, is the fact he was in the middle of writing a letter to his daughter, Mila. The letter was left on his desk unfinished."

Mila?

"How are these two inmates connected to the Aegis investigation?" Maddocks said crisply, anxiety rising in his stomach.

Takumi faced him. "Both men were arrested in a 1993 drug bust. VPD officer lost his life in the ensuing shoot-out. It was thought at the time that the narcotics they were transporting were linked to Russian organized crime, but neither inmate gave up the identities of their associates, two of whom fled the scene. Nothing could be proven. They might have no connection at all with our barcode trafficking case, but the timing of their deaths, especially with the buzz at the port and the club, raises a big red flag." He turned and strode away from Maddocks. "Eden? You got that report for me?"

Maddocks stared after him, sweat pricking over his skin. *Angie? Where in the hell are you? What happened to get you fired? Zagorsky has a daughter named* Mila? *Did you go visit him, too?*

He pushed out of the incident room door and hurried toward the fire escape stairs. He climbed them two at a time to the top floor and opened the door to the roof. He stepped into the chill, misty rain. He phoned Angie on his burner, watching the city below.

His call was flipped straight to voicemail—didn't even ring. Tension crackled inside him.

He dialed Flint.

As soon as his superior answered, Maddocks said, "Can you tell me what happened with Detective Pallorino? I need to know if it's in any way relevant to my case."

A pause. He heard Flint getting up, closing his door. "She was terminated for breach of probation. She visited an incarcerated suspect in an active RCMP investigation using her badge. She was not authorized to do this. She's also being investigated by the RCMP for obstruction. She withheld cold case evidence related to the floating foot case."

"One suspect?"

"Excuse me?"

"She visited just one incarcerated subject?"

A hesitation. "Should there be more?"

"No. I don't know. Has she handed in her badge?"

"No. We don't know where she is. Nor do the RCMP—they're looking for her. Her credit card records show that she checked out of her hotel in Coal Harbour last night and has gone to ground."

Fuck!

He hung up and drew his hand over his hair.

What in the hell are you up to, Angie? Gone rogue? In trouble? Dead?

His work cell rang. He switched phones. It was Eden.

"Sergeant, Takumi needs your input to help prep for the briefing, stat. The ERT officers have just arrived."

CHAPTER 51

It was almost two when Angie pulled up opposite the East Vancouver house of ex-exotic dancer Nadia Moss. She studied the building through the drizzle. Double story. Neat porch. The doors, window trim, and eaves painted an eggplant purple. Stained-glass detail across the top of the front windows. A baby stroller outside the front door. There was love and pride in the appearance of that house. She'd expected something different.

After returning to Vancouver, Angie had checked out of her hotel in Coal Harbour. It had been late, but she was edgy over both Maddocks's and Zagorsky's warnings.

She'd driven to Downtown Eastside and returned to the building that housed the Retro Adult Lounge Club. She'd paid the worn-looking redheaded woman cash for a room upstairs. No credit card record, no name given. All her stuff was in her car now, and she'd muddied up the plates, obscuring the registration. If need be, she'd return to the seedy hotel again tonight, because there she had finally managed to sleep despite the bass thump of the music coming from the basement and reverberating through the walls. It had been almost 10:00 a.m. when Stacey Warrington's call had roused her.

Stacey had gotten Angie's message, and she'd run the DNA profiles and ballistics first thing this morning, in spite of the fact she'd heard the rumors of Angie's termination. She'd called at once with the results. Angie replayed their conversation as she continued to study the house.

"The DNA profile from one of the semen samples is a match to Milo Belkin."

"What about the second sample?"

"Nothing in the convicted offender index, but we did get a hit with an unknown individual in the crime scene index. Blood and saliva evidence were left at a crime scene—"

"Which crime scene?"

"The 1993 drug bust involving Milo Belkin and Semyon Zagorsky."

"You're kidding?"

"Not a chance. The unknown individual appears to have been wounded in the gun battle with police before fleeing the scene. He left blood. Same DNA as the blood was also found on cigarette butts in the cube van when it was impounded."

"The cradle semen contributor could be the 1993 cop killer?"

"Possibly. If he was firing a .45 caliber. You'd need to check the cradle case ballistics against ballistics from the 1993 shoot-out."

"I can't thank you enough, Stace. While I have you on the line, could you do me one last big favor?"

A hesitation. *"Ange, I don't know what's going on, but—"*

"Have they told you yet, officially, that I've been terminated?"

"Not officially."

"Then you don't know, right?"

Another pause, then a soft curse. *"This could be a firing offence."*

"Only if you know. Please. It's just a quick criminal record check."

"What's the name?"

"Nadia Moss. She was the complainant in the sexual assault and battery charge against Belkin that was later dropped."

"Give me a second . . . Okay, yeah, she's got a record. Minor. Possession and soliciting."

"Thanks. What her last known address?"

Another moment of hesitation.

"I promise, Stace—last thing ever."

"Somehow I don't believe you, Angie. Here you go. Last known address, 4527 Rayburn Avenue, East Vancouver."

And that was the house Angie was parked outside now.

After her call from Stacey, Angie had bought another burner phone in East Van. As much as she wanted to call Maddocks and let him know where she was, she also *didn't* want to call him. The less he knew about what she was doing, the less she'd compromise his job, his career. Besides, he'd try to stop her. So would the RCMP—another reason to switch out phones and kill her credit card trail.

She reached for her black cap on the passenger seat and pulled it neatly onto her head, straightening her ponytail in the process. She checked herself in the flip-down visor mirror, although she couldn't say why. Perhaps it was just to prove to herself that she still existed, even though she had no job and was now a cipher erasing traces of her own movements. A pale, haunted face looked back at her. Zero makeup. Zero illusions. She flipped up the visor and got out of her vehicle.

She jogged across the street, headed up the small garden path, and climbed the wooden stairs to the porch. She knocked on the front door. She knew someone was inside—the lights were on, and she'd seen movement in the upstairs window.

Rain plopped from the eaves. She could hear traffic on a busy street a few blocks over and the wail of distant siren.

The door opened a crack, chain lock engaged. A woman peered through the crack.

"Yeah?" she said.

"I'm looking for Nadia."

"Who's asking?"

"A friend. Used to dance with her in the late nineties. I'm visiting town, heard she was still around."

The woman looked her up and down. "She's not here."

"But she does live here?"

"Yeah."

"You a roomie?"

"Pretty much. It's her house—she owns it. I've been renting upstairs from her for six years now."

"Know where I can find Nadia today?"

"She'll be at the club later. Works most nights from ten till late."

"Club?"

"If you danced with her in the nineties, you'll know which club. That much hasn't changed." She shut the door with a snick. Angie heard the lock turn. She ran her gaze over the house one more time. So Nadia Moss still worked at Club Orange B, and clearly she wasn't doing too badly for herself off her club earnings.

CHAPTER 52

Maddocks's hands tensed on the wheel as he drove to the surveillance location. It was already late Monday afternoon, and he hadn't been able to locate Angie. Bowditch's comment to Takumi ran through his brain.

What appears inconsistent with suicide, however, is the fact he was in the middle of writing a letter to his daughter, Mila.

Angie had said that she believed her twin might have been named Mila. Coincidence?

He drew to a stop at a red light. Traffic was snarling up. He turned on his radio to hear what might have caused the backup. He tuned it to the local news channel.

"Breaking news. The *Vancouver Sun* is reporting that the dismembered foot that washed up in Tsawwassen shares the DNA of the Vancouver Island female police officer who recently shot and killed notorious sex killer Spencer Addams, a.k.a. the Baptist. The officer is also the angel's cradle child who was abandoned in 1986."

What?

Maddocks hit the brakes and pulled over into a parking lot. He turned up the volume.

"This revelation came from forensic psychiatrist and true crime author Dr. Reinhold Grablowski, who helped profile the Baptist and who worked with Detective Angie Pallorino. Dr. Grablowski has secured a book deal to tell the remarkable story of an abandoned and abused child turned sex crimes cop who was recently disciplined for excessive violence of her own. Unofficial word is that Detective Pallorino's position with the MVPD has since been terminated and that she has now gone missing. According to Dr. Grablowski, Detective Pallorino had begun remembering pieces of her past, and she may have gone off-grid to search for her biological parents. Tune in to *West Coast Host* for more on the breaking story after the national news."

He called Angie. Still no answer.

Maddocks scanned quickly through his phone contacts, hit *Reinhold Grablowski*.

"What in the hell do you think you're doing?" he said as soon as Grablowski answered. "You could be putting her life in danger. She's a cop, for Chrissakes—"

"Was a cop," Grablowski said.

It hit. Hard. Her career really was over. He drew his hand over his hair.

"Now she's a disgraced ex-cop gone off-grid," said the shrink.

Even better for his ratings. The mystery cradle child was now a missing woman, hell alone knew where. But when the mob got wind of this, if they *were* the same guys who'd offed Belkin and Zagorsky, and Elaine and Stirling Harrison, then Angie was in big trouble. Grablowski had effectively put out a mass message saying, *This is the woman you need to find and silence—she's remembering stuff.* He'd stuck a giant target on her back. Maybe the mob had found her already.

"She had her chance to cooperate," Grablowski said. "She could have been in on my book deal."

Maddocks said, very quietly, rage simmering beneath his skin, "Where did you first get this information that she's the cradle child and her DNA is a match to the floating foot?"

"A friend."

"Which friend?"

"I don't need to reveal my sources to you, Detective. I got a book deal, that's all, to tell her story. And I'm not the only one with the information. If not me, then someone else would have broken the story." He paused. "The truth has a way of seeking light."

It's well past eleven on Monday night as the man sits nursing a Turkish coffee after his customary late-night meal at this establishment, a small brandy on the side. He comes here whenever he's in town. He always chooses a quiet alcove near the back where he can watch entrances, exits, and get a good view of the dancers, as well as note the positions of the security cameras.

There is unusual activity in the club tonight. Men arriving, some in suits. He has an idea what's going down. But it's not his business. He works for one man alone and does not ask questions. He's made good on two parts of the new contract from his boss—he utilized his contacts on the inside last night, and he's been informed that the two inmates are now dead. Two down.

One more to go.

But this remaining one is more complicated, requires some work. He first has to identify *Roksana*, then locate her. His brief is not to terminate her but to deliver her by floatplane to his boss. The boss wants to take care of this one himself. In a place where the subject's body will never be found. This one is special to the boss, and the man knows why—he's put two and two together. He sips his coffee, thinking, watching the dancers.

He's waiting to see whether intel comes from his contacts inside the institutions. They might be able to tell him what name she used to sign in when she visited Belkin and Zagorsky.

His waitress, long legs, nice breasts, brings him the newspaper he requested of her. He wishes to see whether the story of the convicts' deaths has broken, whether he's clean or if suspicions linger. Milo Belkin apparently did not speak to anyone directly about his visitor. He'd been trying to hide the fact she'd come at all. Semy had spoken only to the boss. Now they could not speak at all. Loose ends tied. He's a cleaner.

He unfolds the paper. The lead is a story on the abandoned angel's cradle child from 1986. She's been identified as a Vancouver Island police officer. A sub headline declares that the officer's DNA also matches the DNA of the child's foot found on the beach in Tsawwassen.

Intrigued, he leans closer.

Embedded in the article is a photo of the cop—Detective Angie Pallorino, who worked sex crimes for the Metro Victoria Police Department. Red hair. Scarred mouth. His pulse quickens. He reads faster.

The article quotes a forensic profiler who has secured a book deal to write the story on the angel's cradle child. Dr. Reinhold Grablowski claims that Pallorino is starting to remember her past, and her memories are leading her on a search for her biological parents. Adrenaline whips through him. He glances up.

His boss didn't give him any background on his latest commission, but he knows the legendary stories behind Big Red and the redheaded twins he tried to sell to a Saudi sheikh along with their mother, Ana, his used whore. That was back in '86.

It's all here, he thinks, *in the newspaper. Her identity, everything. Thank you, Dr. Reinhold Grablowski. Except . . .* He returns his attention to the article and reads further. She's gone to ground.

He reaches for his cup and takes another small sip of his bitter coffee. But a movement in the corner of his eye—a sense that the atmosphere in the room has subtly altered—distracts his attention. He looks up. A lone woman has entered the establishment. And her arrival has caused an almost imperceptible ripple through the club's patrons. Only a certain kind of woman does that. The kind who attracts any hot-blooded male's interest, and thus the attention of rival females, too. The man turns his full focus on her. From this vantage point he can see only the back of the woman. She's on the tall side. Dark-red hair hangs long and straight and glossy down her back. Dressed all in black. Leather jacket, slim black jeans. Biker-style boots. Yet elegant. She screams sex appeal. Confidence. Danger.

She turns to survey the establishment. Pale complexion. Kohl eyes. Blood-red lips. He goes stone-cold still. Slowly he sets down his coffee cup. His heart slows. He's a hunter who has just sighted his prey, because it's her. She has the scar.

She has indeed come looking. For her biological parents. And she's good.

Because she's come to the correct place for information—right into this lair.

He watches as she goes to the hostess's stand and asks the hostess a question. The hostess points to Nadia working behind the bar.

CHAPTER 53

It was close to midnight when Angie entered Club Orange B. The place was classy, white linen tablecloths and napkins, low lighting. A lounge singer in a figure-hugging blue dress at a grand piano crooned into an old-fashioned-looking mike. Topless dancers undulated lazily, evocatively against poles. She went to the bar, where the hostess had told her Nadia was working. She ordered a martini from the woman, who looked to be in her fifties. Short blonde hair. Nice-enough looking but well beyond pole dancing at this place. And she walked with a slight limp—consistent, possibly, with the baseball bat beating she'd received after being raped in the alley outside all those years ago.

"I'm looking for Nadia," Angie said when the woman delivered her drink.

She glanced up, locked her gaze onto Angie's. "Who's asking?"

"I need to ask you about Milo Belkin."

The woman paled, set the bottle down. She glanced up at a CCTV camera. Caution whispered into Angie.

"I'm Nadia," she said quietly. "Who are you?"

"I'd like to know why you dropped charges against him."

"Look, I don't know who you are, and—"

"I'm someone who wants to make Milo pay for something he did to my family a long, long time ago, Nadia. He hurt me, too. I'm not a threat to you. I just need to know the names of the guys Milo Belkin and his friend Semyon Zagorsky used to hang with back then."

Two in particular. The ones who evaded the drug bust.

Another nervous glance at the camera. Someone up in headquarters was watching her at the bar.

"I made a mistake," she whispered, wiping the counter around Angie's drink in an exaggerated fashion, for the camera no doubt. "It wasn't him—it wasn't Milo who hurt me."

"Are you certain?"

The woman's gaze ticked up.

"Look, I *can* help you—"

"I don't need help. It's in the past. Over."

A swarthy male in a polo shirt sidled up behind Nadia. "Everything okay, Nadia?" he said, eyeing Angie.

"Yeah, yeah, cool."

The man studied Angie for a moment, then said to Nadia, "Let me know if you need help."

When he left, Nadia went to work the far end of the bar. Angie finished her drink and motioned to Nadia for another. Nadia looked upset. She came over, wiping her hands on her apron. "What now?"

"Can I get a sparkling water?" Angie said.

Nadia returned with the water. As Angie took the glass from her, she said, "How about Semyon Zagorsky, then? Did you know him?"

A frown furrowed into Nadia's brow. She flicked a look behind her back. When she returned her gaze to Angie, she looked scared. "Semy used to come into the club with Milo," she whispered. "Then he got married, had a kid. He didn't come after that."

"Who were Semy's friends? Anyone close who used to come here with him?"

"I don't want trouble."

"Please," Angie said.

"Both Milo and Semy were tight with Ivanski and Sasha."

"They have last names?" Angie said quickly, keeping an eye out for Nadia's polo-shirted boss.

"Ivanski Polzim and Sasha Makeev."

Adrenaline pumped into Angie's blood, her mouth going dry with excitement at the lead.

"Where would I find Sasha and Ivanski?"

"Maybe they come into the club sometimes."

"So they *do* still hang out here?"

The male manager returned. "All good, Nadia?" he said.

"Yeah, all fine."

The man studied Angie for another long moment before leaving. As he disappeared from view, Angie quickly asked Nadia for her check. She was worried Mr. Polo Shirt was going to send in the bouncers, and she wanted to give Nadia a way to contact her before that happened.

Nadia handed her the check. Angie wrote the number for her disposable phone on it and pushed it back across the counter secreted between bills of cash. "Please," she said, "phone me if you want to talk. Or if you remember anything else."

Nadia took the cash, surreptitiously pocketing the note in her apron pocket as she went to attend to customers down the bar. Angie turned on her stool and surveyed the establishment as she finished her water. Couples and groups at the tables were enjoying late meals or desserts, or just drinks and snacks. A man seated in a dark booth at the back caught her eye. He was studying her with an unnerving intensity. He appeared to be dining alone, a newspaper in his hands.

He caught her gaze, then returned his eyes to his newspaper.

Angie finished her drink. She wasn't going to get anything more out of Nadia here. But she had a fresh lead—two names. Ivanski Polzim and Sasha Makeev.

There was a chance they were the accomplices who'd escaped capture during the drug bust that had netted Belkin and Zagorsky. If so, one of them had left DNA at the drug bust scene that matched the semen DNA found on the purple sweater left in the cradle.

One could also be the VPD cop killer.

From the surveillance building across the street, Maddocks watched the monitors over the shoulders of two cops and a technician. The screens all showed live footage of Club Orange B from various angles. They'd been at it for hours—it was hitting midnight now. Something was definitely on the verge of going down, but what and when still remained the question. One monitor showed the outside parking lot next to the club. Another displayed a feed from the back alley. A few more streamed from inside the club.

As he watched, a van pulled into the parking lot and sat idle, exhaust fumes puffing into the wet night. The lot was full with newer model SUVs and cargo vans. He turned to study the monitors showing the interior of the club again. Patrons dining. Dancers at their poles. Lounge singer. Folks sitting at the bar.

His work phone rang. It was Takumi. They were using cells, not radios, which might be listened in to. Takumi said they were on—cargo containers had been unloaded from a vessel out of China. Two of the containers carried human cargo. From them a total of thirty-two females had been moved into two trucks owned by Atlantis Imports. The trucks had left the docks in convoy, following a black SUV with plates registered to Atlantis Imports. Another SUV brought up the rear, plates registered to the same company. Cops were tailing the convoy now. A helo hovered way up high, monitoring progress. Intel from Rollins's UC at the port was that the human cargo was headed toward Club Orange B. ETA around twenty minutes, if a direct route was followed. Emergency response teams were stationed outside and around the club, waiting for Maddocks to give the command on his end. The goal was to storm the joint only once all the women had been taken inside.

"It's going down," Maddocks said to the surveillance team as he killed Takumi's call. "Twenty minutes."

In tense silence they watched the screens. The footage showed several more men entering the club. The males went through the restaurant, past the bar, disappearing through a door at the back. The surveillance team knew from their UC that the door led upstairs, but their surveillance did not extend into that area. Maddocks turned his focus to the footage showing the inside entrance of the restaurant. A woman had just come in. Alone. His body tightened, every nerve in his body suddenly on raw alert as he watched the female. Long hair fell in a sheen as she bent forward to talk to the hostess. The hostess pointed to the bar. The female turned. Shock slammed through Maddocks—*Angie?*

What in the hell?

Tension crackled through his veins. She seated herself on a barstool, ordered a drink, and began conversing with the female bartender. Slap-bang in the middle of their takedown operation. He had to get her out, stat. *Shit.* He rubbed his mouth hard. This was his fault. He'd given her too much information. She'd gone to see Milo Belkin, and Belkin was now dead. Had she gone to see Semyon Zagorsky as well?

Had Belkin and Zagorsky told her something that had brought her here?

Her presence inside that club could send the entire Aegis op sideways.

He should have turned her in to Takumi for everyone's safety, including her own. *This* was why cops in relationships could *never* be partnered on the job—decisions were made out of emotion, not cold, dispassionate logic.

325

Maddocks's heart raced as he considered his options. He reached into his pocket for his burner phone and dialed the number he had for her. No response. Number inactive. She had to have switched out phones when she checked out of her Coal Harbour hotel. He couldn't go into the club, either, and haul her out—he'd blow the entire op himself. The girls could be killed. The UC's life could be put on the line. Other officers, including Angie, would be placed in lethal danger.

He watched Angie write something on a piece of paper, secrete it between dollar bills, and push it toward the bartender. The bar woman pocketed the note and went to the far end of her counter. Angie then angled on her stool to watch the dancers as she finished her drink.

What in the hell is she up to?

He watched as Angie shifted her attention to a male seated at the rear of the establishment. The male was in his late fifties and had a newspaper. He held Angie's gaze across the restaurant. An odd chill of familiarity washed through Maddocks. He leaned closer to the screen.

"Can you zoom in on that guy, there, at the back?" he said quickly to the techs as he pointed to the screen.

As they narrowed in, Angie got up from the bar and made for the exit. The man came instantly to his feet. He folded his newspaper and headed toward the bar, carrying the folded paper in his hand. Angie exited the club doors. The chill in Maddocks turned to ice. The man walked with a very slight limp, like one leg was shorter than the other, and it canted him slightly to the left. Maddocks tried to swallow. The man was the right height, the right build. Except he wore no wig this time. It was *him*. Sophia Tarasov's killer. The man who'd posed as a doctor. His image from the hospital CCTV footage had been burned into Maddocks's brain. Every instinct in his body screamed that *this* was the guy. The hit man. The same killer suspected of having tortured and killed the Russian interpreter.

Angie had walked right into a lion's den.

Maddocks's gaze shot to the monitor showing exterior footage. Angie was walking down the road, past the parking lot, hair blowing in the wet wind, streetlights glinting in the rain.

His attention whipped back to the interior footage. The male was asking something of the woman behind the bar. She looked scared. From her pocket she extracted the piece of paper Angie had given her. She showed it to the man.

The man pointed to it and said something. The woman's body language screamed fear. Subservience. She reached for a cell phone on the shelf behind her. She returned to the counter. The man jabbed at the note with his index finger. She focused on the piece of paper as she punched a number into the phone.

"Closer," Maddocks said, voice thick. "Zoom in more. Onto that note."

The bar woman's hands were shaking. The man stepped in front of the camera's line of view. His shift in position afforded Maddocks a clear view of the headline on the top part of the folded newspaper in the man's hand.

Angel's Cradle Child from '86 Identified as Victoria Cop

A smaller subhead read:

Officer's DNA a match to floating child's foot

Maddocks swung his attention back to the monitor of the exterior. He watched as Angie stopped, answered her phone. She nodded as she spoke, checked her watch, then killed the call. Maddocks switched his gaze to the footage feeding from the inside of the club. The bartender ended her call, too. The outside feed showed Angie turning around and starting back toward the club. But when she reached the parking lot, she crossed through it, threading her way among the stationary vehicles as she headed toward the alley that led to the rear of the club building.

Maddocks could barely breathe. He watched as the male with the newspaper left the bar counter and made for the restaurant exit.

The man headed out the door. The exterior camera picked him up outside. Maddocks scrutinized his gait, the way he held his head, moved his arms, the roll of his shoulders. He was even more certain—*this* was their hit man. The suspect entered the parking lot and approached a black Audi gleaming with rain. He opened the driver's side door, got in. The running lights flared on as he started the engine. He reversed out of his parking spot and drove the Audi around to the alley at the rear of the club.

"Can you read the plate?" Maddocks snapped at the surveillance tech in front of the monitors. "Zoom in on that Audi plate."

"Can't see it," the surveillance guy said. "The dumpster on the sidewalk is obscuring line of sight." Maddocks's phone rang. It was Takumi.

"ETA five minutes," Takumi said. "Waiting for visual confirmation of the convoy on your end."

Maddocks's gaze flicked to the screen showing exterior footage of the dimly lit back alley. Angie came suddenly into view around the back corner of the building. She stopped in dark shadows and looked around as if waiting to meet someone. It happened so fast Maddocks barely saw. The Audi drove into the alley behind Angie just as the bartender stepped out of the club's back alley door.

The bar woman waved and called to Angie, distracting Angie as the Audi door opened behind her. Angie went toward the bar woman. The woman started talking to Angie as the man came out of the car and slipped into the blackness of shadow along the wall. Maddocks could no longer make out his shape. Tension lashed through him. *Where in the hell is he?*

A dark movement loomed out of the shadows and came up behind Angie as she conversed with the barkeeper—*the man*. He flung his arm around Angie's neck, squeezed, and jabbed something in her back. Angie stilled, and then her whole body jerked in wild spasms as if she'd been shocked.

"Fuck!" said one of the surveillance cops. "Did you just see that? Did you see what he did?"

"Stun gun," said the second officer. "He used a fucking stun gun on that woman."

Maddocks stared in mute horror as Tarasov's killer dragged Angie's limp body back toward the Audi, its engine still running and puffing white exhaust fumes into the air. The bar woman went back inside.

"*There it is!*" the tech said, pointing to another monitor. "The convoy. Lead SUV and one bringing up the rear. Two trucks. Atlantis Imports on the sides. We have a visual. We have a visual."

The lead SUV turned into the parking lot and drove around toward the back of the club. The rest of the convoy followed. Maddocks couldn't wait. The killer was pulling out of the opposite end of the alley in his Audi. He was going to exit on the far side of the club. Angie was inside that car.

"Get that damn Audi plate—*there*—there, you can see it now!" The Audi came around the far side of the building, and light fell on it as it turned into the street.

"Sir—the convoy—"

"Yes, you watch the convoy," Maddocks said to the officer who'd just spoken. He addressed the tech next. "You, zoom into that goddamn plate before we lose that vehicle."

The tech obeyed the order. The Audi plate zoomed into view under the streetlight. Maddocks committed the registration to memory as he reached for his work phone and made another call, this time to Sergeant Eden, who was stationed back in the incident room.

"I need a plate run." He gave Eden the registration.

As he waited on the line, he said to the team, "Tell me when all the females from the trucks have been taken inside—all thirty-two, count 'em."

Eden came back on the line. "Vehicle is also registered to Atlantis Imports—a company car."

"Put out a BOLO on a black Audi with that registration. The driver has just abducted a woman from Club Orange B. He's a suspect in the killing of Sophia Tarasov and a Russian translator on the island. Armed and dangerous. Kidnap victim is Angie Pallorino—ex MVPD officer. Did we untangle those holding companies yet? Did we get any key names of the current owners or individuals behind Atlantis Imports?"

"All have ties back to one numbered company that also has investments in Club Orange B—"

"*Who*, dammit, *who* is behind that company?"

"I was getting there, Sergeant," she said coolly. "It's been in the process of being unraveled since you recently brought to the table the MVPD information regarding the possible trafficking route. Until then Atlantis wasn't even on our radar." A brief pause as Eden opened a file. "The company appears to be linked to five BC and Alberta businessmen. All billionaires in their own right. Two are in the oil industry based out of Calgary. Another in mineral exploration and mining in the north. One in commodities trading, and another invested primarily in import-exports. All have at one time or another come to the attention of white-collar crime divisions, but nothing has ever stuck."

"Send me their files, names, photos. Stat."

"Sergeant," the tech cut in, "they're offloading girls."

Maddocks's gaze shot to the monitor. He watched the first woman being taken from the back of a truck. His brain raced, tension ratcheting. His phone pinged—Eden's emails were coming through.

Hurriedly, Maddocks opened the first attachment. It showed the names and photographs of five males, all in their late fifties or sixties. His heart quickened at the sight of the fifth one—a big, pale-complexioned redhead with light-gray eyes. Part of a tattoo was visible down the left side of his neck. His name was Olyeg Kaganov.

Maddocks clicked open the second attachment sent by Eden. He scrolled quickly to the intel brief on Kaganov. The man owned and operated the high-end Semko Fishing Lodge along with several fish farms in the Queen Charlotte Strait. He owned residences on the North Shore but spent most of his time at the lodge.

It was located on Semko Island, which lay north of Vancouver Island.

Fish farms.

When Angie had been taken back under hypnosis, she'd remembered docks. She'd mentioned fish farms. Maddocks replayed their conversation in his mind.

"There was water, ocean beyond the forest. A big building with a green roof where a red man lived. Docks. Several, making square shapes in the water. One with a building on it. I thought of them as fish pens."

"Red man?"

"I have no idea what that means."

"And the docks?"

"A fish farm maybe? They reminded me of the docks outside Jacob Anders's lab buildings . . . The red man . . . I felt the red man was bad."

He clicked open the images of Semko Fishing Lodge contained in the intel brief. Green-roofed log buildings filled his small cell screen. An aerial image showed docks in a grid pattern off the northeast of the island.

It fit—goddammit, it all fit! With Tarasov's testimony, too. Tarasov and the five barcodes discovered aboard the *Amanda Rose* had been taken from the Port of Vancouver by a small boat to a remote holding facility along the coast somewhere. The flying time Tarasov had described from that holding location to Victoria was in the ballpark for the location of Semko Island.

Tarasov had also witnessed ink on the side of her hooded captor's neck. Plus, Queen Charlotte Strait fed into the Strait of Georgia. Angie's twin's foot could have floated from Semko Island.

It all fucking fit, right down to the big "red man's" pale-gray eyes. They were the exact color of Angie's. Ice branched through his chest. *Her father—Kaganov could be her father.*

"Sir, the last five females are coming out of the second truck."

Maddocks's body snapped taut with adrenaline as his gaze ticked back to the screen. He watched as the last girls were being brought out of the vehicle—emaciated, heads bowed forward, their hair lank and dirty, obscuring their faces.

"Sir, the last two females are now being escorted into the club," said the surveillance officer.

Maddocks's thoughts shot to the hit man. He worked for someone. Olyeg Kaganov? He hadn't inflicted a lethal wound while incapacitating Angie. That told Maddocks he wanted her alive. Why? To take her somewhere? To Kaganov?

"Sergeant," said the officer, "the females are now all inside the building. I repeat, all inside. Awaiting order."

When Maddocks didn't answer, the officer turned in his chair to face him, his features tight with tension. "Sir?"

"Call it!" Maddocks barked as he spun around and made for the exit. "Give the go!" he yelled over his shoulder as he flung open the door. "Now!"

"Sir?"

He shoved through the door and left the room. He dialed Takumi as he hurried toward the building's fire escape stairs. Takumi picked up instantly.

"I've given the ERT go," Maddocks snapped. "Cargo is all inside. But a woman—an ex-cop—has been abducted from the club. Her name's Angie Pallorino. She's been independently investigating a case that appears linked to the barcodes. I believe Olyeg Kaganov, one of the men tied to ownership of Atlantis Imports, is directly involved in her kidnapping. Eden's put out a BOLO on the kidnap vehicle. A black Audi. I'm flying up to Semko Fishing Lodge on Semko Island. Kaganov owns and operates the lodge. I think they're taking her there. I'll need backup."

He had no proof, but he had to *do* something apart from waiting for the BOLO to result in a sighting. That alone was a crapshoot now. He had to trust his gut. He'd gotten her into this shit. Now he had to get her out. He believed that if the hit man wanted Angie alive, there was a helluva good chance she'd be transported to Semko.

Takumi started to object, but Maddocks killed the call before Takumi could order him to stand down.

Maddocks knew what Takumi would say—that Operation Aegis needed to move slowly on Kaganov—get proof that Kaganov and the other men *were* actually behind the barcode imports, secure the requisite warrants so that charges would stick in court. Yeah, this was a gamble. It could cost his job. It could cost prosecution of those men down the line.

But if he *didn't* act, it could cost Angie's life.

If he was wrong, if a patrol car picked up the Audi while he was en route to Semko, that was okay—local law enforcement could handle it from there. That base would be covered. In the meanwhile, time was running out. If Kaganov really was Angie's father, and if he was aware from the news that she was now remembering her past and coming after him, she didn't have long to live.

If she was even still alive.

Maddocks burst out of the stairwell door at the rear of the building. Cold rain kissed his face as he ran toward his unmarked car parked in a back alley a few blocks down. As he got into his vehicle, he made another call. To a pilot friend.

CHAPTER 54

TUESDAY, JANUARY 9

Angie came around slowly, confusion clouding her brain. She struggled to place what was going on, where she was. She'd blacked out.

Why? How long? What had happened?

She tried to move her tongue. It felt too large. Her mouth was dry, tasted metallic. Her skull, her brain, her entire body pounded in pain with each beat of her heart. Carefully she opened her eyes, wincing sharply against light filtering down through a window up high. Near the ceiling. With bars.

A chill of recognition cut through her core.

I've been here before. What is this place?

Angie closed her eyes again and tentatively touched her fingertips to the base of her skull. They came away sticky. Blood? Hers? She groaned as she tried to move her head, to reopen her eyes. Her neck felt as though it might be broken. The muscles in her injured arm were afire.

She gave up for a moment, just lying there, trying to figure it out.

She'd gotten a call—that's what had happened. From Nadia Moss. Just as she'd left the Russian club. Moss had whispered over the phone that she'd wanted to meet Angie in private, outside the club in the back alley, where she planned to take a smoke break—she couldn't talk inside. Too risky, she'd said. Moss had sounded desperate.

Tension whipped through Angie. She fought to open her eyes again, to wake fully, to recall with clarity what had happened next.

Nadia had opened the back door into the alley. She'd called Angie over to the lighted doorway. Angie had been grabbed by the neck from behind . . . then a Taser. It had to have been a Taser. After that she recalled nothing, just blackness, apart from a vague recollection of being inside a vehicle at some point, something made of cloth over her head. Then . . . a thudding sound, a vibrating sensation. Chopper? A snatch of memory came to her—the feeling that she was inside a helicopter, flying during the night. It had been dark. Cold. A faint glow had come from electronics, maybe an instrument panel. Her hands and feet had been bound. She moved her legs now. Unbound, she realized. Her boots were still on. Hands were free, too. She tried to inhale deeply through her nose. She recognized the smell of this room.

I've definitely been here before.

Alarms clanged through her. Then Angie stilled. She felt a presence. *Someone is inside the room with me.* Tentatively, she sucked air in through her nose again, and she could smell him. An odor of perspiration underscored by a faint thread of masculine aftershave.

"Welcome home, Roksana."

Electricity shocked through her body. Angie stopped breathing as she was whirled back, back in time. She was in the dank, dim room, the place Alex had taken her with hypnosis.

"I . . . was lying on a bed. In a dark room. There was someone with me in the darkness, holding my hand. A female. Her skin was cool. Soft. She was singing sweetly, gently, like a lullaby . . . those words about two little kittens. In Polish. Then she suddenly stopped singing. Someone had come in. I was scared. The room went blacker . . . There was a man in the room on top of her. Big, big man."

"On top of who, Angie?"

335

"I . . . don't know. The lady singing. He was grunting like a dog on her, and she was crying softly. Very scared. Wasn't nice. Horrible."

Angie lurched up. Her world reeled. Nausea surged up her throat, and she gagged. She was on a bed. She patted the surface around her, still unable to focus properly.

"Welcome home, Roksana," he said again. The voice was low, deep. Sonorous. Terror rose inside her. She swallowed, then blinked frantically. *I know that voice. I know it.*

Her vision focused. She could see the wall opposite her and the barred window up high. She managed to turn her head sideways toward the source of the voice. The pale light coming in through the window shone on a big man. Red hair. Bushy red beard. Pale skin. Pale-gray eyes.

The red man. Bad man. *It was him.*

"Who . . . who *are* you?" Her voice came out hoarse. "Where am I?"

He reached forward and combed his thick fingers through her hair, snaking a lock around his hand. He angled his head, and Angie saw the blue crab ink on the side of his solid neck. "Gorgeous," he whispered. "You grew up so beautiful, my girl." He touched his fingertips to her lips, tracing her scar. She jerked back against the wall.

"Get your hands the fuck off me!"

He grinned. Light danced in his eyes. "This is where I bring all my girls, *Roksi*. Do you recall? This is where I kept the two of you and your mother. I wanted to bring you back here, for you to wake up and see it, and to remember it, and to remember me. I wanted to see and touch you, too, to look into your eyes and have you look back into mine." He studied her. "My progeny," he said quietly. "Resourceful girl. After all these years, you find me. You find my club. Very well done, Roksi. You are indeed my child."

Bile surged into her throat. She could see it—in his complexion. His hair. The light-gray shade of his eyes. She'd found him. She'd found her biological father. And he was the red man. A monster.

"What . . . what's your name?" she whispered.

He smiled. "Oly. Olyeg Kaganov."

"My mother?"

"My whore once. Pretty little thing from Poland. Fell pregnant at sixteen."

Angie's chest crunched with emotions. She glared at him, trying to really *see* him, to absorb his face, the shape of his body, his smell. Trying to understand him. *Her dad.*

"You killed her. You killed my mother, didn't you?"

His smile changed into something darker.

"Ana," she said quietly. "That was her name—her name was Ana."

"Very good. You get this from Semy?"

A pure white hatred filled her heart. It leaked a familiar burn into her blood, and the old taste of rage filled her mouth. It came with sharp, clear edges and restored clarity to her brain. It sliced through her system hand in hand with the pain beating through her body.

"Anastazja Kowalski," he said quietly. "Daughter of Danek Kowalski, a political activist who was imprisoned and then killed during the lead-up to Solidarity in Poland."

A grandfather. I had a grandfather, and his name was Danek Kowalski.

Angie focused fiercely on this news. She had family. In Europe. She was going to get out of this room, out of this prison of her past. She was going to find the rest of her family. She was going to let them know what had happened to Ana.

"Ana told me that her mother died when she was little," he said, his gray eyes locked on her own. "Her father raised her solo. She was fourteen when the violence erupted in Poland and her father was taken. That's when the traffickers got her. Here, see?" Zagorsky reached for a framed photo resting on the small table beside the bed. He held it out to her.

"Take it."

Angie snatched it and stared. A young woman looked back at her. Barely sixteen. A heavily rounded belly. She was a mirror of Angie when she'd been a teen herself—apart from the long, dark, wavy hair and a more olive-toned complexion. Tears pooled in Angie's eyes. She began to shake.

"I thought you also might like to go and see the old fish pens and crab pots again, before we say goodbye." He paused. "Roksi."

Her gaze shot back to him. "Goodbye?" she whispered, tears blurring her vision and obscuring his big face.

"A full family reunion of sorts. It will be fitting, I think, for you to end your life there, where your mother and sister died. Because you see, my Roksana, everything always comes back to the beginning." He drew a gentle circle in the air with his meaty hand. "As it should. But this time"—he grinned—"no shoes that can float."

Angie gagged. She tried to get up, but her world spun again and she slumped back hard against the wall, breathing heavily. "What . . . what did you do to them? How did you kill them?"

"Come, I'll show you." He held out his hand to her. "It's time."

She couldn't move. She'd vomit, pass out—she couldn't afford to black out again. She had to stay present, fight this.

His grin vanished. His eyes turned hard. He took the framed photo out of her lap and returned it to the bedside table. Surging to his feet, he reached around to his back and brought out a pistol. He pointed the muzzle at her, then waved it toward the door. He was tall—well over six feet. Built like a lumberjack. Massive thighs. Abs that looked rock hard. Pecs bulging beneath his shirt and biceps that strained against his sleeves. Olyeg Kaganov might be in his sixties, but her father was still a Goliath.

"Go on. Get up. Move. We're going to take a little walk through the forest where you liked to play with Mila."

The sound of her sister's name speared a jolt of electricity through her. Angie locked her gaze on his as she slowly inched her left hand around her hip to feel the back pocket of her jeans.

"Don't bother," he said. "I took the phone. And the small knife."

As he turned sideways, she caught sight of his knife—a massive hunting blade sheathed on his belt.

He reached down, grabbed her upper arm, and yanked her to her feet. She gasped, eyes watering in pain. But she refused to cry out. Up close she could really smell him—and she remembered his scent in the way that a prey animal recalls the smell of the predator that hunts it. A smell she'd learned to fear as a child. He pushed her, and she stumbled toward the door—the same door she'd opened with Alex's magic key. Except now she had no key, no special word she could utter to return "home," back to the safety of Alex's living room.

Zagorsky reached for the handle and flung the door open wide. Angie blinked blindly into the brightness, trying to orient herself.

"Walk." He rammed the muzzle of his pistol into her lower back. "That way, along the dirt path and down into the forest."

She tried to put one foot in front of the other as she exited through the door, but she staggered forward, almost falling to her knees. Angie stopped. Breathing hard, she righted herself, then attempted once more to negotiate the uneven and twisting path that lay in front of her. As they moved into the trees, the ground underfoot grew springy with moss. She heard a plane engine up high, and she squinted into the sky. A small craft with floats and props flew overhead in the white-gray heavens, then disappeared beyond the tops of trees, oblivious to what was occurring in the forest below.

The path led into a grove of old-growth cedars that towered overhead, branches drooping low, bark hanging in shredded red strips from trunks that spanned wider than the arms of two men joined. Moss and colored lichens grew over rocks. Angie stopped as the sound of a woman singing reached her through the forest.

Little berries, black berries, two gray kittens . . .

The trees above her swirled. Branches rustled. This was it. This was the place. Her and Mila's place.

A child laughed. Angie spun to the source of the sound. In the shadows beneath the cedars, she glimpsed a wash of pink. The little girl was there, peeping around a fat trunk, her long red hair swaying toward the ground. The girl smiled.

"Mila?" Angie whispered, holding her hand out toward the child. But the girl ducked back behind the trunk and vanished into the forest.

Kaganov laughed. "Yes, this is where Semy brought you two to play."

Buy time. I can't match him physically. I have no weapons. I need my wits—that's all I have now. Play him. Buy time to come up with a plan.

She turned to face him. He towered above her, and she tried not to look at the weapon aimed at her chest or the knife at his hip. Instead she focused her eyes on his.

"Who is Semy to you?" she said. *My father's got ego. He brought me here because he wanted me to see him, for me to be impressed by and in awe of and afraid of him. He's a narcissist who wants to show off. Appeal to his ego.*

"My cousin from the Little Odessa side of the family," he said. "By going to visit him at Kelvin, you signed his death warrant. Same with Milo Belkin."

"What do you mean?"

He gave a half-assed shrug with his big shoulder. "Had to have them killed. Loose ends. Need to tie them all up now that you started messing in things."

"They're *dead*?"

A slow smile crossed his face. Bastard was enjoying this. *Play it, Angie, play him.*

"How . . . how did you do it?"

"I have contacts. On the inside."

"Is that how you know that I visited Semy and Milo?"

"No. Semy phoned to tell me. He did it to buy continued protection for his own family, even though he knew his phone call would kill him. And you. That's how much the asshole cared about his family."

It struck Angie. "So it was you—you who ordered the deaths of Stirling Harrison and his wife. I thought they were killed to help Semy attain parole. But I get it now—you wanted that parole board to see him as a continued threat with gang links on the outside. You *wanted* to keep him locked up for as long as you could."

He snorted softly. "Him and Milo. Those two just made trouble for me at a time I was trying to grow the business. I put them inside as a warning to the others."

"How did they make trouble?" *Keep him talking. He's buying into this.*

"Milo was just too stupid—a liability. Semy, he was too soft." Zagorsky's features darkened. "He grew too fond of Ana and you two. Gave you both those pairs of shoes—the one that washed up. Before the opportunity presented to set Semy up in the drug bust, I *made* him watch what I did to little Mila and your mother. Because it was his fault. It was because of *him* that I was forced to kill Ana and Mila. He lost me good money there."

Hatred threatened Angie's clarity. With it came the familiar heat of rage.

Focus. Focus. Don't let the anger blind me.

"It ate at Semy for the remainder of his life—seeing Mila and Ana die. I think it's why he named his own child Mila, born to him before he went into prison. But that's enough talking now. Move."

"That drug haul had a street value of millions. That's a lot to sacrifice just to put your cousin in prison."

"Got a tip through a two-timing informant that the VPD was already onto the delivery. It was tainted. We were going to lose it anyway. So I switched out crews and put Milo and Semy on the job. Move!"

"No." She stood her ground, hands clenching at her sides, clarity crystalizing fast, her mind growing harder, sharper. In her peripheral vision Angie noted various forest paths leading out of this clearing, all possible escape routes through the woods. "Tell me first what happened that night at the cradle. How did Semy and Milo allow us to escape? How was it their fault?"

He moistened his lips.

"Come on, Oly, you brought me all the way here." A sour taste rose up Angie's gullet at the shape of this man's name in her mouth, her own father's name. "Getting me here must have taken some serious effort. So why rush it now? Why not let me know what happened that Christmas Eve before I die?"

He inhaled, a hint of amusement beginning to toy at the corners of his mouth. "Semy and Milo and another man—Ivanski—were supposed to guard you and Mila and your mother plus two others. You were being kept in an apartment in the city while waiting for word to come from contacts at the port so that you could be put aboard a ship."

"What ship?" she said quickly.

"The start of your journey to Saudi Arabia. I'd sold you to a prince there, for his harem. Top dollar. He wanted to groom you and Mila from very young. I threw Ana into the bargain to act as a chaperone. Then, while you were all holed up in that apartment, awaiting the signal, the men were drinking a little too much that Christmas Eve. They were running out of vodka. Your mother saw her chance. She came on to Semy, who was vulnerable to her charms, far too vulnerable."

"He loved her, didn't he?"

Oly's face blackened, and it made his eyes ice-light, like a Viking marauder. But he ignored Angie's question. Which told her that she was right. She knew now—at the heart of it—why Semy had been punished. Why her father had found a way to tip off police to the drug bust. Why Semy had been forced to watch this red man kill Mila and their mother.

"Ana suggested Semy go out in the van to buy more drink. The guys were bored. They'd been there for days. Semy agreed. When he left, Ana dead-bolted the door and, feigning inebriation herself, encouraged Ivanski and Milo to finish the remains of the vodka, and she offered herself to them. She had sex with them both. Then while they were lulled and starting to doze, she grabbed you two from the next room and fled."

The semen on her purple sweater. No time to put my shoes on as we ran into the snow where the Chinese senior at the Pink Pearl restaurant saw us.

"What about the other two women you say were there?"

"In the next room. High as kites. Didn't know a thing."

"It was Milo and Ivanski who chased us?"

"Semy returned with the van at midnight. He saw Milo and Ivanski chasing you all across the street into that alley. He pulled up, heard gunshots, saw your mother fighting with them as she tried to put you and your sister into that cradle. Milo cut your face when he tried to stab Ana. He knew it was you twins that were the valuable commodity. Ana was expendable. But she fought back, and Milo's blade caught your face. She got you into the cradle. Semy drove around to the other side of the alley, and that's when the church bells started ringing and all the churchgoers started coming out. Milo and Ivanski grabbed Ana and your sister and fled to Semy in the waiting van. But you—" He tutted his tongue and tried to touch her scar again. "You were the one who got away, but there, he left his mark."

She took a fast step back from his touch. His eyes narrowed, and his neck corded. A flush of anger colored his cheeks.

Don't break his roll now. Buy time, buy time. Angie forced herself to stand her ground.

"*Why* did you sell us, your own children? Why did you even keep us here in the first place?"

He gave an irritable shrug. "I have a wife. Ana was an indulgence. The Saudi visited and saw you two. Little twin redheads. Fresh as daisies. You intrigued a man with enough money to buy several small countries. He offered me a deal I could not refuse. Now, move." He waved his gun at her. "Or I kill you here now."

Angie turned, walked slowly, her brain racing. Long grass, dewy, dampened the bottom of her jeans. Water dripped from trees. The scent of moist loam and moss was rich, familiar. She'd come all the way back to this place that had been locked inside her memory. Mila's foot had brought her here. Full circle. Back to where her twin had lost her life and her mother had died. Angie had finally found the truth, and now she, too, would die.

As she walked she glimpsed a building through the trees—big. Built of logs. Green roof. A chopper squatted on a tiny helipad near it. That must be the craft she arrived in. An old woman in black watched from the windows in the distance. Angie stilled, pulse quickening.

"My mother," Kaganov said, waving at the woman to shoo her away from the window. "Mothers are important, not so, *Roksana*?"

Rage mushroomed in her. Evil—he was pure fucking evil, enjoying this. She whirled to confront him, but he raised his hand up high and smote the butt of his gun down hard across her face. Pain exploded through her cheek. She staggered sideways under the blow. Bent over, she clamped her hand over her cheek. Blood leaked warm through her fingers. She could smell it, taste it—her own blood. Before she could regroup, he kicked her hard in the side of her leg, forcing her to stumble sideways.

"Go, I said. Walk. We've got to make it across to the other side of the island. I need to return to my guests by lunch."

CHAPTER 55

Through the floatplane window Maddocks scanned the densely forested coastline below with his scopes. His old friend Craig Bennett flew the plane. Bennett was ex-military and had contracted with the RCMP as a pilot. His bird had only visual flight capability, so they'd had to wait until the early light of dawn before taking off.

Bennett's voice came through Maddocks's headphones as he banked his craft to the west. "There she is, Semko Island and the lodge."

Maddocks panned his scopes over the island. He saw the green roof of the expansive lodge, decks stretching out over the water. Outbuildings. Docks, boats. A chopper on a small helipad. Two floatplanes moored out in the water.

Bennett angled the plane as they flew in over the island to come around in the correct wind. Maddocks had borrowed clothes and gear from Bennett, a keen fly-fisher. His plan so far was to walk in the front door of that lodge as a prospective client who was just checking the place out. Yes, it might arouse suspicion, but it was the best plan he had at short notice.

Takumi had finally okayed backup. Maddocks had received the call during flight, just minutes ago. The BOLO had resulted in the hit man's Audi being spotted leaving the heliport in Vancouver. The kidnapper had been apprehended. Evidence of fresh blood and long red hair had been found in his vehicle.

But the chopper that had been awaiting the man had already taken off with the cargo that the man had loaded onto it.

According to heliport staff, the pilot had filed a flight log to Semko Island. Instrument flying—the craft was equipped to travel in the dark.

Heliport staff also informed police that the pilot regularly flew the Semko route, and they'd confirmed that the package that the Audi driver had delivered to the chopper was large enough to be a body. This was the information that Takumi had needed to prove Angie—alive or dead—had likely been loaded onto that chopper. Takumi had gotten the green light for an ERT team to fly in to Semko.

Maddocks was overdosed on adrenaline, his mouth bone-dry. He chose to focus on believing Angie was alive—she had to be. It was all he had to hold on to. It was what kept his mind sharp, his vision keen, every sense on alert. Something suddenly caught his eye in a forest clearing below. He swung his scopes.

His heart spasmed. Shit. *Angie*—alive.

With a man. Maddocks refocused his scopes, trying to stop his hands from trembling as he attempted to get a better view. The male was a redhead. Massive in stature. *Kaganov.* And he had a gun. He was forcing Angie to move ahead of him along a path that led through trees toward the far side of the island, toward docks that ran out into the water in grid patterns. *The fish pens.*

"It's them. He's got her!" Maddocks said through his mouthpiece. "Can you set down on the west side? Around the point north of what looks like fish pens."

"Ten-four." Bennett banked the plane, changing direction.

Maddocks's brain sped like it was on acid. This place looked as Angie had described it from her hypnosis memories. Old-growth forest.

Log house with a green roof. Docks forming fish pens. Surrounded by water.

Kaganov had brought his daughter home. To die.

Kaganov shoved Angie forward through branches that hung low over a seldom-traveled stretch of the path. As she came through the foliage, Angie saw a cove and a beach below. From the shore, old wooden docks stretched out into blue-green water in a grid pattern. A weathered hut listed on one of the docks, faded blue paint peeling from old boards. Beside the hut lay a giant tangle of crab pots.

She knew now why the sight of the docks outside Jacob Anders's window had disturbed her so—it had prodded a buried memory of this place. She and Mila had stood right here, on this path, peeping down at the cove through the branches. And they'd seen something terrible. The recollection gushed into her brain like black, suffocating smoke.

The big red man at the far end of a dock, forcing a thin woman to curl up into a large cage he used to catch crabs. The man wiring the cage tightly shut around the woman, who was crying. The man stabbing her a few times through the gaps in the wires, making blood flow onto the wooden dock. The man shoving the cage with the bleeding woman off the edge of the dock with his foot. The sound of the splash it made. The cry of gulls up high.

Angie swallowed as she studied the scene afresh now, blood still leaking down her face from her split cheek.

The place was clearly disused. The giant crab pots were commercial ones, and they were rusting. On the dock that reached the shore was an old fish-cleaning station. An old gaff leaned against the station.

"Go down." Her father shoved his gun into the small of her back.

She inhaled and began to make her way carefully down the slope toward the pebbled strip of beach. Stones dislodged under her boots and skittered and clattered down the bank. That's what he was going to do—put her into one of those crab pots and drown her. Make her bleed more before pushing the trap into the water. Her blood would attract fish. She'd sink fast to the bottom. She'd lie like that pig carcass trapped on the seabed, her flesh being picked clean by crabs and lobsters and sea lice and octopi. She had to act before he could get her to the far end of that dock where the crab pots lay in a heap.

Cautiously, she moved farther down the slippery path and onto the beach. She stepped onto the old dock. The worn planks wobbled beneath her feet. She found her balance. Tentatively she made her way along the dock toward the fish-cleaning station. Water chuckled beneath the planks. Kaganov stepped onto the dock behind her, and she felt it sway under his weight. The breeze off the ocean was clean and cool and scented with brine. Angie came to a halt beside the station. She couldn't allow him to take her any closer to those crab pots. She had to act now. This was where she had to pick her battle "These . . . these pens are no longer in use," she said, her voice rough.

He snorted, coming right up behind her. "Not for a long, long time. Salmon farming is now a highly scientific, computerized enterprise. My new pens are out at sea—in open water. Deep water. The fish stocks are monitored by techs and live cameras around the clock. My staff live in floating accommodations for two weeks at a time, then rotate shifts. It's a controversial business, of course, feeding the world. Growing protein. Environmentalists wage war on the Atlantic salmon we farm here in Pacific waters, say it kills the local fish, damages spawning in the BC rivers, undermines the entire ecosystem. But I have publicists. Good ones. They offer tours to the public. It all helps the company profile." He nudged her forward. "And now that we're all caught up, my Roksana, it is time. Take off your boots."

Her heart skipped a beat. "Why?" she asked quietly, but she knew why.

"Because maybe they float. Wouldn't want your DNA washing up in Tsawwassen again. No more loose ends."

Slowly, Angie turned around to face him. He had his back to the forested island. Above him, up on the bank between the shadows of the trees, something moved. A ripple of the wind?

Angie tensed as a form took shape in the shadows behind the branches. Her heart stopped. *Men.*

Two.

Armed with rifles.

Then she recognized the blue-black glint of hair. *Maddocks.* What in the—? *He's come for me. He's found me.* Angie tried to level her breathing, to not give him away.

Maddocks waved for her to keep going, to keep moving forward, away from Kaganov. He had his rifle trained on her father. But he needed Angie to put distance between herself and Kaganov in order to give him a clear shot.

"Boots," Kaganov demanded. "Now. Take 'em off."

Inhaling deeply, Angie bent over and slowly began remove her boots.

A rock clattered down the bank. She froze.

Kaganov's head jerked. He spun around. Maddocks ducked back into the foliage, but not before Kaganov raised his pistol and fired. The crack sent a flock of pine siskins scattering from the trees. Silence. Kaganov held still, his back heaving as he watched the trees. Still bent over, heart jackhammering, Angie fingered her hand slowly, surreptitiously, toward the handle of the rusted gaff that leaned against the fish station. Her fingertips touch the old splintered wood of the shaft. She closed her fist around the shaft.

As he registered her movement, Kaganov swung his gun back at her. His eyes looked like ice. Time slowed, stretched, as his finger curled and tightened around the trigger. Angie's vision blurred as a pink glow appeared behind him. Suddenly Mila was there again, standing behind her dad, just like she'd appeared behind the Baptist before Angie had blanked out and emptied her clip into his brain.

Mila reached out her hand. Her voice filled the air, as if the wind itself were speaking.

Come. Come playum dum grove . . . come . . .

Angie couldn't breathe, couldn't think. As Mila came closer, Angie saw that blood was pouring from her eye sockets. The crimson rivers dripped down her white face, soaking into her pink party dress, covering her white legs. Rage exploded, sending blinding shrapnel through Angie's brain. Her mind turned black. Her vision narrowed onto only her father.

Kill him. Kill him. Kill.

She gripped the gaff handle tight and yanked it toward her. With a sharp twist of her body from her waist, using the upward momentum, she swung the gaff hard at her father's face.

The hook met flesh, bone. The impact juddered through her arms. She gripped the gaff shaft with both hands and jerked it downward, and the rusted hook tore through her father's skin from the eye to his jaw.

He howled as he pulled the trigger, but his shot went wild. All Angie could see now was blood. Hot blood everywhere. She placed her feet wide apart and crouched low. She stepped forward and swung the hook at him again, taking advantage of his shock. The hook tip dug into his chest this time, ripping open his shirt and the flesh across his pecs and down to his belly. He gasped, dropping his gun as he clamped both hands to his gut. Staggering backward to avoid her next blow, he slipped in his own blood. He went down hard onto his back. Angie stepped over him, straddling him with a boot on either side of his hips. She flipped the gaff around so that the hook was in the air, and she drove the back end of the shaft into his forehead with a crunch. His arms flailed at his sides. He went limp. Time slid to a halt. Absurdly, she could hear no more birds. No sound at all. The world had been muffled.

Her father's gray eyes blinked as he stared up at her, dazed. His face was a mangled mess of meat and blood. As he breathed, a foam of tiny pink bubbles formed at his mouth.

Panting hard, she stood over him, the gaff handle slick with his blood in her fists.

Kill him . . .

But as Angie reached down and unsheathed his knife, she heard yelling. It seemed to come from far, far away, and she barely registered it. She dropped to her knees beside her father's limp body, exhausted, dizzy. She brought the gleaming sharp edge of his hunting blade to his white throat and pressed it above his Adam's apple, under the red beard. She registered the ginger body hair growing on the white skin of his neck, and the memory of him killing that sobbing, skinny woman flashed through her eyes again.

Roksi?

She looked up. The wind? Mila?

She saw the little girl in pink again—Mila. Standing behind their father's bleeding head. Her sister shook her head. *No. No. No . . . no killumdum . . .*

Angie tore her attention away from the distraction of the little ghost and looked back down into her father's eyes. The color of her own. Full of pain. And hate. He hated her. Her own father hated her and was the most heinous kind of killer.

She pressed the blade across his throat, breaking flesh—

No. No. No, Roksi . . . stop, Roksi!

She shook herself at the sound of the little voice inside her head, the sweet little voice. Tears flooded her eyes. She was better than this. Better than her father. Better than the sum of her past.

Not again, Angie. Not like the Baptist. No more rage. You've found her, you've found Mila. Your sister. You've come home to her. To your mother. They wouldn't want this. They don't want him to make you a killer.

Shudders seized her body.

"Angie!" Maddocks was behind her. "Angie, stop—don't do it!" His voice came into focus. The sound of the whole world came into focus. Birdsong. The ripples of small waves on the beach stones. His

351

hands were on her shoulders, big, firm, pulling her back, away from her father's bloody body.

"Drop the knife, Angie. Don't do it. We've got him. We got him."

But she twisted violently out of Maddocks's grip, shaking herself free. She bent her face close to her father's and said, voice low, her lips near his ear, "I'm not killing you, you motherfucking bastard. That would be too easy on you. I'm going to make you pay. I'm going to put you in a cage, just like you caged all those women. For the rest of your fucking miserable *life*."

Maddocks hauled her brusquely up onto her feet. She didn't have the strength to fight him. The knife fell from her hand. It clattered to her boots. Her whole body shook. Her teeth chattered. Tears streamed down her face.

Maddocks turned her to face him. He cupped her split cheek tenderly, looked into her eyes. "Focus, Angie," he whispered. "I've got it. Focus. Go with Bennett here."

The other male with Maddocks took her hand, drawing her away, leading her down the dock and back to the shore as Maddocks rolled her father over onto his belly and cuffed him. In the distance she heard the thud of choppers.

"They're here," Bennett called out to Maddocks. "Takumi's guys are here."

CHAPTER 56

A female paramedic finished suturing the cuts on Angie's cheek and brow in addition to a gash at the back of her head. She must have hit her head in a few places when she was Tasered and fell to the ground. Or perhaps while being lugged unconscious from the hit man's vehicle to the chopper. She winced as pain sparked afresh under the paramedic's touch.

"Going to want proper stitches from a plastic surgeon for your face," the paramedic said with a smile. "But this should do until you get yourself down to a hospital."

Maddocks was at her side, watching. His presence was like a rock. They were in the living room at Semko Fishing Lodge, and afternoon sun streamed through the windows. The weather had finally broken, and outside bald eagles wheeled against a clear blue sky. Bennett, Maddocks's pilot buddy, was waiting to fly Angie and Maddocks back to Vancouver.

Maddocks had explained to Angie how he'd located her, and she was humbled. By him. By her own recklessness and drive. But she had what she'd come for now. Answers. How she would yet process everything would be new territory, but her relief was profound. She knew who her mother was, and how Ana and Mila had likely ended their lives, and where the rest of their remains might lie—deep in the cold waters below Kaganov's old fish pens. It was the resting place from where the little shoe had probably disarticulated from Mila's foot, floated to the surface of the ocean, and begun its journey, bobbing in currents and winds and storms until it ended up on the beach in Tsawwassen.

The ERT guys had taken off earlier in a chopper with Kaganov in cuffs after the paramedics had flown in to treat him. Crime scene techs were now present and were combing through the lodge. RCMP detectives had also come in via helicopter and were questioning guests, who'd been corralled in another area of the lodge. The old woman in black had been taken away crying. She, too, would be interrogated. A massive forensics dive operation would soon commence at the old fish pens site. If there were remains down there, the team would eventually find them. Police were currently trying to locate Ivanski Polzim and Sasha Makeev. Now that they had names, warrants had been put out for their arrests, and it hopefully wouldn't be long before they were taken into custody. The DNA profile of one of them would likely match the blood of the 1993 cop killer as well as the DNA from the second semen stain on Anastazja Kowalski's purple sweater. The ballistics evidence from the drug bust shoot-out would now be examined in conjunction with the ballistics from the 1986 cradle case. Polzim and Makeev were also key persons of interest in the Squamish arson that had killed Stirling and Elaine Harrison. They were all finally going to go down.

As the paramedic exited the living room, Angie said to Maddocks, "Guess I'll have to go back and face the music myself now."

He smiled, and it lit up his blue eyes like the clear, sunny sky outside. A pang went through Angie's heart. Love. It *was* love, she thought. What else could it be? For this man who continued to save her in so many ways. He had not given up on her when she was so broken that she'd tried to destroy everything good around her. Including him. And what they'd shared.

"Yeah, I'll need to face the shit, too," he said, "after splitting in the middle of the Club Orange B bust and taking off after you. But I've had a few words with Takumi on the phone. I have a feeling he's going to want take all the glory himself for leading an international human trafficking op that cut off the head of the North American arm of the so-called Red Octopus."

Angie's thoughts shifted to the octopus she'd seen in Anders's underwater footage, and a small shiver went through her.

"Nailing Kaganov," Maddocks said, "is also going to send fissures, potentially fatal ones, all the way up through the Prague operation. My gut says Takumi is not going to pursue the fact that I went rogue there for a while, because if I hadn't, this would not have turned out to his benefit like this. RCMP probably won't want to proceed with any charges against you, either."

"I can only hope."

He held his hand out to help her up from her seat. "Let's cross our fingers, then, shall we?"

She managed a smile, but it hurt her face. She clasped his hand and came to her feet. "And engage good lawyers, I suppose."

"That too. You ready to go home?"

"I need to visit that cedar grove one more time first."

"You sure?"

"Dead sure." She hesitated, feeling a little silly, but she said what was on her mind anyway. "That's where they are, Maddocks. My mom and Mila. Not their bodies but their spirits—in the wind that drifts through those ancient trees. I feel as though their voices reach me there. It's from that place that they called me back to find the answers. From that bay that Mila's foot floated south, setting everything in motion. I need to go and say goodbye."

Yellow afternoon sunshine dappled down through the tall cedars as Angie and Maddocks slowly walked hand in hand through the soft, long grass and over the springy moss of the dell. Angie stopped and inhaled the sense of the place once more. Wind rustled, and she felt them—Mila and her mother. Tears filled her eyes.

"It really is beautiful," Maddocks said, sliding his arm around her waist, drawing her closer. Small birds darted through the boughs. It was not the season for blackberries or dandelions, but the berries and flowers were here, beneath the winter earth, pushing up and getting ready to burst forth in the spring and then fall.

"I want that photo of Ana when the techs are done with everything," Angie said.

He nodded. "I told them you'd want it."

"She was so young. She didn't abandon me, Maddocks. She was trying desperately to save us both. I can't tell you how much that means."

They stood in silence for a moment. Just the two of them. The sensation of the old-growth trees surrounding them like ancient sentient beings was humbling. The sound of the whispering wind through their boughs was haunting, spiritual, a murmur of voices in a language not understood by mere mortals. These trees would have been tiny saplings when the construction of the Notre Dame cathedral had commenced, and the mood beneath them was no less reverent.

"If we do find Mila and my mother's remains," Angie said softly, "if the divers manage to bring them up, this is where I will bury them. Lay them to rest. In this cathedral of trees. I did once feel happy here. I—" She swallowed as her throat tightened with emotion. "Maybe I'll return to this island from time to time to just sit with them. To pick the berries and dandelions."

"Only if I come with you."

She glanced up into his deep-blue eyes that had so mesmerized her when she'd first seen him at the Foxy. The look in his features made her heart swell with a warmth, a poignancy that both scared and excited her. "Maybe," she said softly, "we can use that birthday present you gave me. I mean, when things finally wrap up."

His eyes changed. His features tightened. "You mean the voucher? The one for the wilderness lodge? Just you and me, far away?"

She smiled. "Well, seeing as I don't have a job or anything."

His eyes glistened. He swallowed, reached up, and touched his palm gently, so gently, to the side of her face.

"Marry me, Angie," he whispered.

"*What?*"

"Marry me."

Her brain spun. "You . . . you mean, be your . . . *wife?*"

"That's generally what getting married means, Angie Pallorino. I don't ever want to lose you. I came too close. When I thought . . ." His voice hitched as emotion strangled his words.

Angie stared up into those eyes, incredulous. Yet not. Terrified, yet thinking maybe . . . just maybe this was everything she wanted. A chance—a second chance to make things work in her life.

Wind gusted suddenly through the ancient cedars like the breath of giant sleeping dragons being roused. Goose bumps rippled over her skin. She opened her mouth to speak, but he touched his finger to her lips.

"Don't. Don't say a word right now. I just want you to think about it."

EPILOGUE

Two weeks later

As the seaplane came in to land on the waters of Victoria's Inner Harbour, Angie could see Holgersen with Jack-O standing at the dock below. She placed her hand on Maddocks's thigh in the seat beside hers. "Look, down there," she said as she pointed. "Cavalry is here."

Maddocks leaned over her to peer out the window and laughed. "Motley crew is more like it. The deviants."

The pilot banked the plane, came around with the wind, and touched skids to water with a hard bump. They taxied toward the terminal over the choppy surface. It felt good to finally be home after all the debriefings and interrogations and legal meetings with various attorneys. She and Maddocks had been holed up in a Vancouver hotel for the duration, and Angie was more than ready for home. There would be additional questions down the road, followed by legal proceedings, witness statements, and more, but for now Angie and Maddocks were free to go.

They disembarked from the seaplane, gathered their bags, and walked down the dock to where Holgersen shifted from foot to foot, holding Jack-O's leash. It was sunny, the sea breeze fresh. Gulls squawked above them.

Holgersen raised his hand in a salute.

Angie returned his greeting with a wave. "Didn't think I'd ever be happy to see that oddball," she said as Maddocks escorted her along the dock, his hand placed gently at the small of her back.

Holgersen had phoned to let Angie know what Harvey Leo had done—how the veteran detective claimed to have come upon her private meeting with Pietrikowski and Tranquada, and how he'd relayed the information to Grablowski. Angie doubted Leo had just happened to be in the observation room. It was more likely that he'd seen her entering the interview room with the Mountie and IDRU woman, and he'd followed her out of malignant curiosity. She'd bet her ass that he'd turned on the audio feed to listen in. But she'd decided to let it be for now—to let Grablowski write his damn book. But she wouldn't cooperate with him, and she'd refused to take any reporters' calls. Her past was done now. They could make of it what they would. She was going to look only forward from this point on.

"Yo! Boss," Holgersen called as they neared. He dropped Jack-O's lead.

Maddocks set his bag down, crouched low, and whistled, holding his arms open wide. "Heya, boy, come here!"

The animal hobbled wildly over to Maddocks on his three legs, mouth open as he panted in excitement. Maddocks scooped him up, ruffed his little head. The pooch squiggled in his arms with glee. It made Angie's heart crunch. She looked away briefly to hide her emotion. It was so close to the surface still. She'd allowed herself to begin to feel, and what was being released from her heart knew no bounds yet. It was as though she'd opened a dam that had been building since she was a child.

Yes, I think I do love this big, tough, and gentle cop. Love him with all my heart.

He glanced at her. "You okay?"

"Yeah. Wind is making my nose run."

He cocked a brow, set Jack-O back down, picked up his bag, and took her hand.

Holgersen came up and bear hugged Maddocks, slapping him hard on the back. Then he turned to hug Angie, but he stopped short of touching her, looking awkward instead.

"Hey," she said, setting down her own bag. She stepped forward and gave the weirdo a hug. It was a first for Angie, but damn, it did feel good once she'd done it. She stepped back, and Holgersen sniffed and rubbed his stubbled jaw. "Good to see yous, Pallorino."

"Yeah, you too."

"Vee-hickle is this way." He scooped up Jack-O as he spoke. "Thought I'd give you guys a ride."

They walked with Holgersen to where he'd parked.

"So all them new girls that came off that ship is going to be okay?" he said.

"As okay as they can ever be," Maddocks said. "They'll go home, be returned to their families. If Kaganov goes for a plea, Takumi's bunch could use his testimony to nail the Montreal club and the one down in Vegas, plus the one in New York. From there international law enforcement can start working on the Prague bunch. Going to be a long process, but it's gathering its own steam now."

As they walked along the harbor front, a yellow sea taxi chugged by. Colors in the harbor seemed crisp, bright, the air clear. Gulls swirled and squawked above as a young boy dangled a fishing line over the edge of the wall. The Empress Hotel across from the waterfront gleamed like a welcoming grand old lady. Angie felt as if a veil had come off winter—and her world. It was as though she was seeing—properly seeing—things for the first time in full focus. In all kinds of complex beauty. Yes, there was sadness in her soul. But also hope. This, she thought, is what it feels to be properly human, whole.

She'd found out who she was—where she'd come from.

To do it, she'd had to go all the way back to the beginning, look into the eyes of a monster, and rather than kill him, she'd managed to conquer her rage demon. She'd gotten rid of the ghosts that had resided down in the basement of her subconscious.

"So I hear them bones they's been finding down there under Kaganov's old fish pens has gone to be tested for DNA. Several bodies so far, I hear." He shot a glance at Angie. "Including a little one."

She nodded. "All found in an undersea area north of the pens, actually. They'd been washed gradually by a cold current into a deep gulley filled with sediment. It's going to be a complex and protracted operation to properly search the seabed down there and then to try to identify all the remains."

"Those salmon that Kaganov used to farm in that area—they were sent to market all those years ago after they'd been eating human flesh?"

She shrugged. "Probably."

"I s'pose it's like that pig farmer, Pickton, eh? Him feeding human meat to his swine before selling them for bacon. People eating that bacon not knowing it was made of bits of missing women." Holgersen stopped beside his vehicle, beeped the lock. "That was one massive forensics operation out at the pig farm, too. And all them Hells Angels ties to him as well. Guess it'll be some times before they turn over any of the remains from the fish pen, eh?"

"Yeah," Angie said. "And then families can finally lay loved ones to rest."

Holgersen held her eyes a moment, then popped open the trunk. Maddocks took their bags around to the rear of the vehicle and loaded them in while Holgersen opened the driver's side door. Holgersen stood with his hand on the top of the door. "And that Kaganov's mother—she knew everything?"

"Yep," Angie said. "She's cooperating with investigators. Kaganov's wife apparently knew, too. Semyon Zagorsky's wife and daughter also had some idea."

"Holy. They sure keeps it all in the family with that brotherhood-code-of-thieves or whatever. From them gulag days in Siberia."

"Kaganov provided their livelihoods," Maddocks said, coming around and opening the front passenger side door for Angie. "He kept them safe, and he kept them all terrified. He's a controlling narcissist. They knew exactly what he was capable of."

Angie inhaled deeply at the thought of what her father was. She shared his genes. But she also shared her mother's. And her grandfather's. Danek Kowalski was apparently a political hero of his time. Which made Angie at least half good. Just because her dad was a monster did not mean she was one.

"I can sit in the back," she said quietly to Maddocks.

He tilted his head. "Go on, get in."

She climbed into the passenger seat. He bent down to pick up Jack-O.

"Here, let me hold him," she said.

He stilled and met her gaze. An unspoken bond of kinship surged between them. He placed Jack-O on her lap, and then he leaned in, kissed her on the mouth, and he whispered into her ear. "Keep thinking about it."

She smiled. "I am."

Maddocks shut the front passenger door and climbed into the rear seat. As Holgersen started the engine, he said, "So, what yous gonna do now, Pallorino?"

"Don't know yet."

He put the vehicle into gear, pulled out of the lot, and fed into the stream of downtown traffic. "Yous did a pretty good job investigating on your own. Ever thought of getting a PI license, like, specializing in cold cases and shit, finding missing peeps? You could work with that Jacob Anders guy again if you needed forensics stuff done."

She snorted. "Who knows—maybe. But I've got some things I need to take care of first." Like seeing a therapist as she'd promised Maddocks. "Like maybe going over to meet my relatives in Poland. I learned I have an uncle there who is still alive. I contacted him. He said my grandfather was a brave political dissident in the Solidarity movement. Ana fled when my grandfather was carted off to prison. They never knew what happened to her, until now. They want to meet me, Ana's daughter."

"And Kaganov's moms is also your relative," Holgersen pointed out.

She stroked Jack-O's head and watched the scenery go by. She could not think of Kaganov's mother as her own flesh and blood. One couldn't choose one's family, but Angie didn't have to honor that woman, although she was probably a victim, a prisoner in her own way. Maybe time would change how she felt—but not now.

"I gots some things to sort out, too," Holgersen said as he met her eyes briefly.

"Like?" Angie said.

"Like Harvey Leo."

"What about Leo?" Maddocks said from the rear.

Holgersen snorted. "I has a plan. Guy's going down, busted. Hooooo."

"For what?" Angie said. "He didn't do anything criminal in talking to Grablowski about me, if that's what you're referring to."

Holgersen just shrugged, a strange look changing the shape of his face.

Angie studied him a moment, then gave up. Holgersen was an enigma and probably always would be. She turned to look out the window instead, observing her city as he drove. Victoria. A peace filled her heart at the sight of the familiar landmarks.

She had no job, nothing. And yet she had everything, for she had her identity, her biological place in the fabric of things, and her sister and mother would finally be laid to rest. Closure—it was everything it was cracked up to be. She could now look in the mirror and know she'd done justice for Mila, the little ghost girl in pink.

She turned and glanced into the back. Maddocks met her eyes. A seriousness entered his features. And yes, she now had a chance at a future with Detective James Maddocks. They also had a dinner date for tonight with his daughter.

All felt right in the world.

A SNEAK PEEK AT THE NEXT ANGIE PALLORINO NOVEL—COMING SOON.

EDITOR'S NOTE: THIS IS AN EARLY EXCERPT AND MAY NOT REFLECT THE FINISHED BOOK.

A SECRET RUNS THROUGH IT

And out of the ground made the Lord God to grow every tree that is pleasant to the sight, and good for food; the tree of life also in the midst of the garden, and the tree of knowledge of good and evil.

—Genesis 2:9

September 1994

Twilight lingers at the fifty-first parallel, painting the sky deep indigo as tiny stars begin to prick and shiver like gold dust in the heavens. It's cold, winter's frost already crisp upon the breath of the late-September evening. Mist rises wraithlike above the crashing whitewater of Bridal Falls. Fog hangs dense over the forest, playing peekaboo with the ragged peaks of the surrounding mountains. She moves carefully along the slime-covered rocks at the edge of the deep-green eddies and pools of the Nahamish River. Stopping for a moment, she watches a cloud of small insects that have begun to dart just above the water's mercurial surface. Peace is complete, a tangible thing that feels akin to a gentle blanket wrapped about her shoulders. She's in the moment as she crouches down to her haunches and removes a wallet-size fly box from the front pocket in her fishing vest. She opens the silver box, listening to the rush of Bridal Falls just upstream and the more distant boom of Plunge Falls downriver. The wind hushes through the forest up on the ridge at her back. She selects a tiny dry fly that best matches the insects hatching over the water. Gripping the fly between clenched front teeth, she draws the line from her rod with her fist. With practiced movements, she knots her fly onto the tippet attached to the leader at the end of her dry line. A hidden silver hook nestles in the feathers, which are designed to fox the trout into thinking the fly is food. A smile curves her mouth as she thinks of her father. H—he tied this fly for her. He's fished the Nahamish many times. When she told him she was going on this trip with the girls, he'd given her some of his favorite flies. He'd said this one would work best just as the light started to fail at this time of year.

Rising to her feet, she begins to cast—a great big balletic sequence of loops, her line sending diamond droplets shimmering into the cool air. She settles the tiny fly right at the edge of a deep, calm eddy, just where the current begins to riffle along the surface, where she's seen fish rising for the hatch.

But as her fly begins to drift downriver, she senses something. A sentience. As if she's being watched. With intent. She stills, but her pulse has quickened. Her hearing becomes suddenly acute.

Bear?

Wolves?

Cougar?

She can no longer hear the others. They're upriver of Bridal Falls. They all went up to the camping area once the boats had been taken ashore at the pullout. They were around the campfire, waiting for their two male guides to prepare dinner, getting ready to drink and laugh and eat and settle in for the night. But she'd been hungry for more, just a few last casts before full dark on this second-to-last day of their trip. It was a failing of hers—always wanting just one more, of everything, not being able to stop. Perhaps it was not a good idea. Feeding time in the woods. She swallows and slowly turns her head, looks up at the rocky bank. Nothing moves in the dark shadows between the trees that grow shoulder to shoulder along the ridge. Yet she can still feel it—a presence. Tangible. Watching. With malevolence. Something is hunting her—weighing her as prospective prey. Just as she is hunting the trout. Just as the fish are hunting the insects. Nerves tighten. She squints, trying to discern some shape from the darkening evening shadows. A rock dislodges suddenly. It clatters down the bank, unsettling more stones, which rattle and knock their way down to the river and splash into the water. Fear strikes a hatchet into her heart. Her blood thuds against her eardrums. Then she sees it—a form. It shifts and becomes distinct from the forest. Human. Red woolen hat. Relief slices through her chest.

"Hey!" she calls out with a wave.

But the person remains silent, picking a determined route down the bank, making directly for her, something heavy-looking in hand. L—like a log. Or a metal bar, about the size and heft of a baseball bat. Unease slams back into her chest. She takes an involuntary step backward, closer to the water's edge. Her wading boots slip on greasy moss despite the studded soles designed expressly for good grip on surfaces like these. She wobbles, steadies herself, and laughs nervously. "You spooked me," she calls out, trying to chase away her own stupid fear. "I was just wrapping up here, and—"

The blow comes fast. So fast. She spins away, tries to duck out of the reach of the weapon, but her quick twisting motion sends her boots out from under her. Her rod shoots into the air. She lands with a hard smash on rocks and tumbles instantly into the river, entering with a splash. The shock of cold water explodes through her body. It steals her breath. Icy water rushes into her stocking-footed, chest-high waders, seeps into her studded wading boots, saturates her vest, her woolen shirt, her thermal underwear, the weight of it all dragging her down. She flails at the surface with her hands, trying to keep her head above water, struggling to grab at slippery rocks as the current moves her downstream. But her nails fail to find purchase. She gains momentum as the river sucks her toward its heart, where its currents muscle deep and strong toward the thundering boom of Plunge Falls, where mist boils thick above the tumbling water. It's a deadly place, an area people have gone to commit suicide, and their bodies have never been found because the weight and pressure of the falling water traps them deep in pools and pushes them into submerged caves. She tries to kick, to swim, to angle back toward shore. But the Nahamish has other plans. It clutches at her with newfound glee, with impossible strength, tossing her about like a toy, drawing her down and into its churning bowels. Her lungs begin to burst.

With a teasing thrust, the current shoots her briefly to the surface.

"Help!" she screams as her head pops out. She thrusts her clawed hand up out of the foam, pleading.

"Help!" She chokes, goes under again, swallowing water, gagging. Again, the river gives her false hope and shows her the surface. For a moment she manages to keep her chin above water. She can see the person on the bank, growing smaller, face white under the red woolen hat, dark holes where there are eyes. Behind the figure an army of black spruce marches along the ridge, sharp tips like warrior spears piercing the fog.

Why? It's all she can think. It makes no sense.

The Nahamish tugs her back under, smashes her into a subsurface boulder. Pain explodes through her left shoulder. She knows it will take seconds before hypothermia completely steals her brain function, before she loses all motor coordination, all ability to fight, to swim. Wildly, clumsily, she struggles against the current. She must halt her ride downriver before she reaches the falls. But her hands have frozen into cramped claws. Her waders and boots drag her down as if a monster is pulling her by the legs from below, down, down, down into its lair, into to a watery grave.

Lungs burning, she is roiled and bashed against more rocks. She no longer knows which way is up or down, which way to fight for air. But as she starts to pass out, the river once more tosses her to the foaming surface. As her head rises, she gasps maniacally for air. Water enters her mouth. She chokes as she is sucked under again. But she grabs for a fallen log wedged into the bank. This time her claw-hands find purchase.

Hold. Hold, dammit . . . Hold . . .

Her heart pounds against her ribs. She digs her nails into soaked bark as branches trap her like a thing caught in a strainer. But she can feel the spindly branches breaking, her grip slipping in the rotten log detritus. The river yanks insistently at her waterlogged waders.

Should've worn a life vest. W-would it have even helped?

She manages to take a breath, then another. Absurdly, she notices the indigo sky—the brighter points of two evening stars that hover like emergency flares. P—planets, really. *Jupiter? Venus? No idea.* But they give her a sense of the universe, of her tiny place in it. A sense of hope.

Star light, star bright, first star I see tonight . . . It was nights like this, sitting at a campfire with her dad, who taught her to fly-fish when she was little girl—that was the beginning of a journey that has led her to this point, to this river where she is now going to die . . . *Life is like a river . . . Life is absurd . . . The only constant is the water of change . . .*

She takes another breath, then manages to move her hands along the rough log, gaining a better grip, pulling herself toward the bank. Time is strange how it slows, stretches.

She had this experience once before during a head-on collision on a snowy highway. Under extreme life-and-death stress, one really does have occasion to observe things in slow, protracted motion that in real-time occur in a smashing blink of an eye. Claw upon frozen claw, she inches closer to the bank. She gropes for branches of the leafless scrub growing along the river's edge. The bank is very steep here. For a while she lies panting, half in and half out of the water, the side of her face resting in green, slimy green moss and black loam. It smells like compost, like mushrooms. Like a pond with fish.

A sound reaches into her consciousness—a raven. Cawing. It must be close, right above her somewhere in the trees up on the bank. Otherwise, she wouldn't hear it above the boom of Plunge Falls. The raven is a scavenger. It's smart. It knows she is dying. It will go for her eyes first, the soft parts of her body. Her mind begins to go dark.

No. No!

I must keep my brain alive. It's all I've got now. My mind. Use it. To command my body, to live . . . She lies there in the slippery mulch of soil and moss and fall detritus, struggling to comprehend her situation, the sequence of events that sent her into the river. Her brain fades to black again. It's almost a relief now. She welcomes it. But a stray little spark in the blackness does not die. It flares slightly. Flickers. Then bursts to life as fear strikes a jumper cable to her heart.

You.

I think of you. My fear is suddenly for you . . .

Her eyes flare open wide. Her pulse races. Adrenaline pounds through her blood.

What do they say about people who survive against all odds when others would surely die? About that man who sawed off his own arm to free himself from the rock jaws that trapped him; the young woman who descended a snowy mountain after a plane crash wearing a miniskirt and no panties; the female teen who survived feverish, insect-ridden months in the Amazon

*jungle after falling like a whirling seedpod from the sky while still strapped
into the passenger seat of a commercial airplane; the man who drifted for
months in a raft in the ocean . . . They all returned to civilization with one
common refrain. They say they lived, survived, did it for someone. A loved
one. The thought of that loved one infused them with a superhuman strength
to fight death, because they had to go home. To that loved one . . . I must
go home, for you. I must live for you. This changes everything. Everything.
I can't let you down. I am all you have . . .*

She reaches slowly for a clump of roots, drags herself up the bank
an inch. She gathers breath, reaches for a higher clump, pulls. Pain
screams back into her body. She relishes it. She's still alive. She fights
death knowing that one slip, one lost grip, will shoot her back down
the slick bank into the water. And over the falls.

She's almost at the crest of the bank. She stops, gathering breath,
marshaling reserves, retching. Mist creeps over her, thick with moisture
and increasing darkness. She senses something again. She's not alone. A
strange combination of hope and dread sinks through her. Slowly, very
slowly, terrified of what she might find, she looks up. Her heart stalls.

A black shape among the trees. Standing deadly still. Silent.
Watching from the gloom. Observing her struggle.

Or is she hallucinating? Wind stirs boughs, branches twist, and the
shape moves. Coming closer? Or is it just shadows in the wind?

Painfully, slowly, she releases a fist-hold on grass, making precarious
her position on the slick bank. She raises her free hand, stretching her
arm out toward the shape.

"*Help,*" she whispers.

No movement.

"Please. Help . . . me." She raises her hand higher, giving gravity
more power. No response.

Confusion chases through her. Then it hits her. Like a bolt from
the blue. And as she realizes what is going on, why this is happening,

all hope is sucked out of her body. It takes her last vestiges of strength. Her outreached hand has tipped the balance, and she begins to slip. She gathers speed suddenly, gravity thrilled to have her back, tumbling and sliding her in her waterlogged waders and boots all the way back down to the river. She lands with a *splosh*. The current grabs at her with delight as the human figure continues to study her in silence from the trees above. A final thought cuts through her mind as she goes under . . .

It's impossible to suffer without making someone pay for it.

But who will pay if I am drowned?

How will you get justice? How will anyone know?

Because the dead cannot tell.

ABOUT THE AUTHOR

Photo © 2013 Paul Beswetherick

Loreth Anne White is an award-winning, bestselling author of romantic suspense, thrillers, and mysteries, including *The Drowned Girls*, the first book in the Angie Pallorino series. A three-time RITA finalist, she has also won the Romantic Times Reviewers' Choice Award, the National Readers' Choice Award, and the Romantic Crown for Best Romantic Suspense and Best Book Overall—in addition to being a Booksellers' Best finalist, a multiple Daphne Du Maurier Award finalist, and a multiple CataRomance Reviewers' Choice Award winner. A former journalist and newspaper editor who has worked in both South Africa and Canada, she now resides in the mountains of the Pacific Northwest with her family. When she's not writing, you will find her skiing, biking, or hiking the trails with her dog. Visit her at www.lorethannewhite.com.